Sweet Tea With Lemon

A NOVEL BY

SHIRLEY A. AARON

Sweet Tea With Lemon is a work of fiction. All incidents and dialogue, and all characters, with the exception of some family figures and some family friends, are the products of the author's imagination and are not to be construed as real. Where real-life figures appear, the situations, incidents, and dialogues concerning those persons are almost entirely fictional and are not intended to depict exact actual events or to change the fictional nature of the work. In other respects, any resemblance to persons, living or dead, is entirely coincidental.

Aaron, Shirley A.
Sweet Tea with Lemon / by Shirley A. Aaron

Summary: Beulah recalls her friendship with Mavis and Edith, as they deal with the conflicts of family and daily life. The three women share adventures, humor, and tragedies. When Mavis is diagnosed with terminal cancer, the bond between them becomes stronger.

First Edition

1. Alabama—Fiction. 2. Southern Literature—Fiction. 3. Friendship—Fiction. 4. Family—Fiction. 5. Religion—Fiction. 6. Drug Addiction—Fiction. Cancer—Fiction.

Cover designed by Austin Sanderson and Bob Hranichny

IN MEMORY OF

My mother, Hazel, and my sisters, Jeanette, Cindy,
& Billie, all of whom died of cancer; and to my brother, Joe,
who knew how to live and how to forgive.

"The lives of Southern women is like sweet tea with lemon. They understand that much of life's happiness can be full of pain. But, they learn to take the bitter with the sweet."

~Beulah

CHAPTER ONE

It was a long time ago since they'd been best friends. Sometimes, it seemed like a couple of weeks. Sometimes, it was distant and faded, seen through heavy clouds in her mind. Time had lasted for many dark, silent nights and lonely days. But she had adjusted. The adjustment had been slow, as she moved into future time, through light and dark.

She'd been examining herself since Edith's funeral, for signs of loneliness and sadness, for forgotten memories of the three of them. It was often difficult to determine how long Mavis had been gone. Reality told her that it'd been a decade, but her heart told her something different. That Mavis had never really gone away.

Beulah sat, rocking in the dark on her front porch, where she'd rocked as a young child, as a teenager. The world around her was nothing but shadows, as a cool breeze stroked her razor-sharp cheeks. A lump was stuck in her throat and wouldn't disappear. It'd been lodged there for days, making her aware of being caught in between life, in the act of going back and staying somewhere close to the now. She knew that she was in a state of lingering. She tried to understand the whole truth of the lingering, and she knew that the truth was a thorn in a delicate place in her mind.

Her mind chased memories that carried the light and dark, that carried a love beyond comprehension. Memories sneaked from hidden files in her brain and tears saturated her face, making her face feel sticky. A heavy sigh escaped her lips, which tasted salty from the tears that ran like crooked creeks down her face and dripped off her determined chin. A shiver rushed over her body, causing her to tremble in the beginning night. Slowly and methodically, she shifted the pieces of their past lives together. So many years were gone. Vanished like magic. She was the only one caught in between then and now.

Time and age don't always coincide with memories. That was okay. She welcomed the memories that'd taken root in her mind. She remembered so many things about her friendship with Edith and Mavis, the laughter and the tears, the good and the bad, the sweetness and the bitterness. She remembered the illness that took Mavis and stole a part of Beulah. She remembered how Mavis' death broke her heart and how it was still dented and cracked, beaten by years of sorrow.

Mavis died first, after months of suffering. Watching her die was almost more than Beulah could endure. Edith died just four days ago. She was ninety-three and still driving that old navy blue Ford truck. Edith's death was painful, but it didn't sock Beulah in the gut, taking away her breath and making her physically sick, like Mavis' death had done. She loved Edith, but not like she loved Mavis.

In an unexpected instant, as if she were speaking to Mavis, she thought, "Few folks can walk in somebody else's shoes or see the world through another person's eyes. You had that gift. You knew folks. You knew things that could and couldn't be explained. You saw beyond depth and felt deep."

Beulah thought about how Mavis understood her and her people. Edith wanted to, and she tried. God gave Edith a kind heart, but not the gifts that He gave Mavis. Few people had Mavis' gift for comprehending life and people, for getting inside another person's skin, for looking at the world in a panoramic view, and seeing gray between the dark and the light.

Mavis was an incredible observer who had strong instincts and could read emotions. It was almost impossible to get anything pass her. She was vigilant, with watchful eyes that saw through disguises and deception. Beulah totally trusted her judgment and liked the fact that she cared less what others thought about her. But one thing that Beulah liked most about Mavis was her loyalty.

Ever since she'd left Edith's funeral, before darkness began to fall, she'd been caught in the past. Well, even before the funeral, she'd been thinking about her friends. When Edith's son Ferris asked if she'd sing "Old Rugged Cross" at the funeral, she'd hesitated, not sure that she could, but there was so much pleading in his eyes and voice. So, she agreed.

It'd been a nice funeral at Hopewell United Methodist Church, on a late Friday afternoon, as the sun headed west. There was a huge crowd, lots of singing, and people standing up to tell amusing stories about Edith, who was loved by everyone at the church, where she'd sung in the choir for years, in spite of the fact that she couldn't carry a tune in a paper sack and didn't know one note from another.

That was a fact that Mavis never let her forget. She'd say, "Edith, I was coming to church, but I couldn't stand the thoughts of your voice messing up some good music." Edith would roll her eyes, not caring what Mavis said. She kept right on singing, Sunday after Sunday. Edith was like that. What others thought didn't influence her way of thinking or what she did. Her life went on, moving like a train though different scenery.

Beulah's mind had been busy on the way home after the funeral. Thoughts were unorganized, stomping around in her head, loud and uncontrollable. Finally, she let go so that some type of order could take over the storm that raged between ears that lay close to her head. By the time that she'd taken off her large black floppy hat, with the red roses on the left side, removed her one-inch black pumps, plus stockings that were too binding, too controlling, and her sleeveless black eyelet dress that flowed away from her hips and had a narrow red patent leather belt that circled her still tiny waist, the memories had fallen into some type of logical order.

She changed into worn, faded jeans and a man's baggy shirt that had small blue stripes that ran in straight, narrow lines. She rolled the sleeves to her bony elbows and tied the front tails in a knot at her waist. In her bare feet, she walked to the kitchen and poured a large glass of sweet tea. At the front door, she stopped, turned around, and went back to the kitchen. Opening the refrigerator door, she got a slice of lemon from a bag that contained three sliced lemons. She dropped the crescent moon of lemon into her tea. A small smile played at the corners of her mouth.

She sat and watched the sun sink into the earth. The sun bleed across the horizon, and yellow streaks popped through Chinese red. The colors were full of fury, a demanding performance in the West. Death had come and the world was blazing with glory and energy. Beulah found it ironical and amazing, one of those things that escapes comprehension.

As she slowly rocked, she saw a spider web that started at one corner of the porch and extended half the length of the house. Apparently, it'd been a long time since she'd swept off the upper section of the porch. She studied the web pattern and recognized the complex mathematics of it, although she'd never been good at math. Her eyes kept returning to the web's center, the circle.

"There's always a center," she thought. "From the center, things change and become different. If only we could remain in the center." She asked herself, "Is that even possible?"

Time passed, and she rocked, with her hands holding the sweaty tea glass in her lap. The huge hat that she'd worn to the funeral was on her head, but she didn't remember putting it on after she got undressed and redressed. She continued to rock slowly, as the moon sailed high, away from a cloud and cast soft silvery light in front of her bare feet. She watched lightening bugs flash tiny beacons off and on. An S.O.S. Tree frogs made music. A breeze sneaked under the brim of the hat and stroked her face.

An owl hooted in a nearby oak tree, as crickets chirped some place near the porch. The moon peeped from behind a cloud and cast silvery images on the trees and ground. A breeze drifted across the rough wooden porch and gently pushed the wind chimes back and forth. The sound was soft and mellow, a comforter. A few cars, going far too fast, zipped up and down the highway that was at the end of the narrow dirt road that led from her house. The cars' lights were the eyes of monster bugs, searching the darkness.

Tears slid down her cheeks, and the moon made the tears look like silver strings against the ebony of her skin. She continued to recall how the three of them had been friends for decades. Beulah remembered when their friendship started and the differences in their ages when they met. She knew Edith was the oldest…nine years older than Mavis, and Beulah was the youngest…twenty-seven years younger than Mavis, who had daughters younger than Beulah. Often, Beulah felt like she was one of Mavis' daughters. Most of the time, she felt like she was more.

Mavis influenced her and gave her strength, at a time in her life when she felt as if the world was caving in on her. Beulah had never followed anyone in her life, except one mean man, a long time ago. After he left, she swore that she'd never again follow another human being. But, she gladly followed Mavis, who was caring and kind.

Looking back, it seemed impossible that they had become friends. They were so different; yet, they were so unbelievably the same. Beulah sniffed and smiled, thinking about the three of them. Relaxing and rocking gently, she closed her eyes and allowed her mind to take her back in time, when she finally began to embrace life again, to let go of anger and pain, and to begin to hope. To the time that she met Mavis and to a friendship that changed her life in more ways than she could comprehend and that allowed her to laugh, to love.

CHAPTER TWO

I t was 1981. Beulah had been laid off at River View Mill, where she worked the first shift. The brick monolith on the Chattahoochee River was simply called "the mill," and it drew together the people of the small cohesive community, which changed slowly. The cotton mill was their bread and butter; yet, times weren't so good. Production at the mill was slow and people were let go. Most folks were trying to make ends meet.

Since being laid off, Beulah had gotten five jobs, cleaning houses on the Backwaters, where lots of rich folks lived in big houses, with many windows that faced the water. It wasn't enough money to support her teenage daughter, Autumn, and herself. So, she started looking for another job.

It was a Monday afternoon, and she was glancing thorough the classified ads of *The Valley Times*. She noticed that the Mid-Way Café, at McGinty's Crossing in River View, needed a cook. It was the end of May, and a Southern summer wasn't losing any time in making itself known. The temperatures were climbing into the high 80s. A couple of days had already hit 90. There was a definite promise of a hot sizzling summer ahead, which usually brought stormy weather.

Beulah didn't want to waste time inquiring over the phone about the job, so she arrived at the café at eight o'clock sharp the next morning. She pulled her hair straight back into a small bun at the nape of her neck. She wore a cotton dress, with large red and orange non-descriptive flowers. The full skirt swished against her long slender legs as she walked in her ankle-high red Keds tennis shoes. Thin men's nylon socks showed just above the top of the shoes. The socks were covered in tiny red and orange polka dots. In her left hand, she carried a large black patent leather purse that she'd bought at a yard sale for fifty cents.

Her thin face was shiny from the washing it'd taken. Large almond eyes sat wide apart, on each side of a thin, flat nose. High cheekbones jarred out like steep dangerous cliffs over a mouth that had a thin upper lip and a full lower lip. When she smiled, the mouth opened wide and revealed bleached teeth that were close to being buck-toothed. A large dimple flashed in her left cheek.

The cool air from the air conditioner and fans hit her tall, almost skinny body as she walked through the blue door into a slightly dim room that was long and went straight into the kitchen. One small partition prevented her from seeing directly into the cooking area. In spite of the air conditioner and fans, she felt the heat from the kitchen. No one seemed to notice her.

Beulah stood in the doorway and absorbed everything, the shabby furniture and the people who were made up of farmers and cotton mill workers. Soft rock and roll music drifted to the ceiling and fans sent it floating around the room. A young woman with short dark curly hair was at the cash register to the left, where there was a long counter. The bar stools at the counter were full. Five tables with chairs were in the middle of the room. Booths lined the right-hand side of the wall. All of the cushions were covered in red plastic. There wasn't enough room for one more person to sit. The place was packed with people and noise, as everyone talked at once. Some people seemed to be trying to talk above everyone else. Their voices carried and bounced off the ceiling, which sent back echoes of speech that had variations of tone and pitch that were Southern.

In time, Beulah would learn that people came and went, dumping bits and pieces of their lives on the tables, on the counter, and in the laps of anyone who'd listen. Some chose their words carefully and left lots unsaid, but assumed. Some emptied their thoughts and opinions like emptying used dishwater out the back door, not caring or thinking where it flowed.

Breakfast smells filled the air. The odor of fresh coffee hit Beulah's nose and glided down her throat. Smells of lunch food mingled with breakfast food. Beulah's eyes traveled down the long room, into the kitchen, and she saw her. Her sleeves were pushed up to her elbows, as she rolled out piecrust dough. An oversized stained white apron was wrapped around her waist and hooked over her neck. Large gold earrings dangled from her ears. Short wavy black hair was pulled behind her ears.

Suddenly, she turned and saw Beulah. They locked eyes. In spite of the distant between them, Beulah could see bright green eyes that held tiny drops of light, behind silver rimmed glasses. The woman's features looked Native American, except for the green eyes. She had dark hair, high cheekbones and forehead. Her skin was two shades darker than white. Later, Beulah would learn that her great-granddaddy was a full-blooded Creek Indian who was a Methodist minister.

"Don't just stand there in the door. Come on in. You're blocking the door." The woman didn't yell, but her voice carried across the room. Everyone turned to stare at Beulah, who felt a blush sweep across her face, as she stepped further into the room. The young woman behind the cash register looked up. Before she could speak, the woman in the kitchen was crossing the room in Beulah's direction. Her hands were covered in flour.

"Hi. I'm Mavis Agnes Norrell. Call me Mavis. Can we help you? As you can see, it's packed. If you want a table, you can wait. It might be awhile. The early morning crowd likes to hang around. And drink coffee." The woman took the edge of her apron and wiped flour from her hands.

Shaking her head, Beulah said, "No, I don't want nothin to eat. I already ate breakfast. Early this mornin. Bout five-thirty." Then, she stood there, looking at Mavis, feeling awkward and foolish, wondering why on earth she'd said all that stuff about when she ate.

"Oh. Okay. Then, what do you want?"

Looking directly into Mavis' green eyes and without hesitation, she answered, "I want the job. The cook's job that was advertised in the paper yesterday. I'm a good cook. Folks seem to enjoy my cookin. They can tell I do it out of passion." She wondered where all that came from. There was no mistaking the amusement in Mavis' eyes.

Turning to her right, Mavis yelled, "BobbieJo!" She pronounced the name like it was one name, instead of two. Beulah didn't think about that. People in River View and the surrounding area did that. It was "RiverView," said quickly and together. "This here lady wants to apply for the cook position."

She touched Beulah's right arm and said, "Come with me." Together, they walked to the cash register. "What's your name?" Mavis asked.

"Beulah."

"Beulah who?"

"Beulah Faith Burton."

"Are you related to Johnie Pearl and Earnest Burton that lives on the Columbus Road, headed to the Backwaters? They live near the Martins."

"That's my mama and daddy."

"I thought I knew all the Burtons, but I've never met you."

"I been livin in Texas for years." Mavis looked at Beulah. Neither blinked. Beulah didn't know why, but she felt compelled to add, "I left here when I was a young girl." She didn't add that she'd run off with a twenty-eight-year-old no-good devil when she was sixteen or that they'd produced a son and a daughter.

"I'm sorry bout Johnie Pearl's passing. I thought a lot of her. I lost my mama bout the same time Johnie Pearl passed," Mavis said, as she looked over Beulah's shoulder.

This white woman had a way of skipping polite conversation and getting straight to the heart of a matter. Beulah decided that she wasn't going to tell her nothing. There were things that Beulah had locked in far corners of her mind and heart years back. Some things she never told anyone and she didn't intend to start telling a stranger.

Bobbie Jo started to speak, but Mavis cut her off. "Are you a good cook? Oh, you said that you are, that you've got a passion for cooking." There was that twinkle in her eyes again. She quickly asked, "And are you willing to come in bout five-thirty and stay til bout two-thirty or three? I get here every week morning at five. And, sometimes, on Saturdays. When I don't work on Saturdays, Sadie Smith works. Do you know the Smiths that live on Hopewell Road?"

"Yes, to the first two questions. No, to the last question."

"I would've thought that everybody knows the Smiths. They don't live too far from me. Nice people. You'll like Sadie." Realizing that she'd digressed, she continued, "Okay. Now, if you'll come to the kitchen and make a peach cobbler, you've got the job."

Bobbie Jo glared at her mama. "Do you mind, Mama, if I interview her?" she asked, as she raised her eyebrows and put her left hand on a hip that had bowed out.

"No. I don't mind. Go ahead. Interview her."

"Can you cook?"

"Yes."

"Can you get here every week mornin and, maybe, some Saturdays by five-thirty?"

"Yes."

You're hired. If you can make a peach cobbler." Mavis interrupted. "BobbieJo, here, is my daughter. She owns the place. She'll be the one paying you, which, by the way, is fifty cents over minimum wages." She ignored the fact that Bobbie Jo's eyes opened wide and her mouth dropped. "Come back to the kitchen and I'll show you around. You can make that cobbler. The bathroom is to your left. Wash your hands and come on out."

Just like that, she was hired. Everyone declared that the cobbler was delicious. Mavis said that it was almost, but not quite, as good as hers. No one denied it. Beulah suspected that no one dared deny it.

While the cobbler was being eaten, people made sounds of pleasure and praised Beulah's baking skills. "She's a keeper," Fisher Moon declared, as he wiped a dab of cobbler from the corner of his mouth. Everyone agreed. Fisher was the official judge of a cook's skills.

After the cobbler was gone and the lunch crowd had left, Bobbie Jo, Mavis, Irene, the waitress, and Beulah sat at one of the round tables. The kitchen was spotless. The tables were clean, and the floor had been mopped. Mavis left the table and returned with glasses of sweet tea. Each glass had a slice of lemon. She placed a glass in front of each person at the table. "The best sweet tea in Alabama or Georgia," she declared.

Irene took a slow swig and let out a long sigh. "It is the best sweet tea I've ever had. No lie."

Bobbie Jo turned to Beulah. "So, we'll see you in the mornin. Mama gets here bout five o'clock and starts makin biscuits and cookin some things for lunch. I get here bout six-thirty, and we open the door at seven. Irene comes in soon after. Lots of folks stop by early for take-outs. And, as you saw today, we sell a lot of take-outs for lunch."

Beulah nodded. "I'll be here on time." She rose from the table, walked into the kitchen, and got her purse. Returning to the table, she took a final sip of tea and swallowed. "I sho do appreciate the job. You won't be sorry you hired me." She looked from Bobbie Jo to Mavis. A small smile tugged at the corners of Mavis' mouth and there was a twinkle in her green eyes.

◆

Beulah arrived at the café the next morning at five-thirty. It was still dark outside, with a full moon hanging loosely in a sky that was full of diamonds. As she got out of her old tan Plymouth, a dog barked in the distance. Another dog responded, which began a chain reaction.

She stopped at the front fender of the old car and felt the duck tape that she'd used to hold the fender together, after a drunk backed into the side of her car in the parking lot of River View Mill. People had repeatedly told the supervisor that Richie Alley was drinking on the job. Since he was a good weaver, the supervisor let it slide. Come to find out, Richie didn't have any insurance. Neither did Beulah.

A dim light in the kitchen of the café was visible. Through the large window, Beulah saw Mavis rolling biscuits in the palms of her hands. She seemed to be singing and swaying to music. Standing at the hood of her worn-out car, she watched Mavis dance a few steps back, a few steps forward. Then, to the left and, then, to the right, followed by a graceful spin. Beulah noticed that her green eyes were closed the entire time and she kept rolling biscuit dough in her hands.

After two soft knocks on the door, Beulah's eyes followed Mavis as she walked to the door. The tuning of the lock made a soft click, and the door flew open, sending light into the darkness. "Well, ain't you an early bird. Come in. Just put your purse in the same place. You, Elvis, and I will get this show on the road." Beulah recognized Elvis' "Welcome to My World."

"I just love Elvis. Robert...that's my husband...was so jealous of Elvis, when he first starting singing. Why, you'd have thought that Elvis and I had something going on between us the way Robert was so jealous. He didn't even want to hear Elvis' name. I didn't pay him no attention. Finally, I said, 'You're acting like a fool. He's young enough to be my son. Stop embarrassing yourself.' That was the end of that. I just kept on playing Elvis' songs. And dancing." She paused briefly. In a happy tone, she continued, "When I get here every morning, the first thing I do is start my Elvis music. He gets me going." Shaking her head, Beulah couldn't help but laugh, and she got the idea that she was going to become familiar with every Elvis song.

Laughing, Mavis locked the door and motioned for Beulah to follow her. When they reached the kitchen, Mavis turned. "You can start cooking the strick-a-lean, sausage, and bacon. I'll put these biscuits in the oven, and, then, I'll start the grits. Nobody who comes in here orders oatmeal. We'll cook the eggs as they're ordered." She stood still, as if lost in her thoughts. "First, I want you to help me find the garlic. BobbieJo hid it from me. She denies it, but I know she's lying. I can always tell when she's lying."

"Why would she do that?"

"Who knows why she does anything. She's always been a mystery. Probably, somebody complained bout too much garlic. The Turners, an old couple who comes in here almost every single day…Monday through Friday…for lunch, are always bellyaching bout something. And, still, they come back, every single day. They're always griping bout too much garlic. Too much this. Too much that." She stopped talking long enough to put the biscuits in the oven. Afterwards, she started searching drawers and cabinets.

"Help me, Beulah. I want to find that garlic before BobbieJo gets here. When I find it, I'm gonna hide it from her."

They spent the next twenty minutes, searching for garlic. No luck. When Bobbie Jo walked into the café at six-thirty, they were busy preparing vegetables and meat for dinner. Nothing was said about the garlic. Until the breakfast crowd began to thin out.

Only five customers were finishing breakfast or a last cup of coffee. It was quiet, except for the low mumble of conversation among the few lingering old men and the elder lady who lived across the street. Jo Ella Hurst owned the building and came in everyday for coffee or lunch, to talk and to pass away lonely time.

"Where's the garlic, BobbieJo? Now, I'm tired of looking for it. I know you've done something with it." The customers stopped talking to listen, waiting for the bomb that they knew was coming. Mavis' outbursts could be as good as her food. Beulah, too, had stopped turning the cubed steak to listen. After taking one look at Mavis' face, she gave her attention to the cubed steak. But, not her full attention.

"Mama, I don't know where it is. You must have put it some place and forgot where you put it. I've noticed that you're forgettin things. Sometimes. Lately." Bobbie Jo wiped the counter that she'd already wiped. She didn't look at her mama, who was glaring at her.

"Don't play with me, BobbieJo. Don't go telling no lies. Just tell me where it is." She waited a second or two for a response. There was none. Bobbie Jo kept wiping the counter, looking down with total concentration.

"Do you hear me? Answer me. Where is my garlic?"

"I honestly don't know."

"You're lying. Tell me. Now. If you don't give me that garlic, I'm not making no more hamburgers."

Bobbie Jo looked up. Mavis' jaw was clenched and her right eye was dancing. "The customers are complainin that you use too much garlic. I've asked you to stop puttin so much in the food. In everything." She sounded tired and exhausted.

"I don't care what they think. I'm the cook. If they don't like how I cook, they can eat somewhere else. You ain't seen nobody leaving. Have you?"

"No," Bobbie Jo responded, clearing her throat.

"Then, give me the garlic." Silence filled the café. The customers were looking at their plates or cups of coffee. Their bodies seemed to have drawn up just a bit. Beulah took up a large platter of cubed steak and put it in the warming oven. Afterwards, she started battering another batch. Bobbie Jo finally looked up from the sparkling counter.

"Give it to me. Or I'm leaving. Walking right out that door." She pointed to the door.

Bobbie Jo threw the washrag onto the counter. She walked into the bathroom and returned with the garlic. Handing it to Mavis, she snapped, "Here! If I lose my customers, I'm blamin you." Her gray eyes were cloudy with tears that threatened to overflow.

Mavis took a step back. "You had it in the shithouse!" Everyone in the café broke into loud nervous laugher. "I can't use that. Bacteria is all over it. Now, that's whata'll make you lose customers. Throw that stuff in the trash. And I want new garlic. First thing in the morning."

She turned away and, then, she whipped around to point a finger in Bobbie Jo's face. "Don't you pull no more crap with me bout cooking. I'm the cook. Me and Beulah. Don't forget that." As she walked off, she turned the music up real loud. Elvis sang "Don't Be Cruel."

Bobbie Jo looked at the few customers. They all shrugged and went back to talking in low voices. The sound of the phone jarred into Elvis' song. Bobbie Jo answered it on the second ring. She began taking an order. Soon, everyone heard Beulah and Mavis singing with Elvis. Mid-Way Café was rocking

Beulah soon learned that people came to the café for Mavis' food, as well as her occasional outbursts that were highly entertaining. It was entertainment as long as someone else was getting a tongue-lashing. Those who received sharp remarks returned again and again. No one seemed to get so mad that they stopped coming. Mavis kept the customers laughing, terrified, or entertained. And they enjoyed her food.

♦

It was Thursday, Beulah's third day on the job. She arrived at five o'clock, instead of five-thirty. Already she and Mavis had fallen into a smooth morning routine before the sun rose in the East and the morning heat sucked the dew from every blade of grass. It was as if they didn't need to speak. Mavis hadn't asked Beulah one question about her life. Beulah waited. She knew the questions were coming, because she'd quickly learned how nosey Mavis could be. Mavis had no shame or embarrassment when she wanted to know something, but she understood people. That understanding told her when it was the right time to ask questions.

Irene, the waitress who was eight years younger than Mavis, but looked older, came into work about seven or seven-thirty each morning. No one was concerned about the thirty minutes in time that went up and down throughout the week. She was Mavis' ex-sister-in-law. Beulah wondered about that story, and she knew that, in time, Mavis would tell her.

At one time, Irene had been a pretty woman. Too much life had worn on her and left its mark on her face; yet, she carried her tall, well-built body with a cat-like grace that was attractive and sexy. Men flirted with her and left large tips. She laughed at their boring jokes and switched her hips when she knew that they were watching. While serving food, coffee, or tea, she'd move from table to table, gliding in and out of the narrow passages with elegance. She'd glance sideways at some man who spoke of nothing to get her attention. The man would receive a shy wink and a wide smile. When things were slow, she sat at various tables and talked to men who were regulars. Sometimes, she'd sit with a couple. Women envied the ease with which she moved and her liquid laughter that was low and husky.

Irene was refilling coffee cups and tea glasses during lunch. The café was packed. Beulah saw her push an escaped strand of bleached blonde hair from her large brown eyes. Her hair was pulled into a ponytail that bounced as she walked. A man who worked for Alabama Power Company touched Irene on her left arm. He said something and winked. She grinned, said something that made him laugh, and stepped out of his reach. Beulah smiled to herself.

About that time, the door opened and a tiny woman with short bobbed hair came into the café. A wave of heat followed her. Her pink scalp showed through thin hair that looked like pure snow. She had a tanned, weathered face that she'd earned from farming, picking cotton, herding cattle, and driving a tractor. Although her body was thin, small knotty muscles popped on her firm arms and legs.

She wore a sleeveless checked blouse of yellows and browns, a pair of dirty jeans, and black rubber boots that came almost to her knees. The faded jeans were stuffed into the dust-covered boots. In her man's hands that were too large for her tiny body, she carried a worn straw hat, which she used to fan herself. Sweat glistened on a freckled face that'd never made contact with make-up.

Talking, she moved among the tables. Everyone seemed to know her. Talk of planting drifted into the kitchen. Without looking up from the plate that she was filling, Mavis said, "Come on back here, Edith. You can eat at this table. I guess you want sweet tea with lemon?"

A voice, too loud for that tiny body, boomed, "You know I do. You always ask that. And I want a big hunk of that cornbread. And I'm gonna take some home with me. So I can have me some cornbread and sweet milk for supper."

Edith stopped to speak to a woman who was too old to have such long hair, which was gray and held back from her face with a huge red bow. Her hair was as dry as grass that had been scorched by summer heat and lack of rain. She wore an old faded green T-shirt and a long denim skirt that touched the tops of white socks. Her New Balance tennis shoes, which were worn and stained with dried mud, were crossed under the table. A large tattered hobo bag sat on the floor beside her chair.

"Well, hi, Mary Lou Walker. How you been? I ain't seen you at church for some time. How's all them kids of yours doin?"

Mary Lou raised her bushy eyebrows and a sad look sweep over a round face that resembled a balloon. Dark circles were under her watery blue eyes. Small blue veins showed under her pallor skin. She chewed a mouthful of pork chop and, then, sighed deeply, before dipping her fork into creamy mashed potatoes, smothered in rich brown gravy.

"I ain't been much of nowheres. Been down with my back. It just bout kills me most the time. Doc's talkin bout back surgery. I'm just gonna let the Lord take care of it. Most of the kids is doin well, cept for Daisy Lou. You know she's been sickly just bout her whole life. Bless her heart. Doctors don't seem to know what's wrong. But, I say that we just have to trust in the Lord. His will be done. Just wish Daisy Lou had some of Boot's energy. Lord, that boy is all boy. Ain't no tamin him. Lord, help us all."

She chuckled, took a bite of turnip greens that were drowned in pepper sauce and continued in a whiny, nasal voice. "I hope to be back to church real soon. There ain't nothin like a good hell-fire sermon to perk up one's spirits, to get the juices flowin, and to make you wanna dance and praise the Lord. Yes!" she said, raising her arms and looking toward the ceiling. "Praise the Lord!" Several people turned toward the sudden loud praise.

Beulah noticed that Mavis rolled her eyes and shook her head as she moved her mouth, mocking Mary Lou. It didn't help that Mavis said loud enough for everybody in the café to hear, "Most of the time, the Lord gives people sense enough to know when to help themselves. When you ask Him to move a mountain for you, He expects you to show up at the mountain with a shovel and a wheel barrel. And, besides that, when did Hopewell Methodist Church become holiness? I wanna know that. When that happens, I won't be going back to Hopewell

Methodist."

Edith walked into the kitchen and gave Mavis a glaring look. She shook her head and snapped, "Don't you ever know when not to speak? I think you like bein mean." She stood close to Mavis and looked up. Edith was three inches shorter than Mavis, who was five feet six inches. When Mavis deliberately looked down, Edith didn't move a muscle.

Turning to face Beulah, she smiled, showing small, even white teeth. Her pale faded blue eyes danced with life and energy. Offering her rough right hand to Beulah, she said, "Hi. I'm Mary Edith Ferguson. Everybody calls me Edith. I live cross the road from Mavis. We've been neighbors for decades. You're new. What's your name?'

"Beulah Burton. It's nice to meet you. I'm the new cook."

"I know Mavis is sho glad to have some help. She's been raisin cane bout cookin by herself. She needed some help. This place stays busy. Everybody likes Mavis' cookin." She glanced at Bobbie Jo while she was talking.

Mavis was busy filling a plate with two pork chops, peas, creamed potatoes, turnip greens, and cornbread. She sat it on the table that was used as an island. Beside the plate of food that was stacked high, she placed a tall glass of sweet tea with a slice of lemon. Next, she cut an onion in half and put it in a small saucer that she sat next to the plate. "Okay. It's ready. Stop yakking and come eat." She stepped back from the table and surveyed the food. "Beulah's been a life saver. She's a good cook. I don't know what we did without her."

Edith ate while Mavis and Beulah put food on plate after plate. When Edith needed more tea, she helped herself. By the time that she took the first bite of lemon pie, the crowd had gone, except for nine customers. Irene walked among them, pouring tea or coffee. When she finished, she came into the kitchen and fixed herself a plate of food. Bobbie Jo, Mavis, and Beulah did the same. They, along with Edith, who picked up her lemon pie, went into the dining area and sat at a table to eat.

Beulah listened to their gossip and laughed at their funny stories or comments about themselves or about customers. Mavis and Edith punched sharp remarks back and forth as if the words were volleyballs. Now and then, Mavis would laugh loud or give a sneaky grin at something that Edith or someone else said. It was obvious that they were comfortable with one another. They felt free to speak their minds, although Mavis did more mind speaking than Edith.

If Beulah hadn't been told, she would've known that they were neighbors from their comments. They'd lived on Hopewell Road for decades, borrowing sugar, flour, or eggs from one another as the need arose. Edith's sons, Preston and Ferris, had grown up with Mavis' children. Most of their children had left home, except for Edith's Ferris, who was her oldest son, and Johnny Lee, who was Mavis' youngest child. Johnny Lee had been a surprise, arriving years after Mavis and Robert had no plans of having another child.

Edith told Beulah that she still worked at River View Mill, but she planned to retire when she turned sixty-two. She and Mavis had worked there for years. They'd ridden back and forth to work, with Edith driving her truck. When Mavis was laid off four years ago, she'd gone to work for Bobbie Jo as a cook at Mid-Way Café. She said she'd never go back to work in a cotton mill, even if it meant that she might starve to death.

Beulah watched as Irene stood up and refilled their tea glasses, and she noticed the still visible signs that Irene had been a beauty at one time. She was attractive, in a tired sad way. Her best feature was a smile that lit up her sad eyes and lingered in the corners of her mouth.

In another week, Mavis would tell Beulah about Irene, as they prepared food before the crack of dawn. Irene had been married to Mavis' younger brother, and they had three young girls. The youngest girl was three when Irene left. One day, out of the blue, for no reason, or so it seemed to people on the outside, Irene up and left with another man. In a few years, she left that man for someone else. Now, she was married to an older man who wasn't in good health. Mavis didn't know how many husbands or lovers there'd been, and she didn't ask.

Mavis liked Irene. So, when Irene needed a job, Bobbie Jo hired her, and she turned out to be a good waitress. The customers liked her, especially the men who flirted with her and were thrilled when she laughed at their jokes.

The phone cut through the women's conversation. Mavis and Edith were trying to over-talk one another. Everyone suddenly got quiet, waiting. Mavis answered it on the third ring and listened for a full minute. Causally, she held the phone away from her ear and turned to Irene. "It's for you." She handed the phone to Irene and sat down, looking at her empty plate.

"Hello," Irene said in a low, husky voice. Shock ran across her face. "Go to hell, you two-bit son-of-a-bitch! Don't you call this number again!" She slammed the phone down. Anger burned in her eyes and pinched her lips together in a line as thin and straight as a razor's edge.

Facing Mavis, who was still looking at her plate, Irene pointed a finger and said, "Don't you ever do that again! I mean it, Mavis."

Mavis responded by laughing so hard that her body shook. She slapped the table with her left palm. Everyone else wore question marks in their eyes. Finally, Mavis inhaled deeply. "Y'all know those obscene phone calls I've been getting for the last two weeks—off and on. It was him." Laying her hand on Irene's shoulder, she said, "I just wanted to share." Another burst of laughter shook her.

Everyone, but Irene, laughed. "Mavis, I don't think it's so funny."

Bobbie Jo and Edith stopped laughing long enough for both to say, "Yes, it's funny." Beulah couldn't help but laugh, although she felt sorry for Irene.

"I bet he won't call no more," Mavis said as she dapped at her eyes with a napkin. "I've been cussing him out. I think he was enjoying me cussing him. It musta been a turn-on."

Irene cut her cinnamon eyes toward Mavis and started laughing. "Maybe, if we all take turns cussin him out, he'll get worn out and stop callin. Let's clean up this place so that I can go home."

Before they closed the café, Edith, Mavis, and Beulah made plans to go to LaFayette and pick strawberries the next afternoon, which was the one Saturday that Mavis worked. Bobbie Jo and Beulah had agreed that Beulah would work on the Saturday when Mavis worked. Sadie would work the other Saturdays. Edith suggested that after they picked strawberries, they go to Mavis' house and make strawberry preserves. Mavis nodded her head in agreement.

"I make some delicious strawberry preserves," Mavis told Beulah.

"That's a fact," Edith agreed, shaking her head. "I'll pick y'all up as soon as the café closes. The sun's gonna be high. I don't wanna wait til it gets too hot, but there ain't nothin we can do bout that. We'll go in my truck. It might be a tight fit, but we'll make it work."

"You're in for a treat," Mavis said, looking at Beulah.

"Now, what's that suppose to mean?" snapped Edith. She didn't wait for an answer or a smart remark. "See y'all in the mornin. Bye, now."

Soon, they heard Edith gun the motor. Then, they heard the sound of gravel being slung against the building. As the truck reached the railroad tracks, they could still hear Edith slowing down and speeding up. The motor whined in agitation each time that she stepped on the gas pedal.

"Did you hear that?" Mavis asked Beulah. "That kinda driving is what we gonna have to put up with tomorrow. Edith drives like a bat flying straight outa hell or a turtle crossing the road. You're in for one scary ride."

♦

Several weeks later, no one but Beulah was surprised to see Edith at the café at seven-thirty one hot Tuesday morning. But, she often dropped by the café unexpectedly. Every Thursday, she came for lunch and every Friday she came for breakfast. Edith was a creature of habit, while Mavis was spontaneous.

Only ten or twelve customers were in the café when Edith arrived, dressed to work in her garden, where it was apparent that she'd already spent some time that morning. An old straw hat covered most of her face. A dirty freckled hand removed it from her head, revealing hair that was plastered to her head. Her short, thin hair was pushed behind her ears. A spot of dirt lay under her right eye, where she'd brushed away a bumblebee that had landed on her cheek. The knees of her overalls were thick with moist dirt, because she'd been moving on the damp ground, along the rows of vegetables, on her knees. She wore scuffed brown men's boots that were covered in dirt.

After stopping to greet several people, she came into the kitchen and sat at the table. "Give me a sausage and biscuit," she told Mavis. Remembering something, she stood up. "Let me wash some of this dirt offa me."

"It's all over you. You probably need to take a sponge bath while you're in the bathroom," Mavis said to Edith's back. When Edith closed the door to the bathroom, Mavis added, "I wouldn't leave the house, looking like that. Beats all I've ever seen. Edith doesn't care squat bout how she looks. Just hop in that truck and take off when the notion hits her."

When Edith returned, she saw that Mavis had placed the sausage and biscuit, along with a steaming cup of coffee, on the table that served as an island. "Mavis, this here biscuit is burned."

"No. It is not. It's golden brown."

Edith looked at the biscuit as if she might have made a mistake and quickly decided that she hadn't made a mistake. "I know a burnt biscuit when I see one. I like light brown biscuits. Soft."

"Oh, you want an old folk's biscuit. Why didn't you say so. Beulah, bring Edith a half-done biscuit. An old folk's gummy biscuit. Some of her teeth must be loose this morning." Mavis laughed and turned to Beulah.

Ashton Washington, who was eighty-six and who came to the café every morning that it opened, jerked his head so quickly to the kitchen that it was a wonder he didn't get whiplash. He yelled, "Who's callin me old?" His mouth was full of eggs and pieces of egg shone like tiny headlights on his false teeth.

Mavis leaned over the partition and yelled back at him, "Nobody. Nobody's talking to you. Nobody said that you're old."

"What? I'm not old!"

Mavis gave an exasperated sigh. "Eat your food." To herself, she mumbled, "Old fool. Can't hear worth a toot. Butting into other people's business."

"What?"

In a loud voice, Mavis answered, "Be quiet and eat!"

"Girly, you're just too sassy. I like a woman with some fire," old man Ashton replied, with a mischievous grin.

Again, Mavis mumbled something about old fools.

"Tools! What tools? I don't see no tools."

Playing along with Mavis' joke, Beulah called out, "One old folk's biscuit comin up!"

Edith's blue eyes had turned into hard, cold steel. "I did not ask for no old folk's biscuit."

Mavis replied, "Well, make up your mind. We can't carry on this conversation all morning. I've got to cook dinner."

Turning to Ashton, she said, "And I mean you better not say another word. If you can't hear, you can't talk. That's the rule in here."

"I don't understand all this talk bout old folks and tools," he said, shaking a mass of silver hair that fell to his neck. "It ain't like all of you ain't gonna get old one day. Or die." He laughed at his last comment as if it were a joke.

25

After Edith ate her sausage biscuit and drank a cup of strong, black coffee, she poured herself a refill and sat at a table with Bobbie Jo. There were receipts and a calculator on the table. Bobbie Jo stopped clicking the keys and looked at Edith.

Edith wasted no time in getting to the point. She had too much to do before the day ended. "BobbieJo, I want you to think bout talkin to Mavis bout takin it easy. She's been workin too hard and worryin too much bout Johnny Lee. Maybe, she doesn't need to work any more Saturdays. Just take that day to do what she wants. To rest."

Bobbie Jo looked puzzled, but said, "I'll think bout that. Sadie can work most any Saturday. You're right. Mama has lots to do at home." Still, she was surprised at Edith's request. It wasn't like her to interfere.

"Good." Edith patted Bobbie Jo's shoulder. Standing up, she announced,
"Well, I'm gone. See y'all later. Bye."

Mavis and Beulah turned. Beulah waved a long stainless steel spoon and Mavis waved a hand that was covered in flour. "Bye," they said in unison.

On the way out, Edith stopped to talk to Simon Edwards, whose nickname was "Shorty," due to the fact that he was only five feet two inches. About as big around as he was tall, Shorty breathed hard and walked at a snail's pace. He wore his gray hair in a buzz cut and had a habit of running a tiny hand over the bit of fuzz.

Shorty had never lived any place but River View, in a cookie-cutter mill house on the banks of the Chattahoochee River. Fisher Moon described him as "one of the old river rats," who'd spent most of his life camping on Turkey Island or fishing in the river.

In response to Fisher's description, Shorty had replied, "I just couldn't live no wheres without a river. So, I reckon that makes me a river rat."

Shorty remembered when trees stood tall along the Chattahoochee's

26

banks. Now, many of them were leaning inward or falling. Modern dams had been built for flood control and recreation. All of that had altered the river's ecosystem, and Shorty spent hours in the café, complaining about change.

He'd recently retired from River View Mill, where he'd worked since the age of fourteen. He'd often said, "I hated school, like some folks hate rattle snakes." Since his retirement, he'd begun to collect antique clocks. In addition to treasuring old clocks, he sold and repaired them. His wife complained that she couldn't move without bumping into a clock, and the constant announcement of time was driving her "outa her mind." Shorty ignored her.

Edith had taken an antique clock to him for repairs, so she sat at the table with him for a while and discussed the progress of the repairs. As they talked, Bobbie Jo heard Shorty say, "You learn to love these things that's real works a art." Soon after that comment, Edith stood up and patted him on a stooped shoulder. He watched as she walked through the door.

◆

That afternoon was the day that Beulah met Edith's youngest son, Preston, who was in his middle thirties. The lunch crowd had left. The employees had cleaned up for the day and were sitting at one of the round tables, drinking sweet tea with bright slices of lemon that floated near the rims of the glasses. They thought that the door was locked, so they were surprised when Preston walked in, wearing a huge grin on his handsome face. Sandy blond hair hung in his dim blue eyes and a dimple flashed in his chin. Beulah noticed that he was stout, of average height, but well-built. He had the type of body that would turn flabby as he aged, if he wasn't careful.

"Hi, ladies. How y'all doin? I know I'm runnin late, but I was wonderin if I could get bout twelve hamburgers, with chili and cheese. I'll take em to go. And a couple large orders of fries. Please?" He cocked his head and opened his arms to express his mistake in placing an order after closing.

Mavis stood up and spoke for all of them. "We ought to tell you 'No,' but we're gonna do it this time. This ain't happening again, Preston. In the future, get your tail in here before we close. We've done put things away and mopped. Now, just cause you're dragging, we're starting all over." The others groaned and stood up, while giving Preston an amused look.

"I'm sorry. And I want y'all to know I sure do appreciate it. No one at my house wants to cook this afternoon. This is my way of helpin my wife."

"Well, I'm glad to know that you wanna help your wife, cause you ain't helping none of us. That's for sure," Mavis replied. After she stood up, she looked around at the others and said, "Beulah and I'll stay. The rest of y'all go on home. We'll clean and lock up as soon as we get this trouble out the door." No one refused the offer. They quickly put their empty glasses in the sink and headed for the door.

Preston sat down and propped his legs on a table. "Thanks, Ms. Mavis. If there's anything that I can do, let me know. May I have a glass of that good tea of yours?"

Mavis stood with one hand on her hip and glared at him. "If you really wanna do something, you'd take your butt home and grill some hamburgers. Since you've made yourself comfortable, I'll bring you a glass of tea. I apologize that I don't have a magazine or newspaper for your highness."

"I knew you'd understand. Don't worry bout a magazine or newspaper. I'll just doze while I wait," he said, with a wicked grin.

Mavis glared at him. "I think I'll go drown myself in a glass of water." She smiled at his cocked eyebrows and said, "If you say, 'Don't do me no favors,' I'll knock you upside the head."

Beulah liked Preston because he made her smile and because he'd give back to Mavis as much as she dished out. It was entertaining to watch the two of them play verbal games. She enjoyed Mavis' iron tongue and liked Preston's charm.

CHAPTER THREE

By the end of June, Mavis and Beulah had fallen into a morning routine at the café. In the early morning hours, before Bobbie Jo or the first customer arrived, they shared stories about their lives. Mavis was interested in Beulah's life, but she didn't probe. She didn't have to wait too long to hear Beulah's life story. Within a short period of time, she opened up to Mavis, in a way that she'd never done with anyone else.

Beulah told Mavis how she ran away from home at the age of sixteen with Noah Hadaway, a man who was thirteen years older than she. Mavis listened and continued to make biscuits as Beulah described Noah, a man who was six feet two inches tall and built like a heavyweight boxer. His shoulders were broad and his arms were large knotted kettle-black ropes. His shaved head revealed a smooth skull that glowed from the baby oil that he rubbed over it every morning. Small black eyes without depth, a flat nose that occupied too much space on his face, and a large bottom lip that pouted were three things that drew attention to his long face. The chin was square, as it'd been chopped with an ax.

Beulah described large graceful hands that he used frequently when he talked. It wasn't long after she ran away with him that Beulah became more than well-acquainted with those hands as they too frequently delivered sharp blows to her face or body, if she said or did something that Noah didn't like, which was often. It seemed that he derived a great deal of pleasure in using Beulah as a punching bag. Every day he called her stupid and slow, while he laughed at the way she talked. "Just a damn ole country gal," he'd say. "I got me an Alabama stupid cow." Then, he'd laugh and pull her short pigtails until tears filled the rims of her eyes and she begged him to stop.

◆

When Beulah first laid eyes on Noah, he was working with a construction crew that was paving the Columbus Road, from River View to Smiths Station. The road ran in front of her parents' home. Beulah would sit on the front porch and watch the crew as they worked. If she had free time, she'd read. When she didn't have free time, she'd shell peas or shuck bushels of corn. The family garden produced lots of vegetables that Beulah and her mama canned for the winter. Preparation for canning kept Beulah fairly busy throughout the summer.

It was a scorching morning in late June, with the Fourth of July only four days away. Heat filled the air and sticky humidity sucked sweat from Beulah's pores as soon as she walked onto the long front porch. She placed a cardboard box on the floor near a bushel of corn. Next to the box, she placed sheets of newspaper. She made herself comfortable in a rocker, with a large dishpan in her lap.

When she'd shucked half the barrel of Silver Queen corn, she looked toward the road and saw Noah. He glided like a panther to the bottom of the porch steps, stretched out a long leg, and placed a huge foot on the third step. Placing his right arm across a bent knee, he leaned toward her. Circles of sweat showed under the armpits of a faded blue shirt. The long sleeves were rolled above his elbows. Beulah didn't look up, but she felt his overpowering presence. They both waited out the silence.

She'd seen him walk away from the other men and hesitate a minute before stepping into the yard. He swaggered, cocky and sure of himself. As her eyes followed him across the yard, her hands continued to pull the husks away from an ear of corn, revealing the golden silk that lay against the tender kernels of corn. The soft, silky strings of the corn clung to her bare arms and made her skin itch. Green husks covered the newspaper and the sun reflected off the silk. She dropped her eyes and hoped that he'd not noticed her watching.

"Mornin, Missy. It's mighty hot this mornin," and he paused for her to comment. She didn't, so he continued. "I was wonderin if I could bother ye for a glass of ice cold water." She didn't raise her head, only her eyes. His black eyes had no twinkle or teasing lights. He smiled, and she saw large, white teeth. She failed to notice that the smile never reached his eyes.

Something made her move further back in the rocker, but something stronger pulled her inner self to the giant who looked at her as if she was a curious cell under a microscope. Beulah pressed her back against the rocker. She felt the heat of the morning sun and the flames from the solid body in front of her. She looked into eyes that had no depth and didn't respond to words. She suddenly realized that she didn't like his eyes, but it was difficult to look away.

When the sixteen-year-old girl in front of him continued to rock slowly and shuck corn, he thought that, maybe, she was deaf and mute. Or, maybe, real slow, which would be to his advantage.

"I wouldn't ask, but it's gittin so hot already this mornin."

It surprised him when she stopped rocking and laid the ear of corn in the large, round pan that was clasped between her thighs, just above her knees. Her thin cotton dress was pulled above the pan, exposing her upper thighs. His eyes fell on her smooth dark legs as she removed the pan and placed it on the floor near her bare feet. When she bent forward to rise out of the rocker, the scooped neckline of her dress dipped. His eyes locked on her full breasts. She wasn't wearing a bra.

"I'll be back in a minute," she said in a shy voice. His eyes followed her into the cool, dark hall. He noticed that she was tall and slender, that her waist was tiny and that her breasts were a grown woman's breasts. He was thirsty and hungry. The hunger roared in his pelvic area and he ached.

Beulah returned with a tall glass of ice water. Bending over the edge of the porch, she handed him the glass. His fingers closed over hers. Both felt the heat. He didn't let go. He was enjoying the view that the scooped neckline allowed him. Also, he was enjoying her discomfort. A smile tugged at the corners of his mouth. He dropped his hand further down on the glass so that she could remove her hand. He tilted his large smooth head back and gulped the water in one swift swallow, looking at her from under long lashes over empty eyes.

"Just what I needed. Thank you, Missy." He smacked his lips and returned the empty glass to her. "What's yo name?"

"Beulah. Beulah Burton."

"A nice name. My name's Noah Hadaway. Mighty pleased to meet ye. I'm from Texas. I work with highway crews all over Texas, Louisiana, Mississippi, and Alabama. I'm thinkin Alabama's my lucky state."

There was a silence. Beulah didn't respond. "Well, guess I'll git back to work. Mind if I bother you now and then for some ice water?"

"No. It won't be no bother."

◆

And that was how it started. With a glass of ice water. By the end of the next afternoon, Noah was sitting on the edge of the porch, drinking water, while she shelled peas. Before the crew stopped working for the long Fourth of July weekend, he'd met her mama and daddy. No one seemed surprised when he drove up that Saturday about eleven o'clock in a large red pick-up Ford truck. He helped Earnest work in the garden, and Johnie Pearl invited him for lunch. Afterwards, he returned with

Earnest to work in the fields. For the rest of the summer, he was a regular visitor and extra help. Ironically, Beulah's parents didn't seem to be aware of the attraction between their daughter and Noah, a man who was much older and more experienced. They had no idea that by the middle of July Beulah was sneaking out of her window at night, after they fell asleep, to meet him.

At the beginning of August, he told her that the crew was almost finished paving the Columbus Road, and, then, he'd return to Texas. "I want ye to go with me. I ain't takin 'No' for an answer. I done made up my mind I want ye. Be ready to go by the last Friday in August."

"I don't know. I don't think Mama and Daddy is gonna like me marryin so young. They want me to finish high school. Maybe, get some trainin as a nurse." As she spoke, she knew that she didn't have the courage to argue with Noah. He was too strong-willed, too determined when he made up his mind about things.

"We're not gonna tell them. Ye slip outa the house. We'll git married when we git to Texas. Don't leave a note. Ye can call em when we git to Texas."

The index finger of his left hand traced her hairline, from her forehead to her right ear. Then, his right hand circled her slender neck and moved slowly to her left breast. He pinched a firm nipple. He squeezed the firm mound of flesh in his large hand. "It's like a firm grapefruit. Jus the right size."

She couldn't resist. He had a control over her that she didn't understand. There was no question about it. She'd leave with him.

♦

The last Friday night in August a full moon hung low in a smooth dark sky. There were silver shadows around everything that the moon touched. A hint of autumn filled the air and made goose pimples on Beulah's skin as her feet touched the ground outside of her bedroom window. She stood, listening to the sounds of the farm, to the woods behind her house, to a life that she was leaving. For a moment, she thought about climbing back in the window, back to a life that she knew was safe, to a place where she'd known love her entire life.

She thought about the note that she'd left on the kitchen table for Johnie Pearl. Noah had told her over and over not to leave a note, but she couldn't do that to her mama and daddy. It was the least that she could do—let them know where she was going and why.

The moon washed over her and made a small shadow at her feet. She turned and saw the shadow turn with her. A lump came into her throat. Suddenly, she felt nauseous. She told herself to stop acting like a baby. She reminded herself that Noah loved her and that she loved him. She lowered the window as slowly and as quietly as possible. Quickly, she grabbed the suitcase from the ground and ran to a path in the woods. Stars filtered through the tall, thick trees and spilled miniature lights under the branches, blinking like pieces of silver coins. Halfway down the path, Noah was waiting. He took the suitcase and sat it on the ground. He reached through the darkness and pulled Beulah tight to his chest.

"There ain't no goin back. Ye're mine now," he said before his lips met hers.

They rode all night. They arrived in Chandler, Texas, the next afternoon as darkness was falling. Noah took Beulah to a small run-down house in the roughest looking neighborhood that she'd ever seen. When he flicked on the lights, she saw worn-out furniture, dirty floors, and clutter everywhere. A musky smell hit her nostrils and she frowned. Noah watched her face and laughed, "Once ye git through cleanin everything, it'll look a whole lots better. Git use to it, Missy. I don't live no fancy life."

The next morning, Beulah asked Noah when they were going to get married. His hard, dark eyes didn't blink when he gave a hoarse laugh and said, "In time. Don't push me, Missy. I don't like to be rushed. We'll git married when I'm ready."

She didn't respond. She looked at him, assessing his words, his body language. A smirk gave him the appearance of being self-satisfied. She dropped her eyes and her shoulders slumped. He pulled her to him. "Hey, it was a long drive. Let's play. Then, we'll take a nap. The cleanin can wait til tomorrow. Ye can do that while I work."

◆

Days moved into weeks that moved into months. There was no more talk of marriage. It soon became clear to Beulah that Noah had never intended to marry her. In addition to that realization, she became aware that she was trapped in a situation where her strength disappeared and every weakness was revealed. A feeling of isolation overpowered her. In didn't help her confidence to know that she faced the third realization that Noah was as worthless as a Confederate dollar and, in addition, he was an angry man who took no responsibility for his actions.

It hadn't taken Beulah long to become acquainted with the Noah who was shiftless and unreliable, a man who didn't like to be restrained by a woman or by laws. He found Beulah's humiliation amusing, and he laughed at her discomfort. Noah began to slap her and to twist her arms behind her back as he cursed and blew his whiskey breath in her face. At those times, he had a blurry, dazed stare, as if he'd just walked from a dark closet into a room flooded with sunshine. It was a frozen look that was rigid and emotionless. His face was a flat surface as if nothing lived behind the flatness, and his eyes were like black iron skillets.

More often than not, he'd come home and begin to drink, if he hadn't already stopped at some honky tonk. He'd take long swigs of the strong liquid. Beulah would watch his sharp eyes close tightly as the alcohol flowed down his throat, burning a road to his stomach. He'd shake his head and moan softly. The intense look that she gave him didn't cause him any discomfort. Instead, he laughed and made fun of her prissy ways for not drinking with him. Her only hope was that he'd fall asleep in a drunken stupor before he became violent. The violence was constantly escalating to an unbelievable, unpredictable rage.

By the time that Beulah acknowledged the relationship was a mistake, a yoke around her neck, and that she lacked the courage to run away from the muddy rut that she'd gotten into, she discovered that she was pregnant. Thirteen months after arriving in Texas, she gave birth to a son who Noah dominated from the time he held the tiny bundle in his large hands. Beulah looked on helplessly as Silas Ramsey Burton fell under his daddy's control and anger.

When Silas did something that Noah didn't like, he got a sharp slap across his small face. When Beulah intervened, Noah would slam her against a wall and choke her until she almost passed out; yet, each time, Beulah stepped in like a tiger to defend her cub. In return, she was brutally beaten, as Silas watched. She carried many bruises from defending her helpless son. But, she never stopped trying to protect him, even after Silas was later taught to laugh at her tears or to hit her when she corrected him.

When Silas was eleven months old, Beulah found herself pregnant again. She lost the baby, and, in the next year, she lost another child. When Silas was three, she learned that she was once again pregnant. By the end of five months, the doctor was certain that she'd carry the baby full term. She knew it was a possibility, if she could manage to stay away from Noah's large hands.

Life at home had become a house of horrors. The only peace that Silas or Beulah got from Noah was when his job took him out-of-town to work on road construction. It was during those times, alone with Silas, that she tried to instill in him goodness and love. His sweet baby laughter would echo throughout the old house as they played games, and he clung to his stuffed blue rabbit that she'd purchased for him one day when Noah was away. When he slept, he'd hold the rabbit tight to his tiny chest. When Noah returned home, Beulah hid the rabbit, because he'd stomped and ripped apart a stuffed teddy bear that he thought Silas cradled too much.

"I ain't havin no son a mine clingin to no sissy stuffed toy," he said, as he split the grinning teddy bear in two. Silas' tiny face wrinkled like an old man's and he fought to keep the tears at bay as he watched the bear's stuffing fall like large clumps of snow.

Another baby excited her, but it also saddened her, to the point that she cried for days, wondering how she could bring another child into Noah's violent world. Already, she could see her son taking on the personality of Noah. Just as Beulah had learned how to avoid Noah's anger, he'd become a baby who was fast learning not to cry in front of his daddy and to behave in a manner that pleased a man whose idea of pleasure was pain.

During her pregnancy, she did everything possible to make Noah happy, to prevent him from harming her or the unborn baby. When he raised his hands to her, she hovered over her belly, letting most of the blows fall on her back. Afterwards, Silas wasn't allowed to go near her, to hug her. Noah made him sit in a corner and dared him to move. If he disobeyed, Noah slapped him so hard that he fell. It wasn't long before Silas knew not to offer any sign of sympathy to Beulah.

When Beulah was alone with Silas, she'd tell him not to disobey his daddy and not to open his arms to her. "If Daddy thinks you want to hug me, he'll be mean to you. Just know that I love you and that you love me. Understand, Silas? I don't want Daddy to hurt you." He'd nod his little head and she'd kiss his cheeks. "Don't you ever forget that I love you, Silas. I'm so sorry that I don't protect you better. Forgive me."

Silas' tiny, soft hand patted her face. "It be okay, Mama. Me love you."

Three days after Christmas, Autumn was born. Noah made it known that he wasn't happy to have a daughter. From that moment on, he ignored the soft bundle of flesh, except when she cried. Then, he'd yell,

"Beulah, can't ye stop that damn racket? Shut her up! Or I will."

By the time Autumn was five months old, Noah would make Silas slap her if she cried. When they were alone, Beulah told Silas how wrong it was to hit his sister; still, she knew that Silas would be punished if he refused to obey Noah. At that age, Silas was also being told by his daddy to hit Beulah when she wouldn't agree to the boy's demands. Beulah was aware of the conflicting messages that he was receiving from his parents.

She knew that she had to escape in order to save her children. She made the mistake of revealing her plans to Silas, who told his daddy. Afterwards, Noah beat her so badly that both eyes were almost completely closed. Her lips were swollen and purple. Her body ached all over. She spit in Noah's face after the beating, and said, "I'm leavin. Or I'm gonna kill you. You hear me, man? You done turned our son into something evil like you. But, if I take him away now, I can save him."

Noah slapped her and the sound echoed throughout the house. She spit in his face again. "You just best kill me fore I kill you. Cause I swear fore God Almighty I'm gonna kill you. You no-good bastard." She felt a surge of energy and hate that overwhelmed her. In her mind's eye, she saw herself killing Noah and stomping his face until his eyeballs popped out like lottery balls.

He raised his arm, but something in her eyes stopped him. He dropped his hand and walked away. At the front door, he turned to her, and his black eyes were filled with hate. "Leave. And take yo bitch baby with ye. But, ye'll never take my son. He's mine." He slammed the door and the house shook. Silas stood in the doorway to his room, sucking his thumb, a habit that he indulged only when Noah wasn't there.

When Beulah turned, she saw him and her heart broke from the pain in his large brown eyes. A tear slid down his smooth cheek. She swept him into her arms and clutched his tiny body close. "Don't you ever, ever forget that Autumn and me love you. Don't you ever forget." His tiny hand touched a tear on her chin and he kissed her on the lips.

Because of what his daddy had instilled in him, he seldom kissed Beulah. It broke her heart.

On the seventh day, Noah still hadn't returned. Beulah prayed that he'd gone for good or that he was dead in a ditch some place far away. For seven days, she'd seen what life without Noah would be like. Silas was a changed little boy who couldn't stop smiling. For no reason, he'd hug his sister and talk softly to her. He'd climb onto Beulah's lap and ask her to read to him, while he sucked his thumb and clung to his blue rabbit. Now and then, he'd reach up and touch Beulah's face.

When Beulah awoke on the eighth day, the morning light that came through the bedroom window was dim. The house was unbelievably quiet. Beulah listened to the silence. A flood of fear washed over her and she jumped out of bed. She checked on Autumn who was fast asleep, curled up in a ball, one tiny fist against her cheek.

She went into Silas' room. He was gone. The blanket was tossed aside. There was an imprint of his tiny body on the bed and a hollowed out place on the pillow where his head had rested. The blue rabbit was in shreds, scattered over the bed. Her eyes roamed around the semi-dark room. The dresser drawers had been left open. She saw that Silas' clothes were missing. A scream rose in her throat and she clasped her mouth shut to stop it from escaping into the room and awaking Autumn.

Frantically, she began to search throughout the house for a note. Nothing. How could she have slept through the kidnapping of her baby? Why hadn't Silas made a noise to awaken her? She knew the answer to that question. She made a pot of coffee and sat at the kitchen table, watching the dawn enter the dismal kitchen. She put her head on her arms and wept, "Please, God, let my boy be safe. Please take care of my baby. Please bring him back to me. I beg you. Please." It was a prayer that she'd never stop repeating.

The next day, she asked her neighbor to take her to Noah's job site.

When they arrived, she got out of the car, with determination written on her face and in her body language. An employee introduced her to Justin Farr who was Noah's boss. Farr told her that Noah had gotten in a fight nine days previously with another employee who was beaten so badly by Noah that he was still in intensive care at the local hospital. A warrant had been sworn out for Noah's arrest.

"And, by god, if I see that bastard within ten feet of me or my place, I'm gonna call the cops. If I don't kill him first," said Farr.

"When I stepped in to break up the fight, Noah punched me in the nose. I bled like a damn pig. Anyways, I fired him. Then and there. I'm sorry, but I didn't have no choice. And it wasn't the first time Noah has fought with other employees. I've no idea where he is." He stopped talking and took a long look at her, at her wary eyes. "I'm holdin a week's wages for him. I'm gonna give the money to you," he said, looking intensely at her.

"Thank you. And I understand bout Noah. Believe me. I do," she said with acid in her tone. She thought that the trip to Noah's place of employment had given up nothing. Soon, she realized how wrong she was. She'd accomplished two things. One, she knew the reason for his anger the day that he left the house. Two, there was money to live on for a while. And she added another thing to the list. She knew that he'd been fired and she knew the reasons.

She spent the next three weeks searching every inch of Chandler, trying to find Silas, talking to everyone she knew who might know something. No one did or they wouldn't tell her anything. A trip to Noah's Aunt Fannie's home was a waste of time. Fannie Hadaway had raised Noah, defending every low-down and dishonest thing that he ever did, from the time he was a tot until he was sent to a Texas prison at the age of seventeen for armed robbery and almost killing an eighty-year-old man whom he thought that he'd left dead in a rural gas station. Noah drove away from the scene with twenty dollars from the cash register.

But, he'd "whipped that ole man's ass good."

The judge decided that he'd seen enough of Noah Hadaway in his courtroom. If it hadn't been one thing, it'd been another ever since Noah was an arrogant twelve-year-old, terrorizing the neighborhood. At the age of fifteen, he'd been accused of raping an eleven-year-old girl, but there wasn't enough evidence to convict him. Finally, the judge had enough to "throw the book" at Noah, and he didn't carefully select his words when he gave Fannie Hadaway a tongue lashing for being an awful influence on the boy.

Several weeks after Beulah arrived in Texas with Noah, his Aunt Fannie told her about the time he spent in the state penitentiary. There was something grim about the way she spoke, as if she held the truth in a tight fist, releasing only bits and pieces of it when it pleased her. And it pleased Aunt Fannie to see the look of shock on Beulah's face when she learned that the man with whom she'd fallen in love and left home to marry was an ex-con, a violent man who'd almost killed a helpless old man for twenty dollars. Beulah couldn't comprehend why Noah wasn't still in prison, based on the history of Texas' penal system. It puzzled her, but she'd learned how cunning he was.

"The ole fool shoulda gave Noah the money. If he'd a done that, he might not be walkin round with a cane today," she said and spit tobacco juice at Beulah's feet. "That's what he gits for bein stupid." Beulah stood rigid, dumbfounded by such logic.

The woman who'd raised Noah since he was two years old claimed that he stopped coming by to visit and she had no idea where he might be. He'd not been in contact with anyone in her family. Noah's aunt had been lying for him for decades, and Beulah knew she was telling a lie. There was not a thing that she could do to make Miss Fannie tell the truth about Silas' whereabouts. She could only keep an eye on her house, hoping to catch Noah or Silas there.

The police were no help. The chief of police told her that Noah had a right to take his son and that they might return and it was "too early to be gittin all outa gear. Ain't no man gonna burden hisself down with no small young'un. Go on home and wait. He'll bring the boy back when he gits tired a baby-sittin." He showed no interest in pursuing Silas.

When she told him that he didn't have any idea who he was talking about, the chief gave a deep disgusted sigh and recommended that she hire an attorney who might be able to help her locate Silas and bring him home. She'd have to go before a judge. All of that required money, which Beulah didn't have. She felt hopeless, but continued the search for Silas on her own.

The fourth week after their disappearance, Beulah wanted to call Johnie Pearl. She hadn't seen or talked to her mama or daddy since she'd left home, because Noah had demanded that she cut all ties to Alabama. Right after Noah left, she didn't call because she was too embarrassed, and she didn't want to give up hope that he'd bring Silas back to her. Instead of immediately calling her parents, she got a job at a chicken processing plant. While she worked, Hattie Chambers, an elderly woman who lived next door, took care of Autumn and two other neighborhood children.

It'd be almost a year after Silas disappeared before Beulah contacted her parents. They came to Texas and listened to her talk about her life with Noah. She couldn't tell them all of the terrible things that he'd done to his family or explain the deep empty hole in her soul for her son. They begged her to return to Alabama with them. They weren't surprised when she refused. Although they were disappointed that she chose to stay in Texas, they understood the hope that Beulah had of finding Silas. What if he should return and she was gone? She had to be in the same house in case he came back.

♦

Hattie Chambers taught Beulah how to drive a car. After she got her driving license, she purchased an old beat-up green Chevrolet.

Whenever she got a lead about Silas' whereabouts, she'd pack Autumn up on a weekend, and they'd head in the direction of the lead, regardless of how hopeless or small it was.

One lead led them to a small rural town in Arkansas on a cold winter day. The dilapidated trailer park was discouraging. It was full of dogs, whose ribs showed beneath sagging flesh, and scattered, foul-smelling trash blew in the wind. Discarded appliances sat in yards that'd never seen grass; sagging sofas sat on small front porches; an old car sat on cinderblocks, minus tires, with the hood raised and the windows open to catch rainwater. When she knocked on a filthy front door that was beaten inward, a sloppy overweight ebony man with a small head came to the door. His belly cascaded over dirty pants that hung low. He had a fried chicken leg in one hand and was licking the thick fingers of his other hand. Grease from the chicken made a circle around his too full lips. His bare toes were covered in fungus.

He claimed to know nothing about Noah or Silas. "Never heard of em," he told her. It was difficult to tell if he was lying. She thanked him and went from trailer to trailer, asking the same questions and getting the same answers. No one knew anything about Noah or Silas. Or they weren't telling.

Another lead took her to northern Mississippi on a sweltering summer day, to a poor black neighborhood where the houses were small and close together. There were rows and rows of run-down green shotgun shacks, with four rooms each. The rows of houses looked like fields of tall corn.

She stopped the Chevrolet in a dirt driveway and sat looking at a crooked house. It was the only one that was painted barn red. It was worn out by time, weather, and unconcern. An old man dozed in a rocker on the porch. Dead flowers hung from sad baskets that were dry and hot to the touch. The front door was wide open. There was no screen. From where she sat, she could see flies traveling freely in and out

44

of the house. They buzzed unnoticed around the old man's head. In a dim corner of the room, she saw the silver flashing of a TV and two small bodies in front of the magic screen. Her heart skipped a beat and a lump lodged itself in her throat.

Daring not to breath too loudly, she heard jazz float from the house next door. The yells of children playing two houses down drifted into the parked car. She put a hand across her left eyebrow to shield her eyes from the sun that sent long rays of heat over the scorched surface of the yard and into the car. Suddenly, she realized that she was holding her breath, and she slowly released the air that was choking her lungs.

She told Autumn to stay in the car. With caution, she got out of the car and walked to the bottom of the steps. "Excuse me, sir." The only response was a couple of loud snores. In a louder voice, she said, "Excuse me, Sir. I want to ask you some questions." The old man shooed away a fly with a skinny, limp hand and turned his face so that she saw only a profile. "Hey! Excuse me."

Two small children came to the door. Both were girls. Beulah's heart sank. She felt like throwing herself on the ground and screaming. She walked up the steps and stood beside the open door. Looking into the dark house, she saw an exposed bulb hanging on a long wire from the ceiling. The dim light left too much in shadows. A dirty yellow sofa, tattered and torn, sat against the far wall. A TV sat on top of a dresser that had sagging drawers. The linoleum rug was worn bare in spots, and the ridges in the uneven floor had indented the rug, causing cracks. Beulah could smell stale tobacco and dirty diapers; she was assaulted by the stench of a stale, mildew aroma and acid urine. The smell permeated out the door and onto the rotten wooden porch. Beulah's stomach rolled and she felt sick.

Trying to hide her disgust, she asked, "Is your mama home?"

The oldest girl bobbed her head, stuck three fingers into her mouth, and licked something from them. Her large eyes starred at Beulah and moved to the car.

"Please tell your mama that I'd like to speak with her. Okay?" Beulah smiled at the two dirty faces before her.

The small head bobbed again before the skinny girl turned and ran into the house, yelling, "Mama, some lady wants a talk to you."

Soon, a young woman, who looked exhausted, sauntered to the door in slow motion. A small baby nursed one enormous breast. The woman was barefoot and hollow eyed. Her hair had been brushed upward and was left reaching into outer space. A large red pick comb was parked just beyond the hairline of the upward wave. The woman wore a look of indifference, and she gave off a repugnant odor that couldn't be identified. She didn't speak as a fly landed near the baby's mouth.

Beulah explained her mission, while the woman glanced at her out of lazy looking eyes that showed no interest. When Beulah had finished, the woman managed to utter, "I don't know any Noah or Silas." For some reason, Beulah didn't believe her, but she didn't press.

"Thank you," she said, taking a long look at the newborn in the woman's arm. Without thinking, she asked, "Is it a boy or a girl?"

"Another girl," the woman replied in an irritated voice.

"I hope to hell she doesn't know Noah" went through Beulah's mind.

Beulah knocked on every door in the neighborhood. No luck.

The final lead took her to an upper middle class suburb in Houston. It was a gated community, where two-story houses sat back from the road, with expansive manicured lawns and large shade trees. She pulled into a circular drive and stopped in front of a large stone and brick house that seemed to have wings. Sitting in her old faded green Chevrolet, she figured that she'd gotten the wrong address, that her informer was misinformed.

Looking at the slip of paper on which she'd written the address and house number, she realized that it was the same. Butterflies fluttered in her belly and her hands shook. "No way," she thought as she opened the car door and stood looking up at the house. Her shoulders squared and her mouth became determined. Standing wasn't going to tell her anything, so she marched up the steps and pushed the doorbell. She heard it ring softly inside the house. Soon, she heard footsteps on wooden floors.

An elderly plump black woman opened the door. "Can I help you?" she asked in a gentle Texas voice. She was dressed in a black dress with a white collar and cuffs. She wore white stockings and black leather no-nonsense shoes.

"I'd like to speak to the lady of the house, please ma'am," Beulah said calmly and added, "If you don't mind."

"That'd be Mrs. Colleen Chadwick. May I ask who's callin?"

"My name's Beulah. Beulah Burton," she said, trying not to twist her hands.

"Wait here." The plump woman turned gracefully, left the door cracked, and walked into a room to the right of the hallway. Beulah could hear low voices.

Within minutes, a tall, slender woman appeared. Short natural blond hair, with a deep wave that almost covered one eye, swept away from one side of her oval face. A sharp-edged nose lay perfectly balanced between the bluest eyes that Beulah had ever seen. Her eyes were the color of the sky when you looked directly up, not the far away distant blue where the sky stops and the blue begins to fade. The ivory skin looked as if it'd never seen the sun, but the woman wore what looked like riding pants, a pair of highly shined brown leather boots, and a creamy silk blouse that lay against a flat chest. Everything about her, from her high cheekbones to her full pouting lips, screamed elegance and class. Beulah watched as the woman moved forward as if she were on a fashion runway.

When she reached the doorway, Beulah realized that they were both tall, about the same height. The woman held a book in her left hand.

"I'm Colleen Chadwick. How can I help you?" the cool low voice asked.

"Please, come inside," she invited, after a brief silence.

"No, thank you. My daughter's waitin in the car. And I don't wanna let her outa my sight. I'll stay on the porch. If that's all right with you."

"That's fine with me," she said and reached behind her to close the solid oak door, as she looked at the pretty girl in the dusty car.

Beulah explained who she was and the reason that she was there. "A person told me that Noah worked for someone named Chadwick. That person gave me this here address. Can you tell me where he might be? Noah."

Colleen's cool blue eyes never looked away from Beulah as she talked, but there was nothing on her face that Beulah could read. She waited a moment after Beulah stopped talking before she spoke. She again looked past Beulah's right shoulder at Autumn and spoke.

"Noah worked for me for about six months, hauling dirt and doing landscaping work. He was a hard worker, but one day he just didn't show up for work. I never heard from him again." She paused for a moment and looked into Beulah's eyes. "He never said anything about having a son. I'm sorry. I don't recall him ever discussing his personal life."

"And you ain't got no idea where he might be? Where he went to after he left?" Beulah asked hopefully.

"No. I'm sorry. I wish that I could help. If you'll leave me your address and a phone number, I'll contact you. If I hear anything at all."

As Beulah wrote down the information, Colleen said in a wondering voice, "I don't understand why your informer didn't give you the address of my business. Chadwick's Landscaping and Design. My manager would be able to answer your questions better than I'm able to do so. I'll give you the address of the business and my manager's name. If you like."

Beulah looked up, "That'll be nice. I'm interested in every lead that I can get. Regardless of where it ends up."

Beulah gave Colleen Chadwick the requested information and wrote down the information that she was given. As she drove down the long drive, she noticed a smaller, but very nice, house that was hidden among trees. A graveled road led to the house. Beulah thought that she saw a face at a window. She looked back at the large two-story house. Colleen Chadwick was still standing at the closed door, watching as she drove away. The old Chevrolet came to the end of the drive and she took a right.

After she spoke with Marvin Coleman, the manager of Chadwick's Landscaping and Design, one more dim hope was snatched away. Yes, Noah had worked there for almost a year. He'd been a hard worker, but he had a bad temper, which had caused the manager to fire him. No, Marvin didn't know anything about a son. Noah never mentioned a family. And he had no idea where Noah had lived while he worked there.

Beulah believed that there was more than what she'd been told, but there was no way to prove it. She wanted to cry, but she couldn't upset Autumn, who sat in the passenger's side of the front seat, with questioning eyes.

"Another dead end," she said, as she stroked Autumn's head.

Marvin Coleman and Colleen Chadwick had claimed that they knew nothing. Beulah had no way of proving differently, so she left the parking lot and headed to a life without her son, but still searching.

◆

Months turned into years. Nothing. Beulah never saw a boy who was Silas' age that she didn't observe his every feature and mannerism. As the years moved along, one after the other, she wondered how tall he'd be and how he might have changed. And she kept looking, following every lead, traveling through Texas, Oklahoma, New Mexico, and back to Texas. She followed a hopeless lead to a small rural town in Arkansas, where she got another lead that took her to Mississippi. It was as if Noah and Silas had disappeared from the face of the earth.

One day, Beulah was rushing Autumn to pack a bag. There'd been another lead and Beulah was ready to follow it. With tears in her eyes, Autumn, whose body was slim and fragile, stomped her tiny foot and said, "No! I ain't lookin no more. Mama, he's gone. I'm here. We ain't never gonna find him."

Beulah's body slumped, as she watched Autumn storm into her room and slam the door. She heard her daughter's tears, while she sank into the old saggy sofa, with her hands hanging loosely between her knees. It was a long time before she stopped looking at the closed door, listening to the soft sobs that broke Beulah's heart.

The burning heat of the hot Texas September morning sun crawled through the thin curtains and cast a small light at Beulah's feet. The warmth wrapped itself around her motionless body and chilled her bones. She shivered in the heat of the cruel Texas sunshine.

After what seemed like hours, she rose from the sofa and heard the springs creak. Exhaustion filled her body. She knocked on Autumn's door. "Baby, it's okay. We ain't goin. Open the door."

Slowly, a swollen-faced Autumn opened the door. Her head hung down on her chest and her small shoulders were slumped forward. Beulah pulled her into her arms. "We're goin home, baby. We're goin home to Alabama. To my mama and daddy. I'm takin you home. I'm gonna let go fore we both go slam crazy. Maybe, one day, God willin, I'll find him. I ain't gonna put you through no more pain." She kissed the top of Autumn's head.

Autumn looked up from under long lashes and said, "Mama, I love Silas. But, Mama, he's gone."

"I know, baby. I know. Maybe, one day we'll all be together again."

Beulah's mama called the next day to tell her that Earnest had suffered a slight stroke. She wanted Beulah to come home. Beulah agreed and told Johnie Pearl that she'd already decided to return to Alabama, after years of looking for Silas.

The next day she quit her job. She made the rounds, paying her utilities and requesting that they be disconnected within a certain time. Next, she spoke with her landlord, and they agreed that he'd give her six hundred dollars for everything that she left behind. She packed what she was taking to Alabama in the old green car. It'd been two weeks since Beulah talked to Johnie Pearl. Finally, Beulah and Autumn were leaving Texas. It'd be decades before they returned to the state that had swallowed up Silas and erased every memory of his whereabouts since his daddy had kidnapped him.

On a hot day, they waved goodbye to Miss Hattie, who shamelessly shed tears for the two people whom she'd grown to love. Beulah and Autumn hugged her tightly and kissed her soft wrinkled face. Beulah backed out of the narrow driveway and pointed the car towards Alabama, while Autumn hung half-way out of the window, waving to Miss Hattie and blowing kisses.

After driving all day and night, they crossed the Mississippi Delta, late in the afternoon of the following day, just as the sun was sinking. The reflecting surface of the water threw back at them images that were full of life. The windows were down, letting a breeze from the river enter the car. Tears floated in Beulah's eyes, making everything blurry. She looked at Autumn who'd been reading and whose eyes were wide, while her mouth formed a small circle. Autumn had never seen anything like the large muddy river.

"We're almost home, baby," Beulah said, with a catch in her voice. Then, she stuck her left arm out of the window and pressed the horn, long and loud, with her right hand. "Alabama, here we come!" Autumn laughed and waved out the window at the flowing Mississippi.

Both began to shout, "Alabama, here we come!" The sound drifted out the windows and floated down the river, as the dark water made its way to the Gulf of Mexico. Alabama would soon welcome them on the other side of the wide river.

Late that night, they arrived at Johnie Pearl's house. Nothing had changed, except Earnest had given the old wooden house a fresh coat of paint and added shutters to all of the windows. More gravel than Beulah remembered lay on the driveway. The garden appeared neglected in the moonlight. Lights, from the kitchen, the living room, and her parent's bedroom, washed around the house like a halo, throwing out a lighted path for the two who'd returned home.

For seven months, Beulah helped her mama nurse her daddy back to health. During that time, she enrolled Autumn in the local school. When Earnest was almost back to his normal self, Beulah got a job at River View Mill. She began a new life with her daughter and her parents, a life that was spent thinking of her son and praying that he was safe.

CHAPTER FOUR

It was a Saturday morning when Beulah finished telling Mavis the complete story. They were sitting at Mavis' kitchen table, drinking coffee. Both were silent. Then, Beulah added, "That was so many years ago. Still, I can't forget my boy. I think bout him every day." Mavis laid both her hands over Beulah's left hand.

Early that morning, Mavis had called Beulah. "I want you to come over. I'm making biscuits, with sausage and gravy. Robert's gone to look for arrowheads with Winston and Morgan. They won't be back til dark-thirty. Be here in bout twenty minutes." Winston and Morgan were Mavis' two favorite sons-in-law. The other three sons-in-law didn't rank too high in Mavis' opinion.

That Saturday had begun years of Mavis calling Beulah at all hours of the day or night to come have sausage and biscuits or cake and coffee, or to go to Wal-Mart or the dog track in Shorter. Beulah always came, regardless of the time.

After Beulah finished the story, which had seeped out bit-by-bit, she sat hunched over, as tears slid down her cheeks and dropped onto the table. Neither spoke for some time. Beulah wiped the tears away with the back of her hand. Looking up at Mavis, she saw sadness and anger. Mavis got up and wrapped her arms around Beulah and laid her head on

Beulah's left shoulder. "I'm so sorry. Sorry for the hell that bastard put you through. Sorry that you've lost Silas. I'm glad you came home, and I'm glad you're my friend."

Mavis sat back down and picked up her cup of coffee that had gone from hot to warm. "Well, we've got something else in common. You ran away with a man. So did I. I was fifteen. Let me tell you how it happened."

◆

Robert Claude Norrell was a sharecropper on Mavis' daddy's land. He was twenty-five when Dewey Lee Baker and he made a verbal agreement. Robert would lease twenty-five acres of land that he'd use to raise two cows, a horse, three pigs, a dozen chickens, one rooster, cotton, and vegetables. In addition, he'd help Dewey with large acres of cotton, for a percentage and the right to live on twenty-five acres of land.

It was a cold, bleak February day when Robert came to Dewey Baker's house to talk about sharecropping. He was twenty-five years old and had decided to ask for as many acres as he'd lived. The two men sat at the kitchen table, drinking steaming black coffee, and made a deal that satisfied both of them.

Mavis had watched from the kitchen window as a slender, medium height man walked up the dirt driveway. Dark curls whipped about his lean face, and his hands were shoved in the front pockets of tight Levi's. The wind caused him to hunch forward into a dark brown jacket that was zipped to his neck. The corduroy collar of the jacket was turned up for protection. His movements were cat-like quick and almost too graceful for a farmer, but not for a dancer.

When he came to the end of the driveway, near the front porch steps, he paused and looked up at the wooden house that was surrounded by shrubbery and bare rosebushes. Mavis continued to watch as he took two long strides to reach the steps and began the climb to the porch. He disappeared from her vision. Two quick raps sounded on the door. Slowly, she stopped washing dishes and dried her hands on a kitchen towel. Walking to the door, she heard him lightly stomp his feet on the wooden planks to create some warmth.

When the fourteen-year-old girl opened the door, two sparkling sky-blue eyes looked at her. Cheekbones jarred from the man's slender face. His ears and nose were big, but became a memory when he smiled, showing even white teeth. The crooked smile sent cat whiskers to the corners of his beaming eyes. It was like the sun was standing at the door. Mavis' breath caught in her throat. In June, she'd be fifteen. Still, a baby, according to her parents.

"Hi. Is your daddy home?" His voice was clear and polite.

"No. He's in the pasture."

"Well, I wanted to talk business with him. Do you mind pointin me towards the pasture?"

"It's that way." She pointed left. She noticed how his eyes seemed to be laughing.

"Thank you." He turned to leave, but turned back around. "What's your name?"

"Mavis."

"It was a pleasure meetin you, Miss Mavis." He nodded and turned away. She stood in the door and watched until he walked across the yard toward the pasture. Mavis could hear her younger brothers and sisters playing in the back yard, as they took turns swinging on a tire that hung from a tall oak tree. The two older boys were helping her daddy mend fences in the pasture.

Mavis closed the door against the wind and walked back into the kitchen, to finish washing dishes and to help her mama bake bread. Willie Baker's hands were deep in dough. She turned around as Mavis entered the warm kitchen. She looked at her oldest child and saw a flush on her high cheekbones. Turning back to kneading dough, she asked,

"Who was that man and what did he want?"

"I don't know, Mama. He didn't tell me his name. Just said he wanted to talk with Daddy bout business. I told him Daddy was working in the pasture and pointed him in that direction."

By the end of the week, Robert had moved into the shifty sharecropper's house, which was approximately a mile from Dewey's house. Within another week, he began stringing barbwire fences around a ten-acre pasture. Mavis rode with her daddy to take a look at the progress Robert had made. That morning, Dewey let her drive the truck, which she'd been driving since she was twelve. When Mavis parked the truck next to the sloping front porch, Robert was putting up the last fence. He waved to them from a distance and started walking toward the house. Dewey and Mavis stood at the hood of the truck and waited.

Howdy, Mr. D. How y'all doin?" he asked as he got within five feet of the truck. He removed a hat from his head, revealing crushed dark curls. Pulling a red bandana from his jacket pocket, he looked at Mavis and continued, "Good to see you, Miss Mavis. Nice drivin you doin." After wiping his face and hands, he stuck the bandana back into the pocket of his jacket. He extended a dirty hand to Dewey and tipped his hat to Mavis. "Next, I'm startin on pens for the animals. Got to keep them in before I build a shed and a barn."

After pulling the hat low over his eyes, he reached into his shirt pocket and withdrew a pack of cigarettes. As he listened to Dewey, he thumped the bottom of the pack, pulled out a loose cigarette, and replaced the pack in his shirt pocket. He stuck the cigarette into the left corner of his mouth, tilted his head slightly forward, struck a match, and sucked the fire into the tip of the unfiltered cigarette. He leaned his head to the sky and blew out a thin, gray cloud that floated into the wind, sweeping the smoke around his head. He closed his blue eyes and inhaled a second time.

Mavis leaned against the hood of the truck, watching Robert go through the process of smoking. Dewey had never smoked and didn't approve of the habit. She noticed him frown while Robert completed the ritual. The two men discussed the fence, pens, animals, and planting cotton. As they talked, she watched Robert, with the openness and innocence of a child. It didn't occur to her that the open evaluation of the handsome man was anything but the curiosity of a child. Robert felt her green eyes and kept glancing at her. Something about the way that she looked at people, intense, without blinking or speaking, intrigued him. He'd never met anyone, young or old, who seemed to be intruding inside your head, analyzing and defining.

"Well, we best be lettin you get back to what you're doin. Thought I'd stop by and see how things are goin. If you need anything, let me know," Dewey said as he headed to the passenger's side of the truck. "Okay, Mavis, back it out slow. Ain't no need in tearin outa here like some bat outa hell."

In a voice that revealed she'd been insulted, Mavis poked back, "I know how to drive, Daddy." Robert gave a crooked grin and his eyes twinkled. Turning to Robert, she continued, "Daddy drives like a turtle. Why just last week the police stopped him for driving so slow. And, of all things, Daddy said, 'It's my damn car. I'll drive it anyways I wanna drive it.' Now, don't that beat all? Talking to the police like that?"

Dewey snorted, "Git in the truck, Mavis. You talk too much."

◆

In June, Mavis turned fifteen. Willie gave her a birthday party on a Saturday afternoon, two days following her birthday. All of Mavis' friends and relatives were invited. Robert came and stood in the distance, watching. He'd given Mavis a small heart that hung from a delicate gold chain. It'd cost him every cent that he'd been saving. When he got ready to leave, he wished Mavis a happy birthday and bent to kiss her forehead. Her face turned crimson and she avoided his laughing eyes.

Willie wasn't pleased with Robert's gift and insisted that Mavis return it. Mavis cried and pleaded until Dewey took her side, telling Willie that it was only a gift and that she was getting too upset over small stuff. Mavis threw her arms around her daddy, while Willie's lips pressed firmly together.

By the beginning of August, Mavis was at Robert's house almost every day, helping with chores. She'd bring two or three of her siblings, who were too young to recognize what was unfolding before them. Most of the time, Robert would be in the fields when she and her siblings came. He'd return home to find a clean house and a warm meal.

Willie wasn't happy that her daughter spent time cleaning and cooking at Robert's house. She had several discussions with Dewey, to express her disagreement. Dewey wanted to know if Mavis and the other kids were failing to do chores at home. When Willie admitted that nothing was being neglected at home, he told her to let it go. It didn't hurt the kids to offer a helping hand and Robert was working from daylight to dark. He needed some help. Finally, Willie sighed and stopped complaining.

When fall arrived, Mavis began to find excuses after school to "check on things." Soon, she was sneaking out of the house at night to meet Robert. By that time, he'd purchased an old black Ford truck that had rust spots on one door and several fenders. On the weekends, he took her and one or two of her siblings for long drives down dirt roads. Often, they'd stop by the creek that was on Dewey's land, not too far from his house. As Mavis' siblings fished, Robert often hinted that he wanted her to run away with him. At first, she laughed and told him that her parents had big plans for her. It wasn't long before she began to listen to his plans and nod her head.

The first frost arrived. The days got shorter and winter began blowing in from the north. It was October, and everything was beginning to decay, to become food for new beginnings. The woods were filled with brilliant colors that danced in the sun. Soon, leaves would become brittle and begin the process of decomposition. They were already covering the ground, crunching when stepped upon and releasing woodsy odors of musk and mold. Something about the beginning of fall gave off energy, and Mavis could feel it in her blood.

Halloween was a week away. Mavis' Aunt Lolly, who lived six miles away, was planning her annual Halloween party. Neighbors within miles would come and bring their families. They'd roast wieners and marshmallows. There would be dancing in the barn. Later, everyone would sit around the fire and tell ghost stories. It'd be midnight before the first guest left.

Robert and Mavis made plans to slip away from the party. The plan was to run away and get married. Robert's family lived in Dadeville, and they'd go to his Aunt Vera's to spend the night. Bright and early the next morning, when the doors opened, they'd be at the courthouse. Mavis' mama and daddy wouldn't have time to find them or to stop the marriage.

Everything went as planned. As people settled down around the fire to roast marshmallows and listen to stories, Mavis and Robert moved behind the crowd, sitting quietly until they were certain that no one was paying any attention to them. Then, they crept silently into the darkness and ran a half-mile down the road, where Robert had left the old truck.

A brown cardboard suitcase was on the passenger's side. Robert sat it on the floorboard under Mavis' feet. Then, he handed Mavis a large brown paper sack that she'd placed in the ditch, earlier that day. When Willie asked what was in the sack, Mavis replied that it was shucks from the fall field corn that Dewey raised to feed the animals. The kids liked the corn as well; therefore, Willie would often roast it for them. It made sense that Mavis was taking the shucks to the barn for the cattle. Willie had no idea that the sack contained a nightgown and clothing, as well as a dress for the wedding.

Robert hesitated before closing the door. "Are you sure that you want to do this?" he asked.

"I'm here, ain't I? Let's go." She touched his cheek.

He closed the door and smiled. A slice of moon sailed in and out of a dark cloud. The engine purred to life and its headlights shot straight lines of light into the darkness. Mavis slid across the seat and rested her head on Robert's shoulder. She began to hum softly.

By the time that the first guest left the party, they were almost at Vera's house. She was waiting. When they arrived, she immediately opened the door and hugged Mavis. Robert was given orders to sleep on the sofa and Mavis took the guest bedroom. Vera reminded them that they had to get up early, in order to drive to the courthouse, to be there when it opened. She'd be a witness.

"Dewey and Willie are gonna be mad as wet hens with me. For a long time," she told them. "And at you," she added, looking at Robert. "I suggest that y'all stay with me for a while. Maybe, by that time, things will have cooled down."

They agreed. Vera said that she'd take Mavis for a visit with Dewey and Willie, after some time passed. "It'll be best if you don't come with us," she told Robert. "They're gonna be mad, but, by that time, y'all will be man and wife. I think they'll come around."

◆

After three weeks, Vera drove Mavis to her parents' home. Neither spoke much as they left Tallapoosa County and entered Chambers County. Vera turned the car in the direction of Lee County, where Hopewell Community ran along the Lee County line. Empty cornfields and cotton fields came into view.

Mavis had heard how Dewey had sat in his truck, every afternoon for days, at the end of the long driveway. He'd park the truck at the edge of the highway. A shotgun stood on the floorboard of the passenger's side. Its barrel was pointed toward the roof of the truck, within easy reach.

He was waiting for "that sonofabitch, Robert Norrell" to drive by. Finally, one afternoon, the sheriff came by and told Dewey "to let it go, cause they're married now, and there ain't a thing you can do. Anyways, now, she's his wife. In every sense of the word."

Willie blamed Dewey for being "stubborn" and for "refusin to see what was happenin right in front of their eyes." She reminded him over and over that he should've listened to her. She'd seen the signs, but Dewey had refused to pay attention, because he was too concerned about land and cotton and making money.

Every night, while Dewey sat at the edge of the road, Willie cried. She recalled how everyone had spoiled Mavis, from the time that she was a small child. Willie would never admit it, but the love that she felt for her first-born child was a special love. Thinking of Mavis made Willie recall how she'd never liked Robert Norrell. She'd never liked how he looked at Mavis when he thought no one else was watching. She saw those looks and tried to warn Dewey. Because her husband had refused to see what was going on in front of him, she'd lost her daughter to a man whom she hated.

It was almost dinner when Vera pulled into the driveway and drove slowly to the side of the house, near the kitchen. Mavis knew that Dewey would still be somewhere outside, doing chores that were never-ending on a farm. She saw Willie looking out the window and felt a chill that no winter could produce. She drew her coat tightly across her chest before she opened the door and stepped out of the car into the bright sunshine. Taking a deep breath, she began mounting the steps to the back porch, while her heart began a rapid beat.

When she reached the porch, Willie opened the door. They looked at one another for what seemed like hours. Willie felt overwhelmed and tried to hide her emotions. She wanted to grab Mavis and hold her close, but she was a woman of self-control. And she was still hurt, still angry.

Vera stepped between them and extended her hand. "Hello, Willie.

I'm Robert's Aunt Vera. I've brought Mavis for a visit."

Willie said flatly, "I know who you are. I've known Norrells all my life. Ain't too many of them worth killin." Acid was in the tone of her voice, and she looked at Vera as if she were an insect crawling on Willie's skin.

Choosing to ignore the vinegar in Willie's voice, Vera's blue eyes crinkled when she smiled and she continued, "Mavis wanted to come. She wants to talk to you. And to Dewey."

Mavis felt Willie's nasty disposition and stepped around Vera. She hugged her mama and whispered in her ear, "I love you, Mama. Please don't turn me away. Please."

Willie's response was non-committable, but a lump lay in her throat as her heart beat fast in her chest. "Come inside, outa the cold. Dewey will be comin for dinner in a minute. Your younger sisters are outside, gatherin eggs. The others are at school." She paused for a moment and said, "Where you need to be."

Vera and Mavis stepped into the warm kitchen. A large pot of vegetable soup simmered on the stove. Willie had just removed a black skillet of cornbread from the oven. The smell of sweet potato pie drifted among the room. A gallon jar of sweet tea sat on the counter.

"Mavis, sat the table. Add plates for yourself and Vera. Y'all might as well eat since you're here and the food is ready," Willie instructed, without looking at Mavis.

"Yes, ma'ma," Mavis said. "Mama makes the best cornbread and tea in the world. And, just wait til you taste that pie," she added, smiling at Vera who had pulled a chair away from the table and was sitting as far away from Willie as she could get.

Willie's back was to them. A smile crept into her dark green eyes. Suddenly, she wanted to dance with Mavis across the floor, to tell her how happy she was, now that she was home. Instead, she turned around and said, "Mavis is a good cook herself. I guess that's a good thing since she's done run off and married. Before she's even started shavin her legs."

"Mama, you know I've been shavin my legs for a year. Don't you remember how mad it makes Daddy when I use his razor?"

No sooner had she spoken than her sisters, Betsy and Rosa Bell, came into the room. Betsy was carrying a large bowl that contained eggs. When she saw Mavis, she sat the bowl on the floor and ran to Mavis, wrapping her arms around Mavis' legs. Rosa Bell clung to Mavis' other side. Mavis bent down, hugging and kissing both.

"Did Robert come with you?" Rosa Bell asked. Silence filled the room, as Rosa Bell looked into Mavis' eyes that were so much like Willie's.

"No. It's just me."

"Are you stayin?" Betsy asked, bouncing on her feet and clasping her hands together as if she were about to pray.

"No. I just came to visit," and she turned to Willie, "and to talk with Mama."

From the doorway, Dewey spoke, "Well, for goodness sake. Who is this? Come here, Mavis. Give your daddy a hug." Mavis flew into his outstretched arms. She laid her head on his broad chest while he stroked her hair and caught Willie's eyes that were bright with unshed tears.

Still holding onto Mavis, Dewey walked across the room and held out his hand to Vera. "Hello, I'm Dewey Baker. Mavis' daddy. Thank you for bringin my girl home."

Vera stood and extended her hand. She was almost as tall as Dewey. "Nice to meet you. I'm Robert's Aunt Vera. They've been stayin with me. In Dadeville. I brought Mavis for a visit."

"I see," Dewey said, through tight lips. Mavis noticed that his left eye began to twitch, which was an involuntary habit that he had when he was mad.

Quickly, Mavis said, "Daddy, I want to talk with you and Mama.

Later, after dinner." She locked eyes with Dewey. He saw a determined look in her eye that reminded him too well of Willie.

"Okay. Well, let's eat. I'm starvin," he said and sat at the head of the table.

After dinner, Vera helped Betsy and Rosa Bell wash dishes, while Mavis sat with Willie and Dewey in the living room. Willie closed the door so that Vera couldn't hear the conversation. Vera Norrell had interfered too much already in things that were none of her business.

After the dishes were washed, dried, and put away, Vera went outside with the girls to see the playhouse that Dewey had recently built for them. It was over an hour before Willie called them inside. Vera was apprehensive, but tried not to show it as she walked into the kitchen. Willie's face didn't look as grim, and Dewey had a broad smile on his face.

Mavis ran to Vera and hugged her. "Robert and I are coming home. We're going to live in his house. Well, Daddy's house that he's letting us live in. I'm so happy. I want to be near my mama and daddy. I want to be near my sisters and brothers."

"That's wonderful," Vera said, looking from Willie to Dewey.

"Thank you for bringin our girl home," Dewey said to Vera. "You tell Robert Norrell that I'm gonna have a long talk with him when he gets back. Just let him know."

"I'll do that." Vera looked at Mavis and said, "I guess we'd better start back." She looked around the room. "It was nice meetin all of you."

Everyone followed them to the car. Vera watched Mavis hug and kiss each one. Mavis looked at Willie just before she got into the car. "We'll be home tomorrow. Daddy and Robert can talk, while you and I get my stuff together. I love y'all."

Mavis rolled down the window and waved until they were out of sight. Once they'd gone down the steep hill below her family's home, she rested her head against the seat and sighed deeply. "What a relief! I didn't know if they'd kill me or hug me."

Vera touched her arm. "There's nothin stronger than a parent's love for a child. They might not be happy bout you marryin Robert, but I don't think they want to lose you. Sometimes, you take what you can get. Some things can't be changed. It's gonna be okay. I can feel it in my bones."

"I hope so, Ms. Vera. I hope so."

♦

The next morning, Mavis made coffee. Robert and she talked about the planned meeting with her parents, which was to take place at one o'clock that day. When Mavis spoke the day before with Dewey and Willie, they'd all agreed that Robert and Mavis would live in the sharecropper's house and that Robert would continue working the land. Dewey had been taking care of the animals since Mavis and Robert had left. He couldn't see ignoring creatures that didn't have a thing to do with Robert's lack of responsibility.

Mavis knew that she was pushing her luck, but she intended to suggest that her parents sell the house and land to Robert and her. After all, she'd told them about the baby. She knew that they'd never turn her and her child away. Robert feared that Mavis was asking too much, too soon, but he left the decision to pursue the subject entirely up to her.

After the meeting with Dewey and Willie, Robert walked to the sharecropper's house to catch up on the chores that he'd neglected. As he walked through the barn and the hen house, he noticed that someone had been gathering eggs and feeding the animals while he was gone. It made him feel good to be outside, where he could think while he worked. Work would help clear his head. As he performed one task after another, he tried not to think about how much Willie disliked him. It was going to be more difficult to come to a meeting of the minds with her, than with Dewey. Robert was aware that Willie, a strong determined woman, influenced her husband.

While he worked outside, Mavis had driven the old truck to the house. It was parked near the kitchen door. As soon as she entered the house, she began to clean and dust. She rearranged what little furniture there was. About three o'clock, she heard a vehicle stop at the edge of the porch. Looking out the window, she saw Dewey get out of his truck and head toward the barn. She didn't go outside. This meeting was strictly between her daddy and her husband. How Robert reacted to Dewey would be critical, but she couldn't be involved.

Mentally, she checked off a list of items that she planned to ask Willie to give her. The list grew, until, finally, she decided to write down everything that she planned to request. Between Robert's truck and her daddy's truck, they could deliver everything on the list in one morning. As she finished the list, she heard Dewey's truck back out of the driveway.

When Robert came into the house for supper, Mavis was sitting at the kitchen table, going over the list that she'd made. "Whatcha got there?" he asked, removing his hat and coat before sitting at the table.

"I'm making a list of furniture and stuff that I'm going to ask Mama to let us have. Also, I need to make curtains for the windows. Mama can help me with those," she said with confidence. "How did the meeting with Daddy go?"

"Well, after he called me a 'low-down-son-of-a-bitch' who he'd kill if I ever mistreated his daughter, he was nice before he left. Not too much, though. They'd not happy bout our marryin. And he made it clear he's not doin me any favors. So, that list is useless."

"We'll see," she said, not looking up. "And, we gotta build a bathroom. So, I'm gonna talk to Daddy bout that."

"Mavis, don't you think that you're askin too much? I mean your folks ain't exactly thrilled bout us marryin. It might be too early to ask for stuff. The land, the house, furniture, a bathroom—"

"No," she interrupted him, "it's not too early. I might as well ask now as tomorrow or next month. Regardless, the answer will be 'yes' or 'no.'"

He gave a sigh. "Okay. I trust you. I just hope Mr. D's not standin in the door with a shotgun pointed at my head."

The next day when Robert and Mavis paid a visit to her parent's, Dewey wasn't standing in the doorway with a shotgun, but if looks could kill, Robert Norrrell would have fallen dead. He felt the cold hostility in the kitchen and was aware that Dewey didn't offer to shake his hand. Willie stayed as far away from him as she could, while she gave her complete attention to Mavis and Dewey.

The four of them sat around the kitchen table, and Mavis took it upon herself to serve coffee to everyone. When she sat down, she smiled at Willie and took her hand. Then, she smiled at Dewey. "Thank y'all so much for meeting with us." She looked around the room and said, "I've always loved this room. It's so cozy. And I'm so happy that I can just walk up for a visit. That means so much to me."
No one spoke.

"You're my parents, and I love you both. Robert's my husband, and I love him. I'm his wife. I appreciate so much that you've let me come back." She stopped talking and looked at each one of her parents. She noted the sour look on Willie's face at the mention of Robert's name. Dewey dropped his head and stirred his coffee.

Directing her next comment at Dewey, she said, "I know that you've made it clear to Robert how you feel. That's okay. He understands. And the favors that I'm bout to request are for me and the baby." Then, she went into the list of things that she wanted, starting with purchasing the house and the land. Needless to say, Dewey and Willie were caught completely off guard.

When Mavis finished, she added, "I just want y'all to know this is all my idea. Robert thinks I'm asking for too much. I told him I might as well ask now."

Dewey and Willie looked at one another. Finally, he spoke. "It's a lot. Willie and I need to discuss it. As far as furniture and the other stuff, that's up to Willie. The both of you can talk bout them things. After Willie and I've talked bout the house, the land, and the bathroom, I'll talk to y'all.

"In the meantime, while you talk with your mama, Robert and I need to step outside and discuss mendin some fences on the north side of the property." He rose and waited for Robert to stand. Willie and Mavis watched them put on their coats and leave.

When the door closed, Mavis said, "Okay, Mama, what can you let me have?"

By the end of the week, most of the things that Mavis had asked for her home were delivered. Two weeks later, Dewey paid them a visit late one afternoon. He laid out a plan for them to purchase the house and ten acres, as well as adding a bathroom to the house. Mavis hugged her daddy and clapped her hands. Robert sat in total shock.

◆

For the next two years, Robert worked the land and raised animals. A daughter, whom they named Janet, was born before the end of the first year of their marriage. Two years later, a son, whom they named after Robert, was born. The family was growing, and it was becoming apparent that Robert wasn't the farmer that Dewey was. They were barely making ends meet. And, they needed to add several bedrooms to the house. Money was tight.

It was Mavis' idea for Robert to apply for a job in one of the local cotton mills. She'd take on more farm chores while he worked. Two days after this discussion, Robert applied for a job at Langdale Mill. He was hired as a loom fixer. Things became easier, but babies kept coming. Before they could bat an eye, there were seven children. They decided that'd be the last baby.

"I spent a lot of time pregnant. Five daughters and three sons.

They're all married now. Except for Johnny Lee. The baby that we didn't anticipate. And, as you know, he's still at home." Mavis took a sip from a fresh hot cup of coffee. "And, as you know, he's a drug addict. Lots of time I wonder what Robert and me did wrong. I worry bout him, but worrying hasn't stopped the drugs."

Beulah laid her wide hand on Mavis' shoulder. They looked at one another. "I know. He's your boy. You think you gotta protect him. We do what we think we gotta do."

"Yeah. But, the others can't understand. They think I oughta just throw him out. I can't do that, Beulah. My parents didn't throw me out.

"I blame myself. You know?" she continued and took another sip of coffee. "Maybe, I shouldn't have had him when I was forty-two. Robert and me were just too old to raise another child. Anyway, I had him." She looked out the window. "He was a sickly baby from the beginning. Always crying."

A sigh escaped from her nostrils, and she looked at the clock on the opposite wall. The kitchen was filled with sunshine and the quiet that comes with waiting. Beulah traced an unseen pattern on the table with a finger.

"You don't give up on your kids. Sometimes, you've only got hope and faith that things will get better. That's all I've got left...hope and faith. I don't talk bout Johnny Lee to his brothers and sisters, cause they're too judgmental. They all think they've got the answers.

"And I'm not gonna listen to their remarks. What I do is none of their business. I gotta do what I gotta do. Nobody but Robert seems to understand. And Laura Faye. She understands."

"I understand. I really do. And you can always talk to me," Beulah said.

She understood Mavis' commitment to Johnny Lee. Although there was a gap in their ages, there were many similarities between the two women. The age difference didn't influence their friendship.

From those first weeks at Mid-Way Café to Mavis' death, they shared secrets and talked about everything. They came to understand one another's political and religious views. If they didn't agree, they respected the other one's opinions. Now and then, one would switch to the other's point of view. When there were long minutes of silence, they felt a non-verbal communication and subsumed one another's emotional state.

◆

Beulah recalled the conversations that dealt with hers and Mavis' marriages, as well as the many other topics that they'd discussed. Their long discussions and the tone of Mavis' voice when she talked about her life were some of the reasons that Beulah always came in the early morning hours when Mavis called after Robert's death.

The phone would ring between twelve and two o'clock in the early morning. "Beulah, I've made biscuits and gravy. Come on over," Mavis would command when Beulah picked up the phone that'd cut into a deep sleep. She'd dress and drive to Mavis' house. Always, Mavis would be standing at the kitchen window, looking for her.

Sometimes, Mavis called because she couldn't sleep. She had a terrible habit of awakening in the early morning hours, unable to go back to sleep. Most of the time, something was nagging her mind, making her restless for answers or confirmation. It was like an insect that kept chewing and biting inside her head. Talking with Beulah helped to drive away the insect, to bring peace.

Usually, Mavis wanted to talk about Johnny Lee, his drugs, his anger, his women, or the failed attempts to stop his drug habit. The problem was never solved. As time progressed, it was more drugs and increased violence, demanding behavior that Mavis tried to hide from Johnny Lee's siblings.

Often, when times were good with Johnny Lee, Mavis just wanted company, a friend who understood her and who listened. During those times, the women discussed family, work, politics, and community gossip. They laughed and joked about the world and the people around them. Over time, a strong bond of loyalty developed between the two women, as they joined their separate worlds together and supported one another.

CHAPTER FIVE

It was the end of June when Beulah met Johnny Lee. She'd heard about his drug addiction, about how irritated Mavis' other children were with his behavior and his selfishness. It was obvious to Beulah that the more Johnny Lee's siblings resented him, the more Mavis and Robert defended him. According to Mavis, her daughter Laura Faye, who was closer to Johnny Lee in age, was the only sibling who protected and coddled him. Beulah didn't say so, but she recognized three people who were enablers.

Johnny Lee was born when Mavis was forty-two. Too old, she thought, to be having another child. Seven was enough, but she never contemplated anything but giving birth to the baby whom she wanted; yet, whom she resented to an extent. An abortion wasn't an option, although she didn't fault anyone else who made a different decision. Who was she to judge?

Johnny Lee was twenty-one when Beulah first saw him. It was during lunch at Mid-way Cafe when he arrived. He'd been to an early morning interview and had just gotten a job at Langdale Mill, where Robert worked. Up until then, he'd worked in a garage as a mechanic. He didn't have any training to be a mechanic, but he was a quick learner when it came to working on vehicles. It helped, too, that he was a hard worker.

Eugene Clark, who owned Clark's Auto Mechanics, hired Johnny Lee two days after he quit school at the age of sixteen, and he'd worked there ever since.

Eugene was aware that Johnny Lee smoked marijuana. So did Eugene. Sometimes, after hours, they'd light up a joint together. As the years went by, Eugene wasn't aware that Johnny Lee was dapping in other drugs. Mavis and Robert knew and told Laura Faye. The three of them covered for Johnny Lee. It became a topic among the three of them that was never shared with anyone else. Until Mavis told Beulah.

The day that Johnny Lee was hired at the mill, his truck came flying into the parking lot of Mid-Way Café. It missed hitting the front door about a foot before it screamed to a stop. The brakes squealed loudly and some gravel hit the large window. Everyone inside thought the truck was coming through the front door, right into the café.

They heard a loud, slurred voice say, "Damn! Shit a'mighty!" Then, they heard a door slam loud enough to wake a nearby sleeping dog.

Several people, along with Irene, looked out the window. "It's Johnny Lee," she informed everyone. "BobbieJo, he barely missed hittin the buildin. Another two inches and he'd be sittin in here with us. So would that truck."

Bobbie Jo just shook her head and didn't look up from the cash register. When she heard the squeal of the tires and the gravel hit the window, she knew that it was Johnny Lee. And, yeah, one day, he and his truck would probably end up in the middle of the café.

The door swung wide, letting cool air escape like air from a balloon. Everyone turned to look at the tall, well-built handsome man who swaggered through the door. He was wearing faded Levis, with holes in the knees, and a crooked grin crawled up to his crystal blue eyes that twinkled with mischief. His chest and feet were bare. On his middle right finger, he twirled the keys to an old black Chevrolet truck that ran like a charm, in spite of rust spots on the left front fender and the hood.

The fact that it could run at all was a testimonial to Johnny Lee's skills as a mechanic. As soon as he entered the room, he spread his long legs, put his huge hands on his hips, slightly twisted his shoulders, and said in a husky voice, "Hi, y'all. What's up?"

After everyone had returned the greeting, he added, "And, I want y'all to know I got a new job. I'm gonna be workin second shift at Langdale Mill, startin in two weeks. Gotta give Eugene a two weeks notice. He's gonna miss my talents." He said the last sentence in a cocky voice that was sluggish.

Mavis's face gleamed with pride, but she made no comment. She turned toward him as he said, "What you been up to, Fisher?"

"Well, not much of nothin, if you wanna know the truth…and can take it," grinned the man who was a disabled veteran, with a noticeably bad limp. He was a regular at the café. He never missed a morning sausage biscuit and four cups of strong black coffee. Every weekday he'd hang around until lunch, smoking long thin Marlboros, drinking coffee, and talking to anyone who'd listen. There was one subject that he never discussed. Vietnam. He'd spent many hot, humid days in the jungles of a place he despised. For long days, he hunched in narrow, wet ditches, daydreaming of River View, where he'd lived all of his life. After returning home, he swore that he wouldn't live any place else, except perhaps the Hawaiian island of Kauai, which he saw while he was in the military.

At eleven o'clock, every weekday, he ordered a dinner to go and left in a beat-up old black Jeep that looked as if it hadn't been washed in years. Most café regulars knew that he'd spend the rest of the day drinking beer, listening to blues, and watching cars go by his front porch.

"I can take it, Fisher. I can take anything," laughed Johnny Lee. "Where's that favorite woman of mine? Mama! Will you, please, give me two biscuits with sausage gravy? BobbieJo, just charge it to Mama." He turned to wink at Irene when she sniggered. Bobbie Jo's lips tightened and she kept her head down. She made no comment.

"Yeah. I guess I'll be a lint head like all these other Valley folks. Get lung disease and die cause I can't breathe worth a shit. I ain't complainin. Hell, we start dyin the minute we're born. Gotta go sometimes. Anyhow, it's gonna be a better check than the one I been gettin." Turning to wink at Fisher, he said, "And it means I can buy more smokes. If you know what I mean."

"If you got a job this mornin, why don't you have on different clothes? You didn't wear them old jeans with holes in them to apply for a job. Did you?" asked Irene.

"Hell, no, honey. You know I got more sense than that. Course, I didn't go for no interview with the boss turds, barefoot and no shirt. Afterwards, I went straight home to change and to celebrate. I want to be loose and free fore that jail claims my soul. Plus, it's too hot outside to be wrapped up like a Eskimo. I'm gonna be hot enough once I start workin in that furnace."

"I think it's got AC now," Fisher said. "So, no more open windows, with cotton flyin out like snow. Years back, a stranger comin here for the first time would've thought it was snowin like hell in the middle of a heat wave. What with the windows of the mills open and cotton whirlin out and floatin all over the place. That damn cotton would land everywhere. In trees. In people's yards. In your hair. In your mouth, when you spoke. Everywhere."

While the conversation continued, Mavis beamed. Although breakfast had stopped being served, she was busy frying sausage and making white gravy. A hot pan of biscuits had been taken from the oven before Johnny Lee walked in the door. Beulah watched as Mavis split two biscuits in half. On top of the biscuits, she put four large spoons of gravy. Finally, she placed three pieces of sausage on the side of the plate. "What do you wanna drink?" she yelled at Johnny Lee.

He stopped listening to Fisher long enough to say, "A large coke, with lots of ice."

Mavis took the food to him, where he'd joined Fisher in a booth near the kitchen. She didn't say a word as she sat the plate in front of him.

"Thanks, Mama," he said in a low voice and smiled at her.

Mavis stood beside him. She waited until he took a large bite. "Beulah, come here. I want you to meet Johnny Lee."

Beulah dried her hands on her apron and walked to the table. She nodded at Johnny Lee. His blue eyes sparkled as he smiled at her. "Hi you doin, Ms. Beulah? Mama told me bout you. What a nice lady you are. Ain't forgettin...she also told me that you're the best cook she's ever seen. Now, comin from Mama, that's a lot."

Beulah smiled. "Thank you. I appreciate that." Her eyes held a sadness that Johnny Lee recognized, but he couldn't identify its source. There was no way that he or anyone in the room knew that she was thinking about her own son, that he would be younger than Johnny Lee. She was wondering how he looked, how he was doing, where he was and if he was okay. Or was he an addict like Johnny Lee?

During the time that Johnny Lee was in the cafe, it became clear to Beulah that he'd charmed all of the women who worked there, except Bobbie Jo. Before long, Beulah, too, had fallen under his charm. Women, young and old, just couldn't say "No" to Johnny Lee Norrell. She'd already realized that Mavis and Robert hadn't been able to say "No" during his entire life.

After Johnny Lee wolfed down the sausage and biscuits, along with a second glass of coke, he stood up and announced, "Be seein y'all. I gotta get to the shop. Eugene gave me a half-day off."

He walked into the kitchen and touched Beulah on her shoulder. "It's a pleasure meetin you. Mama thinks the world of you. Daddy's lookin forward to meetin you. Take care."

To her surprise, he kissed her forehead. Again, she wondered about her own son as Johnny Lee walked out the door, closing it gently behind him. He had entered the cafe like a whirlwind and had left quietly like falling cotton.

♦

Beulah met Robert several weeks after she met Johnny Lee. It was a Saturday morning in early July, while the dew still lingered on the grass. Although it was seven-thirty, the sun had long risen from the hill beyond Osanippa Creek, which ran below Mavis' house. Now, the sun was blazing its way across a cloudless blue sky that was the color of Robert's eyes. It'd dawned on her when she met Robert that his eyes also reminded her of Colleen Chadwick's eyes. Only, the eyes of the beautiful blond were as cold as steel, not warm and inviting like Robert's eyes.

Beulah thought about how much Johnny Lee looked like his daddy. They had the same sparkling intense eyes that seemed to be cut from the sky. When they smiled or laughed, tiny wrinkles grinned at the corner of each eye. Both had a lopsided grin. The slim build was the same. Only Johnny Lee was at least three, maybe four, inches taller than Robert. Before she left, Beulah realized that they smoked a cigarette in the same way, tilting their heads to one side when they blew out smoke, and that they held a cigarette in the same manner, pinched between the thumb and middle fingers.

A few bees buzzed around Beulah's head as she got out of her car. She noticed immediately that Mavis and Robert were in the garden that lay to the right side of the driveway. Mavis looked up and waved. "Grab one of those buckets beside that first row of beans. Then, come over here and meet Robert."

Beulah waved back. "Thank y'all for lettin me pick some beans. They'll come in handy this winter. Autumn loves string beans."

"Come on and join us," Robert said. He was squatting on the ground, picking beans that grew low on the vines. "We got enough to feed an army."

He rose in one quick, catlike movement and walked toward her. She couldn't help but notice that he wasn't wearing a shirt and that one strap of his overalls was left hanging, exposing a slender, but firm, tanned chest. "Nice to meet you, Beulah. I'm Robert. Aggie's better half." That was the first time that Beulah had heard anyone call Mavis by her middle name. It wasn't long before Beulah learned that Robert always called her Aggie, unless he was mad.

They laughed. Both knew that he adored Mavis and thought that she was the best thing since moonshine, which he'd made and sold years back. He handed her a five gallon white plastic bucket. "Fill this up as many times as you want."

"Thanks," she said as she followed his slim frame into the tall tepee rows of beans that grew up slender strips of brown strings and created heavy green curtains as the vines climbed the stalks that seemed to touch the sky. As the sun rose higher, the tall green curtain shielded them from the sun, offering a small degree of shade. The green leaves felt like rough velvet that had been washed and left to dry in the sun. The leaves tickled their hands and faces as they moved slowly among the coolness.

They talked for a while, but the talk stopped as each one concentrated on the task of filling buckets to the rims. After they'd picked the beans, they walked among the rows of butterbeans, peas, and okra, filling more buckets. When each bucket was full, the contents were dumped into large brown paper sacks. The bags were adding up, proof of how long they had been bending over row after row of vegetables.

Afterwards, they sat in the shade on the back porch and shelled peas. Mavis brought large glasses of sweet tea. Robert had taken off his worn boots and socks. He stretched his legs and wiggled his toes. From a pocket in the bib of his overalls, he withdrew an unfiltered cigarette. Placing it in one corner of his mouth, he picked tobacco from a thumb and flipped the small dark dab onto the floor. He bent over a match that was cupped in one hand and inhaled deeply. Beulah watched the tip of the cigarette glow a strawberry red. Then, Robert threw the match off the porch and onto the ground, as he leaned his head against the rocker and exhaled a cloud of smoke to the rafters of the porch.

The smell of strong tobacco assaulted Beulah's nostrils, as the end of the cigarette began to burn. The small red flame was a miniature sun, hanging from Robert's lips. A fan that was sitting on the floor make a slight swooshing sound and rearranged the heat. A bumblebee drilled a hole in one of the beams above Beulah's head and sawdust fell on her shoulders. In the far left corner of the porch, she noticed that dirt dauber nests were scattered along the beam over the swing.

Robert talked about the weather and how well the garden was doing that year. He told funny stories and they laughed at his irony. He was handsome, with strands of gray that zagged like streaks of lightning throughout his thick curly hair. His personality was that of a charmer. As Beulah got to know him, she learned that he flashed his charming smile and friendliness on anyone. But, if he didn't like the person, he'd say, "That low-down son-of-a-bitch ain't worth a tinker's damn," as soon as the person disappeared from his presence. If Mavis didn't like someone, she didn't pretend. No way would she smile and be friendly. She'd keep quiet and glare at the person, not be gracious and polite.

At twelve o'clock, Mavis made tomato sandwiches and served them with more tall sweaty glasses of tea. Robert squeezed lemon juice into his glass and took a long swallow. The juice from the lemon landed on his wrist and an arm of the rocker. He rocked back and forth gently.

"Good, Aggie," he said and winked at Mavis.

Talk switched to the mills. Beulah told them how she'd worked there until people were laid off. She was one of the last groups of people to be let go. Since then, it'd been hard on her. The job at Mid-Way Café helped, and she still cleaned houses for folks who lived on the backwaters. She was managing. Mavis and Robert listened, making a comment now and then.

"I'm seventy-one years old. Two years ago, I decided that I'd worked long enough in the mill, inhalin junk in my lungs for years. It got so bad I could hardly breathe. So, I retired." Robert stopped talking, to blow a cloud of smoke at the rafters of the porch. He blew a dot of tobacco from his lower lip. "In the summer, I grow a garden. Enough food to feed me and Aggie, our kids and their families, and to give some away. In the winter, I hibernate." He laughed.

Silence filled the gap in the conversation. They'd finished eating and slowly rocked as bumblebees buzzed around their heads. The sun had begun to claim the sky, making its presence known for miles. It'd been hours since it'd sucked the moisture from the earth. Taking and giving was what the sun did best. Its rays reached under the tin roof of the porch and bit into their flesh.

Reluctantly, Beulah stood up and sat her glass down on a nearby table. "Well, I guess I best be goin. I wanna get home and put up these vegetables fore they start dyin on me. I sure do thank y'all. This helps a lot."

"You come any time you want and get whatever you want," Robert said. "We're happy to share. It was nice meetin Aggie's new friend. Hopefully, we'll be seein more of you. Don't be surprised if she doesn't try to drag you off to the dog track at Shorter fore long. I don't go, cause I've got no interest in gamblin of any kind. But, Aggie loves it. Suits her personality." He laughed. Mavis gave a little sniff.

"It was nice meetin you, Robert. And, again, thanks for the vegetables," Beulah said with gratitude.

The three of them held stuffed brown bags in both hands and walked to Beulah's car. They made two trips. Beulah opened the trunk for sacks that wouldn't fit on the back seat. After they'd filled the back seat with more sacks, she slid into the driver's seat. Robert closed the door, while she turned the ignition. Waving, she backed out of the drive. As she reached the top of the hill that dipped to the creek, she looked in her rearview mirror. Mavis was still standing in the driveway.

As the car crossed the bridge, Beulah realized that she'd not seen Johnny Lee. Neither Mavis nor Robert had said a word about him. It was a Saturday, and he was probably sleeping late.

◆

Near the end of July, peaches became the topic of discussion at the café one day during lunch. Customers smacked their lips over Beulah's peach pie. She stood at the stove and smiled as she listened to the praises. Edith placed four take-out orders of pie and laughed when the group accused her of snatching the pie from under their mouths.

"This has gotta be the best peach pie I ever ate," Fisher Moon declared, wiping his mouth with a paper napkin. "Beulah, we got lucky when BobbieJo hired you." He quickly added, "You, too, Mavis. Mid-Way Café's got the two best cooks in the state."

"Fisher, you just want another helping of pie," Mavis said, with a wide grin.

"Well, don't mind if I do. Thank you, Ma'am," and he held up his empty plate.

As Irene brought him another helping of pie, he said, "Mavis, why don't you bring us some more a them peach preserves that you make? Them was sho enough good."

"I don't have any more. They disappear from my house faster than cool air. But, I do need to make some more," Mavis replied.

"Hey, Mavis, why don't you, me, and Beulah go to South Georgia this Saturday and get some peaches? We can make a day of it. Sunday afternoon we can peel peaches for preserves and freezin. What do y'all say bout that?" Edith asked enthusiastically.

Mavis looked at Beulah who nodded. "That sounds good to me. Let's leave early before it gets too hot," Mavis said, as she loaded a dinner plate.

81

"I'll drive. Be ready at seven," Edith said, heading toward the door.

Mavis rolled her eyes and shook her head.

"Okay, smarty pants, what's wrong?" Edith demanded. "You always do that when I mention drivin, but I notice that you always go."

"Of course I go. I go to make sure that you don't have an accident or get stopped by the police," Mavis laughed. "Don't get your panties in a wad. I'm teasing. See you at seven." She waved Edith out the door.

"One day you gonna push Edith's button too hard, Mavis," Fisher warned.

Mavis dismissed him with a wave of her hand. "Ugh! Don't you worry bout that, Fisher. Edith and I understand one another. I make her laugh, and that's more than that sorry husband of hers does."

Fisher didn't comment. He knew not to get Mavis started about John Ferguson who wasn't one of her favorite people. She seldom mentioned his name. When she did talk about him, it wasn't positive. Everyone, as well as Edith, knew that Mavis didn't like Ferguson because he'd been active in the KKK and because he ignored Edith, "treating her like a piece of shit stuck to his shoe," Mavis would say with contempt.

John Ferguson was a man of average height and broad shoulders. He had hypnotic brown eyes that gave condescending looks to those whom he disliked. His often cold, sardonic glances spoke louder than words. In spite of the fact that his light brown hair was thinning on top, leaving a bald spot, he was handsome, in a rugged rough way that appealed to men and women.

It wasn't that John gave Mavis a personal reason to dislike him, because he was always nice to her. She didn't like the way that he flirted with women in Edith's presence. She resented that every Friday night he took his very attractive single sister to dinner at some fancy restaurant, while Edith sat home watching TV or playing solitary. Nor did she approve of the many stories that she'd heard about his womanizing. She gave him credit for being a good provider who worked in one of the mills and who managed, with lots of help from Edith, to run a successful farm.

Mavis had quickly learned when she and Edith became friends not to say anything negative about John. Edith always defended him. Mavis had long ago given up trying to convince Edith to put a stop to some of John's ways. Actually, she stopped when Edith flat told her that it was none of her business. So, they reached an unspoken agreement not to discuss one another's spouse. For Edith's sake, Mavis was friendly to John and stopped saying negative things about him to Edith. Still, she couldn't help but wonder why a strong woman like Edith tolerated such behavior. Some things simply were beyond comprehension when it came to men and women.

CHAPTER SIX

The sun burned through the early Saturday morning like a furnace that was desperate to reach an elevated temperature. It was as if all the coal mines in Kentucky had been thrown into a ball of fire. As Mavis looked out her kitchen window, she saw a half-circle of blazing gold, resting on top of the hill, on the other side of Osanippa Creek. The brightness caused her to blink and look away, focusing her attention on last minute things that she had to complete before Edith's GMC truck came flying down the driveway, across the road, and into Mavis' driveway.

She buttered a half-dozen biscuits for Robert and Johnny Lee. Then, she wrapped a towel around them to keep them warm until they were eaten. Robert was already in the garden, hoeing and pulling weeds. Johnny Lee was still in bed and would probably be there when she returned. Still, if he decided to get out of bed before the end of the day, the biscuits would be waiting.

Just as she finished making a fresh pot of coffee for Robert, she heard the sound of Edith slamming on brakes, as the truck skidded to a stop at the end of Edith's long gravel driveway. Then, she heard a loud honk, which was Edith's way of telling Mavis to be at the door and ready to ride. Mavis sighed and thought to herself, "Does she have to do that?"

She took her purse from a chair and opened the kitchen door. She was wearing knee-high jeans, one of Robert's shirts, and tennis shoes with white socks. Her hair was swept away from her face with a thin headband; her makeup was flawless, and her favorite lipstick, a shiny blood red, made her lips full. By the time that Edith stopped the truck, Mavis was standing on the porch.

As Mavis got into the truck, she couldn't help but notice that Edith was wearing a pair of John's overalls, one of his white shirts, with the sleeves rolled to her elbows, and her garden boots. Her thin short hair was pushed behind her elf ears. As usual, she didn't have on a dab of makeup or lipstick.

Edith said, "I got us some ice water, some green apples, and some tomato sandwiches behind the seat. We can eat whenever we get hungry."

Edith heard Mavis grunt. "What's that grunt mean?"

"Nothing. I just hope the sandwiches aren't soggy before we decide to eat them. That's all."

"Well, I like soggy tomato sandwiches myself. If you're hungry enough, you won't care, anyway."

"I suppose not. I was hoping that, maybe, we'd find us a nice place to eat so that we could enjoy a real girls' day out. You know?"

"We can do that, too. I mean eat the sandwiches and eat at a café or someplace. Be prepared is what I always say."

"Be prepared for what?" Mavis asked in a sarcastic tone.

"Anything," Edith replied, and they both remained silent, until Beulah's house came into view. As they pulled into the drive, Edith tooted the horn loud enough to wake up everyone within a quarter of a mile.

"What in tarnation! Edith, do you have to honk the horn loud enough to wake up the dead? It makes my ears hurt," Mavis complained.

"Uhmm!" was all Edith said.

Beulah came to the door, wearing jeans, a sleeveless printed shirt, Keds, and a straw hat. Mavis slid to the middle of the seat. It'd be a tight squeeze, but they'd be comfortable. When Beulah sat down and closed the door, Edith put the truck in reverse and flew out of the driveway, slinging dirt over the back of the truck. Her passengers' heads snapped with the sudden surge of energy that Edith gave the big truck. Beulah's straw hat clawed at Mavis' right eye.

"Beulah, you're gonna have to take off that hat or you're gonna put out my eye. Especially with Edith jerking this truck around like she does."

"Sorry," Beulah said and placed the hat in her lap.

"Throw it behind the seat," Mavis instructed.

"So, exactly where are these famous peaches?" Beulah asked.

"They're in Fort Valley, Georgia, which is a small place in the middle of nowhere. We can pick them or buy them already picked. I don't mind pickin them, myself." Edith looked at Mavis.

"I'm not picking mine," Mavis quickly informed Edith.

"Whatever you want to do. I don't care," Edith responded, in a tired voice, as if she was talking to a hardheaded child. Mavis thought that Edith was just determined to have the last word.

Beulah laughed. She knew that the two women would try to out-do one another all the way to Fort Valley and back to Chambers County. They enjoyed arguing too much to stop. No longer did Beulah think that they were about to attack one another when their comments sailed through the air like paper airplanes, with sharp tips. Each one wanted the last word and both worked hard to have it.

As the truck rattled along, not anywhere near to breaking the speed limit, the three women talked and laughed. Now and then, Beulah sang for them. When Edith joined in, Mavis asked her politely to "stop ruining the song and let's just enjoy some good music." Edith looked at her and laughed. She continued to sing along with Beulah.

They crossed the Chattahoochee River that divided Alabama and Georgia. They were in Columbus, the town of Fort Benning, one of the largest military posts in America. Edith pointed the truck on an eastward journey, through the town and into flat meadows and cornfields that glowed bright green and swayed gently in the stuffy summer breeze. They passed pastoral landscapes that contained few houses or barns. Green grassy pastures, with gazing cattle, passed in slow motion.

Soon, the long road ahead meandered up and down hot asphalt hills, stretching for miles between Georgia pines that touched a blue highway that ran between the tips of the tall pines. It was an overhead highway as far as the eye could see. The truck climbed steep hills and coasted down at a faster speed than it'd been going. No one seemed to have noticed that they were no longer moving along flat surfaces that would lead them southeast.

The sun was high in the distance, and heat waves rippled in the still suffocating heat, creating a mirage and giving the false appearance of a sweeping breeze. The stuffy breeze blew into the windows, but it didn't prevent sweat from popping out on the foreheads of the women. Mavis feared that her makeup was a mess. After wiping her face more times than she remembered, she was certain that no make-up remained. She no longer cared.

As they talked, their minds wandered away from the twists and turns in the road, as well as the signs that told them the direction in which they were traveling. All of a sudden, a stop sign loomed out of nowhere. Edith slammed on the brakes, and the truck stopped with a jerk. Rubber burned as the tires pressed into the hot pavement. Their heads almost hit the windshield. Just as quickly, their heads went backwards. Everyone stopped talking and looked at the three signs beside the road. One read "Stone Mountain, Georgia…35 miles ahead."

"Stop the truck, Edith!" Mavis ordered.

"In case you're ain't payin attention, Mavis, I've already stopped the truck," Edith barked back.

Ignoring Edith's comment, Mavis ordered Beulah to get out of the truck. Then, she got out and walked up to the signs.

"Give me the map, Beulah. It's in the glove compartment," she said, turning around and walking back to the truck.

Beulah handed her the map. Mavis spread it out on the hood of the truck. By that time, Edith was standing next to Beulah and Mavis. They were all looking at the map, watching Mavis use her middle finger to trace a route. Three pairs of eyes looked from one to the other.

"How did you manage to drive almost to Stone Mountain? Almost to Atlanta? When we were supposed to be going south." Mavis waited for an answer and didn't get one.

"You must have taken a left some place, instead of a right," she suggested, as if one turn had gotten them so close to Stone Mountain and so far from their designated journey.

Edith shrugged her shoulders and said, "I have no idea. We was talkin bout that Lawson baby. You know. How he don't look nothin like his daddy. And I been thinkin, Mavis. You're right. He looks slam dab like old man Turner. I've heard rumors that he's been hangin round that gal's house for months now."

Mavis stared at her. "Edith, nobody cares bout that now. There are no peach trees in Atlanta. Although, there's a Peachtree Street." She looked into an empty field in front of her and said, "And I've always wondered why they named it Peachtree, when there are no peach trees on the streets."

Edith threw in, "Is 'Peachtree' one word or two words?"

Beulah answered in a calm voice, "It's one word."

"Well, I question the intelligence of people in Atlanta who don't have sense enough to name a street after peaches, when the street don't have any peaches on it. That's all I've got to say bout it," said Edith, determined to have the final say.

Beulah looked around. "I don't see nothin for miles and miles."

Mavis was looking at the map again. "I'm thinking if we turn right here and go on down the road, there's a road that we can take east and head toward Fort Valley. Maybe." No one said anything. "Well, we might as well. Or just keep going to Stone Mountain. If we go to Atlanta, hopefully, we'll find a peach tree on Peachtree Street."

Edith folded the map into a small square where Mavis had pointed. "Okay, girls. Let's take a right turn." They got back in the truck and Edith gunned the motor before she made a sharp right turn. Mavis didn't take her eyes off the map. No one spoke for miles. Finally, Mavis looked up and yelled, "Take a right on the next road!"

Edith stopped the truck at the next right. She turned toward Mavis and in a shocked voice, she said, "It's a dirt road, Mavis. Are you sure?"

"Yes. I'm sure. I've been reading the map, and this seems to be a short cut, back to the road that we need to get on." Edith looked at her. "What are you waiting for? Christmas? Go on. Turn right."

"It's a dirt road, Mavis," Edith said in an exasperated voice. Too, she wasn't so sure that Mavis knew what she was talking about. "And what's the road that we need to get on? The one that this one runs into?"

Beulah kept quiet and looked out the window at the dusty red dirt road that was narrow and filled with ruts. She was sure that it wasn't the road that they needed to travel, but she was leaving the decision-making to Mavis and Edith. No way was she going to be caught in the middle of their discussion.

"So. According to the map, it'll take us where we want to go," Mavis said, making it sound more like a question than a statement.

"Okay, but I'm lettin you know right now that this is all on you. Don't blame no one but yourself if we end up in China," Edith declared as she pointed a finger at Mavis.

"China? Are you serious? We'd have to cross an ocean—maybe two—to get to China. Somebody doesn't know nothin bout geography."

"And, we're bout to find out how much geography you know, smarty pants," Edith snapped as she made the right turn.

They bumped along for at least twenty minutes, without anyone speaking. Red dust whirled behind the truck, as it bumped over the ruts at twice the speed it should have been moving. The fact that Edith was going over the speed limit told Mavis that she was mad. The women bounced up and down on the seat. Dirt flew up from the road and entered the windows of the truck, causing them to cough. The dirt settled in their lungs and clung to the body of the truck. It stuck to the windshield, causing Edith to turn on the wipers until the dirt flew away and landed on some other part of the truck. When the windows were free of the red Georgia dirt, Edith cut off the wipers.

"Stop!" Mavis yelled.

Edith slammed on the brakes and everyone went forward. "Now, what? Do you see another road that we need to take? If you say, 'Yes,' you're imaginin things, cause there ain't no other roads in sight."

"No," Mavis glared at Edith. "I've got to pee."

"You're gonna pee? Where?"

"Right here. I'm gonna open the door on the passenger side—near the ditch. I'm gonna squat and pee. While you and Beulah keep a lookout. Why don't you get those sandwiches out and we'll eat after I'm finished?" she suggested, looking at Edith.

"For goodness sake," Edith moaned and got out of the truck.

Beulah moved around to stand beside Edith who was spreading the food on the hood of the truck. They could hear Mavis begin to pee. "My, god, she sounds like a horse pissin," Edith said. "I wish I could pee like that. I dribble. If I peed like that, I'd lost five pounds."

"It might have something to do with your age," Beulah suggested, with a grin. They both laughed.

Above the peeing, Mavis said, "Old folks only talk bout pee and poop."

"Well, I'm not old. Thank you," Beulah laughed.

Pee splattered in the dirt, which was as soft as baby powder. Just as Mavis stopped peeing, a dusty new red Chevy truck came barreling down the road ahead of them. The truck went past the women. Suddenly, the driver slammed on the brakes pass the tailgate of Edith's truck. Quickly, he shoved the truck into reverse. It flew backwards, until it was in front of Edith and Beulah. Each was holding a tomato sandwich.

Two raggedy young white men were sitting in the truck. They wore dirty baseball caps that had "Braves" in bold red. The driver wasn't wearing a shirt, and his skinny arms were covered in tattoos that ran from his shoulders to his wrists. A soaring eagle flew across his bony chest, and it looked as if his ribs kept the eagle in the air. There was no hair on his smooth tanned skin. He leaned out the window and spit a wad of tobacco juice toward the women. Slowly, he wiped his mouth with the back of his right hand. His left elbow stuck out the window and his hand rested on a steering wheel knob that was shaped like a naked woman. Black dirt was under his fingernails.

He grinned and asked, "What do we have here, Digger? Two nice little old ladies out for a drive." He looked toward Digger and slapped him on the shoulder. He winked and Digger winked back. "Now, what cha make a that? And they got samwiches. How bout that?"

Digger laughed and showed teeth that were stained from too much tobacco or a lack of brushing. Long blonde hair poked from beneath his cap in the front and on the sides. Pimples covered his long face. He wore a sleeveless shirt that was one big design of the Confederate Flag. The long sleeves had been cut out, leaving fringe around the shoulder seams. Muscles rippled in his upper arms.

"Yeah. All a sudden, Weez, I'm sho enough hungry for a mato samwich." He giggled.

Mavis had heard the truck coming, heard it stop and back up. She listened to the two men for a few minutes. She heard two doors open and close loudly. Weez began to call Edith and Beulah old vanilla and chocolate. "Hey, old vanilla and chocolate, how bout y'all do a little dance for me and my bud here?" Digger giggled.

"Hand me that shotgun off the rack there, Digger," Weez instructed. "We gonna have us some fun." Digger giggled.

As soon as Mavis heard the truck back up, she stayed in a squatting position and reached for her purse that had been sitting on the floorboard at Beulah's feet. Slowly, she removed a twenty-two caliber pistol, stayed low and moved around the door. By the time that she reached the other side of the door, she heard Weez ask for the shotgun. She stood up and shot toward Digger, just as Weez took the sandwich from Beulah's hand. The bullet missed Digger's foot less than an inch. A rock flew up and hit Weez on his right thigh, just as he took a large bite out of the sandwich.

"Hot damn a mighty!" Weez yelled and started hopping around on his left foot. "What the hell!" he said, throwing the sandwich on the ground.

"Either one of you makes a move toward that truck, and I'll shoot the holy hell clear out of you. Understand?" Mavis asked as her eyes hardened.

"Wee, doggy! Another vanilla old lady! With a little pistol," Weez mocked. "Like I said, 'Hand me that shotgun.'"

Looking at Weez, she said, "Stop your yakking. I've heard enough out of you. You piece of chicken shit." Her green eyes had gotten greener and her mouth was a straight line. "You make one move, and I'll blow your jewels into the next county."

Edith and Beulah looked at Mavis. She was bracing the gun with both hands on the hood of the truck. Edith couldn't see that Mavis' jeans and panties were below her knees. "Edith, get the shotgun out of the truck and point it toward those two ill-mannered sons-of-bitches who ain't worth a sack of cat shit."

Mavis didn't want her to leave it on the hood, too close for one of the men to grab. She watched as Edith moved carefully to the truck and lifted the gun from the rack. Moving slowly backwards to her truck, Edith kept the gun pointed at the two young men. One's eyes held fear and the other's eyes held hate.

"Beulah, come around here and get that other gun outa my purse. Point it at those young fools," Mavis instructed, without taking her eyes off of Weez and Digger.

As Beulah walked around the truck, she noticed that Mavis' jeans and panties lay around her ankles. She heard Edith ask, "Why are you totin two guns? Who needs two guns in her purse?"

Beulah couldn't help but smile at Mavis' answer. "Apparently, I do. Are we gonna discuss gun control or are you two gonna help me handle these young idiots who have the mistaken notion that they can bully women?"

Looking Weez in the eyes, she added, "And you, you bastard, we ain't old. Not too damn old to put a bullet in your stupid brain."

Beulah got the gun and cocked it. She walked around the truck, spread her legs apart as if she was getting ready for some target practice, and pointed it at Weez.

"Make sure those guns are ready to shoot," Mavis commanded.

"I know what to do with a gun. For goodness sake, Mavis," Edith whined.

Mavis gave instructions to Edith and Beulah. "Point the guns at their chests." She waited until they followed her orders. "Now, if they move, shoot to kill. Kill em dead."

In shock, Edith said, "Shoot to kill! Who said anything bout killin?"

Beulah answered, "I think Mavis did."

While they talked, Mavis reached down, without moving the gun an inch. Taking her eyes off the men for less than five seconds, she pulled up her panties and jeans.

"The First Commandment says, 'Thou shall not kill.' It's a major sin," Edith reminded Beulah.

Beulah nodded her head and said, "You right, Edith. It sure does say that. It's a sin. A big sin." She rolled her eyes at Mavis, lowered her head and looked up.

Mavis came around the truck. "For crying out loud! You two beat all I've ever seen." She stopped, but didn't take her eyes off the men. There was a moment of quiet. "Y'all are right. Give them the guns. Let them shoot us. Let them commit a major sin."

Together, Edith and Beulah looked at her as if she had lost all her brains. "What? Do what?"

"Give them your guns."

Beulah said, "Let's just think bout this for a second. Aint no need in bein foolish." Edith nodded her head.

There was a long silence. A crow could be heard nearby. A plane from the Atlanta airport flew overhead, leaving a long streak of gray behind. The two men grinned, and Weez stepped forward. Mavis shot between his legs, so close to his private parts that he grabbed himself and looked as if he needed to pee.

"So, we keep the guns. And shoot them if we have to. Is that what y'all want? Mavis asked, still watching the men.

Edith and Beulah nodded. The men rolled their eyes and shook their heads.

"Don't just stand there. Tell me what you want," Mavis demanded.

"Yes," they said together.

"We'll keep the guns," Edith said.

"Good. Now, I want both of you to take off your pants and shoes," Mavis told the men.

"You're kiddin. Right?" Weez asked, with his mouth hanging open and his cold blue eyes stretched wide.

"Don't test me, fool. Start taking off your pants and shoes. Now!"

Mavis shot a bullet into the air.

Realizing that she was the one who was going to have to do the shooting and that three of the bullets in her gun were gone, Mavis looked at Beulah and said, "Give me your gun. You take mine." The two women exchanged guns.

Weez unzipped his pants, and they fell to his ankles. He stood naked, chewing gum and sneering at Mavis, with a twinkle in his hard blue eyes. His head was cocked to one side, turned so that it appeared to be dangling from a rope. His skinny legs were wide apart, and he placed one hand on his penis. Suddenly, he held it up and started to pee, making a McDonald arch that ended in front of the women's feet. Several drops spattered onto Mavis' legs. The smell of strong urine drifted upward, and she wanted to gag. A smirk slipped across Weez's face. Amusement was evident in his icy eyes.

Edith made a gasping sound. Beulah rolled her eyes. Mavis raised the pistol and pulled the trigger. A bullet barely missed Weez's right ear. He heard a swishing sound and felt the heat from the energy of the spinning bullet as it sailed through the air and into the cornfield behind him. As the bullet traveled over the cornfield, the muffled gunfire was a vanishing sound that sent birds flying and ladybugs running down the stalks of corn.

"What the hell!" he screamed. Arrogance had transformed into shock, as all color left his face, which was as white as the clouds above their heads. His penis shrunk to a pink satin wrinkled button.

In a disgusted voice, Mavis said, " If it's a pissing contest you want, I just won it. Now, I'm getting damned tired of your bad manners. Next time, my hand might shake so bad that I can't control where I shoot.

"Now, that we've seen your little boy thang, take off your shoes," Mavis mockingly added.

Digger giggled nervously, and Weez shot him a look that was full of snake venom. His bony hands made fists, and he spit tobacco juice at

Digger, who was wearing briefs, with pictures of bats flying in and out of his crack.

"Beulah, get their pants and shoes. Put them in the back of Edith's truck. Edith, take the keys out of the truck and give them to me."

Mavis watched Beulah get the clothing and place it in the upper left-hand corner of Edith's truck. Edith handed Mavis the keys and watched in surprise as Mavis threw them into the field behind her. Edith had no idea that Mavis had such a good arm. A dedicated fan of the Braves, Edith watched or listened to every game; therefore, she knew a good throwing arm when she saw one.

"Edith, get the rope that you keep behind the seat." After Edith got the rope, Mavis continued, "Okay. Tie their hands behind their backs."

She watched Edith tie the men's hands behind their backs. Each time that she tied a knot, she pulled the rope tight, jerking it downward so that the men frowned. Watching, Mavis thought that Edith was having way too much fun.

"Boys, I want both of you to get back in the truck. Move!" she ordered in a drill sergeant's voice. When the men were in the truck, she said, "Now, Edith, close the doors."

After Edith returned to stand beside the two women, she lifted the gun from the front seat of the truck, where she'd laid it when she tied the men's hands. She was in the process of placing it behind the seat, when Mavis fired twice. Beulah and Edith looked in amazement as the tires of Weez's truck started to collapse and the contained air was slowly released. Mavis walked to the other side of the truck and fired two more shots. A soft hissing sound escaped as the tires began to deflate. Five bullets were gone, but it didn't matter. There were two more guns and more bullets.

"How are we gonna let the windows up, if it starts to rain?" Weez asked in a sarcastic tone.

Mavis proceeded to give him a lecture about greed and wanting too many new toys, like trucks that had to be running before a window could be let up or down. If he had an old truck, like Edith's, he could roll the windows up or down. The entire time that she talked, Weez's eyes were rolled to the roof of his truck. He was biting his bottom lip, which was dry and chapped. About that time, a mosquito bite his penis, and he gave a sound like a puppy that had been kicked.

"Holy, shit!" he yelled as another insect pestered him by landing at the tip of his eyelashes. He shook his head and his cap fell forward.

Weez and Digger watched helplessly as the three women climbed into the now dusty GMC. Edith drove down the road about two hundred yards, made a U-turn and headed back toward the main highway. When they passed the two men, they waved. By the time that they reached the main road, they'd decided that they'd just drive until they came to a house or a service station—some place that they could ask directions to Fort Valley.

They'd ridden in silence for almost ten minutes, when Edith said, "I feel bad bout leavin them tied up and no clothes."

Mavis said, "Pray. God will forgive you."

Edith took her eyes off the road and looked at Mavis. "You're makin fun of God. Again."

"No, Edith. I believe in forgiveness. God's in the business of forgiving. He loves to forgive. He likes for us to be humble and meek and ask Him to forgive us. Hey, just look at the Catholics. They sin and ask forgiveness almost every day. It's a hobby with them. The Methodists and Baptists could learn a few things from the Catholics."

Edith replied, "He wants us to live right. To not sin in the first place. And He wants us to be serious bout our faith."

"I don't know bout you, Edith, but I'm as serious as sin on Sunday when I ask for forgiveness. I don't play with God." Mavis took a tube of lipstick from her purse and, without the help of a mirror, painted her lips perfectly. "Do you think God wasn't helping us out back there?"

Edith didn't answer, instead she said, "It don't seem right, somehow. God might not like what we just done."

"He'll get over it. He likes to forgive," Mavis said in a wary voice.

"That's right, Edith. He sho does enjoy forgivin. What was we supposed to do?" Beulah asked.

"I just feel soooo bad," Edith almost whispered.

Beulah spoke up. "Edith, look at it this way…they could've killed us. Buzzards would be pluckin out our eyeballs and suckin our tits."

"Stop! Stop the truck!" Mavis shouted in Edith's right ear.

Looking surprised and holding her ear, Edith slammed on the brakes. The truck slid and turned sharply toward the ditch. "What's wrong?"

"Turn the truck around. We'll go back and untie them. That might not please God, but it'll please you," Mavis said, as if she were talking to an idiot.

"Are you crazy? Go back! Untie two nuts who was goin to do God knows what to us. Are you for real, Mavis?" Edith asked in shock.

"Well, I don't want to be responsible for your soul. We'll do what you think is the right thing to do," Mavis said, turning to give Beulah a lopsided grin.

Edith looked at her calm friend for what seemed like a long time. Slowly, she said, "Are you batshit crazy, Mavis? We ain't gonna go back. Understood?"

Mavis shrugged her shoulders and said, "Whatever you say. You're driving." After a moment, she added, "A peach would be real tasty now. Let's go and get some peaches."

Beulah added, "It sure would. I can taste a sweet Georgia peach. I can feel it slidin down my throat." They all laughed.

Mavis looked at the map and said, "I wonder how far those peaches are. I sure do have a taste for a fresh Georgia peach. Keep driving til we find a place to stop and ask directions to Fort Valley."

Edith glared at Mavis out of the corner of her right eye. Beulah started singing. Soon, Edith and Mavis were singing alone with her. Beulah was the only one who was singing on key. For once, Mavis didn't make a comment about Edith's voice.

Edith stopped singing and said, "Oh, my goodness. If John finds out bout this, he'll take my truck."

"Don't tell him," Mavis said. "Anyway, you let John boss you around too much. You need to put him in his place and stop kissing his ass." She regretted it the minute that it left her mouth. "I'm sorry, Edith. I shouldn't have said that."

Beulah interrupted the silence. "We ain't tellin nobody bout this. The only thing they need to know is we got peaches." Edith and Mavis agreed.

Mavis added, "Right. When we get to the first town, look for a trashcan. We'll get rid of those clothes in the back."

"What bout the shotgun?" Beulah asked.

There wasn't a reply from Edith or Mavis. "Maybe, we can throw it in the Chattahoochee when we cross the state line," Beulah finally suggested. The other two nodded in agreement

"Although, that's a nice shotgun. John and the boys would love to have that gun," Edith said.

"It's a sin to tie up two fools who mighta killed us, but it's okay to steal a shotgun and give it as a gift?" Mavis asked with exaggerated sarcasm.

Edith replied in a low voice, "Well, I'm just sayin it'd be a shame to throw a nice shotgun in the river. When someone could use it."

Mavis didn't respond, and Edith was glad that she chose not to comment. The gun had to be thrown in the river. Too, there was no way that she could explain to John how she'd gotten possession of a gun.

No one spoke for several miles. The sun had risen higher in the sky. The heat was making them tired and hungry. The sandwiches had been knocked to the ground at some point during the confrontation with

Weez and Digger. No one had thought about food until now.

"Hey, I've got an idea—"

Edith interrupted Mavis, "Oh, no. I'm not so sure I want to hear this."

Mavis gave her a sour look. "Just listen for once. Why don't we find a fruit stand on side of the road and buy a bushel of peaches. Nobody will know the difference. We'll make peach preserves tomorrow and serve them at the café on Monday. It'll be our secret."

Edith and Beulah thought that was a good idea. "Be on the lookout for a stand on side of the road," Beulah told them.

About nine miles down the road they saw a stand that proclaimed "Georgia Peaches and Other Stuff." Edith parked the truck under an oak tree that branched out like a large tent. An old man sat in a straight back wooden chair that had a straw bottom. The chair was tilted against a tiny shed. Fruits and vegetables surrounded the chair. The lopsided shed was built from scraps of lumber that'd been stored for years in the old man's barn. The boards had begun to fade from too many summer suns.

The old man observed the women as they walked toward him. A pipe was firmly gripped in a corner of his mouth. A gray handlebar mustache rested above his upper lip. Silver-rimmed glasses covered brown eyes that held light and laughter. He wore overalls and a faded blue dress shirt. Scuffed brown Georgia boots were planted on the dirt floor of the shed. A large raggedly straw hat covered his forehead. Gray hair lay on his neck.

As the women walked toward him, he lowered the chair and removed the pipe from his mouth. Only then, did they realize that there was no smoke coming from it. "Hello, ladies. How y'all doin? I got all kinds of stuff here…vegetables, watermelons, peaches. Whatever you want. You name it. I got it."

Edith spoke first. "We're lookin for some good peaches."

"You come to the right place. My peaches are so sweet you'd think bees been kissin em."

The women began to move among the vegetables and fruits, squeezing something now and then. Mavis was the first one to come to the peaches. She picked up several and smelled them. "We'll take a bushel of these," she said, without consulting Edith and Beulah.

"You won't be sorry. There ain't no better peaches within miles," the old man said, with his hands in the bib of the overalls.

"What else is within miles of this place?" Mavis asked. "And how far are we from Fort Valley?"

"Well," the old man laughed, "you're a long ways from Fort Valley, but bout three miles down the road is a little town. Nothin big. There's a fillin station, a grocery store, a bank, a pool hall, and a café that closes at three o'clock every day, but on the other side of the wall is a bar that opens up at four o'clock. They serve hamburgers and sandwiches til closin. There's a parkin lot in the back.

"Not much of nothin, but all the folks round here need." He continued, "There's a police station and a volunteer fire department. In case you need to ask for directions. Where you ladies from?"

"We're coming from Atlanta and got a notion to go to Fort Valley for peaches." Mavis smiled at him. "But, since these peaches look good and smell so good, I don't think we need to go all the way to Fort Valley."

He smiled back, liking the pretty woman with the green eyes that looked into his soul. For some reason, he didn't believe that she was telling the whole truth. "There ain't no need in drivin all the way to Fort Valley. I got better peaches."

"We also need directions to get to Columbus, Georgia. Do you know where that is?" Edith asked.

"I sho do. If you got a map, I'll try to tell y'all the best route to wherever y'all wanna go. Are y'all headed to Columbus...If y'all not goin on to Fort Valley?"

Mavis walked to the truck and got the map. She unfolded it and gave it to the man whose eyes were laughing. "We're going home. To Chambers County, Alabama. That's across the river, on the west side, from Columbus," she said.

"Okay. Just let me take a look see at this here map for a second or two." The women watched as he studied the map. Finally, he looked up and said to Mavis, "Give me that pencil off the table over yonder. I'll mark the best and quickest route."

"Thank you," Edith said, and Beulah repeated her words.

With a twinkle in his eyes, he said, "If y'all was headed to Fort Valley this mornin, I don't know how on earth y'all ended up here, comin from Atlanta. But, stranger things have happened. I guess."

"Edith took a wrong turn some place—," Beulah said.

"It wasn't totally my fault. We was all talkin and cuttin up. Nobody was payin attention to where we was goin. Don't blame all of this on me," Edith said with indignation.

"It doesn't matter. I just want some peaches, something to eat, and to go home," Mavis sighed. "So how much do we owe you for the peaches?"

The old man gave them a deal on the peaches and told them that the café would still be open. "I've marked your route from the town. Just follow my directions. And don't talk or cut up too much," he said with a note of humor in his voice. He loaded the bushel of peaches into a cardboard box and placed them on the back of the truck

As they climbed into the truck, he waved and said, "Be careful. Don't stop for no buzzards." They waved as the truck pulled onto the highway and headed toward the small town.

◆

Monday morning, Irene gave peach preserves to all of the customers at Mid-Way Café. No one turned down a second helping. They all smacked their lips, closed their eyes, and sighed deeply. Several said that they'd never gotten such good peaches from Fort Valley. Mavis said, "I guess they just had a really good crop of peaches this year." She winked at Edith, who'd come in for breakfast and was sitting in the kitchen at her usual place, eating a buttered biscuit with peach preserves.

"Did you gals pick these here peaches?" Fisher teased, licking a middle index finger that was covered in dripping peach syrup.

"No, we didn't want to ruin our manicures," Edith answered, looking at Mavis whose long nails were always polished and manicured. Edith's hands had never known a manicure. Her fingers were knotted ropes, weathered, chapped, and brown from the sun, from the hard labor of working on a farm.

"Mavis, how bout lettin me buy a couple pint jars of em peach preserves," Fisher said. He turned his head toward the radio and held up his right hand, as if he was about to swear on the Bible. "Hold on, everybody. What's ole Speedy Chevis sayin bout some young boys found half-naked in Georgia?"

Everyone stopped talking and looked at the radio. Mavis, Edith, and Beulah didn't move a muscle as the local DJ at WCJM told how two young men were found walking along the side of a dirt road in Georgia, with their hands tied behind their backs. One was wearing nothing but his underwear. The other one was "buck-naked, wearin nothin but his birthday suit."

Speedy continued giving information, between sarcastic remarks and lots of laughter. "They said several men robbed them and tied them up, after throwin away the keys to their truck. In addition, the men took a shotgun that was in the truck and shot out all the truck's tires. They drove off in a green Cadillac. The police have been unable to find a car that matches the description of the Cadillac. Except for mosquito and chigger bites, as well as bein dehydrated, the young men appeared to be in excellent condition.

"I got one question for the audience. How did they get chigger bites?"

Speedy asked.

His sidekick, Bubba Farr, answered, "The only way I can thank of is that they squatted in a field somewheres." The two men laughed.

"Wonder what they wiped with?" Speedy asked and added, "Hey, ain't no need in any of y'all callin the station to answer that question. Let's just imagine."

When Speedy went to a commercial, Fisher asked, "Is that all?"

Irene asked, "What do you mean by that question, Fisher?"

"Oh, I don't know. It seems to me that there's a lots more to the story."

People began to laugh and make comments about a green Cadillac. "Hey, Ms. Jo Ella, you sure that Cadillac ain't yours?" Fisher asked and slapped his thigh. Ms. Jo Ella gave him a crooked grin and dismissed him with a wave of her slender hand, as she took another sip from her third cup of coffee.

Before Jo Ella could answer, Mavis said, "Whoever heard of a green Cadillac?"

"My Cadillac isn't green, thank you," Ms. Jo Ella said with a smile. "But, I wish I'd been there. Why do y'all think they were made to strip naked?"

"I don't know, ma'am. But, why take their clothes and shoot out all the tires?" asked Fisher. "That seems a bit extreme. Who knows?" He took another bite of buttered biscuit, with peach preserves dripping onto the plate. After thinking for several minutes, he looked at Ms. Jo Ella and asked, "Why do you wish that you'd been there? To see naked men?" He laughed.

Again, before Ms. Jo Ella could answer, Mavis said, "I doubt if there's anything special about those naked men."

Edith added, "I bet that's the truth."

"We don't care bout two naked men in Georgia. Just enjoy them peach preserves," Beulah said to no one in particular.

"Amen to that," Fisher said, holding a second buttered biscuit in the air. After a couple of big bites, he asked, "Hey, do any a y'all know why Speedy Chevis is called 'Speedy'?"

Hoody Alley, who was over six feet, with a donkey mouth and a chin that couldn't be distinguished from his neck, grunted loud enough for everyone to turn and face the man who had flared nostrils like a snarling bull and a mouth that looked like it ate corn on a cob through a chain link fence. One of his eyes was crossed, and it was difficult to see the other eye because a torn baseball cap was pulled low over it. Big elephant ears stuck from beneath the battered cap.

Everyone looked and waited for Hoody to stop eating. It was almost more than they could endure since he chewed with his mouth wide open, smacking more than was necessary. Several customers turned away, unable to bare the large gaping mouth with yellow teeth.

"Well, hell, Hoody, are you gonna tell us or are you gonna make us sick watchin you chew like a cow?" asked Fisher.

"This here's what I heard some time ago. Old Speedy was runnin round with the preacher's wife. Y'all remember that time Old Speedy was into goin to church and preachin ever now and then. All the ladies was just eatin it up. Couldn't get enough of Old Speedy talkin bout God and religion. Them women'd get all carried away when he preached, a dancing and shoutin. I saw it myself. It was a pure sight to see. Let me tell you. Well, anyways, him and the preacher's wife got a thang goin. You know what I mean?" Hoody gave a large wink with his one good eye, but few people saw it because of the cap.

"Yeah! I think we all know what you mean," Fisher interrupted. "Continue."

After giving Fisher a disgusted look, Hoody said, "Everbody knowed they was messin round. Everbody but the preacher. If I rightly recollect, the preacher was invited to preach a revival up round Clay County somewheres. He ain't no sooner left than Old Speedy and the preacher's wife start gettin it on. This goes on for three nights. Damn if that preacher didn't git sick and have to come home early. He walks into the bedroom and there they are. Goin at it. The preacher grabbed his shotgun and fired. The bullet barely missed Old Speedy's head. He jumped outa that bed, naked as the day he was born, and took off a runnin. He ran faster than a bullet and he didn't stop til he fell out on his kitchen floor. He never did give his wife a sensible answer bout why he was runnin round naked as a jaybird." He took a large bite of eggs and added, "He's been known as Speedy ever since."

By the time Hoody finished the story, everyone was laughing. They'd completely forgotten about two naked young men in Georgia.

CHAPTER SEVEN

I t was a hot, humid day, and summer was almost at an end. Customers at Mid-Way Café talked about planting turnips and collards, about spending more time fishing at Goat Rock Dam before the cool weather arrived, about cutting firewood, and about school starting soon. Most of the customers had children or grandchildren, and they complained about the cost of sending kids back to school. They discussed the teachers and decided which teachers that they wanted their children or grandchildren to have for the coming year. They were aware that they could ask for certain teachers, but the final decisions wouldn't be left up to them.

During one of the discussions about school, Miss Nellie Bea Davis, a ninety-two-year old retired teacher who regularly attended Hopewell Methodist Church, came in for her usual breakfast of two poached eggs, gravy, and two slices of wheat toast. She'd retired at the age of seventy-six, and she wouldn't have retired then if she'd not gotten some strong encouragement from the superintendent of education. She'd taught eighth grade English at River View School, before the seventh and eighth grades throughout the Valley area were sent to the fairly new middle school over in Fairfax.

Ever since Bobbie Jo had opened Mid-Way Café, Miss Nellie Bea came every morning, rain or shine, for breakfast. Regular customers knew that she was more predictable than a ground hog. They got worried if the short, tiny bent lady, who still dyed her hair a raven black to match her goal black eyes, was a second late. A tight bun rested on the nape of her neck, and her hair was parted in the middle. Her hands were large for her body and her fingers were shaped like claws. She always dressed in dark colors. That morning, she wore a dark navy dress with a white lace collar, dark stockings, and black shoes that were laced. In spite of the fact that the shoes looked as if they'd been ordered from a twenties Sears-Roebuck catalogue, which was possible, they were shiny and clean. It made people in the café sweat when they looked at her dark dress and stockings.

When she entered the café, Fisher, whom she'd taught so long ago that neither one remembered, jumped up and held the door wide for her. Irene took Miss Nellie Bea's left bony elbow and led her to her favorite table, where she could see everyone in the café. Years of teaching had given her an instinct for locating the best place for a bird's eye view. As she slowly sat down, everyone greeted her. Almost all of the customers had been her students, and each one had a story to tell about Miss Nellie Bea.

Bobbie Jo took her order as usual and yelled it to Mavis, while Miss Nellie Bea pressed her lips together and frowned at Bobbie Jo. Miss Nellie Bea didn't like loud outbursts. Too, she remembered that Bobbie Jo had been a quiet student, but one whom Miss Nellie Bea considered to be sneaky, although she didn't have any reason to support that belief.

Mavis' response was, "You don't have to yell, BobbieJo. I know what she wants. The same thing she's been ordering for years." A slight smile curved Miss Nellie Bea's lips upward. She liked sassy Mavis.

The talk quickly returned to the subject of school. Miss Nellie Bea listened and slowly chewed her food. "Fools," she thought. "All of them are fools. They don't know doodle about how a school operates." She continued to listen.

Fisher's voice rose above the others. "Hey, Miss Nellie Bea, whata you think bout the new principal? And do you think parents oughta have a say-so in who teaches their young'uns?"

Fisher had been hell on wheels when he was one of her students. She'd told him dozens of times, "You'll never learn anything under the shining sun. In a million years." He was a constant clown and smarty mouth, wandering around the room whenever he took a notion. She finally whipped the day lights out of him, hitting his skinny butt so hard that he was sure it'd caught fire. But, that didn't stop him; it only slowed him down a bit. Also, she recalled that he didn't bite his tongue. Just said whatever he wanted to say. Like now. In spite of that, she admired Fisher because he'd told no one but her about his awful experiences in Viet Nam. Few people knew that he'd received a Purple Heart for bravery. So, she supposed all that spunk of his had come in handy.

Miss Nellie Bea finished chewing her toast before she answered. "I don't know anything about the new principal, and, if I did, I wouldn't gossip about him. He'll have a hard enough time, without folks bad-mouthing him. And, no, I don't think parents should be running the school, telling the principal how to do his job. If parents think that they can do better, they need to keep their kids at home and homeschool them. Why do you think educators are required to have a college degree? They've been taught to handle things that pertain to education. That's all I've got to say about the subject." Turning to Irene and holding out her cup, she said, "Pour me another cup of coffee."

There was silence, and the subject of school was quickly dropped. Mavis grinned and winked at Beulah. Mavis said, "When Miss Nellie Bea leaves, remind me to tell you a story bout her, when Marley Jane was in her class." Beulah hadn't met Mavis' daughter, Marley Jane, who had recently moved back to Chambers County.

While Miss Nellie Bea was drinking her second cup of coffee, she ordered a take-out of the blue plate special for lunch. Mavis always gave her an extra helping of everything because she knew that Miss Nellie Bea would stretch it into two meals and because Miss Nellie Bea no longer cooked, due to her bad eyesight. It was a known fact that she'd almost burned down her kitchen twice. After the fire department came the second time, she decided that her days of cooking were over.

Miss Nellie Bea patted Mavis' hand when she placed the blue plate special on the table. Mavis' eyes twinkled. "I gave you an extra slice of strawberry cake cause I know how much you like it."

Fisher held the door wide for Miss Nellie Bea, and everyone waved bye. Fisher had overheard Mavis tell Beulah about the story. As soon as Miss Nellie Bea was no longer within hearing distance, he instructed, "Okay, Mavis, tell us that story bout Miss Nellie Bea."

Mavis still laughed when Marley Jane talked about having Miss Nellie Bea for English in the eighth grade, which had been long past twenty years. All of the customers stopped talking when Mavis walked from behind the partition and began to tell the story.

As the story went, it'd been a rowdy class. Benny Hollis slept through almost every English class. Miss Nellie Bea wouldn't allow anyone to disturb him. One day he woke up, rubbed gook that had formed crusties in the corners of his watery gray eyes and yawned with his mouth open wide enough for a squirrel to crawl through. He blinked and squinted when he looked at the overhead florescent lights. His forehead wrinkled with concentration and irritation at being awake.

He stared around the room at his classmates. Several were passing notes. Marley Jane was designing evening gowns. Two boys were shooting spitballs at the blackboard. One boy who sat behind a gorgeous redhead was playing with her curls, twisting them in and out of his fingers, while he appeared to be in dreamland. Two boys were poking one another with pencils under the desks. One homely looking girl was writing a love letter, which she'd never send to a tenth grader.

She worried that her mama would find the passionate letters in a secret place at home. The other students pretended to pay attention to Miss Nellie Bea.

Benny's appearance was disheveled. His jeans had a small rip in one thigh and needed washing. His shirt looked as if someone had used it for a ball. He wore tennis shoes that had once been white, but were caked with muddy streaks. A close inspection revealed a hole in the heel of one dingy sock.

Dried spittle had taken up residence in the corners of his mouth. A thin strip of snot glowed like a sheen of thin ice on a mirror. It made a tiny ravine from his nose to his left cheek. On his right cheek was a large red pressure point that had been made by sleeping on his left fist. He wiped his nose on the back of his hand, pulling away most of the snot. After he saw it clinging to his hand, he wiped his hand on the sleeve of his flannel shirt.

"Benny I'm so glad that you can join us," said Miss Nellie Bea, as she attempted to draw him into the circle of intellectual enlightenment. It was a failure, but a roaring success for the students. An interaction to accomplish academic achievement between Miss Nellie Bea and Benny was like a mixture of oil and water.

"Ugh?" he asked, shaking his long sticky blond hair that badly needed shampooing. With a quick, jerking motion, he brushed a lock of greasy hair out of his right eye. Grim peeped from beneath his fingernails that were bitten to the quick. Raw skin surrounded the cuticles.

"Benny, we were discussing common nouns and proper nouns. Can you tell the class the difference between the two?"

"What?" he asked, attempting to subdue a yawn.

She repeated the question in a patient, sweet voice. Several students sniggered.

"Nope. Don't think so." He sounded bored as he yawned again, opening his mouth wider and revealing decayed teeth.

"You know what a noun is. Right?"

"Nope. But, what bout it?" Benny asked with absolutely no interest in the answer. He squirmed in his seat as if his butt itched.

"I'll give you a hint. It's a person, place, or thing. Does that help?"

"Nope. Sorry. It don't ring no bells," he answered, scratching his left armpit and sniffing snot back into his nostrils.

"I'm going to help you. Tell me your name."

"Why? You know my name."

"Just tell me your name," she said, with a forced smile and clenched false teeth that were at the point of grinding.

"What does my name have to do with any old noun?" he asked, while the class sniggered and poked one another. They were impressed by Benny's lack of grammar knowledge and by his frank admission that he didn't give two tooty hoots.

"Tell. Me. Your. Name," she repeated through teeth that were clamped firmly together. Her small black eyes held a dot of fire.

"Hey, don't get yourself in no knot. Okay? My. Name. Is. Benny," he told her, slowly saying each word and leaning forward on his desk. He added in a gentle tone, "Maybe, you need to write it down, Miss Bea, so you won't forget."

His classmates were in stitches. They hooted with exaggerated laughter, glad to have a break from nouns. Two boys fell on the floor, laughing and holding their sides. Their knees were drawn up as they rolled back and forth. They remained on their backs and kicked their legs in the air.

Miss Nellie Bea went into freaky mode and began to shout at the class, "Stop the noise! Can't you see that Benny wants to learn. And the rest of you won't learn anything in a million years! Not under the shining sun!"

Her tiny body quivered and she shook a long, skinny finger at them. She was never more than five feet two inches tall, but age had shrunk her to barely four eleven. Her body was bent. She had a skeleton's face, with rawhide flesh pulled tightly over each bone. Enormous black eyes glared from hollow sockets. Once luscious lips were now crooked pencil thin lines that were always chapped.

"Benny, don't you pay them any attention. It's going to be you and me, because I know that you want to learn. They don't want to know anything under the shining sun."

"Well, I don't know nothin bout no English. Or no other foreign language. I speak American. And I know all I need to know to speak it. English is like....some kinda foreign language. Ain't nobody needs all that fancy, proper talk. Not in RiverView. Cause we talk American." After that insightful opinion, he dropped his head onto his folded arms. The two boys, who were still on the floor, howled louder and held their sides.

Within minutes, the sound of Benny's snores filled the room, while Miss Nellie Bea failed to gain control of the class. Benny suddenly farted so loud that Miss Nellie Bea stumbled backwards. She retreated to the far corner of the room, near the door, as if she planned to escape. The entire class burst into hysterical laughter. Miss Nellie Bea spent the next ten minutes, trying to stop the laughter, but it had become hopeless.

Following an old plan that the class had used throughout the school year, one student asked for individual help. With her back to the rest of the class, Miss Nellie Bea bent over the student's desk. Benny's low snores, followed by loud snores that sounded like foghorns, filled the room. One by one, the other students tiptoed out of the room and down the long, narrow hall to the library that didn't have a librarian and had never had a librarian and would never have a librarian.

It was the end of class before Miss Nellie Bea realized that there were only three people in the room. She knew where the students were, so she left the room, headed to the library, where she'd pick up where she'd left off, talking about nouns. It'd become a routine that she no longer fought. Before she got to the library, she heard Mr. Mayfield, the principal, giving the students a tongue-lashing. Until that morning, the students had gotten away with sneaking out of the room, because Mr. Mayfield always left campus during their English class. He returned early that day and stood inside the door of his office, watching the students as they tiptoed down the hall.

Marley Jane laughed when she told the story, because "it was just too funny, and you had to be there to get the full impact of the humor." At the end of the story, Marley Jane said to Mavis, "I felt so bad about laughing. I didn't want to laugh, but it was one of those times when you couldn't stop laughing, although you knew that it was wrong. So, to make up for my laughing, I gave Benny my cheese sandwich and apple at lunch. He was always hungry. I still feel badly about laughing, but I still laugh when I tell the story."

After Mavis finished telling the story, different customers told stories about the times that Miss Nellie Bea was their English teacher. By lunch, anyone standing on the other side of the street could hear the laughter that came from the café.

That morning was certainly not the first time that Miss Nellie Bea had been to the café since Beulah began working there, but it was the first time that she'd heard one story after another that concerned Miss Nellie Bea's years as a teacher.

◆

Beulah had met almost every customer that came through the doors of Mid-Way Café, except for a few. She'd heard a lot of talk from the customers about Samuel Franklin, who, according to the customers, no one but Mavis, Miss Nellie Bea, and his mama could handle. Everyone had been wondering why Samuel hadn't been to the café in months. Someone said that his mama had sent him to Harlem to spend the summer with her sister.

Fisher laughed, slapped his thigh, and said, "Lord! Don't you know the Big Apple done slap gone crazy with Samuel ridin his damn bike all over the city, cussin people, and givin em the bird?"

Irene injected, "I doubt he took his bike to New York City. But, I betca he walked all over that place, cussin and shootin birds at folks who made him mad or got in his way."

The next morning, following the stories about Miss Nellie Bea, Samuel surprised the customers and stopped by the café. He parked his purple, three-speed bike against the building and stomped in, slamming the door behind him. The customers stopped eating and stared at the six foot two inches of dark massiveness who wore cut-off jeans that rested beneath a huge belly. A white T-shirt had a large orange stain from an orange crush soda, and he held in his left hand a New York Yankees baseball cap that'd seen better days. Sticking out of an enormous afro was a black hair pick.

Fisher was the first to speak. "Hi, my man. What's up? Where you been? Long time no see."

Samuel grinned as he headed to a booth that he had to squeeze into. "I been travelin the world. Been to New York City. What y'all been doin?"

"Nothin much. Waitin on you to give us a report bout city life. Tell me. Whata you think bout New York City? Be honest, now."

"It ain't worth a penny is what I think. Too many folks all over the place. Too much noise. You can't even hear a bird sing. Don't think there's no birds there. And I don't blame em. I wouldn't live there either." He added, "Ms. Irene, give me what I always order." He gave her a smile that revealed large crooked teeth.

Samuel ordered a full breakfast of three scrambled eggs, four slices of bacon, a bowl of grits, two buttered biscuits, syrup, and a large glass of milk. Samuel was not too bright and had never gone beyond the fifth grade, where he was three years older than his classmates. His bad habit of picking his nose and wiping boogers on everything and everybody had worn thin the teachers' patience. On top of that, he had a habit of rocking violently back and forth, causing his desk to dance around the room, bumping into other desks and the teacher. The one straw that broke the camel's back was the long stream of curse words that'd erupt from his mouth at the most unexpected times. There wasn't a vulgar name that he didn't know to call anyone or any curse word that wasn't a close acquaintance of his.

Several teachers had threatened to quit, and one had walked out after Samuel called her a "mother-fuckin stupid piece of shit-eatin trash" whose "pussy smelled like rotten fish." It was too much for the pretty young teacher who'd done her absolute best to treat Samuel nicely. The board members had a meeting and called Samuel's mama to come for a visit, where they kindly informed her to keep Samuel at home.

After then, he spent most of his time riding his bike from one end of River View to the other. When school was in session, he made it a point to peddle down to the front parking lot and circle the flagpole, over and over. As he rode around the flagpole, he'd lift his right middle finger high in the air and curse the school and everyone in it. It was all that the teachers could do to keep the students in their seats. Most of the time, the principal ignored Samuel. But, once in awhile, he'd go out and tell him to leave.

After the seventh or so time of asking Samuel to leave, the principal came outside. He pointed a nervous finger near Samuel's face, which proved to be too much for Samuel, so he began to chase the angry principal with the bike. It was a sight. The rotund principal, who hadn't run in decades, ran around and around the flagpole, trying to stay ahead of the bike. It occasionally bumped his behind, causing him to almost lose his balance. But, he continued to yell, "Now, Samuel, I mean it! Go on home! Don't let me have to call the police. You hear me?"

Samuel cursed louder and called the principal every name in the book, as well as some quiet creative ones. The students ran to the windows, laughing and cheering Samuel on. The teachers lost control. The principal broke to the right and ran up the steps, into the school. He called the police, who came and calmly explained to Samuel that he couldn't be cursing on school grounds and chasing the principal. That didn't stop Samuel from continuing to ride over to the school and circle the flagpole, cursing softly under his breath and shooting birds high in the air. The principal and the teachers were glad that he'd toned it down a bit. Needless to say, the students were disappointed.

Samuel didn't listen to many people, because he sensed their negative feelings about him, but Mavis was kind to him. His mama liked her and he liked her. She always gave him a free glass of orange juice. After finishing his breakfast, he'd drink it in one long swallow and smack several times. Then, he'd belch loudly to express his gratitude.

Instead of leaving that morning, as he usually did, he took the large black pick from his afro and began to pick his hair. Hunks of hair fell on the table, the floor, and flew through the air. Samuel shook his large head and more hair flew. People looked on in shock and made weird, disgusting faces, as they bent over their food to protect it from flying hair.

"Stop that!" Mavis said, standing in front of him.

"I ain't stoppin nothin!" Samuel said in a calm voice, looking at Mavis with cold dark eyes. New York City had given Samuel a new streak of stubbornness, and he wasn't letting anyone, including Mavis, tell him what to do.

"Samuel, now, I mean for you to stop picking your head," Mavis said, getting madder. Her hands were on her hips and she held a long wooden spoon in her right hand. At the moment, she wanted to whack him upside the head with the spoon.

"Don't be tellin me what to do, Ms. Mavis," Samuel shot back.

"I want you to leave. Now!" Mavis said, pointing a finger at him, and, then, at the door.

"No, bitch, I aint' goin no wheres," Samuel flatly stated, while new hunks of hair like slim worms fell on the table and floor.

The more Mavis talked, the more Samuel picked his afro. The more he picked, the more hair fell. Customers backed up, but they couldn't help but laugh at Mavis who, for once, couldn't control a customer.

At that moment, Miss Nellie Bea opened the door. Fisher jumped up to hold it for her. She stopped inside the door and watched Samuel sling more hair to the floor. She heard him let out a string of curse words that'd shame a sailor. And, she'd never seen Mavis so frustrated.

Miss Nellie Bea took cautious steps toward Samuel and Mavis, not because she was fearful. Just old. When she was standing beside Samuel, she pointed a bony finger in his face, so close to his nose that when he turned to look at her, a long fingernail poked his nose, and he said, "Darn burn it! Whata you tryin to do, Miss Bea? Poke out my eye?" He noticed that her black eyes were hard and that her thin lips were in a line as straight as a ruler.

"I'm going to do more than poke out your eye, if you don't behave yourself. Got it?" and she made a question mark with her arms by bending her right elbow and pointing her arm to the ceiling. She bent her left arm across her waist so that her fist was beneath the right elbow. Anyone who'd ever been a student of hers knew when she jerked her arms into that position, she was asking you to explain or simply stop the foolishness. It was quite intimidating.

Samuel didn't like for Miss Nellie Bea to make the question gesture. And he respected her. After the board members told his mama not to let him return to school, Miss Nellie Bea was outraged and offered to tutor him once a week...free of charge. She'd been tutoring him for five years now.

Exhausted, Mavis said, "I'm gonna tell your mama. I'm gonna call her right now. And I'm gonna tell her to keep you at home. Not let you come back to the café."

Just as suddenly as he had begun to pick his afro, he stopped and put the pick in his shirt pocket. He dropped his head. "I be sorry, Ms. Mavis. Don't call my mama. I promise I won't sass no more or pick my head." Hesitating a moment, he looked at Miss Nellie Bea and said, "I'm sorry. I'll behave."

Miss Nellie Bea nodded her head and patted his arm. Mavis said, "Okay, I won't call her, if you leave. Before you go, I want you to vacuum up that mess of hair on the floor. And don't you come back in here doing no such as that again. Do you understand?"

"Yes, ma'ma. I promise. Are you gonna tell Mama?"

"No. Not if you clean up the mess you made and not come in here combing your head again."

"Oh, Ms. Mavis, Samuel's a good boy who keeps his promises," said Miss Nellie Bea, as she smiled at him, showing large false teeth. "Samuel, you vacuum. When you finish, I'm going to buy you a coke. How about that?"

Samuel smiled at her and clapped his large palms together. "Whee, doggie. I sho do like cokes. Mama don't want me to have no cokes. You won't tell her, will you, Miss Bea?"

"It's going to be our little secret," smiled Miss Nellie Bea.

Beulah was amazed at how quickly Samuel stopped and became nice. Two women, other than his mama, seemed to have some influence over him. Beulah had seen Mavis go from stormy angry to amicable calm. It wouldn't be the last time that she'd witness Mavis change gears in a difficult situation.

◆

By the end of August, Beulah had met most of Mavis' children, who had on various occasions come to the café for breakfast, lunch, or to drink coffee and chat. Until the second week in August, Marley Jane hadn't been to the café. Mavis had told Beulah that Marley Jane and her husband, Winston Steele, were moving from Notasulga, in Macon

County, Alabama, to Chambers County. Winston had taken the job as head football coach at the local high school, where Marley Jane had graduated. She was given a position, teaching English at the middle school. They'd be moving the second week in July.

According to Mavis, two weeks before they moved, Marley Jane said to Winston, " I don't want to go. Call the superintendent and tell him that you've changed your mind. That we're not coming."

Winston's reply had been, "I'm going, with or without you." And that'd been the end of the discussion, but Marley Jane resented coming back to the place where she'd grown up. She told her mama that she'd followed Winston every time that he wanted to move and she was tired of moving. Plus, she'd grown to love the small rural town of Notasulga, where they'd fought so hard, along with many others, for the survival of the school and to fit into the community that was divided over desegregation of the schools and racial issues in the 60s and 70s. Sure, it was true that she didn't want to go to Notasulga at the beginning, but fourteen years there had become home. Winston believed that she'd adjust to coming back to her hometown.

It was the last Tuesday in August when Beulah first saw Marley Jane, who'd come to the cafe for a sausage link biscuit and to visit with Mavis and Bobbie Jo. When she quietly entered the café, everyone turned to look at the petite attractive woman whose blond naturally curly hair fell to her shoulders. Few people there knew or remembered her because she'd been gone so long from Chambers County. When she came home for visits, she didn't visit anyone but family members.

As soon as she walked through the door, Edith, who was sitting at the kitchen table, turned and yelled, "Well, hi there, Marley Jane! Come on back here and meet Beulah. You're the only one of Mavis' young'uns she ain't met yet."

Beulah watched as the small woman moved gracefully in and out of the tables, greeting Irene and hugging Bobbie Jo. She wore Mavis' green eyes, but they lit up with smile wrinkles like Robert's. By the time that she entered the kitchen, she'd locked eyes with Beulah. She had her mama's same intense stare that seemed to grip a person, to know more than the person wanted known.

Mavis wiped her hands on her apron and hugged Marley Jane. "This here is Beulah. She's a dog-gone good cook. And friend. Beulah, this is my daughter, Marley Jane Steele. The one I been telling you bout."

Beulah was stirring a pot of stew. She stopped stirring and extended her left hand. "Hi. I'm glad to meet you. Seems like I know you already."

Laughing softly, Marley Jane extended her right hand and said, "Well, I hope Mama's told you good things about me. One thing I'm sure of is that she didn't lie. Like it or not. She's told me about you and how glad she is that you're working here and that you're her friend. I'm happy for both things. Now, she has two good friends," and she hugged Edith.

Edith patted Marley Jane's back and said, "Sit right here beside me." She stood up and poured Marley Jane a cup of coffee. "Here you go. Whata you wanna eat? Beulah's biscuits are as good as the ones Mavis makes. And Beulah made the biscuits this morning."

Marley Jane noticed her mama's wrinkled nose and grinned. "Well, if they're as good as Mama's, they're delicious. I'll take a sausage link biscuit, please."

"A sausage link biscuit comin right up," Beulah announced and smiled at the woman whose eyes held tiny stars.

The morning crowd thinned out, giving the employees a much-needed break before the lunch crowd was scheduled to come through the door. The women sat at the largest table and drank coffee. They listened to Marley Jane talk about the upcoming school year and Winston's job as head football coach. She never said a word about not wanting to return to her hometown. It was a done deal, and Marley Jane didn't fret over done deals, unless they could be changed or altered in some way that'd be a benefit.

When the first lunch customer placed an order, Marley Jane stood up and placed her cup in one of the large kitchen sinks. "I'll let you all get back to work. I've got tons of things to do before school starts, so I don't have any idea how long it'll be before I can come back for a biscuit." Then, she hugged all of the women at the table. When she hugged Beulah, she said, "I'm glad you're one of Mama's friends. I'll see you soon. Bye, everybody."

CHAPTER EIGHT

It was 1983 before Beulah knew it, and she was still working at Mid-Way Café. Several times in the past two years she'd applied for a job at one of the mills, without any luck. There were rumors among the employees at the cafe that Bobbie Jo's husband wanted her to close the cafe so that they could start a motorcycle business in one of the small adjoining towns. When asked about it, Bobbie Jo just shrugged her shoulders and said, "I don't know."

Edith retired from the mill in December of 1981, and her husband passed away the following July. It was the morning of July 3rd, and John had planned an annual barbeque at their home for the next day.

It was always a spectacular event, with food throughout the day and blazing, brilliant fireworks after dark. During the day, children rode a wagon over the dirt road that weaved pass fields of corn and cotton, into a thick forest that was shaded by trees older than their great-grandparents. Men and women fished on one side of a five-acre lake beyond the forest, while teenagers swam on the other side. Friends, family, and neighbors had been invited. If you didn't get an invitation, it was a sign that, for a minor reason, you weren't in favor with John Ferguson. Those people went out of their way to be nice to John, in hopes that they'd get an invitation the following year.

Edith got up early on the morning before the big event. She'd made a list of all the things that she needed to do that day. As she slipped out of bed, careful not to wake John, the darkness outside the window was thick. Looking out the window, she noticed that only a few stars blinked in the shiny blackness. A slice of a moon hung on a limb of the tall oak that shaded the barn. Turning away from the window, she looked at John, asleep in a fetal position. At some time during the night, he'd kicked off the sheet and lay naked, enveloped in darkness.

Edith found her house shoes, shoved her feet into them, and tiptoed across the floor. Closing the door behind her, she felt her way down the hall, to the kitchen. The room filled with glaring light as she flipped the switch. After she made a pot of coffee, she began pulling out cake pans and baking ingredients. When that was completed, she poured herself a cup of coffee. She figured that she'd get the cakes in the oven and start breakfast before she woke John. By the time that he shaved, breakfast would be on the table. He didn't like cold food that was meant to be hot.

The cakes were in the oven, and a pan of biscuits sat on the counter, ready to be put in the oven as soon as the cakes were removed. Edith gulped the remaining coffee in the cup and slowly pushed her chair away from the table. She checked on the cakes and removed them from the oven. Then, she placed the pan of biscuits in the center of the middle rack. Taking a deep breath, she walked down the hall to the bedroom. A dim light came through the windows, letting her know that the beginning of another day was about to start. For a moment, she stood at the foot of the bed and looked out the window, into the dim light that'd soon be so bright you couldn't look into it.

She turned her attention back to the room and John, who was still in a fetal position. He'd not moved a muscle. Edith listened. The only sound that she could hear was the singing of birds, outside the bedroom window. Their singing was a routine, so common that Edith and John

124

no longer heard it. She gently called his name. There was no response. A knot formed in the pit of her stomach and fear crept along her skin, as she gently shook him and called his name again. Edith shook him harder and called his name louder. Still, no response. She bent to listen to his breathing and heard nothing.

In the stillness of the beginning dawn, her screams bounced off the walls and ran down the hall into the room of their oldest son, who still lived at home. He sat upright in bed, unable for a moment to trace the sound. It dawned on him that Edith was screaming his name, over and over. He dashed down the hall and into his parents' bedroom. Edith stood over John. Her hands were on her cheeks and her eyes were wide. Ferris noticed that she was trembling.

"He's dead! My god, he's dead!" she screamed.

Ferris' heart beat fast as he gently moved Edith to the side and bent down to listen for a heartbeat. There was no air escaping through John's nostrils or open mouth. Ferris couldn't feel a heartbeat. He stood up and looked at Edith. "He's dead, Mama. I'll make the call. Stay here." He left the room, and Edith heard him talking on the phone to someone. She sat on the side of the bed, beside John, and looked at the floor as sunlight fell at her feet. It was a long time before she smelled biscuits burning. Slowly, she went into the kitchen, removed the charred biscuits, and turned off the oven. She returned to the bedroom and sat in the rocker. Unaware of what she was doing, she began slowly to rock back and forth, as she hummed "Amazing Grace."

It seemed like forever before she heard Preston's truck come flying into the yard. He ran across the long back porch and opened the door to the kitchen. Ferris sat at the table, surrounded by the smell of burnt biscuits. Before Preston could ask, he pointed to his parents' bedroom. Preston started down the hall. Neither brother had spoken a word.

Edith rocked back and forth, humming. Her eyes were closed and her head rested on the back of the rocker. A streak of sunshine fell across her face, blurring Preston's vision and preventing him from seeing her clearly. First, he touched John's head, standing beside the bed as tears ran down his cheeks. The clock beside the bed ticked softly, and he wanted to throw it at the window, to hear the glass break and fall on the wooden boards of the back porch. A need to slam his fist into something filled him with rage.

After a long time, he went to Edith. He bent down and held her tightly, until she pushed him away and pointed down the hall. "Go talk with Ferris. Y'all make plans bout your daddy. And bout tomorrow. Let me know what y'all decide. I don't wanna talk to anyone now."

He left her and went to the kitchen, where his brother sat at the table, drinking coffee and waiting. Preston poured himself a cup of coffee and sat across the table from Ferris. For a long time, Edith heard their low voices, making arrangements. After they finished talking, Preston called Mavis. He told her to come that afternoon when Edith would feel more like talking. And, no, there wasn't anything that she could do. Just be there for his mama. Later, Mavis called Beulah and Sadie. They visited Edith that afternoon, as the sun was sinking behind a hill.

Edith and her sons decided that the Fourth of July event would continue, in honor of John. It'd be the last big celebration that John had planned. He'd want it that way. Many people who came to the event weren't aware that he'd died the day before. Preston made an announcement shortly after everyone arrived. He told them the news and asked that they make it a happy day, in memory of his daddy. Everything was already planned. It'd be a celebration of America's independence and the life of John Ferguson.

During the weeks that followed, Mavis and Beulah spent more time than ever with Edith. Although Edith never talked about John's death, Mavis saw the pain in her blue eyes. Edith had never talked much about her marriage to John, but she'd often tell more than she realized in comments that she made now and then. She'd said enough, and Mavis had seen enough, to reveal that John was a man who controlled everything and everyone around him. He ignored Edith as if she didn't exist, doing whatever he wanted.

Mavis had learned from Edith's now and then comments, as well as from others, that John Ferguson was five years younger than Edith when they met. He'd just returned home from basic training, wearing an Army uniform, fully prepared to go to Germany "to kick some Nazi ass." He walked into his parents' home unannounced, wanting to surprise them, and Edith was there. She was visiting John's older sister, Ruth, who was Edith's best friend.

After hugging all of his family, he was introduced to Edith. She stood at the far end of the room, her hands folded in front of her like a schoolgirl, with her head slightly bowed. Her blue eyes locked with John's dark brown eyes as he moved across the room to her. His mere presence dominated the room. She thought he was the most handsome man whom she'd ever seen.

John was immediately drawn to the shy woman in front of him. He liked her honest blue eyes and pale skin that was covered in freckles. When she laid her hand in his, he felt the rough skin and large knuckles. She was wearing short cut-off blue jeans and a white sleeveless shirt that was tied in a knot at her waist. Although her body was small and slim, well-defined muscles rippled in her arms and legs.

Like a wolf, John sensed her meekness, and he knew that she was innocent in every way. In spite of the shyness and meekness, there was a toughness about her that couldn't be mistaken. John Ferguson liked all of those things. He was a man who enjoyed a good hunt. From that moment on, he decided that he'd own her. Marriage wasn't part of the plan, but Edith couldn't resist the magnetism of John Ferguson.

When Ruth learned that they were seeing one another, she became furious. Edith was older than John and certainly not the woman who deserved to be seen with her younger handsome brother who could have any woman in Chambers County that he wanted. Why settle for a mouse? Ruth liked Edith as a friend, but she didn't want her to become a part of the family. John laughed when Ruth expressed her opinion to him. "Do you think I'm a fool, girl? Hey, I'm just gittin ready to go overseas. I wanna have some fun." He laughed, as he messed up Ruth's perfectly styled black hair.

"I guess you know that she's five years older than you. I don't want to see her hurt. After all, she's my best friend. John, she hasn't dated much. Be careful," she cautioned him. "And don't get too involved."

John's grin was wicked. "You don't have to worry bout that. I just wanna have a little fun. Maybe, show Edith a little fun. You know?" His laughter boomed off the walls of the kitchen where they sat, drinking cold beer. Ruth smiled at him and shook her head.

To Ruth's surprise, John married Edith before he went to Germany. When Edith announced several months after John had left that she was pregnant, Ruth thought that there'd been too much careless fun. In spite of his many faults, Ruth knew that he was an honorable man in many situations. He wouldn't abandon his child or leave the woman whom he'd married. And he could've done worst. He married a woman who adored him, who was a hard worker, and who'd already saved enough money to purchase a farm that wasn't too far from his parents.

Edith and John were married in the living room of his parents' home three days before he left for Germany. It was a cold rainy day in December, two weeks before Christmas. You could hear the rain drizzle off the rooftops. Raindrops fell through the branches of trees and drops of silver liquid hit the hard ground, making a sound that could barely be heard inside the warm house. That morning, frost was on the windows and clung to the roof. It'd be a blistering cold day.

John's daddy was his best man, and Ruth was the maid of honor. Edith's parents wore their best Sunday clothes and looked on with pride as their oldest child finally said the marriage vows that would take her from their home to her own home. They'd almost given up hope that she'd ever find a man. They believed that it was her duty to make sure that John was happy and that her marriage lasted.

After the wedding, John and Edith went to the small farmhouse that sat on an incline, far back from the road. Together, they'd signed the deed to the property the day before the wedding. A grove of small pecan trees lay to the right of the driveway. An open field to the left of the driveway stretched far in the distance, until it met a wall of trees. A large well-built barn sat approximately two hundred yards from the back of the house. Pastures, large enough for horses and cows, stretched behind the barn and it, too, met the wall of trees that wrapped halfway around the land.

The day that they purchased the land, with money that Edith had saved from working in River View Mill, John pointed out to Edith where he'd grow cotton and have a vegetable garden. He talked about the cattle that he'd raise and the lake that he planned to build. Edith didn't give any opinions, and it never enter John's mind to ask her opinion.

She was lucky that he wanted to marry her. The marriage sealed her dedication and loyalty to a man who wouldn't always be dedicated and loyal to her, but he never considered leaving her. There was never a time in her marriage that she wasn't in awe of the fact that he'd chosen her, an unattractive woman. When he could've had any woman that he wanted, he chose her. It was a mystery that she never understood and didn't want Mavis or anyone else to explain to her.

Ferris was born in August. He was a huge red baby who came into the world, yelling at the top of his lungs. Edith thought that he was the most beautiful thing that she'd ever seen. It amazed her that she'd given birth to another human being. It was something that she'd decided, long before she met John, would never happen.

John and Edith exchanged letters that seemed to creep across the

SHIRLEY A. AARON

ocean. John was proud of the son whom he'd not seen. Ferris' birth caused John to look at life and death differently. It became more difficult for John to pull the trigger and shoot a young man who made him think of his own son.

One day, John's troop was surprised in an open field, as bullets sailed from the roof of a large barn. The American soldiers took cover or fell to the ground behind tall grass. John crept on his belly toward the barn. When he was within close range, a young German soldier stood at the open window of the barn's roof and aimed at John. Without thinking, John looked down the barrel of his gun, located the young man's head in the crosshairs, slowly pulled the trigger, and watched as the young man fell, hitting the ground with a thud. At that moment, John Ferguson became a changed man. Anger filled him; he hated war and the survival instinct that men must have to live in a world of conflict and discontent. But, he became, at that moment, some of the evil that war brings. The anger and confusion would live in his mind until the day that he died.

Before Ferris was five, the war had been over for a year. Preston was born near the end of that year. His first cry was soft and lasted only long enough for him to inhale the breath of life. As the nurse laid him on Edith's belly, he looked into her eyes and yawned. He stuck two tiny fingers into his mouth. When John held him for the first time, Preston gripped one of John's fingers in his small fist and looked deep into John's eyes. Then and there, Preston became John's favorite. John had already decided that Ferris was too meek like Edith. He wasn't the rough and tumble boy that John had hoped to have.

As the boys grew, it became apparent to everyone that Preston was a leader. He was more like his daddy, while Ferris was more like Edith. Both boys were hard workers. Although they were both rough and demanding of other children, Preston was the one who was usually in control, and he quickly became a bully. If he didn't get his way, he

130

sought revenge. When charm didn't work, his other side could be seen. Like John, he fooled a lot of people. He never fooled Mavis. She liked Preston, but she wasn't blind to his ugly side.

Soon after John's death, Edith learned that he'd left everything in Preston's control. She'd have to ask Preston for money to purchase a washer, a dryer, or a new vehicle…anything that cost more than two hundred dollars. Edith didn't complain. That was what John wanted, so it was okay with her. Plus, she'd saved most of her own money and had a nice egg nest. Ferris lived at home and worked in one of the mills. He helped with household expenses; therefore, they'd not have a problem with money. And she trusted Preston to provide for her when she needed something.

According to Alabama law, Edith could've challenged the will and won. She chose not to do so. The attorney made it clear to Preston that she'd win in court, if she decided to contest the will. Based on what the attorney said, Preston knew it was in his best interest not to argue with Edith when she asked for something. He knew how to maintain control and how to manage Edith.

◆

It was the summer of 1985, and John had been dead for two years. There was more talk than ever about Bobbie Jo closing the café. In June, Beulah applied for a job at River View Mill and was hired to work on the first shift. She gave a two weeks notice, and Bobbie Jo began searching for another cook. Mavis didn't think that she was looking too hard, and it dawned on Mavis that it was highly possible that Bobbie Jo was planning to close the café and go to work for her husband Trent, who'd recently opened a motorcycle business near Interstate-85. To Mavis' surprise, Bobbie Jo soon hired Sadie Smith as another full-time cook. Since Mavis and Sadie were neighbors, she rode to work each day with Mavis.

The first week in September, Bobbie Jo announced that she was thinking about closing Mid-Way Café at the end of the month. First, she told her employees. Then, she posted a handwritten sign on the front door. It stated, "Mid-Way Café will close at the end of September. Thank you for your business."

No one was happy, least of all the employees. They had less than twenty-seven days to find another job. Customers were disappointed or angry. After grumbling for days, Fisher asked, "BobbieJo, what are we supposed to do now? Go all the way up the Valley to McDonalds? You know can't nobody cook like Mavis. Folks in RiverView is sho gonna miss this place."

Unruffled, Bobbie Jo calmly replied that she was going to help Trent operate the motorcycle shop. In an off-handed manner, she gave another reason for closing. Ms. Jo Ella had raised the rent for the second time in a year. Business was booming, but the rent was making a deep cut in the profit. It was time to close the doors.

She ended the conversation by saying, "So, I'm doin what's best for me."

◆

The day that Mavis got the news, she left work worried and exhausted. Working as a cook at her daughter's café had been more than a means of helping earn a living. There was a lot more than the loss of a job that concerned her. Work was an escape from an almost daily ordeal that she faced with Johnny Lee. She was getting older, not an ideal time to begin looking for another job. Robert was in bad health. Unable to verbalize it, Mavis felt the oncoming doom of his death.

Together, they'd protected one another and Johnny Lee. She didn't know how she'd managed, trapped in the house with a son who was unpredictable from one day to the next. Robert grew weaker as the weeks passed. Johnny Lee realized it and took advantage of the lack of energy that he recognized in his daddy. Mavis was more likely to give in to his demands, but Robert didn't tolerate his rude behavior.

There had been a silver lining. When her youngest daughter Laura Faye opened a mobile home dealership in Opelika, she asked Johnny Lee to quit his job in the mill and work for her as a handyman, setting up and installing mobile homes for customers. Johnny Lee was a certified plumber and would be a benefit to her business. He accepted the offer. That'd been some years ago. Johnny Lee handled Laura Faye the same way that he handled Mavis. He got his way and stayed out of work when he felt like it. It didn't help that Laura Faye never docked his pay.

Robert's health took a quick downhill dive, with one small stroke after another. Each stroke was more severe than the previous one. Someone needed to be with him at all times, so Laura Faye asked Johnny Lee to stay home and take care of Robert. She continued to give him the same salary. At the time, some of her siblings agreed that it was a great idea. The other siblings thought it was foolish. They didn't believe that Johnny Lee would give their daddy the care that he needed. They all worked and couldn't stay with Robert; therefore, they remained quiet.

That agreement didn't last long. It was no time before Mavis began coming home to find Robert unattended. Johnny Lee and his present girlfriend would be in his room, behind a locked door. As soon as he began staying home with his daddy, he moved his girlfriend in with him, without asking his parents. It didn't surprise his siblings that he didn't ask permission for the woman to move in with him. It was a known fact that he never asked permission for anything.

The girlfriend was a curvy bleached blonde, with a round doll face and cupid lips that seemed to be sulking all the time. A soft voice and lazy amber colored eyes reminded Mavis of a cat that never stopped stalking. Mavis had no use for the woman and even less after she learned that she'd abandoned her husband and three children for drugs and sex. Johnny Lee told Laura Faye that the sex was hotter than a one hundred degree temperature on a tin roof in July and that there were no limits to what the woman wanted. He gladly accommodated her.

They'd lock the door, smoke weed, and have sex all day. Often, music would be so loud that the walls vibrated. When Mavis came home and found the door locked, with music pouncing the floors, she knew that they were as high as a Georgia sky on a sultry summer day. Nothing she said convinced Johnny Lee to change his behavior and threatening the latest girlfriend only enraged him more. He told her to mind her own damn business and leave him the hell alone.

After he told her that, she remained silent and plotted. She meant, by god, the bitch was going to leave her house. It wouldn't be the first time that she'd gotten rid of a sorry woman whom one of her sons had brought home. Her daughters shook their heads at Mavis' attitude toward any woman who was involved with one of her sons. No one, it seemed, was good enough. All of Johnny Lee's siblings agreed with Mavis. The present girlfriend was a real piece of cake, a scumbag. She needed to go back to her nice home, with her nice husband and three small children.

Although the news about closing the café disappointed Mavis, she was glad that she'd be at home with Robert. She told herself that it was time to have a lengthy conversation with Laura Faye, the only sibling who defended Johnny Lee, the only one who agreed with Robert and Mavis about him. The three of them were his enablers, a fact that he took full advantage of at every opportunity.

Mavis called Laura Faye and told her that she'd be at the dealership the next day, after she left work. The following day, she stopped by the house to check on Robert before she went to the lot. She was pleased to see that Johnny Lee and the girlfriend were sitting at the table with him. They appeared to be drug free. Johnny Lee had just sat a bowl of ice cream in front of Robert. He smiled at Johnny Lee.

"I'm gonna run down to see Laura Faye for a little while," she told them. "Johnny Lee, make sure you put Robert in his easy chair. I won't be gone long."

"Don't worry bout it, Mama. We're gonna be fine. Ain't that right, old man?" he laughed, winking at Robert. Robert rewarded him with a grin.

♦

Mavis told Laura Faye that Bobbie Jo was closing the café, and they talked about the effects that the closing would have on Mavis. Laura Faye listened as her mama talked. Plans began to form in her head, as she mentally looked for ways to financially help her parents. No one knew the depth of love that Laura Faye felt for Mavis. All of Mavis' children loved her, but none of them adored her like Laura Faye.

They talked about Johnny Lee, about his present girlfriend, and about him not taking care of Robert. Mavis told Laura Faye that Johnny Lee stayed behind a locked door most of the day, unaware that his daddy was in another room. Music could be heard below the house, when Mavis crossed Osanippa Creek on the way home from the cafe. Laura Faye listened and told her mama that she'd talk to Johnny Lee, that she'd lay down the law and demand that he return to work the first week in October. Since Johnny Lee listened to Laura Faye more than he did to anyone else, Mavis agreed.

Laura Faye talked with Johnny Lee the next day, while his bleached blonde sat in the waiting room, twisting her hair and reading magazines. In the days that followed, his behavior got better. When Mavis got home from work, the house was clean and Robert's lunch had been prepared. The woman made an effort to be friendlier, but Mavis was having none of it. She considered several options to make the woman leave.

After a week, Johnny Lee returned to some of his old habits. But, Mavis told no one that many days he and the girlfriend were high when she got home. Most of the time, at least, they weren't behind a locked door, and loud music didn't shake the house. Robert was pleased that they sat with him and talked. It didn't matter that the talk made no sense and jumped from one topic to another, without rhyme or reason.

♦

The end of September came, and it was the last day that Mid-Way Cafe was open. The place was packed. Elvis sang, while the crowd laughed, recalling memories about the café and about the people who'd frequented it through the years. Fisher sat for a long time, not talking. His face wore a cover of sadness as he thought about how so much of his life revolved around the café and the people who came and went, leaving pieces of their lives behind. The realization hit him that they were his friends, closer to him than his own family. Finally, Irene pulled him to the floor and insisted that he dance with her. Tears hung on the rims of his eyes as they weaved in and out of the tables, while everyone clapped and joked. Several couples joined them, moving cautiously among the small space.

Beulah came at five o'clock that morning and helped Mavis make breakfast. She stayed and cooked until it was time for her to go to work. As she laid her apron on the kitchen table, she told Mavis that she'd call her later. They hugged. Then, Beulah hugged Edith who was sitting at the table in the kitchen. People stopped Beulah as she moved across the room. She spoke briefly with each one. Finally, she reached the door and turned to wave. The sound of "Bye, Beulah" could be heard as she walked to her car. For several minutes, she sat and looked at the door of the cafe. Looking back was too painful, so she shook her head, started the motor, and backed into the highway.

Riding home that day, Mavis breathed a deep sigh and exhaled slowly. Now, Johnny Lee could return to work. Mavis would be home with Robert. Maybe, she thought, all of this was God's will, because Robert was getting worse and Johnny Lee was getting antsy. This would be better for everyone. Mavis would take one day at a time. There was no need in worrying about things that she couldn't control, but she knew of one certain bleached blonde who would be controlled.

When Mavis walked into the house, the first thing that she did was to check on Robert. He was asleep in his lounge chair, with his mouth slightly open. His bony hands were folded on his chest. The TV was on, but the sound was muted. The only sound in the room was Robert's gentle snores. There was no sign of Johnny Lee. The door to his bedroom was closed.

Mavis stood in the middle of the room and absorbed it all. Slowly, she untied the apron from around her waist and removed it from her neck. She placed it on the back of a chair and sank into the soft cushions of the sofa. After several minutes, she removed her tennis shoes and wiggled her toes. As she massaged her feet, she realized that she was getting too old to stand all day on a concrete floor. It was time that she slowed down. As soon as the thought entered her head, she dismissed it. She sounded old and worn out.

It all became overwhelming. She placed her head in the palms of her hands and began to weep softly. Everything was happening too fast. Life was coming with the force of a strong gusty storm. A feeling of doom washed over her, and she wanted to be taken away by the storm, to be destroyed by the storm, to escape in the storm.

"Babe, are you okay? What time is it?" Robert asked in a weak voice.

She looked at him. He'd lifted his head. Fear shone from his beautiful sky blue eyes. His pale, thin-skinned hands gripped the arms of the recliner. Mavis pressed her fists into her eyes to catch the tears. Looking up, she smiled. "I'm fine. Just a little tired. How are you feeling?"

"I'm feelin good. Now that you're home. Where's Johnny boy?" he asked, looking around the room. "He was sittin on the sofa when I dozed off. Is he okay?"

"He's fine. Taking a nap in his room." She pushed herself out of the plush sofa. When she stood near him, she kissed his face.

"I'm going to change clothes. Then, I'll start supper. What would you like?"

"I don't too much care. I'm not too hungry. Plus, you know. I gotta watch my weight." He smiled, and the light from the lamp, near his recliner, was caught in eyes that appeared weak.

It wasn't really a joke about his weight. He'd always watched his weight, based on the feel of his clothes. Until he became sick and skinny, he'd never been anything other than slim, with lean defined muscles. Oh, he wanted Mavis to cook all of his southern favorites, but he might eat only a small portion. No one could remember a time when he'd been anywhere near overweight, while Mavis fought a constant battle with the scales; yet, in spite of her love for food and eight babies, she'd kept her weight down.

Robert told her it was because she was so vain about her looks. She didn't deny it and was proud that she was still an attractive woman who turned people's heads. It was true that she took too much pride in her appearance. She knew it and didn't care. After all, everyone had a vice or two.

She took the almost empty glass from the table beside Robert and went into the kitchen. She returned with a fresh glass of water and sat it on the table. "I'm going to put the chicken in the oven and start the vegetables. Don't go anywhere," she ordered, stroking his lean face.

"You don't need to worry bout that. I'm stayin here with you, Aggie."

CHAPTER NINE

Johnny Lee returned to work at Laura Faye's mobile dealership the day after Mavis' last day at the cafe. He was the first employee to arrive. Laura Faye called him into her office as soon as she heard his footsteps in the hall. She noted that he appeared clear-headed, and there didn't seem to be any indication that he'd indulged in drugs before leaving home.

"Sit down, Johnny Lee," she told him, looking up from a stack of papers on her desk. "I want to talk with you bout a few things before you start work today." She stopped talking long enough for him to flop down in a chair. As she watched, he stretched his long legs out in front of him, touching the bottom of the large mahogany desk. Getting comfortable, he slumped in the chair, ready for a lecture.

"All right," he sighed, "just get it over with. First, let me tell you this: there ain't no need in you tellin me not to do drugs on the job. I know not to do that. And, for your information, I don't mix drugs and work. Now, have I said it all? Or is there something else you wanna say fore I get to work?" He gave her a big smile to soften the sarcastic tone that he'd used.

"I hope we have an understanding bout work and drugs—"

He interrupted her, "We do. I told you. I don't mix drugs and work.

You don't need to worry bout that, Laura Faye." He dragged the words out in slow motion so that she'd be sure to comprehend. It only pissed her off.

"Don't get smartass with me, Johnny Lee. I'll slap you upside the head." For seconds, as they looked at one another, the only sounds were traffic that rushed by the lot and coffee that brewed in a small kitchen down the hall. Finally, Johnny Lee laughed and sat up straight in the chair.

Laura Faye laid down the pen that she'd been holding. "I'm concerned bout the drugs that you're doing at home and bout the way that you're behaving with Mama and Daddy. They're getting too old for your shit. I want things to change. We all want things to change. Things are gonna change—"

"Let's get one thing cleared up," he interrupted her, leaning across the desk. "Right now. You're my boss at work, but you ain't my boss at home. I don't need to ask you or any damn body else what I can or cannot do in my own house. You got that?" he said, getting angry. He blew a cloud of smoke in her face to punctuate his rhetorical question.

She ignored him and continued, "Things are gonna change in the way you treat Mama and Daddy. I love you, Johnny Lee, but I love them more. If you ever hurt one of them, I'm personally gonna kick your ass." He rolled his eyes to the ceiling, and she went on, "And, the girlfriend has got to go. She can take her ass back to her husband and three kids. Her big-shot daddy can deal with her. Not Mama and Daddy."

"Again, Laura Faye, you're talkin bout something that ain't none of your business. She ain't goin nowhere. That's a fact, Jack." He stood up to leave. "Anything else you got to say?" He smothered the cigarette in a crystal ashtray on the desk. His lop-sided grin made her furious.

"Don't test me, Johnny Lee. I mean it," she said, pointing a finger at him. He turned his back on her and walked out the door.

Picking up the pen, she looked down at the stack of papers in front of her. She didn't see Johnny Lee turn and come back down the hall, but she heard the loud slam of her office door. She mumbled under her breath, "One day I'm gonna have to kick his ass."

♦

After Johnny Lee left for work that morning, Mavis washed his breakfast dishes and, then, walked to the door of her bedroom to check on Robert. He lay on his back, and she watched as his chest rose up and down. His breathing was shallow. Walking away, she knew that he'd sleep for at least two more hours. That'd be enough time for her to carry out her plan.

When she opened the kitchen door, the coolness of the morning gave a hint of the coming fall. She closed the door and looked at the tall walnut tree near the driveway. Its leaves were changing colors. Some leaves drifted slowly to the ground as she walked down the steps and headed to the barn, where she selected a hoe and a shovel. With determination, she walked to the other side of the driveway, where Robert always planted his garden. But, he'd not planted one the past spring because his health hadn't allowed it.

She marched directly to the center of what had been the garden. First, she took the hoe and made a large circle. Over and over she traced the circle, digging deeper into the ground, until there was a distinct circle, which was at least four inches deep. After she laid down the hoe, she picked up the shovel and began to dig out the dirt from within the circle. The dirt formed a small mound around the hole that became approximately twelve inches deep. Mavis stood back and evaluated the hole. "That'll do," she said to the emptiness around her.

Next, she dragged the hosepipe to the hole. Afterwards, she returned to the barn and replaced the tools in a large wooden barrel. She removed Robert's thick gloves and laid them on a workbench. On second thought, she returned to the hole with the hoe and shovel. She placed them on the ground near the hole. As she walked to the house, she wiped her hands on her jeans.

She stopped in the kitchen long enough to get a large plastic bag. Next, she went into the bathroom and put all of the girlfriend's products into the bag. Afterwards, she went into Johnny Lee's bedroom. The girlfriend was tangled in the sheet that covered most of her face. Bleached blonde hair fell across the pillow. For several minutes, Mavis watched her with contempt. The girl was in a deep sleep.

Mavis walked to the dresser and dropped everything that belonged to the girl into the black garbage bag. Opening one drawer after another, she dumped all of the girl's underwear in the bag. When there was nothing left that belonged to the girl, Mavis moved to the closet. One by one, she removed the girl's clothing from the racks. Once she turned to look at the girl. She hadn't moved and her mouth hung open, slack and wide, with spittle drooling out one side of the full lips.

One last trip around the room told Mavis that everything the girl owned, except her purse, slippers, and robe, were in the large bag. Mavis picked up the purse, which was sitting in a chair. Quickly, she looked through the contents and took out the girl's wallet. The only pictures were of three beautiful blonde-haired children, two boys and a girl. The oldest boy had lost a front tooth, and the gap filled a part of his smile. The younger boy had a lop-sided grin that reminded Mavis of Johnny Lee. An adorable baby girl's smile revealed dimples in both cheeks. The bright-eyed children appeared to range from two to six years old. Mavis shook her head and wondered how any woman could abandon such beautiful children. She decided that there was only one reason. The mother was as sorry as four hundred hells.

Mavis considered throwing the purse in the bag, but she decided that the girl needed her identification. And Mavis couldn't bring herself to throw away the photos of those innocent smiling faces. Gently, she laid the purse on the chair, took one final look at the sleeping girl, and walked out of the room.

Mavis thought, "I can't call that girl a woman, in spite of the fact she's had three precious babies. There ain't an adult thing bout her."

Again, she walked to the garden. She took a few items from the bag, threw the bag into the circle, and, then, she threw the items on top of the bag. Back to the barn she went. A metal gasoline can sat on the floor, near the door. She took the can and felt in her pocket for the matches. They were there, where she'd put them when she'd started a fire in the wood heater that morning, to take the chill out of the living room before Robert got up.

At the edge of the circle, she stood and poured gasoline over the items. She stepped back, just far enough for her to throw a match onto the gasoline. There was a popping sound like a small explosion and the contents in the hole burst into flames. The plastic bag gave off waves of dark smoke. Mavis watched until the fire had almost burned itself out. She turned on the faucet to the hose and drenched what was left of the contents. She heard a sizzling sound as the water hit the fire. Bits of black particles floated upward. Mavis stood and looked at the charred wet mess in the hole. Using the shovel, she began to cover the hole with the dirt that formed a circle. When she finished, she took the hoe and smoothed out the mound of dirt. When that was completed, she returned the hoe, the shovel, and the gasoline can to the barn.

She turned off the faucet near the porch, walked into the house, and stood still in the kitchen, listening. After washing her hands, she made a phone call. After the call, she went into Johnny Lee's bedroom. The girl had turned onto her back. One arm was flung across the bed. A strand of blonde hair fell across her eyes. Mavis shook the girl's shoulder. Nothing. She shook it harder and said, "Wake up! Get up!"

The girl opened her eyes and frowned at Mavis. "Leave me alone. Go away." She closed her eyes.

Mavis slapped the girl's face enough to make it sting. "I said, 'Wake up!' and I'm not gonna keep saying it. Get your sorry self out of bed."

"Leave me alone," the girl growled, slinging an arm and kicking a long shapely leg. "Go away!"

Mavis pulled the girl's long bleached blonde hair as hard as she could. The girl sat straight up in bed and tried to fight, but each time that she almost made contact with Mavis, a downward jerk on her hair stopped the contact. "Get outa bed and come with me to the kitchen. Put on your robe and slippers. Bring your purse with you."

The two women looked at one another for what seemed like a long time. Mavis never blinked. The girl looked away and pushed her feet into her slippers. It irritated her that Mavis stood watching, with her arms folded and a look of pure hatred on her face. She put on her robe and got her purse. After one final glare at Mavis, she walked out of the bedroom and went to the kitchen, with Mavis following her.

"Sit down. You and I are gonna have a talk. Before your husband gets here. I need to make things clear—"

"What the hell are you talking bout? When my husband gets here? You called my husband? You bitch!" The woman, who was still standing, raised her purse in the air.

Before the purse began to move toward her, Mavis picked up a pistol from the counter near her and pointed it at the woman. "Go ahead. Hit me. Leave a mark so that I can say I was defending myself. Hit me hard. Give me a reason to blow you to hell."

The girl lowered the purse and sat in a chair. "You're one crazy bitch. You know that?"

"I'm sure you don't want this crazy bitch to put a bullet in your scarred heart. Now, do you? So, let me talk. While you listen."

Mavis began to tell the girl that all of her belongings, except for what she was wearing, had been burned. Next, she told her that she'd called the girl's husband and what she'd said to him, ending with "He's on his way to get you." At last, she told the girl that Johnny Lee was history, that they'd not see one another again, and that she'd need to find another drug addict to hook up with. At the end of the long talk, the girl just stared at Mavis.

"I hear a car in the driveway. That's probably your husband. Get up." Mavis still had the pistol in her hand.

The girl got up and walked out of the house, with Mavis close behind her. The gun was in Mavis' right hand, which was behind her back. The huge white truck that the girl's husband used in his father-in-law's business was parked near the porch.

The man who stepped onto the ground was of medium height, with balding sandy hair. His face was long and narrow. Thick black-framed glasses made his eyes look large. There was something about him that made Mavis feel sorry for him. She knew that he cared about the girl or he wouldn't have come to get her. And, too, Mavis had learned that this wasn't the first time that the girl had run off with another man, leaving her babies behind.

When the girl reached the last step, the man took her arm and walked with her to the other side of the truck. He opened the door for her and waited until she was seated before he closed the door. She never said a word.

After he got into the truck, he rolled down his window. "Thank you for calling. She won't be back. I assure you of that."

"I hope not. For her sake," Mavis said, looking into his blurred brown eyes. "Thank you for coming." He nodded and drove away. Mavis walked into the house. It was time to get Robert up for his breakfast.

When Johnny Lee got home, Mavis told him that the girl called her husband and that he came to get her. The girl started packing her stuff almost as soon as Johnny Lee left for work. Johnny Lee wanted to know if the girl had said anything, given a reason why she left.

"Not a word, except that she called her husband to come get her. He came. And she left with him."

Johnny Lee watched Mavis as she talked and took cornbread from the oven. He was sitting sideways, with his legs stretched out and his right elbow on the table. Tilting his head back, he looked at Mavis from under half-closed eyelids and blew smoke to the side. Mavis noticed the lop-sided grin on his face. He knew that she wasn't telling him everything, that most of what she said was bullshit.

When she finished talking, he looked at the floor. He didn't say anything for a long time. "Well, it's probably just as well. I'm gonna be workin, and I'll be tired when I get home. I won't be havin time to entertain." He laughed. "How bout fixin me a bowl of them collard greens and cornbread, Mama?"

CHAPTER TEN

It was the summer of 1986. Every summer, since 1981, Beulah, Edith, and Mavis had canned fruits and vegetable most Saturdays, from the time the sun opened its huge large eye until it began to move west, to end the day in a blaze of brilliant glory. By the time the sky was filled with primary colors, they were following the sun, almost every Saturday afternoon, to Shorter, where they bet on the dog races. Mavis was always lucky. Not so much Beulah and Edith. When Mavis won, she shared a percentage with the other two women. None of them had money to burn, but they enjoyed one another's company and the escape from the routine of their lives.

Since Beulah had gone to work in the mill, she didn't go with them as often to Shorter, especially if the mills were working overtime to meet demands. Soon, Edith began working on Saturdays for Preston who'd opened a small store on the backwaters, selling gasoline and food that boaters were interested in eating with their fingers. That left Mavis without her companions, but one of her children would accompany her. Her oldest son Claude and her oldest daughter Janet enjoyed the dog track almost as much as she did.

Summer ended in fewer heat waves, while fall sneaked into time, with cool temperatures in the mornings and nights. It was a matter of days before the first frost settled on the pumpkins that Edith had planted and planned to share with family and friends. She couldn't wait to bite into one of Mavis' pumpkin pies.

Most nights, Beulah threw a light blanket over Autumn's bed. It was hard to believe that her baby was a grown woman who'd completed four years of nursing and worked at the local hospital. Autumn had been dating Tyrone Upshaw for three years. She'd told him about her brother and daddy. He'd asked her to marry him several times, but she kept putting him off. Tyrone didn't push her to make a decision.

Every morning, in order to take away the chill, Mavis started a fire in the wood heater that was in the living room. Robert couldn't get warm enough, and he contacted a bad cold, with a cough that rattled in his chest. The cough wouldn't respond to any homemade remedies. As they lay in bed late at night, Mavis listened to his labored breathing. During the day, he'd sit in his recliner, bundled up in his winter jacket, his eyes red and watery. Mavis wondered how he survived, because he ate very little. There was no mistaking that he'd lost weight, and he didn't have much weight to lose.

When Robert awoke one Tuesday, Mavis noticed that he couldn't find the right words for chair or for coffee. He became angry and knocked a cup of coffee onto the kitchen floor. Steam rose from the hot liquid that remained in a puddle on the linoleum rug. They both stared at the stain. When Robert began to speak, he couldn't form a sentence. He looked at Mavis, his eyes pleading for help.

She soothed him, cleaned up the spilled coffee, and poured him a fresh cup. She added cream and sugar, just the way he liked it. Afterwards, she stood beside his chair and stroked his head. "I'm taking you to the doctor. Finish your coffee and get dressed." She added when he shook his head, "We're not arguing bout it. You're going to the doctor. Something's wrong."

He laid his head on her breast. His head nodded in agreement.

Although she couldn't see his tears, she knew they were on his cheeks. She took his hand and kissed it. Then, she stroked his silver curls. Fear ran through her body like streaks of lightning and gripped her heart in a tight fist.

When she called the doctor's office, the nurse told her to go straight to the emergency room at the hospital. The doctor would meet them there. Before Mavis left the house, she called Bobbie Jo and told her to meet them at the hospital. Bobbie Jo called Janet. They were waiting at the emergency room when Mavis and Robert walked through the door.

The doctor examined Robert and asked him some questions, like "What day is it?" and "Who's the President of the United States?" and "How many fingers am I holding up?" He instructed Robert to touch his nose with his tongue and to smile. Mavis frowned when Robert gave the wrong answer or hesitated too long before answering. After the examination and X-rays, the doctor asked to speak to Mavis and her daughters in the hallway.

"Mr. Robert had a stroke. Until he's had more tests, I can't tell you the extent of the stroke. In my opinion, this isn't the first stroke. Also, I want to run some tests to check his lungs. I'm admitting him to the hospital this morning and ordering some tests." He looked at Mavis and waited.

"Do whatever needs to be done," Mavis said in a false brave tone.

"Good. Someone will take him to a room before long. I'll be by this afternoon, if you have any questions. Let's step back into the room and let me speak to him," he said, touching Mavis' arm.

They walked into the room, where Robert lay on a narrow hospital bed, a white sheet and warm blanket pulled to his chin. Fear made itself known in his eyes and his rigid body. "Well, doc, what's the news?" he asked, attempting to laugh.

"It looks like you've had a stroke, Mr. Robert. Right now, I don't know the extent of it. That's why I'm admitting you to the hospital. I want to run some more tests. Is that okay with you?" the doctor asked, laying his hand on Robert's right shoulder. "I don't want you to go home, until I have some answers."

"Do what you need to do. I'm here now. Guess I might as well find out what's goin on."

Robert stayed in the hospital for four days. Tests revealed that he'd had many mini strokes and one that'd come close to being serious. His lungs were in terrible condition. One lung had almost stopped working. Oxygen would be a necessity for the rest of his life. The strokes would probably become worst over time. A serious one could kill him.

The doctor told Mavis the signs that she needed to be aware of and to call 911 immediately if she suspected a stroke. "Make sure that he uses the oxygen all of the time. Day and night. Call me, if you need me."

◆

Before Robert left the hospital, oxygen was ordered and delivered to the house. Four days in the hospital had convinced Mavis that Robert wasn't going to be an ideal patient. It had become obvious while he was hospitalized that the last stroke had affected him more than she thought the day that she took him to the emergency room. He became frustrated and angry over the least thing. To make matters worst, he despised the oxygen. It was a chore to keep the tube in his nose. Mavis would turn her back and Robert would fling the oxygen tube to the foot of the bed or onto the floor.

Johnny Lee stayed out of work to drive Mavis and Robert home from the hospital. When they arrived, all of his siblings were there. His sisters had cleaned the house, and they had also cooked dinner. His brothers sat in the living room, drinking coffee and talking. They all met their parents and Johnny Lee at the kitchen door. Richard put his arm under Robert's left arm and almost carried him to the recliner, where the plastic tube for oxygen lay on one of its arms.

As Robert settled into the recliner, Laura Faye turned on the oxygen.

Robert heard the soft hissing sound and felt the air from the tube hit his left hand. Mavis took the tube and placed it in his nostrils, while he gave her an evil look. By the time that he'd sunk into the chair, he was out of breath. He laid his head back, closed his eyes, and greedily inhaled the oxygen. In a moment, he felt his heart rate slow down to a regular rhythm.

Before long, he was asleep, stretched out in the recliner. Mavis placed pillows under each of his arms so that he'd be more comfortable. She checked to make sure that the bottle attached to the oxygen machine was filled with water and that the oxygen was set on the correct level. After she made certain that the machine was correctly adjusted, she joined her children in the now crowded kitchen. They ate, sitting at the table and standing at the counter, as they talked in low voices. While the others ate and talked, Johnny Lee went to stand by Robert's chair. He touched Robert's cheek and bent to kiss his forehead. Tears welled up in Johnny Lee's eyes, and he went to the bathroom to wash his face.

In the months that followed, the children came more frequently and offered to help in any way. Claude came every afternoon. Concern for Mavis was written on his face, as they drank coffee and talked. Laura Faye provided financial assistance and came by almost every day after work. She listened to Mavis pour out her feelings and thoughts. She laughed and joked with Robert, whose eyes lit up when she walked into the room. She talked privately with Johnny Lee and watched him cry. His tears were real, but she knew that, in spite of his love for their daddy, the drugs were strong and owned him.

There were many frustrating and tiring times for Mavis. Dealing with Robert could be like handling a rebellious child who refused to listen and who indulged in temper tantrums. He threw things at her and refused to give up the cigarettes that he'd been smoking since he was a teenager. Several times, she caught him about to light up. The oxygen tube would be in his lap, hissing.

One day she left Robert alone to start dinner. She was gone for about ten minutes. When she walked into the living room, he wasn't in his recliner. The cut oxygen tube lay on the floor. She checked the bathroom. He wasn't there. She started down the hall and saw him wobbling from the bedroom, the cut oxygen tube dangling from his nose and stopping at this chest. An unlit cigarette was gripped firmly in one corner of his mouth. He wore a big devious smile as he winked at Mavis.

"What have you done?" she asked, near tears. "Robert, you cannot smoke with the oxygen in the house. I've told you that over and over." She led him back to the recliner, while he blew invisible smoke into the air.

"The hell I can't," he replied, with a wicked grin. "Just watch," and he blew more invisible smoke toward her face.

"What am I gonna do with you?" she asked, as she took the cut tube from his nose. She hooked another tube to the machine and placed it in his nostrils. He jerked it from his nose and threw it to the floor. Near tears, she picked it up and wiped off the tips. Slapping her hand was the last straw. She put the tube in his lap and left the room. For a long time, she sat on the edge of her bed, biting her upper lip and refusing to cry. When she went back into the living room, Robert had put the tube in his nostrils and was asleep, while the unlit cigarette lay on the floor.

Once, he spit in her face. She walked away so that she wouldn't slap him. There were good days, but the bad days came more frequently. Often, Mavis sat at the kitchen table and cried quietly so that Robert couldn't hear her. Her body ached for rest, and the headaches split her head as the pain flashed behind her eyeballs. It was almost more than she could tolerate to keep up a front for everybody. Only Beulah and Edith knew how tough things were.

When Beulah left work, she'd come to sit with Robert, while he slept in the recliner and Mavis went to bed. Johnny Lee would be in his room or gone. No one knew where he was or when he came home. He went to work almost every day. Beulah would turn the television on low or she'd read. Often, she washed and dried clothes. She did what she could to make life easier for Mavis.

Before she left to go home, she'd wake up Mavis. They'd put Robert to bed. Sometimes, they'd sit at the kitchen table and drink coffee. Beulah heard about Mavis' concerns for Robert and Johnny Lee. When Mavis cried, Beulah cried with her. Mavis told Beulah things that she couldn't tell her children or Edith, who came often to help in some way. Bringing food was Edith's way of comforting Mavis.

Autumn came several times a week to check on Robert. He liked the pretty young woman who understood him when his language was almost incoherent. She laughed at his jokes and waited patiently for him to complete a sentence. Later, as he grew sicker and had more strokes, she bathed him. Other than Mavis or Johnny Lee, she was the only one whom he'd let bathe him.

Johnny Lee liked Autumn and flirted with her. That's as far as it went. Autumn thought of him as a friend. She admitted that he was charming and handsome, but he was definitely not someone with whom she'd get involved. She knew about his addiction, but she never mentioned it to anyone.

◆

By December, 1988, Robert's body had reached a stage that hovered too close to death's door. Every bone was clearly defined beneath a thin layer of skin. There was no muscle tone. His blue eyes were sunk in hollow dark holes and his bushy gray eyebrows hung over the dark spaces like silver clouds. The cheekbones were sharp planes that supported thin skin and blue veins.

On a cold day in late January, he awoke and became furious when he couldn't pronounce anything. He called a chair a cigarette. No word was the right word. Sentences were jumbled nonsense. One eye looked weaker than the other eye. He couldn't lift his right arm and his head titled to one side. His one good eye begged Mavis for help. Tears rolled down his bony cheeks, as she held his head to her breast and stroked his head.

"It's gonna be okay. I called the ambulance." He raised his head and tried to shake it.

Mavis took his chin in her hand and said, "You've got to go to the hospital. You need help." They looked at one another and she continued. "I can't help. I don't know what to do." Tears dropped from her eyes onto his lap. He tried to touch her face and couldn't lift his hand. Then, he tried to nod his head.

The doctor took one look at Robert and told Mavis that he'd had a serious stroke. After several tests, he confirmed on the third day that Robert's lungs were failing. In addition, the doctor suspected that gangrene was in his system. It was definitely in his legs, which had begun to split in places. Most of Robert's speech returned, if he spoke slowly and considered each word. He'd look at his legs that were stretched out in front of him on the bed and shake his head. The doctor told him that the only means of saving his life was to remove his legs above the knees.

On the fifth afternoon, Mavis and several of his children were in his room. Marley Jane stood by his bed, with her hand on his head. He looked at her and at his legs, skinny and split open in places. "That's a damn pitiful sight. Ain't it?" he asked Marley Jane. He looked at her and smiled. "It's not a good sign. Is it?"

Marley Jane replied, "No, Daddy, it's not a good sign. But, there's hope."

"Yeah. There's hope. Cuttin off my legs," he responded with tears in his eyes. But, there was no anger in his voice, just sadness. "I don't know bout that."

No one spoke. Marley Jane wished that she'd kept her mouth shut. It was so quiet in the room that only their breathing could be heard. Each person's head was bowed. Except Marley Jane, who looked into her daddy's beautiful sky-blue eyes and nodded her head.

"I don't wanna live like that. I don't want Aggie to have to take care of me," he said in a low voice, as if he were talking only to Marley Jane. Again, Marley Jane nodded her head, determined that she'd not cry.

That was a Friday. The doctor made his rounds late that afternoon, while the children were still there. After checking Robert, he motioned Mavis to join him in the hall. "If he lives, I've got to amputate his legs Monday morning," he told her. She didn't speak. "I need your permission."

"What will happen if you don't operate?" she asked, looking at the wall on the opposite side of the hall.

"He'll die a painful death. Gangrene is painful. It'll move over his entire body. The pain will be unbearable." His voice was soft and comforting.

Mavis looked at him and said, "Operate, but let me tell him."

She told him Sunday morning, when they were alone. Repeating what the doctor had said, she watched his face. While she talked, he looked out the window at the Chattahoochee River and the naked trees on the far bank. A small whirlpool in the river caught his eye.

When Mavis stopped talking, he said, "I don't wanna be a burden on you." He kept his eyes on the whirlpool.

"You won't be a burden on me. Johnny Lee can help." She waited. When he didn't speak, she said, "There's no other choice. If you don't have the operation, the gangrene will be a painful death."

"Okay," he finally said, still looking at the rumbling river.

◆

Sunday night Zelda's husband, Hector, stayed the night with Robert. They sang one religious song after another. Hector had no idea that Robert knew so many old religious songs. He'd never heard Robert sing, and he was surprised to hear a deep bass sound coming from a man whose lungs were in such bad condition.

The nurses smiled at one another as they listened to the two men vocalize song after song. None of the other patients complained. At ten o'clock, a nurse came into the room and gave Robert a sleeping pill. It didn't work. She called the doctor and asked if she should give him another pill. He told her "No."

Shortly after two o'clock, Robert fell asleep. Hector stood at the window and looked into the black river as it flowed to Columbus, Georgia, and on to Florida. He prayed as he glanced up at the sky, filled with millions of diamonds that sparkled on the cold river in the moonlight. Finally, he lay down on the cot that'd been brought to the room for family members.

When Hector awoke, the sun was shining in his eyes. He turned to look at the clock beside Robert's bed. It was seven-thirty and Robert was wide-awake, starring at his covered legs. There was nothing on his face to reveal his thoughts.

"Good morning," Hector said, sitting upright and running his fingers through his dark hair. "It's a bright, sunny day." Without knowing exactly why, he felt foolish.

They talked for several minutes before a male nurse came into the room. "Hi, Mr. Robert. I'm Charles Jackson. Do you remember me? I was here the first day that you arrived. I took a few days off."

Charles was a medium-size black man whose hair was cut close to his head. His face was square and clean-shaven. Large eyes, the color of soot, sat wide a part. All of the patients adored him. They liked his wide smile, energized eyes, and his friendly bedside manner.

Robert smiled and nodded his head. "Yes, I remember you." He didn't, but he saw no need in saying otherwise. Like many people who suffer strokes, he had an extra sense that he relied on to say the right thing so that his answers wouldn't be questioned.

"I'm gonna bathe you and get you ready for surgery. First, I'm gonna give you a shot that'll relax you. Okay?"

Their eyes locked. Hector watched, as the two men seemed to be silently communicating. To Hector's surprise, Robert said, "Okay. Let's get the show on the road." He smiled and his blue eyes twinkled. Robert had never allowed any of the nurses to bathe him. No one did that but Mavis, Johnny Lee, or Autumn.

Charles turned to Hector. "You go have breakfast. Take your time."

Hector looked at the nurse. He looked at Robert. "Okay." He patted Robert's shoulder. "I'll be back fore you know it." Robert winked. Hector unwillingly left the room.

Hector ate breakfast and read the *Columbus Ledger*. When he rounded the corner to Robert's room, he noticed that the door was closed, and Charles stood outside, talking to another nurse. When he saw Hector, he walked toward him.

"I'm sorry. He's dead. He died quietly, while I was bathin him. I'm sorry."

Hector didn't know what to say. He'd just left Robert, less than an hour ago. Robert was smiling. He seemed fine. "What happened?" Hector asked, unable to grasp the meaning of "He's dead."

"I'm not sure. It could've been a stroke or heart failure. He closed his eyes and passed away."

"Can I see him?"

"Yes. Take your time. I'll be here."

Hector opened the door and stepped inside the room, which was now flooded with sunshine that bounced off the walls and shone directly on Robert's closed eyes. His face was peaceful. The covers were pulled up to his neck. Hector touched Robert's face, and a lump caught in his throat. He knew that he had to get to the elevator and wait for Mavis. It was important that he be the one to tell her, to prepare her. He didn't want her to walk down the hall and be met by a nurse.

As he walked through the door and headed down the hall, he saw

Mavis and Bobbie Jo getting off the elevator. He stood and waited for them. They greeted one another.

"How's Robert?" Mavis asked. Without waiting for an answer, she asked, "Did he sleep well last night?"

"He slept well. We sang religious songs most of the night," Hector answered her second question.

Mavis watched him closely. "What's wrong?" She could hear the sound of fear in her voice.

"I don't know how to tell you this. Charles, you know the male nurse who was here the day Mr. Robert was admitted, came in to bathe Mr. Robert. And he told me to go to breakfast. When I got back, he told me that Mr. Robert died while he was bathin him." Hector's words seemed to be tumbling out of him.

"What?" she asked in shock.

"I'm sorry, Ms. Mavis," he said as she pushed him aside and hurried down the hall. Bobbie Jo was close behind. Hector followed them.

◆

Four days later, Robert was laid to rest in the cemetery at Hopewell Methodist Church. It was a graveside service. Bitter cold competed with the long bright rays of sunshine, as people shivered and crossed their arms to stop the trembling. The family sat under a huge blue tent that didn't keep out the Arctic wind. Beulah and Edith stood just inside the tent, next to the row on which Mavis sat, between Claude and Johnny Lee.

Beulah looked around and saw that cars lined both sides of the road as far as her eyes could see. As the minister talked about Robert, a hawk circled overhead. It'd swing wide and high. It'd dip and make another circle. Large wings spread across the perfect, cloudless, but cold, sky. After the minister closed with a prayer, he asked Beulah to come forward. As her voice rang out across the cemetery, the hawk seemed to be moving in time to the song.

After the funeral, everyone went to Mavis' house. They filled the kitchen, dining room, living room, and back porch. People whom no one had seen for years were there, listening to stories about Robert or sharing their own stories about him. All of the regulars who'd frequented Mid-Way Café came. Laughter filled the house and the porch as people celebrated Robert's life.

Wash Fuller, one of Robert's first cousins, told the story of how the two of them had spent six months in Florida, when they were eighteen and nineteen years old. As he told the story, those who were gathered around stopped talking. No one had ever heard the story. Robert never talked about living in Florida.

Wash said that they'd gone to a bar in Tallapoosa County, drank too much, and ended up in a barroom fight. He wasn't exactly clear how the fight started or who started it, but he did add that the two of them had a reputation for enjoying a good fight. Wash had a small gun that he carried inside his jacket. When someone else fired a shot, Wash fired at the opposite wall. No one could tell exactly when a heavy man hit the floor. Was it after the first or second shot? Wash heard someone yell, "He's dead!" The fighting stopped. Men were looking over one another's shoulders to get a glance at the man stretched out on the dirty wooden floor.

Wash and Robert looked at one another. "Let's get the hell outa here," Robert said and headed toward the door, dragging Wash by his arm.

"What if I shot him? We can't leave," Wash said, pulling back.

"We don't know who shot him, but we're gettin outa here. Come on," Robert said in a stern voice.

They jumped into Robert's old Ford. As the car rushed down the road, dust whirled around them. When they reached the paved road, they saw a far-away blue light flashing to their left. Robert took a right. First, they went to Wash's house and threw his clothes in a paper sack.

He had thirty dollars, hidden in a sock that he grabbed. Next, they went to Robert's house for his clothes. Quickly, he told his mama what had happened. She gave him forty-five dollars that she'd been saving for Christmas. They promised to keep in touch.

They drove, stopping once for gas, RCs, and moon pies, until they reached a town near Jacksonville, Florida. After finding a dirt road, Robert pulled the car to the side of the road so that they could sleep. Wash got in the backseat. When he woke up, they were back on a paved road. They rode into a small run-down town and started looking for jobs. By noon, they were both employed at an auto repair shop. The owner pointed them in the direction of a boarding house, with cheap rates and okay meals. They rented a room together and paid for two weeks.

At the end of six months, Robert received a letter from his mama. It was good news. The man who'd fallen in the bar wasn't dead, and he hadn't been shot. He'd suffered a small heart attack, as a result of too much booze, too many cigarettes, and too many fried foods. Robert read the letter aloud. When he finished, the two men did a dance in the middle of their room.

"Well, whata we waitin for? Let's get the hell outa Florida," said Wash.

As he began packing, Robert said, "Here we come, Alabama."

On the way home, they discussed their life style. Bar hopping was going to have to stop, especially the bar fighting. It was time to change their ways and, perhaps, grow up a bit.

"Well, we both know it's gonna be hard to give up the whiskey," Robert said.

"I ain't givin up my whiskey. But, I'm damn sho gonna stop totin that gun round everywhere I go," Wash declared with sincerity.

Wash ended the story by saying, "I never again toted a gun. And I never again left Alabama."

Mavis listened to the story, which she'd heard many years ago from Robert. He'd shared lots of stories that made her laugh and some that made her shake her head in amazement. He'd been an entertaining man, a man who made her laugh at herself and at others. And, he'd adored her. She'd already begun to feel the empty spot in her heart that his death had caused. Melancholy swept over her.

CHAPTER ELEVEN

Before any of them were aware of the rapid passage of time, it was the first of July, 1992, and a lot had happened. Edith retired from the mill. Bobbie Jo closed Mid-Way Café. Beulah went back to work on the first shift before the café was closed. John and Robert were dead. Laura Faye was taking care of Mavis financially, making her life as comfortable as possible. Johnny Lee still worked for Laura Faye. He hadn't given up marijuana. Instead, he'd begun to experiment with various types of drugs. Mavis' other children were disgusted that Laura Faye and Mavis continued to make excuses for him and to cover for him. It was useless to say anything.

Laura Faye's business was growing. Most of her employees were family members, which she'd say, years later, hadn't been such a good idea. But, she wanted to share her success with her family. She needed them and they needed her. It seemed to be a win-win situation. But, things aren't always the way that they appear to be.

One Saturday night, she called Mavis. "Mama, I want to talk with you tomorrow. Can I come by for lunch?"

"What's wrong?" Mavis always assumed there was trouble if any of her children wanted to talk.

"Nothing's wrong. I just want to talk to you bout something."

"What?"

"We'll talk tomorrow. Love you so good."

After Laura Faye hung up, Mavis listened to the soft sounds of nothing. She held the receiver away from her face and looked at it. "Wonder what's wrong now," she thought to herself, shaking her head. "She could've just come by and not said anything bout talking. Young'uns like to worry folks. They never get too old for that."

The next morning, Mavis got up early. She made a pound cake, cooked some vegetables, and put a roast in the oven. After taking a bath, she got dressed for church. During the time that Robert was sick, she hadn't gone too often. But, in the last five months, she'd started going back to church, riding with Edith, who'd almost given up asking Mavis to go with her.

Edith came flying into the driveway, slamming on the brakes so hard that gravel shifted and hopped along the ground. Mavis stood on the back porch, wearing a black, wrap-around dress of soft jersey. A strand of pearls circled her ivory throat. She carried a large red leather purse on her left arm, and she wore black leather pumps.

Getting into the dusty truck, she said, "Edith, I ain't got time to pussy-foot around after church today. Having tea and cookies with every Tom, Dick, and Harry. No socializing. I gotta get home. Laura Faye's coming for dinner. She wants to talk."

Edith glanced at Mavis. "No problem. What does she wanna talk bout?"

Mavis gave her a "duh" look. "Well, I don't know. She didn't say. I mean absolutely no gum wacking after church. No hugging and shaking hands with everybody. No kissing babies. I gotta get home."

"Understood."

"Good. As long as you understand." After a pause, she added, "What do you think she wants to talk bout?'

"I've no idea. Do you think it's serious?"

Mavis gave a heavy sigh. "Edith, of course, it's serious. Young'uns don't call you up and say, 'I wanna talk to you,' unless it's serious." She threw Edith a dark look.

"Well, I wouldn't know. Preston and Ferris never want to talk to me. Bout nothin. So, I'm the wrong one to ask."

"Maybe, you don't listen. Maybe, you're too bossy or interrupt too much."

"Are we talkin bout you or me? Cause you're the bossy one who interrupts. And might I add that you always interrupt to talk bout something that has absolutely nothin to do with what's bein discussed." She saw Mavis open her mouth to deny it. Before she could say a word, Edith added, "You are and you know it." Mavis glared at her and noticed that Edith was griping the steering wheel with both hands. Edith continued, "Whatever she wants to talk bout, don't get all bossy. Just keep quiet and listen."

"I think I know how to handle my own kids. I'll listen. It makes me worry, wondering what she wants to talk bout."

"Forget it. There's nothin you can do, until you hear what she has to say." Changing the subject, she asked, "Why don't you sing in the choir today? We need some more voices."

"What are you talking bout! Me? Sing? No way! And y'all do need some more voices. Some good voices. Speaking of voices. Edith, your voice needs some help. You don't sing. You squeak and squeal like a dying pig. I'm just telling you as a friend. Not to hurt your feelings."

"You're not hurtin my feelings. Not a tad. I've heard all of that from you before, and I don't pay you no attention. Cause I'm gonna raise my voice to the Lord and sang His praises. No matter how insultin you are bout my singin."

"Oh, for goodness sake. Edith, I'm sure God wouldn't mind—like the rest of us, if you just sat on a pew and hummed. You know He has very sensitive ears. And He adores good music."

"How come you're such an expert bout God? All of a sudden."

"Well, I'm trying to project myself in His place and understand how He feels bout bad singing."

"That's your problem, Mavis. You put God on the side of negative too often. Stop tryin to guess what He thinks. Leave Him alone. He's just happy we're goin to church."

"Now, who's guessing what He thinks? He's not doing no such thing. He's got more important things to think bout. Like running the universe. Has it ever occurred to you what a job that is? As a matter of fact, He's probably on the other side of the moon, in another universe, right now, wondering why those people are doing what they're doing."

"Do you actually believe there's life on another planet? Or there's another universe?"

"Why not? Do you know something scientists don't know? If so, please share it. I think it's arrogant of us humans to think we're so almighty important and special."

"Well, we are. Important and special."

"How? Just tell me how. A few people might be, but most of us ain't squat. Most of us are a pain in God's royal behind. He probably threw up His hands on us a long time ago."

"Now, you're bein cynical."

"He probably created another species of beings because we disgust Him so much." Since she'd run out of things to say, she looked out the window.

Edith still had plenty to say. "Mavis, you need to pray more," she taunted, as a smile came alive in her eyes.

"I pray enough. There's no need in bothering God bout every little thing."

"God wants us to talk to Him."

"Yeah. Talk to Him. Not at Him. In my opinion, He doesn't have time for silly prayers that are a waste of His time."

"What do you mean, 'silly prayers'?"

"Oh, you know. Like, 'Oh, Lord, I know You are here with me, Lord. Yes, Lord, I feel You in my heart. In my soul, Lord. And, Lord, I know You care about me. About all my needs. Whatever they might be, Lord. I know You know that I need a new car cause that old car of mine embarrasses me so. Oh, yes, Jesus! Oh, Lord, I know how You love me and want me to drive a shiny new car. I know Your love for me will never die,' and on and on, saying a whole lot of nothing. Just tea and cookie talk. God ain't got no time for tea and cookies. For useless chit-chat or listening to a prayer that's all bout 'me' or 'I.' He wants to hear how you care bout other folks and how you want their lives to be better." She stopped talking and seemed to be in deep thought.

Looking at Edith, she continued, "And there are some needs that people have that they shouldn't have. So, why would He condone those things? Now, if the person said, 'I've got a strong need for drugs or raping children, and I want You to take away that need,' I'd understand that request."

Edith didn't reply. She knew that Mavis had often prayed for God to take away Johnny Lee's need for drugs. When it didn't happen, Mavis didn't give up. She kept asking God for help. It stood to reason that Mavis would pest God just like she did anyone when she wanted something done. Edith wondered if Mavis asked God how she could help Johnny Lee give up drugs.

They were approximately one mile from the church. The morning sun that rode behind the truck was beginning to heat the highway. It'd be a scorching day before it ended. Edith hoped someone had turned on the AC at the church. Otherwise, the old, poorly insulated wooden building would be toasty before services began. Her mind ran over the Sunday school lesson that she'd planned. Mavis, who usually didn't attend Sunday school, had come early so that she could support Edith. That worried her. If she made a questionable comment, Mavis would call her out on it. Arguing with Mavis wasn't on Edith's Sunday school agenda. And, it appeared that Mavis was in a mood this morning to question anything. The lesson might go to hell in a New York minute.

Silently, Edith said to herself, "Please, God, don't let Mavis say a word. Just this one time. Please."

As she finished her private prayer, Mavis' voice cut into her train of thought. "And, for goodness sakes, I can't stand those prayers that tell God what He already knows. Do people think they're talking to an idiot? I remember the last preacher we had."

There was a hesitation as she waited for Edith to comment. When she didn't speak, Mavis continued, "I didn't like him. He prayed like that all of the time. I wanted to tell him to shut up, go back to school, and take a course on how to talk to God."

Mavis looked at Edith, who stared straight ahead. Then, she asked, hoping to draw Edith into an argument, "Is there such a course, you think?" Edith refused to take the bait.

Edith couldn't help it. She laughed and beat her left fist on the steering wheel. "Mavis, I swear, God's gonna strike you dead one day. Talkin like that. Although I agree with you bout that preacher."

Mavis' face was fake surprise. "You mean He's gonna kill me for telling the truth? Don't be ridiculous."

Edith began to hum. "Sing, if it makes you happy," said Mavis. "I enjoy having something to smile about."

"Really, Mavis? Really?" Edith laughed and began to sing "What a Friend We Have in Jesus." Mavis clapped her hands and rocked from side to side.

By the time that they'd sung the first verse, Edith made a sharp left turn onto the gravel parking lot. Several people were standing at the front door, talking to the young minister who, apparently, found something to smile about with each conversation that he was having. He was positive and upbeat. Mavis liked that he didn't scream about hell and damnation, about how America was going to hell in a jet, and about every negative thing that was happening in society. She understood that a man of God should be concerned about all of those things, but it was important how he approached those subjects.

Edith liked him because he was friendly, visited sick members, called members who hadn't been to church in several weeks, and showed genuine concern about every aspect of the church. She also liked the fact that membership and tithes had doubled since he became their minister.

He met them halfway on the steps. He shook Edith's hand and hugged Mavis. "Two very pretty ladies. Y'all are going to make preaching a pleasure today. There's nothing like looking at beauty while preaching. I appreciate you coming, Mavis. We've missed you. And you let me know what you think of my sermon. Hear me?" He patted Mavis' shoulder and laughed.

Edith and he knew that Mavis would give an opinion. It might be no more than "A good sermon" or "Umph!"

Mavis amused him. Also, he respected her quick wit and her ability to zero in on a subject and "Hit the nail on the head," as he would say. There was no fooling Mavis, and she didn't get caught up in emotions and myths. Her type tested ministers, because she saw through people as if they were glass cages. When she gave someone an intense stare and said nothing, that person probably didn't want to know what she was thinking. Her silence and her thoughts were as profound as her quick, witty comments.

The two women walked into the cool sanctuary, greeting people as they made their way to the classroom, where Edith would give her monthly lesson. When they walked into the classroom, they saw Beulah who'd come to hear Edith's lesson. Also, she would sing a solo during the service. Occasionally, she'd miss her church service so that she could sing at Hopewell Methodist Church. She was the only African-American in the room, surrounded by some people who'd come just to hear her sing.

Mavis sat beside Beulah and squeezed her hand. Edith took her place at the wood podium, arranging papers and her Bible. Someone had sat a glass of water nearby. She was a bit nervous, but she knew that the nervousness would disappear as soon as she began with an opening prayer. She went over the prayer in her mind, to make certain that it didn't include any of the negatives that Mavis had talked about on the way to church. It irritated her that she was slightly concerned about what Mavis thought, when it often appeared that Mavis didn't give two flips what anyone else thought. But, Mavis was Mavis, and Edith was Edith.

Beulah and Edith knew that Mavis totally accepted Edith, even when she was poking fun or arguing with her. Edith knew that Mavis was one of her few, real true friends and would go to bat for her in the blink of an eye. She was a loyal friend. Just look at how she stuck up a friendship with Beulah. And Mavis was the reason that Beulah sang solos in the church.

◆

Edith recalled the first time that Beulah came to Hopewell Methodist Church. She came with Mavis, in September of the first year that they met. Church had begun, and they were more than five minutes late. As they walked down the aisle, Mavis greeted people to her left and right, with a smile and a nod of her head. She patted old man John West, who she always said smelled like last year's garbage, on his shoulder; she said something in Ada Moore's ear that made her smile; she kissed the wrinkled sunken-in right cheek of Miss Nellie Bea Davis, who patted Mavis on her cheek and whispered in her left ear.

Mavis liked Miss Nellie Bea, but she couldn't understand why the Chambers County Board of Education had continued to employee an old lady, whose marbles rolled around loosely in her head, long after she should've been put out to pasture. Mavis liked Miss Nellie Bea's spunk, her determination, and that she was a strong woman who'd survived on her own, without a man.

Although Miss Nellie Bea lived in River View, she attended church in the Hopewell Community, because her neighbor was a long-time member of the church and she'd invited Miss Nellie Bea to church one Sunday. Since Miss Nellie Bea could no longer walk to the River View Methodist Church, and no one there offered to give her a ride back and forth to church, it made sense for her to hitch a ride with her neighbor to Hopewell Methodist.

Edith smiled as she observed Mavis patting shoulders and whispering in some people's ears. Taking her time, Mavis waltzed right down to the front pew. She never sat near the front. Several old men pursed their thin dry lips and looked as if they'd been sucking sour pickles. Some of the women sneered and raised questionable eyebrows. Mavis wasn't offended at all. Not even mad. As Edith watched, Mavis appeared to be enjoying herself. For months afterwards, Mavis laughed about the looks on people's faces. She knew how to upset an apple cart, to create conflict, and to make people question things.

Beulah questioned Mavis' invitation to visit the church, but there was no arguing with Mavis. "I just dare anybody to say one word bout you being there. They'll get a big piece of my mind. Beulah, you can't run from things that aren't right. You have to butt heads with them. Don't be afraid. Don't ever be afraid of doing what's right."

So, Beulah went that day. The first song was "Blessed Assurance, Jesus Is Mine." Beulah's sweet, clear voice hit every note with precision, rising high above every other voice in the church. People turned to that beautiful voice and many stopped singing so that they could listen. Beulah's eyes were closed as she swayed back and forth. Once she raised her right hand high above her head, threw back her head, and the notes rippled out of her throat.

The last song was "Mine Eyes Have Seen the Glory." Again, Beulah's voice rose above everyone else's voice. It reached the high ceiling of the old church and vibrated off the walls. It seeped into the hard hearts of those who'd glared as she walked down the aisle, with her head held high and her eyes focused on Mavis' back. The sound of her voice brought tears to many eyes. It made restless children pause and listen. Mavis smiled.

After the service, the choir director swooped over to Beulah and invited her to "Please come sing a solo for us. Anytime you like." Well, she did, the following Sunday. That'd been years now, and she was a regular once-a-month visitor. No one made sour faces or lifted their eyebrows. Beulah was the darling at Hopewell Methodist Church.

Edith brought her attention back to the room that'd filled up as her mind wandered. She cleared her throat and asked people to bow their heads for a word of prayer before she began the lesson. After the prayer, she glanced at Mavis whose face was an empty page.

At the end of class, Mavis hugged Edith. "I'm proud of you, Edith. You did good." Edith smiled like a child who'd won the prize Easter egg.

After church, Edith and Mavis spoke briefly to Beulah. They were in a rush. Laura Faye was coming to Mavis' house for dinner. "Laura Faye wants to talk to me. I don't know what it's bout. I'll call y'all tomorrow and let you know what's so darn all fired important. I hope it's not bad news. I'm not in the mood for bad news."

"None of us are ever in the mood for bad news, Mavis," said Edith. Mavis looked at her in wonderment. Beulah laughed and waved goodbye.

On the way home, Mavis bragged on Edith's lesson and Beulah's singing. Edith listened as Mavis said, several times, how glad she was that she'd gone to church that day. Just before Edith pulled into Mavis' driveway, Mavis turned to her and said, "I really enjoyed hearing you teach and sing."

Edith was going to make a snappy reply until she saw the serious look on Mavis' face. "Thank you, Mavis. I appreciate that," she said smiling. "Don't forget to call us tomorrow and let us know what's goin on."

"I won't. You and Beulah come to the house tomorrow bout five o'clock. I'll cook supper, and we'll talk. If that's okay with you, I'll call Beulah and tell her."

"That's fine with me. See you tomorrow."

♦

Mavis was taking the rolls out of the oven when she heard Laura Faye come in the side door. "Mama, I'm here." She threw her purse on a chair and headed for the kitchen. Smells that were good enough to eat drifted through the house and met her as soon as she opened the side door.

When Laura Faye walked through the kitchen doorway, she saw Mavis, holding the pan of rolls. Laura Faye hugged Mavis tight and kissed her cheek. "You're looking pretty. Did you go to church today?" Without waiting for an answer, she said, "That was a silly question. You're still dressed up. Let me take those."

Mavis handed her the pan and told her to place the rolls in the breadbasket on the kitchen table. "Since it's just you and me, I thought we'd eat in the kitchen. Most everybody else will come dragging in throughout the day. I made enough for everybody." By "everybody," she meant some of her other kids, their spouses, and children. Two or more families came by every Sunday to eat and to visit. Unless it was a holiday, no one came at the same time. Mavis never knew who'd show up.

Laura Faye sat down. While Mavis poured tea, neither of them spoke. After sitting the tea pitcher on the counter, Mavis sat down. "Say grace," she commanded Laura Faye, who hesitated for a moment. Then, she said a few words to bless the food and reached for the roast.

"Mama, I got some great news and some more great news. I'm so happy." She chewed for a while, smiled at Mavis, and said, "As always, this is soooo good." Stabbing the fork into a juicy slice of tomato, she said, "Sooo good," and gave a big sigh.

Laura Faye's eyes were closed as she chewed and made a humming noise. Mavis took a long look at her. The glow on Laura Faye's face couldn't be mistaken. Happiness seeped over her entire body. Mavis continued to stare as her youngest daughter did a happy upper body dance, alone in her own world. Watching her sway, Mavis knew that the excitement wasn't caused by good food. Still, she wasn't exactly looking forward to hearing "great news" and "more great news."

There were eight children in the family, three boys and five girls. Johnny Lee was the youngest child. Laura Faye was the youngest girl. She was also the tallest girl, which reminded Mavis of how much Laura Faye resembled Robert's mama who'd been a tall, slender beauty. When she was eighty-two, Minnie Norrell was elegant and gorgeous. Laura Faye had her grandmother's smooth skin, full lips that always pouted, and high cheekbones. Both had graceful hands, with long slender fingers. Their eyes were different. Minnie had large, lazy-looking violet eyes that caused people to take a second look. She often spoke with her eyes, and men loved it. Laura Faye had small eyes that told nothing and kept secrets.

In spite of the fact that before finishing high school and marrying a man whom Mavis considered to be a long-haired hooligan who smoked too much pot, Laura Faye had done well for herself. She got her GED, after she left the hippie in California, boarded a bus, using money that her oldest sister Janet sent to her, and came home.

She was three months pregnant when Mavis met her at the bus station. Six months later, she gave birth to a baby boy and got a divorce. She remained friends with her ex-mother-in-law, whose only child was the long-haired hippie whom Laura Faye abandoned in California, after he tried to choke her to death, while high on drugs. Years later, Laura

Faye became friends with her ex.

Five years later, she married Mark Rogers, an older man. They opened a mobile home dealership in Smiths Station. A year later, they opened another one in Opelika, which Laura Faye managed. Two years after opening the second dealership, she filed for a divorce and got the dealership in Opelika. She'd turned it into a six million dollar a year business.

For almost a year, she'd been dating a smooth talker who had a gift for persuasion, flamboyant ways, and expensive tastes. He saw himself as a charmer, and he charmed Laura Faye the day that he applied for a job as a salesman. It turned out that he could sell ticks to a dog. He was the number one salesman at the end of his first month, and he never lost that title, increasing the sales of mobile homes at the dealership to a surprising level.

Although he saw himself as a charmer, Mavis saw him as a snake, which didn't surprise anyone, since she seldom liked the people whom her children chose, especially Richard and Johnny Lee. Although Mavis didn't like any of Richard's first three wives, she adored Bella, his present wife. She approved of Janet's husband, Morgan, and of Marley Jane's ex-husband, Wendell. Her vote hadn't been cast for Marley Jane's second husband, who was an attorney. There were too many things about him that reminded her of Robert and that rattled her mind. She thought that Bobbie Jo's husband was too old for her, but she never shared that opinion with anyone, other than Robert and Beulah. It was no secret that she didn't care for Zelda's husband, who impressed her as being lazy and whiny. In spite of that, she liked the fact that he was crazy about Zelda.

Mavis toyed with her food. It was her nature to be suspicious. "Why are you so happy?" she asked, with a hint of curiosity. She wasn't sure that she wanted an answer.

Laura Faye opened her eyes, shoved a forkful of potato salad into her mouth, chewed, swallowed, and answered, "First and most important, Felton and I are getting married in two months. I'm going to have the large wedding that I've always wanted. A long, white gown and a band. The works."

Too quickly, Mavis said, "This will be your third wedding. A white gown is a little too extreme. If you ask me."

"I don't care, Mama. I'm having it. And, I didn't ask you. I'm also having a big cake that I want Janet to make for me. I want her to cater the reception. We're going to the Bahamas for our honeymoon. And I want lots of flowers, candles, and lights." She'd stopped eating to talk; she looked out the window that was across the table.

"Well, that all sounds fancy. A little late. But, fancy," Mavis said, with zero enthusiasm.

"Now, Mama, don't you start spoiling my plans. You're going to have to behave....or stay home. I love you, Mama. But, I'm serious."

"What makes you think that I won't behave? I know how to behave."

Laura Faye looked at Mavis, giving her a stare that said, "I know you didn't say that. Stop with the bullshit." Instead, she said, "I know you know how to behave. But, will you behave?"

They locked eyes. Mavis looked away. "Okay. I'll behave. Was that the 'great news' or the 'most great news'?" She reached for a roll and jumped when Laura clapped her hands. "Good grief. Scare a person to death."

"I'm remodeling my condo in Panama City. Felton and I have been down there three times, talking to contractors and designers. We've decided on what we want and can't wait to start remodeling. It's gonna be absolutely gorgeous. Between the wedding and remodeling the condo, my plate is so full."

"That's nice. I love the beach."

"I know you do, Mama. That's the reason I'm telling you. You've got a key, so you can go, like always, whenever you want. And take Ms.

Edith and Ms. Beulah. Stay as long as y'all like. I want you to be happy, too, Mama. I want you to have fun."

Mavis didn't look up because she didn't want Laura Faye to see the tears that covered her eyeballs. But, there was no missing the single tear that slid down her cheek. Laura Faye reached out and wiped it away. "I've got one more surprise for you. It's another key, to a new car so that you don't have to worry bout an old car breaking down on you on the way to the beach. BobbieJo's gonna bring you to the lot tomorrow morning, for you to pick it up. It's your favorite red color."

"Oh, my goodness. Laura Faye, you shouldn't have. You're spending too much money." Mavis's hands covered her cheeks and she forgot to hold back the tears.

"Well, that's not all. From now on, in addition to paying all the utilities here, I'm giving you a credit card. There's a limit. So, be careful." Laura Faye stood up and hugged Mavis who was openly crying. "I love you so good, Mama. More than you'll ever know." She took Mavis' left hand. "Be happy for me, Mama. Even, if you have to pretend. Please."

Mavis touched Laura Faye's cheek. "Don't be foolish. I love you, and I'm happy, if you're happy. Now, come on. Let's eat some pound cake and ice cream before the crowd starts coming." Mavis said the things Laura Faye wanted to hear, but they both knew that nothing would make Mavis like Felton Wheeler.

◆

Bobbie Jo took Mavis to the lot the next morning. When they turned into the driveway, Mavis saw a shiny red SUV Ford, parked in front of the office. A big white bow rested on the roof. Mavis's eyes were bright and large. A crooked grin settled on her face as she walked around the car. She opened the door to the driver's side and slide onto the black leather seat. By that time, all of the employees stood on the porch. Half of them were family members whom Laura Faye had hired as soon as she began managing the dealership. Mavis smiled when they clapped.

She noticed that Johnny Lee couldn't stop grinning.

Cake and sandwiches were inside. But, Mavis was too excited to eat. "I want to drive it," she told Laura Faye.

"Let's go," Laura Faye said. "All you girls come with us. You guys stay here and hold down the fort. We'll be back when we get back." The words were barely out of her mouth before the women put down their plates and headed for the car.

Mavis drove to downtown Opelika. She left downtown and headed for Interstate I-85. She got off at the first Auburn exit and went to downtown Auburn. She drove past Auburn University. Finally, she returned to the Interstate at the third Auburn exit and headed back to the lot. The women laughed and joked, while Mavis smiled, not saying a word.

When she parked the car, everyone, except Bobbie Jo and Laura Faye, got out and went into the building. Laura Faye was sitting behind Mavis. She leaned forward and kissed Mavis' cheek. "I love you so good. Now, here's the card I was telling you bout. You can spend up to seven hundred a month. That's the limit. Give me another kiss. I gonna get to work to pay for all of this."

Laura Faye stood on the porch and waved as Mavis left the lot, followed by Bobbie Jo, in her old brown station wagon that was considered an antique.

CHAPTER TWELVE

After Robert's death, Beulah's phone would ring at one or two in the morning. "Beulah, I've made biscuits and gravy. Come on over," Mavis would command when Beulah picked up the phone.

Beulah would get dressed and drive to Mavis' house, as darkness covered Hopewell Road. It was during those early morning hours that Mavis told Beulah things that she'd never told anyone, even Robert. Based on those conversations, Beulah would say decades later, "No one, but me, really knew Mavis. Her young'uns didn't know her a tall."

Usually, it was to talk about Johnny Lee, his drug habit, his rages filled with anger and demands, his women, or a possible drug rehabilitation program that Mavis never seemed to approve. The problems were never solved. As time passed, it became more drugs and increased violent, demanding behavior that Mavis hid from Laura Faye.

One night, on a bitter cold early February morning, as rain drizzled among the empty branches and the chilly breath of the wind fogged the windows, the shrill ringing of the phone cut into Beulah's sleep. Rolling over in the darkness and the warmth of the bed, she lifted the receiver on the third ring. Mavis' voice was coarse and low, filled with fear. "Beulah, you've got to come. Now! It's Johnny Lee. I think I mighta hurt him. Bad. Come quick!" Beulah heard a click as the phone on the other end of the line was dropped in its cradle.

"My, Lord. What's that boy-man done gone and done now?" she questioned the darkness. She rolled out of bed and reached for a pair of jeans that was slung over the back of a chair. After she zipped them, she opened a dresser drawer and pulled out an old gray sweatshirt with "Hang in There" in bold black letters on the front. Quickly, she shoved her large feet into loafers, not bothering to put on socks. She buttoned her worn wool coat and grabbed her purse. Then, she ran to her car, hurrying into the now raging rain that pounded her body and pelted the earth.

She turned the ignition, and, at first, she thought that the car wasn't going to start. It seemed to resist the cold rain and howling wind. It finally grumbled into a loud purr. She sat for a moment, letting the engine idle. Squinting into the cold darkness, watching the rain run down the windshield, she turned on the wipers and began to back out of the driveway. Once she was on the main highway, she pointed the car toward Hopewell Road.

The headlights cut through the silver drops of rain and cast a beam on the wet, slick pavement that glistened in pools of light. As she came up the steep hill near Mavis' house, she saw a light in Mavis' bedroom window. As she pulled into the circular drive, the light in the kitchen fell across the back porch and spilled onto the wet yard. Beulah saw Mavis' face, peeping out the window, searching the darkness, as she glanced into the cold and windy rain that slanted as it continued in a furious fall.

Before Beulah cut off the motor, Mavis was standing in the kitchen doorway, bathed in bright yellow light. She stood tall and straight, in a flannel nightgown that was covered in tiny pink rosebuds. Her feet were bare. A baby's well-worn cloth diaper was tied around her head. Beulah knew that she wore the diaper around her head when she suffered terrible headaches.

By the time that Beulah got to the opened door, Mavis was shivering, but Beulah suspected it was more from what had happened than the cold. They hugged, and Mavis clung, trembling, to Beulah. When they stepped apart, Beulah saw Mavis' compressed lips and lack of color on her face. Her green eyes were large and filled with bewilderment.

"I zapped him, Beulah. He came at me in a rage, demanding money. And I zapped him. I don't even know where I zapped him. He fell to the floor. He's still there. On the floor."

"Is he okay? Is he breathin? Movin?" Beulah placed her hands on Mavis' shoulders and looked into her watery eyes. "Where is he? Show me?"

Mavis took Beulah's left hand and led her into the bright bedroom. Johnny Lee lay on the floor at the foot of his mama's bed. There were signs of visible agitation. Moaning escaped his sagging mouth, as he gently rolled back and forth in a fetal position. His eyes darted furtively, and Beulah noticed that they flickered between blue and green. He wore only pajama bottoms, and his feet were bare. On his face, he wore a look of helplessness and fear.

Johnny Lee had felt the jolt seer through his body, had felt himself falling, as he gasped for air, stunned, unable to move as his blood sugar turned to lactic acid, leaving him without energy. He became weak, confused, and disoriented. He was unable to make his body move, and his brain gave orders that his body refused to obey. He was dimly aware that he was entering darkness. Suddenly, his head and body were too heavy for him to move, as he lingered in the darkness behind his eyeballs.

There was movement near by, and he realized that it was Mavis, crying and calling his name in a tunnel. Her fear crawled into his disorientated mind and became his fear. An attempt to speak, to tell her that he was okay, failed. So, he closed his eyes and surrendered to the darkness.

When Beulah arrived, his disorientation was beginning to disappear. His muscles were slowly starting to work, as they began to follow instructions that his mind issued. Beulah knelt beside the tall twisted body and brushed damp hair from his sweaty forehead. She took one of his limp hands in one of her wide, strong hands. "Johnny Lee, it's me. Beulah. It's gonna be okay. You hear me?"

His eyes blinked. She took that as a yes. "I want you to try to relax, to stay still. Close your eyes. Breathe slowly and deeply. The pain's gonna soon go away. I'm gonna put a pillow under your head. After awhile, I'm gonna put a blanket over you. I want you to try to relax. Understand me?"

He blinked again. "I'm gonna get you some water. Don't try to get up. Mavis is gonna stay with you." She rose and turned toward the living room. Turning around to face the lump on the floor, she reminded him, "Your mama loves you, boy. Whatever she did, she never woulda done unless she felt she had to. And we gonna take care of you."

Beulah looked at Mavis and left the room. She heard Mavis say, "I love you, Johnny Lee. I didn't have no choice. You threatened me and came toward me." Beulah didn't see the slight nod of agreement that Johnny Lee gave his mama or the forgiving look in his eyes.

When she returned with the glass of water, Mavis was kneeling beside Johnny Lee, stroking his face. His body had begun to relax and his eyes were closed. Tears glistened on his pale cheeks and dripped off the sides of his face onto the creamy carpet. Beulah lifted his head. "Take a couple of small sips. Then, lay back and relax. Mavis and me is gonna get you to your bed in just a little while. After you've relaxed and can move."

He looked at her smooth dark face that was soft with compassion and blinked away the tears that filled his restless eyes. He reached for Mavis' hand. Found it and squeezed. No one said anything for several minutes. Beulah watched Mavis watch her son, the long, lost boy whom she kept trying to save, hoping that he'd one day conquer the demons that he'd willingly invited into his life at the age of fourteen.

Beulah knew the only moral support that Johnny Lee received came from Mavis and Laura Faye. His other siblings felt anger and frustration and impatience with their younger brother. They believed that he was selfish and spoiled. Which was true. Always, they shared their opinions and quickly gave unwanted advice, never once offering any type of help or assistance. Mavis and Robert became tired of their chatter and anger, so they stopped discussing Johnny Lee, except with Laura Faye. It had become a "hands-off" subject.

Now, Robert was gone and Mavis confided more often in Beulah, who listened and understood. She had a son who was lost to her, taken by her brutal common-law husband, in the dark of night, while she and her baby girl slept. She still felt the terror that swept over her in the early morning when she discovered Silas missing, along with his belongings. She recalled how, for years, she searched for him, never giving up hope. Still, she believed that one day she'd locate him.

Beulah understood Mavis' love for her son. She knew how difficult it is to let go of a child, to turn your back on a child who might be suffering. They'd discussed their sons, their feelings, and their need to protect a weak child. Their sons united them in a way that nothing else in their lives could. The love for their sons was a bridge that crossed culture, race, kinfolks, politics, and opinions.

"I think we can take him to bed now, Mavis," said Beulah in a soft voice. Mavis nodded.

"Johnny Lee, I'm gonna help you up. Your mama and me is gonna put you in your bed. Okay? Just lean on us." Beulah instructed the man whose body had stopped shaking and whose eyes were closed.

"Yes, ma'ma. I think I can stand now," he said in a weak voice.

Beulah helped him to a sitting position. A low, soft moan escaped his open mouth. She watched as he tightly squeezed his eyes. "I'm gonna count to five. Then, Mavis and me will get a grip under your arms and lift you to your feet. Can you move your legs?"

Johnny Lee moved his legs up and down on the floor. First, the right leg. Then, the left leg. "Yes."

"Okay. When we put our hands under your arms, bend your knees. Help push yourself up. You got it?"

"Yes." He sounded exhausted.

When Beulah said, "Five," Mavis and she tugged and lifted. Johnny Lee bent his knees and pushed upward. He stood, leaning forward, as if he'd fall face down onto the floor. They held him up, although he was almost dead weight. When he managed to straighten up, he towered over Beulah by two inches. Slowly, they walked into his bedroom and laid him gently on his bed. The room was cold and dark, except for a small lamp beside the bed. A heavy, black curtain hung over the window, blocking the sound of the whipping rain.

Johnny Lee's tall slender frame welcomed the comfort of the bed. His arms were stretched out so that he made a large cross on the white sheets. The lamp gave off a small circle of light and revealed the small red wounds on his chest. Mavis had zapped him twice on his upper torso. She saw the puncher marks for the first time. Putting her hand over her mouth, she gave a gasp. Her pale face turned away from the spots and she looked helplessly at Beulah.

"I'm so sorry, Johnny Lee," she said in a pinched voice, while Beulah stroked her head. "I'll put something on those places."

"Mama, don't be sorry. You had to stop me, but it damn sure does hurt. Remind me not to piss you off again," and he gave a lop-sided grin that reminded Mavis of his brother Richard. He reached for Mavis' hand and drew it to his dry lips. "So sorry, Mama." His eyes closed. No one spoke for a while.

"Can I have some water? Then, if you don't mind, pull the blanket over me."

Mavis pulled the blanket up to his chin. Beulah left to get the water, and Mavis got some salve to put on the small red burns on his chest. After he drank the water and the salve was administered, they left the room and closed the door, leaving a small crack, where the light from the lamp crept through. He'd fallen into a deep sleep before they reached the kitchen.

Beulah made strong coffee, while Mavis sat at the table with her face in her hands. All energy seemed to be drained from her bent body. She heard Beulah pull out a chair and sit down. She reached across the table and touched Mavis' left hand. "Here's a nice cup of hot coffee. Okay, Mavis, tell me what happened here tonight."

Mavis pulled the cup closer and wrapped both of her hands around it. The cup was hot, and she felt the warmth move along her arms. When she looked at Beulah, tears floated in her bright green eyes. She inhaled and exhaled slowly before she began to relay the horror of Johnny Lee's attempt to kick down her bedroom door, as he demanded money for drugs.

Beulah knew that since Robert had died, Mavis had taken to locking her bedroom door out of fear and that she kept a baseball bat beside her bed, because Johnny Lee had entered the room before in a violent rage, demanding money. There was never enough money for drugs. Mavis always gave him money in order to make him stop yelling and cursing, but the last time that he'd stormed into her bedroom, at one o'clock in the morning, there'd been a heated argument. Beulah sensed Mavis' fear when she told her about that incident, and they agreed that Johnny Lee's violent outbursts were getting worst; therefore, Beulah installed a lock on Mavis' bedroom door. Only, tonight, Johnny Lee kicked in the door, leaving it hanging useless on its broken hinges.

Beulah listened as Mavis told her how the night before, at two o'clock in the morning, a drug dealer pounded on the kitchen door. Mavis heard Johnny Lee walk from his bedroom to the kitchen door, heard it open, and heard Johnny Lee's low scared voice and a low response that was a far-away mumble. She listened to Johnny Lee's bare footsteps cross the wooden floors. He knocked softly on her bedroom door.

His voice shook with fear. "Mama, the man wants three hundred dollars that I owe him. I don't have it. He's threatenin to kill me. I need the money, Mama. Now. Open the door," he demanded in a louder voice.

Mavis got out of bed, put on a blue fuzzy housecoat and took a pistol from beneath the mattress. She slipped it into the deep right-hand pocket of the housecoat. Then, she walked into the closet and took a shoe box from the far right corner of the top shelve. She counted out three one hundred dollar bills. It was almost everything that she had left from her last trip to Biloxi, Mississippi. She shoved the bills into the left pocket of her housecoat. She stood at the locked door before she opened it. When she opened the door, she saw the terrified eyes of her son. A light from the bathroom fell across his frightened face. He looked like a terrified little boy. Her heart melted with love and sadness, but the adrenaline from anger rushed through her body, making her bold and fearless.

"Stay behind me when I open the kitchen door. And don't say a word," she said in a firm, flat voice.

Taking her time, she walked to the kitchen door. Mavis stopped so quickly that Johnny Lee almost bumped into her. "Stop that damn racket? I'm coming," she screamed with venom, through clenched teeth. She pulled the pistol from the pocket of her housecoat, turned the knob, and jerked the door open with her left hand.

Seconds before she opened the door, Johnny Lee whispered in her ear, "What the hell! You wanna get us killed?"

When the door swung open, the pistol was pointed at the jewels of a large, short man who looked like the TV character Fat Albert. A full moon revealed a smooth ebony face that had small dots for eyes, a large nose, and ears that stood out on each side of his head. Dreadlocks hung down his back and over his shoulders. His lips were too full. He wore saggy pants and expensive tennis shoes on large feet that didn't fit his height.

For a brief moment, he looked shocked to see Mavis. They both recognized one another. He was known as Big John Alley, but his real name was John Lincoln Alley. He'd stopped by Mid-Way Café every morning for breakfast, after he left his job at River View Mill. When he came into the café, he greeted people, slapping the men on their backs and smiling politely at the women. People liked Big John. Mavis liked him. He liked her.

"So, you're the bastard who's beating on my door at two o'clock in the morning. I'm going to give you what Johnny Lee owes you. If you ever come back to my house—or threaten my son—I'll kill you. I'll hunt you down and kill you, deader than four hundred frozen hells. You understand me, Big John? Anyways, what damn smart businessman sells drugs on credit to a drug addict? Are you stupid or what?"

She pulled out the three hundred dollars and shoved it into his shocked face. "Take it! Don't you ever come here again. Or I'll blow your fat ass to hell and back. Now, get off my property."

Big John looked down at the money and for the first time, saw the gun that was pointed at his private parts. "I didn't know he was yo son, Ms. Mavis. I swear. No one told me. It won't happen no more. No more credit," and he looked at Johnny Lee. "And I won't be back here. You got my word."

"You damn sure better mean it. If not, I'll blow your sorry ass to hell and back. I'm not gonna tell you not to sell him no more drugs. Cause he'll get them somewhere else. But, no more credit. And don't come back here. Now, get!" She slammed the door in his face.

After Mavis closed the door, she lowered the gun as her hand trembled. Turning to Johnny Lee, she ordered, "Go to bed. I don't wanna be disturbed again tonight."

The very next night, Johnny Lee needed more money for more drugs. Again, he was high, and the drugs gave him a false sense of grandiosity and delusions. Mavis was tired, angry, and embarrassed. She wasn't tolerating any more threats—from her son or his drug dealer.

When Johnny Lee kicked the door and broke the lock, his eyes were glittering and dilated. His mouth had a hard and wicked look. His voice was sluggish, slurred and loopy. It echoed with curse words that bounced off the dark ceiling and fell on the bed like bombs. As his anger escalated, he yelled more obscenities, using threats to manipulate in order to control. It was difficult to deal with his rages and his illogical demands.

Coming closer to the bed, he said, "By, god, how many times I gotta say it? I need some fuckin money. And, I mean right fuckin now! I ain't gonna take no damn bullshit bout you ain't got no money. You hear me, old lady?"

Mavis was sitting on the edge of the bed, waiting. She'd been sitting in that position since the second loud bang on the door, watching it shake. As the door shook, she became aware of the pounding rain on the roof. Lightning flashed in the windows and lit up the room with neon brightness. The windows shook in rhythm with the shaking door. The sound was a rapping of loud drums. Suddenly, the door sagged on its hinges. Mavis' lips formed a thin, tight line. She gripped the black object in her lap, as a cold sternness moved over her body.

"I don't have any more money. Go back to bed."

"The hell you don't. You're always lyin bout havin money. I need some money. Damn it! I ain't gonna keep on askin. Got it, Ms. Mavis?" he jeered.

"I'm telling you the truth. Now, go back to bed."

"You're tellin an outright lie. I know it. You know it. No more talkin. Do you understand? I want some money." He snarled and moved toward her.

She raised her right hand and pressed. It wasn't a time for her to indulge in sympathy for her lost son who was already flying as high as a Boeing 747. He was hell bent on getting his way, regardless of what he had to do. It was time for fearlessness. No emotions. It was time that she drew a line.

Without any show of regret or hesitation, she watched as his body jerked and twisted. He'd been pissing vinegar, but one zap took the vinegar out of him. His eyes widened in disbelief and anger. He took another step toward her. Again, she pressed the black object. She watched him shake violently, grabbing his chest, before he hit the floor at the foot of the bed. The screams of a wounded animal ripped out of his mouth, but she heard only one word. "Bitch!"

"You call me a bitch one more time, and I'll zap you til you can't move or speak for days. Enough is enough. And I've had enough of your bullying, smart-ass mouth."

It seemed like forever that they were glued in the same positions. Frozen in space and time. Mavis was in a daze, looking at Johnny Lee's body, as it twisted back and forth. Moans seeped from his mouth. Then, it hit her that she might have done some serious damage. Fear engulfed her. She felt helpless. Only one word entered her head. "Beulah."

"Johnny Lee, stay still. I'll be back. Don't move," and she stepped over him. She made the call, from the kitchen phone, to the one person whom she knew would come. After the call, she alternated between checking on Johnny Lee and looking out the kitchen window.

"Please, God. Please, God," she prayed over and over.

♦

As she finished the horror story of the last twenty-four hours, tears rolled down her hollow cheeks. Her shoulders slumped and she laid her head on her crossed arms. Beulah came around the table to Mavis' side and wrapped her arms around the pitiful, shaking body. She stroked

Mavis' hair and began to sing softly, rocking back and forth, until the weeping stopped.

She lifted Mavis' chin. "How bout another strong cup of coffee? You feel like makin me some of your biscuits and gravy? I bet Johnny Lee will want something to eat when he wakes up."

Mavis gripped Beulah's right hand in both of hers. "Yeah. I've got some fig preserves we can have with our biscuits. If you want." She raised herself tall in the chair and cocked her head. "Listen. The rain has stopped. Before long, it'll be daylight." She looked into Beulah's dark eyes. "Stay til daylight. Okay?"

"Okay," and she squeezed Mavis' hand that remained soft, in spite of washing dishes, working in gardens, and planting abundant flowers and shrubs.

As they finished eating, the first streak of light burst into the room and covered the windows in glowing white. The wind was no longer a wild dancer, moving among the trees. The kitchen was warm and cozy. They could hear the crackle of the fire in the iron potbellied stove in the living room. Before cooking, Mavis had coaxed a fire from the ashes that she'd blanketed before going to bed. Throughout the last hours, she'd periodically checked on Johnny Lee to make sure that he was breathing. He had rolled onto his left side soon after he fell asleep and had remained in that position.

Beulah and Mavis talked in low voices as they drank the last of the strong coffee. Suddenly, there was a comfortable silence. They both looked into their coffee cups. They glanced at one another. Mavis spoke first. "Thank you for coming. I was so scared. I didn't have anyone else to call. No one I could trust. No one who'd understand."

"Mavis, that's what friends do. Real friends. I got your back." She looked out the window and blinked from the brightness. With a sigh, she said, "I can't say 'no' to you."

Their eyes locked. Mavis broke the spell. "Thanks, Beulah. Hey, let me get these dishes in the sink. You go on home. I know you're tired. We're both tired."

"After I help with the dishes." She raised her hand to hush Mavis. "Don't say nothing. I'm helpin with the dishes."

Mavis lifted one perfectly arched eyebrow and grinned. "Okay. Let's do it. Then, you're going home to bed. No more arguments. Thank goodness it's Saturday."

♦

Johnny Lee stopped his extreme violent behavior. The drug dealer no longer gave him drugs on credit or knocked on Mavis' door. But, Johnny Lee still got high, often ranting and cursing. He still stomped through the house, kicking things in his path. At times, he called Mavis bad names. Usually, it took one hard, steel look from her to make him back off.

He repaired Mavis' bedroom door, swearing he'd never "be that stupid again."

And he never was.

Mavis kept the deadbolt on her door, a bat beside the bed, the stun gun under her mattress, and the pistol in the drawer of the bedside table. Experience had taught her that there were no limits to what a person high on drugs would do. There was no more trust or denial. She'd never let down her guard. Only Beulah would know. It'd be years before Johnny Lee's siblings learned of the electrical jolt their mama had given Johnny Lee one cold, rainy February night.

CHAPTER THIRTEEN

Four months after Mavis zapped Johnny Lee with the stun gun, her daughter, Zelda, who was a Holiness minister, invited Laura Faye, Bobbie Jo, Edith, and Mavis to attend a Wednesday night service at the Fellowship Holiness Church of God, which was located in a one room white wooden building, near Little Shelby, an African-American community that was infested with drugs. Concrete steps led to a small porch and a steeple sat on top of the building. A sign near the highway and the steeple were the only clues that the building was a church. An old trailer sat behind the church. It served as Sunday school rooms and an office.

Zelda had issued an invitation various times to Bobbie Jo and Mavis. Each time, they turned it down, with some lame excuse. Mavis' response to Zelda's last invitation was, "Why in tarnation do I wanna go listen to a bunch of folks, screaming and carrying on? And jumping over benches cause the Holy Ghost is after them? Or laying hands on folks that don't want to be touched by strangers? Now, answer me that. I'm a Methodist, and we don't do no such as that."

"Quit being ugly, Mama. There ain't nothing wrong with people praising the Lord. It might do you some good," Zelda said. There was a long silence, while Mavis stared at Zelda. "What are you thinking,

Mama?"

"I'm thinking," and she stopped for a long pause, "it don't appeal to me." She saw the hurt in Zelda's eyes and watched as the hurt was replaced with anger. "Hey, I'll come. Why not?"

Zelda's delicate features softened and lit up with a warm smile. "Good! Laura Faye will bring you to church Wednesday night. And, Mama, I'm so glad you're coming. Preacher Zach Bell is gonna give the sermon. You know him."

"Who? You mean that dried up, tight-lipped mean ole jackass who puts locks on the cabinets in his house so that nobody in his family can eat a thing without his permission? The same son-of-a-bitch that made his wife sit outside on the doorsteps, in the freezing cold, without even a sweater, cause the gas bill was so high? Hell, he ain't no preacher! That's for sure. Yeah, I'd like to hear what that fool has to say. I can tell you now that a fly has more sense than he does. I'll be there," she said with unexpected enthusiasm.

Zelda began to have second thoughts about giving Mavis an invitation.

Two days later, Laura Faye picked up the three women in her new beige Yukon that had leather seats and fancy gadgets. Mavis sat in the front passenger's seat and turned every dial on the dashboard. She wore black pants and a ruffled red blouse that she hoped would irritate old man Bell. Her nails and lips were burning flames. Her make-up was perfection, and she'd gone to the beauty shop to have her hair done. More attempts to irritate Bell.

Edith and Bobbie Jo sat in the backseat, chatting back and forth about people whom they knew. The discussion got to old man Bell. "I used to work with his wife in the mill," Edith informed everyone, as she erased a wrinkle on her plaid full skirt that fell to her ankles. She straightened the collar on a purple pokey dot blouse. "She was a mousey woman and walked round like she was afraid of her own shadow. If

192

anybody spoke to her, she'd jump a mile high. I felt sorry for her."

"I feel sorry for her. Married to that toad. Well, she was probably exhausted from havin one kid after another. He kept her workin and pregnant all the time," Bobbie Jo added. "She looks twenty years older than she is."

Mavis turned around and said, "She's plum pitiful. When he says, 'Jump,' she asks, 'How high?' It beats all I've ever seen in my life. And he ain't never worked a single day of his lazy life. Just called himself a preacher." She turned back around. "It seems just bout anybody can do that. Give em a Bible and watch em start thumping it, saying all kinds of stuff that they insist is in the Bible."

No one responded. It was useless to argue with Mavis when she got on a hobbyhorse. Plus, a lot of what she said held some truth. And there was too much evidence on Mavis' side to argue with her about that subject.

As they pulled into the dirt parking lot, they noticed that there were only seven cars and one beat-up blue truck that had a huge dent on the rear left bumper. Music floated from the open windows. Someone was banging the hell out of an upright piano. The service had recently begun.

Walking into the sanctuary, Mavis saw women whose hair was drawn back in severe buns or pulled from their faces and held with large bows. Young girls had long hair that was combed away from their innocent faces and fell down their backs, racing to reach their butts. All of the females wore long skirts, long-sleeved blouses with high necks, and cheap cloth shoes with ankle socks. No one wore make-up. Not even lip gloss.

Mavis, Bobbie Jo, and Edith knew almost everyone who had, at one time or another, eaten at Mid-Way Café. Bobbie Jo led the small group of women to a pew on her left that was halfway down the aisle. She sat near the window and watched as the others sat down, one-by-one.

Each woman took a fan from the trays that were attached to the pew in front of them. On the front side of the fan was a picture of Jesus, knocking on a door that didn't have a doorknob. On the back were advertisements for local businesses. One read, "Be the woman that you can be. Merle's beauty shop can transform you." Another one read, "Let Jimmy's Tires spirit you away on tires that will take away your breath." The one that made Mavis smile proclaimed, "We got all that you need— for any need—at Dude's Pharmacy. We can satisfy you."

The women gripped the thin wooden paddles on the fans and began a back and forth rhythm with the music. Five ceiling fans did little to cool the stuffy room that the sun had roasted throughout the day, as it beat pass the glass windows. The western sun was savage on those who sat on that side of the aisle.

Zelda, the piano player, a heavy-set woman with gray hair that was in a large bun, and old man Bell sat on a small stage that was elevated approximately three feet off the floor and seemed to float in front of the congregation. A ceiling fan turned at full speed above the three of them. They sat stiffly, facing the small crowd.

When the music stopped, Zelda walked to a homemade wood podium that stood in the middle of the stage. Her hair wasn't long like the women who sat before her, but it was pulled back from her face, which was void of make-up. Mavis twisted her shoulders and grunted softly. A long white ruffled skirt fell to Zelda's ankles, and she wore white sandals. A soft pink blouse, with elbow length sleeves fit loosely.

"Let's stand for prayer." Everyone stood, and Zelda began a prayer that Mavis thought went on for too long. She released a loud sigh and peeped under her lashes at Zelda who ignored the deep sigh that had rippled above the fans. After she said, "Amen," she gave Mavis a warning look, which Mavis pretended not to see. Then, Zelda introduced old man Bell.

He strutted to the podium like a cocky rooster on a mission, took the microphone in his right dried wrinkled hand that was covered in age spots, thanked Zelda, and walked to the edge of the stage. "Praise the Lord! Amen! Praise the Lord! Raise your hands and praise the Lord! Ain't God good? If you know God's good, say, 'Amen.'"

Everyone did as he commanded, except for Laura Faye, Bobbie Jo, and Mavis. When Edith raised her hands, Mavis poked her in the ribs. Edith gave Mavis a frown and lowered her hands.

"Amen! Thank you, Jesus! Praise the Lord! Praise His holy name!" old man Bell screamed from the pulpit, as he began to pace back and forth, with the Bible in his left arm that was raised high above his thrown-back head, which was bald on top. Stringy strands of gray hair hung to the worn collar of a faded blue shirt. Wrinkles like crevasses cut across his face and his excited eyes looked at the ceiling.

Some women had begun to sway from side-to-side. Their hands were lifted above their heads and their eyes were closed. Some clapped and made strange sounds. One older woman bounced on her toes and spoke in tongues. In Mavis' opinion, it was a bit early to start speaking in tongues, which proved to her that speaking in tongues was a whole lot of nothing.

"Oh, for goodness sakes," thought Mavis. "If these silly women start swaying now, they'll be dancing and laying on hands before long. I don't want nobody touching me."

Old man Bell stopped as quickly as he'd started and motioned for everyone to sit and get quiet. They obeyed. "Now, let me jus warn all y'all right now. I'm a gonna be preachin gainst sin. And sin ain't no purty sight no which aways you look at it."

Several people yelled, "Amen! Tell it like it is, preacher!" The words echoed in the building and ran out the windows.

"I'm a gonna be talkin bout some sins that done got this here country in a big ole mess. This here country—this here United States of America—is off the track. Cause we ain't got Jesus in our lives. We need God back in the United States of America! I say, 'Bring God back to

195

America!' We need to git back on the right track, fore this here country ends up in hell. The track that's gonna lead us to Jesus. Amen! Praise His name! Praise His holy name!

"I'm a gonna be talkin bout sins that done influenced a whole lotta folks and made em vain and wicked. And selfish and self-centered. Done ate away at their greedy souls and done made em children of Satan. Amen and hallelujah! I'm a talkin bout the sins of vanity and bad habits and greed! Worthless thangs on this here earth. Thangs God don't like a tall!" He pranced across the stage, looking at the floor, as if he was deeply concentrating. He didn't speak for several minutes.

Everyone waited. Some of the women leaned forward, watching and anticipating his next words. Only the fans could be heard. Suddenly, he stopped and loudly slapped a calloused open palm on the podium. Some people jumped. Mavis looked bored. Soft "amens" could be heard.

"Y'all women folks, listen up. Cause I'm a gonna mainly be talkin to y'all. Too many women today wanna wear make-up, paint their lips like a Jezebel, wear flashy nail polish, and loud perfume. They hang that there fancy gold from their ears and necks. It dangles from their arms like wicked enticin snakes. They cover their fingers in big flashy diamonds. Em's the thangs of Satan."

Laura Faye twisted the two large diamonds on her fingers and touched the expensive gold necklace at her throat. Then, she held her hands in her lap so that the diamonds couldn't be seen. As she did so, the odor of Joy perfume drifted upward from her wrists. She began to feel uncomfortable and assumed that everyone was secretly glancing at her.

Mavis didn't respond to the comment about her red painted lips and nails, as she glared at the small unkempt man in front of her. Instead, she deliberately touched her face and neck, hoping the red caught his eye. She gave a disgusted look at his baggy trousers and soiled blue shirt that was open too far and revealed a thick mat of gray and mousey brown chest hair. She noticed as he walked that the inside soles of his brown dusty shoes were worn down. The top of his head glistened with sweat. What hair that he had was thin and hung low on his neck. In an attempt to disguise the bald spot on his head, a long strand of hair from the back was combed forward and kept moving as he walked.

Bobbie Jo and Edith, who didn't wear make-up or nail polish or jewelry, didn't bat an eye as the red-faced man before them shook his fist now and then at the audience and glanced too often at Mavis.

"Em ain't thangs that's a gonna git y'all up to heaven. To save y'all's souls. Em's thangs a Satan."

On and on he talked about sins that were directed at women. The more he talked, the more excited he became. Sweat began to drip down his face so that his skin glowed under the harsh lights. Dark spots appeared under his armpits. He rocked back and forth on his toes. Now and then, he quickly grabbed his penis. People stood up and shouted, "Amen! Tell it, preacher! Tell it like it is!"

Mavis' attention had long drifted away, and she was planning what she'd cook for dinner the next day. Suddenly, her ear caught the word "snuff," and she focused on the sweating, bug-eyed man in front of her.

"People who dip snuff is headed to hell! It's a sin to dip the brown bitter medicine of the Devil. It's a drug that the Devil uses to take yo soul, to steal yo life. Folks, it's a sin! Make no mistake bout it! It's a sin!"

Without thinking, Mavis spoke up loud enough for everyone to hear. Her words cut straight into the "amens" that filled the room. "He needs to mind his own damn business." Everything came to a grinding halt. All eyes looked at Mavis. Quiet settled over the crowd, and time waited.

People who knew Mavis well weren't surprised that she'd spoken out. Also, they knew that old man Bell had focused on the women who'd walked in late. In addition, they were too aware that Mavis knew a great deal about their own sins. No one wanted to tolerate a lecture from her about sins. They certainly weren't about to throw rocks at Mavis who could throw a rock or two herself.

Old man Bell stopped dead in his pacing, with his finger pointed in the air, and shock on his wrinkled face. His eyes shot scorching fires from the depths of hell. Laura Faye and Bobbie Jo started to laugh like schoolgirls. Edith didn't move, but looked at a spot above Zelda's head. She wanted to laugh, but bit her tongue. The only sounds were the laughter of two women and the whisk of the fans. From the back of the church, a man laughed. Embarrassed, he coughed.

Mavis' eyes connected with the cold gray eyes of old man Bell. Her eyes were hard emeralds, void of fear, that challenged him. He dropped his hand and seemed to shrivel into his small body. Anger was a storm on his face, and hate, along with the burning fire, shot from his bulging eyes. Mavis' glare was an artic icy winter, daring him to respond. Two forces were at play. The laughter had stopped. Mavis heard herself thinking, "Come on. Say something. I beg you. Say something."

Old man Bell looked at Zelda. She stood up and walked to the podium. The two brushed one another as he returned to his chair. "Led us bow our heads in prayer." Mavis didn't bow her head. Instead, she looked at the bald spot on the bowed head of old man Bell. It was a brief prayer.

Zelda caught them as they were going down the steps of the church. "Thank y'all for coming. Mama, thank you for coming. I didn't know that he was going to talk bout those things." She hugged Mavis.

"Don't' worry bout it. I don't think he knew what he was gonna talk bout, until we walked in. He's always been an idiot. I've got only one thing to say. If you're going to invite someone to preach, get a real preacher. Not a toothless, rotten mouth hypocrite who's heaven and hell stupid."

On the way home, Laura Faye, Bobbie Jo, and Edith couldn't stop laughing. They'd never seen anything like it. Edith said, when she could stop laughing long enough to talk, "Now, do y'all see what I put up with every Sunday that Mavis comes to church? I never know what she's gonna say. If old man Bell knows anything bout Mavis Agnes Norrell, he shouldva known better than to say some of the things he said. Lord, I ain't laughed so much in months."

Grinning, Mavis said, "I betcha Zelda won't be asking me to come back to church. That man's a nut case. A fool and a hypocrite. Poor Zelda. Where does she find these loony bins?" Everyone laughed.

After several minutes, Mavis proclaimed, "I'm sticking to the Methodist church. And when they get a nut-job like that, I'm leaving the church. Period."

The conversation turned to another topic. Looking out of the window, Mavis considered the different personalities and complexities of each of her children. They were full of surprises; they were a wide assortment of variety, and she didn't think that was a bad thing. Each one was his or her own person. Without understanding the reasons, it made her proud. And, yes, she was proud of Johnny Lee. Not that he was a drug addict, but that he was a good person, with a kind and forgiving heart. Those things were worth something. He'd never really hurt anyone but himself.

Some of her children weren't forgiving. And some were jealous of one another.

One by one, she named them in her head. Janet, the oldest child, was headstrong, determined, and bossy. Mavis understood the reasons. Robert and Mavis had left her in charge too often, with too many responsibilities for a young girl. Janet and Marley Jane were close, more like mother and child than siblings. It was Janet who watched over Marley Jane and took care of her after she was born. Mavis remembered Marley Jane, barely a year old, resting on Janet's hip, under a tall shade tree in Dewey's cotton field. Janet changed her younger sister's diapers and saw that she had a bottle.

Marley Jane was a mystery that Mavis never could quite solve. She always seemed to be outside the family, looking in, by choice. When she was born, she was given to another woman who nursed her for almost twenty-four hours before the mistake was discovered. After the nurse placed the baby in Mavis' arms, Marley Jane refused to nurse. An elderly nurse suggested that a bottle might be the answer. Marley Jane accepted the bottle, but she never acquired a taste for milk. Mavis often wondered if that episode had somehow affected Marley Jane, made her stay on the outside edge of the family circle.

When she announced that Winston and she were getting a divorce, Mavis was shocked. They were all shocked, but Marley Jane refused to discuss the reasons with the family. And she wouldn't speak about Winston in a negative way. It reinforced Mavis' belief that no one in the family really knew Marley Jane.

Bobbie Jo and Mavis had been close when Bobbie Jo was a teenager. Almost too close…more like sisters. Time had changed that. Bobbie Jo was very opinionated and stubborn to the point of absurdity. She never let go of a belief or an opinion, regardless of facts that supported something different. But, she was a dependable and caring person. Sometimes, she seemed to understand Johnny Lee, to have a degree of compassion. At other times, she seemed to be disgusted and angry with him, but she had a kind heart.

Laura Faye was the only one who deeply cared about Johnny Lee and who believed that he needed her protection. She'd supported her parents one hundred percent when it came to her youngest brother. Mostly, she didn't want her parents to worry about Johnny Lee, that he'd not be taken care of. As long as she lived, Johnny Lee would have someone to care about him. Mavis knew that to be a fact.

Laura Faye had a strong love for Mavis that was almost possessive and needy. She wanted to be Mavis' favorite, wanted all of her love, wanted her approval. And, she couldn't do enough for her mama. Laura Faye was loving, kind, and good-hearted. But, she also had a terrible temper when she was crossed.

Zelda was a challenge, always testing, saying things that didn't make much sense to Mavis. Often, she seemed to be in total contradiction with herself, and Mavis wanted to shake her, to make her leave the pretend world that she'd created when she was a child. This was the child whom Mavis wanted to lecture, while holding her close and reassuring her that she was loved. Mavis had decided that nothing she did or didn't do would have much impact on Zelda's opinion of her mama, of Mavis' love. Zelda was searching, feeling in the dark for something that eluded her. Mavis hoped that one day Zelda would find what she was seeking. She knew that Zelda would tell her that she'd found what she was seeking. The Lord. And that was probably true, but Mavis believed that Zelda was still searching.

There were the boys whom Mavis felt that she had to protect. The girls were stronger than the boys, by a long shot. Claude had been immature and foolish up to the time that he married, which was the best thing that ever happened to him. He was a quiet, good man who was a hard worker. He harbored too much anger against his daddy. Mavis didn't know how to repair that and hoped that one day he'd resolve his anger. Like Zelda, it seemed that he clung to one or two negative incidents in his youth and refused to release them to the past. She hoped in time that he'd let those things go.

Richard had been handsome and wild, from the time that he was a teenager. Women, old and young, adored him. He was a charmer, with a dark side. He'd gone through three wives and a lot of alcohol. Mavis had spent more time than she liked to recall, dealing with one wife or one woman after another, one drunk episode after another, while chasing down Richard's demons that took her to honky tonks and bars, where she'd find her middle son drunk and on the verge of a fight. Several times, Mavis had whipped out her gun and pointed it at one drunken fool or another who was intent on stomping Richard to hell and back.

Now, he was happily married to Bella, a wonderful woman, and he no longer drank. Like his older brother, he was a good man who had a kind heart and who was a hard worker.

Johnny Lee was the baby. He, too, had a kind heart and a gentle soul, but he couldn't walk away from drugs, which was his crutch. Mavis and Robert had done all the wrong things for what they thought were the right reasons. Too often, they prevented Johnny Lee from suffering the consequences of bad behavior or bad choices. Although Mavis knew of those mistakes, she continued to make them, again and again. Mavis believed that there was something else that no one, not even he, knew about his personality. She believed that there was something that drove him to immerse himself in drugs; yet, she had no idea what it could be.

"Mama, didn't you hear me?" Laura Faye cut into Mavis' thoughts.

"No. What were you saying?"

"I'm planning a cruise to the Bahamas. I want you, Ms. Beulah, and Ms. Edith to go. And I'm asking all of my sisters. I'm paying. Would you like to go?"

"Well, I don't know. I'll see."

"I'm taking that as a 'yes,' so you talk to Ms. Beulah. We'll go in bout three months. That'll give me time to make plans."

"What bout your wedding?"

"That's five months away. We'll have time. Or, if y'all like, we'll wait til after the wedding."

Bobbie Jo spoke up. "Let's wait til after the weddin. Maybe, bout April or May. That way, no one will be rushed." Edith and Mavis nodded their heads.

"Okay. That's settled. We'll go next April. How's that?" Laura Faye suggested. The others agreed, but the idea didn't excite Mavis like it might have done at one time. She was too tired for a cruise.

CHAPTER FOURTEEN

It was soon September, and Tom Jones had scheduled a concert in Macon, Georgia. Next to Elvis, Tom Jones was Mavis' favorite singer. Bobbie Jo and Laura Faye made plans to take Mavis, Beulah, and Edith to see the famous entertainer. The three friends spent hours talking about the big night, planning what they'd wear.

The day of the concert arrived. It was a Saturday, with a steady rain that began before daylight and fell throughout the day. Edith and Beulah arrived at Mavis' house at three o'clock, dressed in cowgirl outfits. They wore large straw hats, boots, bright vests, and skirts that were barely below their knees.

Edith had cut around the bottom of a denim skirt so that long strands of fringe flapped as she walked, and she wore one of John's faded shirts, as well as his favorite cowboy boots. On one side of her hat, she'd stuck an enormous yellow rose. Her velvet vest was covered in rhinestones. The most shocking thing that Edith wore was too much blush that stood out in small dots on her cheeks. She wore the brightest red lipstick that Mavis had ever seen in her life. The mismatched outfit didn't surprise Mavis, but that red lipstick and the blush made Edith look like a clown—or a rag doll. It wasn't clear if Edith wanted to be the rhinestone cowboy, the yellow rose of Texas, or Raggedy Ann. Mavis vowed to herself that she'd keep her mouth shut and not make any comments.

Beulah wore a leather skirt, and, Mavis could only guess where that came from. She'd borrowed some child's toy gun and belt. It fit snuggly around her waist. A couple of pigtails stuck out from beneath a large hat. A plaid shirt of bright orange and blue, along with a red bandana around her neck, completed the outfit. Except for silver brackets that lined both arms and jingled each time she moved a hand. Mavis thought, "Good grief! With all that jingling, nobody's gonna hear one peep outa Tom Jones."

Mavis looked classy in a new navy blue suit, a white silk blouse, with a bow at the throat, and perfect make-up. Black leather ankle boots, with one-inch heels, completed the outfit. Gold earrings dangled from her tiny earlobes and her favorite red lipstick shined on full lips. She'd been to the beauty shop that morning for a perm and color. Edith and Beulah decided that she looked as if she'd stepped from the pages of a fashion magazine.

Still, Edith said, "Why ain't you dressed up? Like us. I thought we agreed to wear cowgirl outfits. Where's yours?"

"I put it on and decided that I looked slap awful. I know we agreed, but I didn't feel comfortable. So, I took everything off. And, here I am!" she said, throwing her arms wide and slowly turning around.

"Well, you sho do look good," said Beulah. "We gonna have fun anyways."

By the time that Laura Faye and Bobbie Jo arrived, it looked like the rain might stop. But, when the Yukon crossed the Chattahoochee River, a deluge of rain fell. The further that they traveled, the harder the rain slapped the roof of the vehicle. By the time that they got to Macon, Laura Faye could barely see the highway in front of her. She slowly pulled into the packed parking lot. They sat for several minutes, hoping that the rain would slow down.

While they were waiting, Mavis looked at Bobbie Jo and said, "I hope you got some more shoes, besides those fuzzy house shoes you're wearing. Anyway, why did you wear those things? Are you planning to spend the night here?"

"No, I'm not! I wore them cause I like them. And I wanna be comfortable."

Mavis gave Bobbie Jo a cold stare and didn't say anything, because she knew that Edith and Beulah were waiting for her to make a comment so that they could use the word "comfortable" against her. Instead, she thought to herself that it was just like Bobbie Jo to dress as sloppy as Edith. For more times that she could recall, she wondered what had happened to her beautiful daughter who had, at one time, looked like Elizabeth Taylor and had cared about her appearance. Again, she kept quiet. It'd amaze most people how often Mavis kept quiet, which was more times, actually, than she spoke out.

Realizing that the rain had no intentions of slowing down, the five women held large umbrellas and splashed through puddles of water to the entrance of the auditorium. By the time that they entered the building, Bobbie Jo's fuzzy slippers were soaked rags. She took them off. She pulled a pair of fuzzy socks from a large brown leather bag that she carried. Without a care in the world, she pranced across the floor. As they headed to their seats, they were met by loud music, as people cheered and whistled. Several couples danced in front of the stage. Excitement and anticipation filled the air.

They made their way down the long, slanted aisle to the front and located their seats on the third center row, near the aisle. Mavis, Beulah, and Edith were already bobbing to the music, snapping their fingers and nodding their heads. Laura Faye and Bobbie Jo got tickled. No one else seemed to pay attention to three older women who were jiving to the beat of the opening band.

It seemed like forever before Tom Jones appeared on stage, and the crowd went wild. Mavis, Beulah, and Edith were bumping butts and clapping. Edith made a "V" with her fingers and whistled so loud that the people who sat near her felt their eardrums pop. Afterwards, Beulah and Mavis gave Edith a high five. Laura Faye was certain that Tom Jones and every member of his band looked at Edith and grinned. Tom Jones ground his hips, and the crowd went insane. Mavis thought that it was a good grind, but not as good as an Elvis grind.

Bobbie Jo was surprised that the dark-haired handsome man, whose curls fell across his forehead, wasn't very tall. It didn't matter. His smile was charming and his voice was sexy. Raw sexuality dripped from his pores. Tight leather pants and a white silk shirt that exposed his chest intoxicated the crowd. He was slender, but well-built. When he began to sing, "She's a Lady," the crowd stood up. They began to sway, cheer and clap. A couple of young women screamed and threw panties on the stage.

Before Laura Faye or Bobbie Jo could bat an eye, Edith and Beulah were following Mavis to the small empty space between the audience and the stage. As the two younger women watched in shock, the three older women boogied like nobody's business. When they began to twist, the crowd cheered louder. It was obvious to Tom Jones that the three elderly women were stealing his thunder.

Twisting his hips toward the edge of the stage, he motioned for them to join him. Three of his bodyguards appeared out of nowhere beside them and extended their hands. Pair-by-pair, they walked up the steps to the stage. Tom Jones got in the middle of the three women and crazy took over. The crowd loved it, as movements became more suggestive. At the end of the song, he asked each woman to introduce herself and to tell the audience where she lived. Then, he kissed each one on a blushing cheek. His bodyguards escorted them to their seats, hoping they'd remain there for the rest of the show.

As the five women left the building, a dark sky that looked like wet asphalt hung above the tall Georgia pines. The rain had stopped, but small ponds of water were scattered across the parking lot. The women made their way around one pond after another. They were exhausted, but happy and hungry. Laura Faye located an all-night diner, and they ordered cheeseburgers, fries, and milkshakes.

By the time that they arrived at Mavis' house, everyone was past ready for bed. Laura Faye and Bobbie Jo waited until Mavis was inside her house. Then, they watched as Beulah and Edith drove away in their vehicles. "I think they had a good time," Bobbie Jo said, with a smile, as Laura Faye turned the car towards Bobbie Jo's house.

"Me, too. I've never laughed so hard in my life," Laura Faye said. "I'm glad we went. Mama seemed real happy. But, did you notice how tired and quiet she was on the way home?"

"Yeah, she was tired. But, we're all tired. It's been a long day."

"I hope she'll be half as happy at my wedding," Laura Faye sighed.

CHAPTER FIFTEEN

Mavis often seemed tired after the Tom Jones concert. There were less late night calls to Beulah when Mavis couldn't sleep. Beulah would frequently stop by after work to check on her friend and would find her in bed, with the familiar diaper wrapped around her head. Mavis would say that she'd cleaned house, ironed, or cooked and was simply tired.

Too, the days were getting shorter, and Mavis said that depressed her. The fact that Mavis had lost her appetite and weight concerned Beulah. When she mentioned it, Mavis waved her hand and said, "It's nothing. I'm getting older."

At the end of October, Beulah called Edith and expressed concern for Mavis. Edith had observed the same things that Beulah had noticed. No matter what time of the day that Edith knocked on Mavis' door, she'd find Mavis in bed or curled up on the sofa, wrapped in a blanket. Edith worried that Mavis wasn't as perky or quick to comment when Edith talked about people and subjects that, at one time, had sparked an immediate response from Mavis. It wasn't like Mavis. Maybe, there were more serious problems with Johnny Lee that Mavis didn't want to discuss. Whatever it was, there was a change in Mavis.

"I'm concerned bout Mavis. Has she talked to you bout feelin tired all the time?" Edith asked Beulah in a whisper, afraid that her loud voice would carry across the road and into Mavis' range of hearing. She looked over her left shoulder as if she was making sure that Mavis wasn't standing nearby, listening.

Beulah hesitated. She had noticed that Mavis was tired and had seen the dark circles under her eyes. Too, her appetite hadn't been so good. Edith and Beulah were aware that Mavis had lost weight. Also, Mavis had repeatedly told Beulah that she was tired all the time. She complained that she didn't seem to be able to do simple chores like cleaning the house, ironing, cooking, or tending to her flowers. Nothing interested her any more.

"She hasn't said anything bout bein tired to me. Has she said anything to you?" Edith spoke softly into the phone. Beulah heard the concern in Edith's voice. "Do you know that some Sundays she sleeps almost all day? She's been missin church a whole lots lately. And she ain't been goin to the dog track as much. I thought at first she didn't have the money," Edith continued in a whisper.

"Yes. Lots a times," Beulah answered, "and I've noticed other things. I spoke to BobbieJo bout it, but she shrugged her shoulders and said it was probably all Johnny Lee's fault. That he's probably drivin his mama crazy with worry. She did say that Mavis had been in bed or on the sofa a couple a times when she'd visited. But, she didn't think it was anything to get concerned bout. That she did that herself. Take a nap durin the day. Especially in the afternoons or on Sundays."

"Well, I don't know. I think she needs to see a doctor. It's not like her. She enjoys goin too much."

"BobbieJo did say that she'd start payin more attention. And Mavis was sho nough tired after that concert. I told her Mavis needs to go to the doctor, and BobbieJo said she'd talk to Mavis, but she wasn't gonna make a promise that Mavis wouldn't allow her to keep. And, she added that puttin up with Johnny Lee's crap was nough to make anybody tired and not have an appetite."

Edith and Beulah decided to pay Mavis a visit to talk about Laura Faye's upcoming wedding. Edith said that she'd ask Mavis the best day for them to get together. The call was made, and Mavis insisted that her friends stop by two days later for biscuits and gravy.

Two days later, it was a cool morning. A light frost was still on the ground when Edith arrived before Beulah. It was the first time in weeks that Edith had seen Mavis in something other than a housecoat. Mavis' hair was styled; she wore makeup and her favorite lipstick. Still, her green eyes were sunken and her cheekbones were more prominent than ever. But it pleased Edith that Mavis was cheerful and spunky.

The morning flew by, while the three friends laughed and talked. Beulah and Edith began to imagine that they'd over-reacted. Mavis seemed like her old self as she joked about the upcoming wedding and how she thought that she was finished with weddings. But, every time that she thought she was done with a wedding, one of her kids or grandkids got married. As Mavis poked fun, her two friends smiled at one another and thought how foolish they'd been.

As soon as they left, Mavis put on her pajamas and went to bed, exhausted. She didn't wake up until six o'clock the next morning. Still tired.

◆

One week later, Laura Faye married for the third time, to her "knight-in-Shining Armor." The remark made Mavis snort each time that she heard it. Aloud, she said nothing. To herself, she grunted, "Knight in shining armor, my ass. What a joke! If he's wearing armor, it's as rusty as nails on a rotten old barn."

The wedding was a large event. Flowers and candles were everywhere. Mavis complained that there were too many varieties of flowers and that

Laura Faye should have chosen only one or two types. Too many scenes interfered with one another. She made certain that Laura Faye didn't hear her complain.

The day of the wedding, Mavis wore a beautiful silk champagne suit that had tiny pearls on the collar and cuffs. Satin one-inch heels, died to match the suit, peeped from beneath a long skirt. A light radiated from her pupils and a Mona Liza smile clung to her lips. In spite of that, Beulah heard her silence and knew that Mavis' mind objected to the wedding.

Beulah understood most of the reasons that Mavis objected to the people whom her children married. Past comments had made it clear to Beulah that Mavis liked Marley Jane's first husband, Winston Steele, who still stopped by now and then to visit. The jury was still out as to whether or not she liked Marley Jane's second husband.

Everyone in the family adored Janet's husband. He was the favorite of Mavis and Robert. Robert and Morgan got along better than any of the other sons-in-laws, except for Winston, who'd also been a favorite.

Mavis believed that Bella had tamed her wild son, as well as his love for alcohol; therefore, Mavis liked her. For the rest of them, Mavis wouldn't give you five cents for the whole lot. It seemed that they were always supplying Mavis with something that she used against them or used to mock them. Mavis once told Beulah that all of her children had married too young or too quickly, and she questioned what she should've done differently in raising them.

All eyes in the church faced Laura Faye as she walked down the aisle, in a beautiful form-fitting white wedding gown. Mavis' grin became crooked and threatened to turn into a snarl. When Zelda sang, "At Last," Mavis gave a peaceful smile. She always enjoyed listening to Zelda sing.

After the ceremony, the wedding party remained for photos. Mavis smiled and tried not to grit her teeth. By the time that they entered the reception hall, she was tired. Her head and feet ached. After thirty minutes, she asked Johnny Lee to take her home. They sneaked out before anyone realized that they were gone. The band was playing "Mustang Sally," which was Laura Faye's favorite song.

On the way home, Johnny Lee touched his mama's hand. "Mama, are you okay? You look tired."

"I'm fine. Just a tad tired. I'm not used to standing in heels for hours. I'll feel better, when I get in something that's comfortable." She leaned her head against the seat and closed her eyes.

Johnny Lee looked hard at her. He noticed how much weight that she'd lost and the tired lines that lately never seemed to disappear. He patted her hand. He'd never seen his mama so fragile, and he'd noticed how quiet that she'd been after the wedding. He assumed that she'd decided to play nice and behave like the classy lady whom she could be. That didn't explain her lack of energy. Too, he'd watched recently as she rested after cooking or doing housework, which she wasn't doing as often as she once did. It was a fact that she was getting older. Still, he was worried and made up his mind to talk with Laura Faye about their mama.

◆

When Laura Faye and Felton returned from their honeymoon in Hawaii, Mavis noticed that her daughter glowed and couldn't stop talking about her wonderful new husband. Mavis said nothing, which worried Laura Faye. The silences spoke louder than any words, and, combined with empty long stares, meant that Mavis' thoughts didn't need to be expressed.

Thanksgiving was the first time after the wedding that the couple spent with Laura Faye's family. Felton wasn't the type of man to be nervous. Talking to people was his best gift, although Mavis believed that his gift of gab bordered on deception and false pretenses, but she never expressed her feelings to anyone, except Beulah.

Mavis invited Beulah and Edith for Thanksgiving dinner. Beulah's daughter, Autumn, was a nurse and she was working overtime on Thanksgiving Day. Beulah's mom and dad had died years ago, one immediately after the other. So, Beulah would be alone at Thanksgiving. Edith's oldest son Ferris was dating a widower who had three children. He planned to spend the day with them. Preston's family was going to Gulf Shores for the holiday, and Edith hadn't been invited; therefore, she, too, would be alone. Both were grateful for the invitation to spend Thanksgiving with Mavis and her clan.

Johnny Lee watched for days as Mavis cooked and froze desserts. He helped when she asked for help, and he noticed that she took long breaks. At night, she'd go to bed as soon as darkness came. The old cloth diaper would be wrapped tightly around her head to ease the pain. The next morning, long after Johnny Lee had gone to work, she'd leisurely get out of bed and cook a cake, a pie, or more cornbread for the dressing.

Thanksgiving arrived on what felt like a summer day. Beulah and Edith came early to help Mavis. They were shocked at how pale and thin she looked. They'd spoken to her on the phone, but it'd been over a week since either one of them had seen her. They were surprised to hear the exhaustion in her voice. As Mavis moved in slow motion about the kitchen and dining room, they exchanged glances. At last, they convinced her to sit down, while they put the food on the long table and completed any unfinished chores. While they worked, Mavis' eyes grew heavy and closed; her head dropped to her left side and she dozed for a while. Suddenly, she jerked awake and looked around the room that was filled with the fading day. Everyone would soon arrive. She made a feeble attempt to look alert, but not before Beulah and Edith saw the tired look on her face.

Bobbie Jo and her husband were the first ones to arrive. They found the three women sitting in the living room, watching an old movie on

TV. Mavis had fallen asleep on the sofa. Beulah had placed a blanket over her, because, in spite of the warm day, Mavis had complained about being cold.

Others began to barge into the room, and voices became louder. Mavis sat up and looked embarrassed. She smiled and greeted everyone, before she disappeared into the kitchen to pop the rolls into the oven. Beulah followed her and said, "Now, Mavis, I can do all of this. You go rest. You've done enough."

"I'm fine. There's only a few things that need to be done. Then, I'll rest," she said with a weak smile. "As soon as everybody starts eating, I'm going to bed. I guess I'm getting too old to cook so much." She gave a soft chuckle.

"No, it ain't that. I'm worried bout you, Mavis. You need to go to the doctor. You've been tired for a long time now."

"I know. To be honest, I'm worried. I'm afraid of what the doctor's gonna say," Mavis answered, with tears in her eyes. "You're right. I need to go. And I can't get rid of this cough." On cue, she began coughing and holding her side. "Gosh! It causes a pain to shoot straight through me. I must have a really bad cold."

Beulah hugged her friend. "You go on to bed. Edith and I'll take care of everything."

"Thanks, Beulah. I'll do that. As soon as everybody starts eating."

During the meal, Marley Jane became aware that Mavis was nowhere to be seen. She asked, "Ms. Beulah, have you seen Mama? I can't find her in the kitchen, living room, or on the porch."

"She went to bed bout twenty minutes ago. She's done slap wore out. I just checked on her. She's sound asleep." She sighed. "She's got that old diaper round her head. So, she must have another one of them awful headaches. And she can't stop coughin. That worries me."

"Let's check on her," said Marley Jane. They walked down the hall. Marley Jane carefully opened the bedroom door. The room was dark.

Mavis was under two quilts that she and her mama had made when Mavis was a young girl. The sheet was pulled over her head, but Marley Jane could see the white of the diaper. She softly closed the door.

"Is she still sleepin?" asked Beulah.

"Yes. Don't tell anyone or someone might disturb her. We'll let her sleep." She started to move away, but stopped and touched Beulah's arm. "Ms. Beulah, I'm worried. Mama's not been herself for months. She's always tired. And she's lost weight. Now, she's started to cough all the time. I've told her to go to the doctor, but she won't listen." Marley Jane wasn't aware that she'd repeated much of what Beulah had said.

"I know. Edith and me done told her the same thing. You know yourself that your mama can be stubborn. But, somethin's got to be done. Somethin ain't right."

"I'm coming back to tomorrow. I'm going to try to talk to her. To get her to see a doctor."

◆

The next day, after church, Marley Jane went unannounced to Mavis' house. When she knocked on the door, no one answered. So, she got the hidden key and entered the house. The wood heater that sat almost in the middle of the living room floor—for as long as Marley Jane could remember—was putting out enough heat to warm the North Pole. There were no signs in the kitchen that anything had been cooked that morning. Everything was exactly as the sisters, Beulah, and Edith had left it the day before.

Marley Jane walked past the open door to Johnny Lee's room, without peeping inside. It was unusual for him to leave his door open, but she decided that he'd done so in order to hear Mavis. Her door was slightly open, enough of a crack for the light from a bedside lamp to shine through. Gently pushing the door, Marley Jane tiptoed inside the room. The shades were drawn, but shadows from outside sneaked through and moved across the walls. Mavis was curled in a ball beneath the heavy quilts.

Marley Jane stood beside the bed, looking down at her mama's curved back. She reached out to touch Mavis' shoulder and threw back her hand. Just as she turned to leave the room, Mavis rolled over and opened her eyes.

"What are you doing here? What time is it? Are you by yourself?" Mavis asked one question after the other, without waiting for answers. She sat upright and tossed the quilts to the side.

"It's one o'clock. I'm by myself." Sitting on the side of the bed beside Mavis, she asked, "Are you okay, Mama? I came to check on you. I'm worried about you. Being tired all the time. And coughing."

"Move, so I can get out of bed. Let's go sit in the living room. It's too cold in here."

Marley Jane got up and watched Mavis swing her legs off the side of the bed. She sat for a moment and breathed deeply. Marley Jane took the housecoat that lay at the foot of the bed and wrapped it around Mavis' shoulders. She put Mavis' feet into slippers that were half-hidden under the bed. As Mavis stood up, Marley Jane held her left arm, and they took their time walking into the living room. Mavis sat on the sofa.

"Turn on one of the lamps. And put some wood in the heater. I'm freezing to death."

"I'll need to bring in some wood before I leave," Marley Jane thought to herself. "Why can't Johnny Lee keep the wood box full?" She didn't say that aloud.

After stroking the fire, she said, "I'll fix you some breakfast or some left-overs. Or do you want soup or something else?"

"Give me a glass of buttermilk and cornbread. That settles my stomach. I'm not really hungry. Are you?" Mavis smoothed her housecoat and continued, "I don't seem to have a taste for much of anything."

Giving Mavis a worried look, Marley Jane walked into the kitchen.

Mavis could hear her, preparing the buttermilk and cornbread. Before long, she returned and sat a plate that contained a glass of the mixture and a spoon on the coffee table in front of Mavis.

"I hope I didn't put too much cornbread in it. If I did, I'll fix you some more."

Taking a small bite, Mavis said, "No. It's fine. Did you say you're by yourself? Is Johnny Lee here?"

"I'm by myself. I guess he is. Do you want me to check?"

"No. That's okay. Let him sleep."

Neither one said that he might be knocked out on drugs. Marley Jane knew that Mavis didn't want to deal with an irritated Johnny Lee. And she surely didn't want to listen to a drug induced rant.

"Why did you come?" Mavis asked, sitting the glass on the plate.

"Aren't you going to finish that?" Marley Jane asked, ignoring her mama.

"After while," Mavis replied. "Why did you come?"

"Because I'm worried about you, Mama. You're tired all of the time. And I wanted to talk with you, without everyone around. You've been tired for a long time. You can't stop coughing. And I think you need to go to a doctor for a good check-up."

Mavis looked at her daughter until Marley Jane looked at the floor. "I'm tired. A lot. I don't know what it is. And I've got so much pain. Sometimes, I can't stand up for more than ten minutes at a time." She sighed and looked at the wall behind Marley Jane. "Maybe, I'm getting old."

Some of what Mavis said was a lie. She had long suspected what was wrong with her. One day, over a year ago, while she was bathing, she noticed a lump in her breast. "Maybe, cancer," she thought, but quickly pushed that word into a dark corner of her mind, as she touched the lump again. It was the size of a butter bean, and it rolled like a child's smooth marble. The thought of cancer made her single-minded, selfish for time, greedy for life and more daylight hours, but she'd easily become fatigued, unable to stay awake or do things that she'd once enjoyed.

She thought that cancer, too, was greedy, snatching a person's energy and life. It wanted everything that one desired; it sneaked into a body, without giving a warning and invaded organs; it was stronger than anyone's will. Cancer became an unacceptable word, and she used all of her mental power to push the word out of her mind.

Marley Jane got up and sat beside Mavis. "It's not because you're old, Mama," she said, taking Mavis' hand. "I don't know what it is, but it's not that. Promise me that you'll go to the doctor. I'll call tomorrow and make an appointment. Okay?"

Mavis rested her head on the back of the sofa and closed her eyes against the light from the lamp. She was aware that she was becoming weaker each day and that her world had become a bed, four walls, two windows, and a door. She was as tired of that as she was of being just plain tired.

She opened her eyes and sighed wearily, "I'll make the appointment myself. Tomorrow. And I'll get Edith to take me to the doctor. Don't worry. I'm sure there's nothing wrong. Now, how bout a slice of that sweet potato pie? If any's left."

"Okay. I'm calling you tomorrow to remind you to call the doctor. And don't tell me that you did when you didn't. Because I'm going to call Ms. Edith, too. I'll get the pie."

After they'd eaten pie and drank a cup of freshly brewed coffee, Marley Jane washed the few dishes and put them away. She sat near the heater with Mavis. They talked for a little over an hour, and Marley Jane realized that Mavis was getting tired.

"I'm going to fill the wood box, and, then, I'm leaving. Can I do anything for you before I go?"

"No. I'm going back to bed. Just lock the door when you leave." By the time she'd finished talking, she was halfway down the hall. Marley Jane followed her into the bedroom and helped her into bed. She kissed Mavis' forehead. Next, she closed Mavis' door, filled the wood box, turned off the lamp, and locked the kitchen door behind her. As soon as she left, Mavis was sound asleep.

The next day Mavis made an appointment with her family doctor. Edith drove her to the doctor's office and sat in the waiting room, while Mavis saw the doctor. He told Mavis that her iron was probably low and that she was worn out from worry and work. For pain, he recommended Ibuprofen several times a day. Edith was surprised that he didn't order any tests or blood work.

Everyone was busy preparing for Christmas, so no one but Beulah and Edith were aware that seeing the doctor hadn't accomplished anything. They sympathized with Mavis when her children asked about her health and she became upset. It was clear to them that Mavis was trying hard to put up a front.

♦

Christmas dinner was at Mavis' house. All of her children and most of the grandchildren came. Again, Mavis spent weeks preparing. Again, Johnny Lee, Edith, and Beulah observed an exhausted Mavis drag from one day to the next. Mavis had developed a cough that wouldn't go away and kept her awake at night. Another trip to the doctor yielded little of nothing.

Mavis' daughters discussed her cough soon after they arrived for Christmas dinner. They whispered among themselves as they went back and forth from the kitchen to the dining room with food. A comment was made that the cough had become more intense since Thanksgiving. What benefit had the doctor visits produced?

Changing the topic when Mavis walked up to the tight group, Bobbie Jo said, "I had a dream last night." Everyone stopped talking to listen. "It was a dream bout Daddy. It's the first time, in all the years since he's been dead, that I've dreamed bout him."

Before she could continue, Mavis said, "That means I'm gonna die. He came to get me."

No one spoke. They knew that Mavis believed in dreams and analyzed them. She had an Elizabethan belief in dreams, and she was as good as Shakespeare in determining their symbolism.

"Mama, no, I don't think that's true," Bobbie Jo said in shock, sorry that she'd mentioned the dream. She should've known better, because she knew how much value Mavis placed on dreams.

"Yes. It's true."

Beulah felt a jab at her heart and fear filled her throat, because she, too, believed in dreams. She tried to erase Mavis' quiet statement by saying, "It ain't nothin but a dream, Mavis. It's Christmas. Naturally, BobbieJo—or any of us—might have a dream bout somebody who's dead."

Mavis gave Beulah a crooked grin, but there was no denying the sadness in her eyes, when she said, "Well, anyway, Edith, will you ask the blessing? Janet, tell everybody to come in here."

After grace, the noise level rose while people talked and bumped into one another as they made their way around the long table, filling their plates. They drifted into the living room, kitchen, and onto the back porch to eat. The day was sunny and much cooler than Thanksgiving had been. Still, it was the South, and the weather often changed in the blink of an eye.

When it was time to open gifts, Marley Jane didn't see Mavis. "Where's Mama?" she asked Zelda.

"I don't know, but I don't like that cough she's got," Zelda said, as she cut a slice of Italian cream cake.

"BobbieJo, where's Mama?" Marley Jane asked.

"I don't know. I saw her a minute ago. Has anyone seen Mama?" she asked those who were nearby.

Laura Faye said, "She told me that she was going to bed."

Word spread that Mavis was tired and had gone to bed. Gifts were exchanged, and Janet placed Mavis's many gifts to the far left of the tree. Afterwards, the women cleared the table, filled the dishwasher, and washed the pots and pans. The men stood or sat on the back porch and continued to talk. The younger children chased one another and tumbled on the wide back yard, while the older ones played tag football or sat in the living room, watching TV.

Within two hours, everyone had left, except Edith and Beulah. They stood outside Mavis' bedroom door and listened to the cough that had gotten worst in the past weeks. Then, they tiptoed quietly away and sat around the wood heater with Johnny Lee, who listened to their concerns and shared their feelings.

The next morning, he called Laura Faye to tell her that he wasn't coming to work. Instead, he was taking Mavis to the doctor. He gently shook Mavis awake. "What's the matter?" she asked, in a low hoarse voice.

"Get up, Mama. Get dressed. I'm takin you to the doctor. Come on. I'll help you," he instructed, holding her left arm.

Mavis sat on the side of the bed and looked at Johnny Lee. She'd realized that reality refused to step aside or to take a vacation so that she could continue to ignore the cough, the fatigue, the pain, or the lost weight. The headaches were almost unbearable. Sleep was the only thing that eased the pounding in her head or made her forget the pain that cut through her body.

Three hours later, Johnny Lee called Laura Faye to tell her that Mavis had been admitted to the hospital. Johnny Lee had raised hell with the doctor, demanding that something be done, that "By, god, this is the third time she's been to see you, and you ain't done a damn thing, but talk shit."

Laura Faye had recommended this particular doctor who didn't like being ordered around by a smart-ass. But, in spite of his feelings, he ordered a series of tests as well as blood work to be drawn, just to satisfy Johnny Lee and to shut him up. By that afternoon, all of Mavis' children were at the hospital.

Two days later, the results of the tests were complete. Things didn't look good. Mavis' white blood count was extremely high; therefore, her body was fighting something. Fluid had settled around her lungs, and they needed to be immediately drained. The doctor scheduled a PET scan.

Everyone began to worry, because, by now, they'd begun to suspect that cancer might be the enemy that'd been robbing their mama of energy and weight. Mavis stayed calm and made few comments. Beulah wouldn't leave her side and firmly held her hand. In the afternoon, Mavis insisted that Beulah go home. She couldn't stay out of work any longer.

When all of the test results were received, the doctor took the charts the next morning and went to Mavis' room. She was alone, staring out the window at the fog that was a cold blanket over the Chattahoochee River. Although at least one son or daughter had been with Mavis since she'd been admitted to the hospital, no one was with her at the moment. Janet, Zelda, and Marley Jane had gone to the cafeteria for breakfast. The children had made it clear to the doctor not to give Mavis any bad news, unless at least one of them was present. He wasn't the type of doctor who listened to his patients' children.

Mavis turned her head to the door as the doctor entered. She steered herself for something terrible, for horrible news. Weeks ago, she'd assumed the worst scenario in her head, and she wished that someone— one of her children or Beulah—was with her. Looking at the doctor's face, she knew that today was a turning point in her life.

In a faraway place, covered in fog, she heard the doctor's voice, giving her a life sentence. Her eyes grew cloudy as she listened to the diagnosis of cancer that was in stage four and had begun to spread throughout her body. The doctor's words came out of the heavy fog, which seemed to have stolen into the room from the Chattahoochee. "Not long. Maybe, six to nine months. It's spreading throughout your body" became tattooed on her brain. The fog was in her head, smothering her breath. She looked out the window, but she couldn't see anything for the fog. It crept across the windowpane. It crawled inside her head and perplexed her thinking.

"Mrs. Norrell, did you hear me? Do you have any questions?"

She lay stone-faced, trying to accept the truth that death would soon arrive, an unwanted visitor. It wouldn't be an acquaintance that merely came and went. Death, a power beyond control, would leave and take his prey. No one was safe. No one escaped. No one could flee death. Everyone was exposed to the entity of death.

Mavis knew, of course, that there are no guarantees in life. Strings were attached to every aspect of living. She knew that death stole a person's bodily possessions, leaving, in the end, material things that didn't matter. Finally, it left only bones. The flesh—the soul—gone. Gone to an unknown. Away from everyone and everything, good and bad, that you'd ever known. It was terrifying, and she knew it was the terror that she had to conquer before she died. She might be able to conquer the fear, but never death. Already, she felt its presence. Suddenly, she had a tenacious desire to live.

Salty tears slid down her cheeks. There was no sound of crying. Mavis thought, "What's the next phase of being, of existence? Is there really anything beyond this world?" She'd never been the type of person who pondered questions that deal with the hereafter. Until now, it'd not really mattered, not been real, not something that she worried about too often.

She turned to look at the pudgy doctor who had a full moon face and a small head that sat on his stocky body, making it look as if something had pushed his head into his shoulders. His hair was curly and dry. He wore black-rimmed glasses and his eyes looked empty behind the lenses. For the first time, she noticed that his small eyes were almost black and that his lips were thin and straight. Suddenly, she despised the man whom Laura Faye had insisted she see. He was a freak whom the other doctors distrusted. Mavis made a note to insist that her regular doctor be contacted. She didn't want anything further to do with the stocky doctor whose nails were bitten to the point that his fingertips were raw and peeling.

"Any questions?" he repeated, without once having touched her hand or shoulder. She was glad that he'd not touched her, because he'd brought into the room the icy hand of death. And death's coldness clung to him like a loose garment.

"No," she answered in a dull voice. Her eyes turned away from him and she looked out the window at the thick fog as it gripped the window.

"I'll be back this afternoon. If you have any questions, we'll talk then," the small, tight mouth said.

Mavis didn't respond or turn her head. After several seconds, he left the room and closed the door. Only then, did she allow the tears to come freely and the malevolent noises to escape from her open mouth.

◆

Janet, Zelda, and Marley Jane returned from the hospital cafeteria and found Mavis crying. They ran to her bedside. All asked the same question, "What's wrong, Mama?"

"I'm dying. I was right about BobbieJo's dream. The doctor just left. He says I've got six—maybe, nine—months to live." She erupted into loud sobs and her body shook.

"We all told that fool not to talk to you, unless one of us was here!" Zelda said in anger.

Janet, who'd never stopped bossing her siblings, looked at Marley

Jane and ordered, "Call his office and make an appointment for us to go down there and talk to him. Now!"

The three sisters were furious. While Janet and Zelda expressed disdain for the doctor, Marley Jane called his office. Her voice was calm, giving no indication of the anger that raged inside of her.

"To whom am I speaking?" A pause. "I'm Marley Jane, Mrs. Mavis Norrrell's daughter. Doctor Ruthledge left my mother's room approximately thirty minutes ago. She's upset. My sisters and I are upset. He didn't follow our instructions about discussing my mother's illness, with at least one of her children present. My sisters and I would like to meet with him as soon as possible. Before I contact the administrator of the hospital, the medical association, and, possibly, an attorney. How soon can we meet with him?"

After listening for a while, she said, "Okay. Call me at this number as soon as he returns to his office." She gave the number for the phone in the room.

"His secretary will call me as soon as he arrives at his office," she told her sisters.

At that moment, Laura Faye arrived. It broke her heart to watch Mavis cry. It scared her when she heard the diagnosis. Also, it infuriated her that Doctor Edward Ruthledge had heartlessly given her mama a death sentence, while she was alone. She wrapped her arms around Mavis and cried uncontrollably.

Two hours later, they received a call from the doctor's office. By that time, all of Mavis' children, plus some grandchildren had arrived. They stayed with Mavis, while Janet, Zelda, and Marley Jane walked down the hill to the doctor's office. Janet and Zelda talked angrily about how they intended to give "that crazy doctor" a piece of their minds. Marley Jane said nothing, as she rehearsed what she planned to say to the man whom she decided probably shouldn't be practicing medicine. She'd heard rumors. Maybe, the rumors were true. Good doctor or bad doctor,

Marley Jane hated him at the moment.

Doctor Ruthledge sat behind a large oak desk, with his medical degrees from a northern university on the wall behind him. His eyes were hard and his lips were tight. It was obvious that he was ready for three little nobodies from a cotton mill town. Lent heads. Uneducated. Mill workers. He didn't stand or speak when they entered, but continued to write on a pad in front of him.

Marley Jane sat down and her sisters followed suit. They waited until he finished writing and looked up, with a bored expression on his full face. He got straight to the point. "I understand that some of you are upset that I discussed your mother's medical condition without one of her children being present," he stated in a flat, condescending tone.

Janet immediately said, "Marley Jane's not happy. She wants to talk with you."

Marley Jane sensed that her jaw was about to drop. She pressed her lips together and glared at her oldest sibling.

Zelda quickly added, "Marley Jane wants to talk with you." She puckered her voluminous lips, crossed her slender legs, smoothed her dress, and tilted her head in an innocent child-like pose.

"What the hell!" thought Marley Jane. She quickly realized that they didn't want to question the decision of an authority figure, which she had absolutely no hesitation about doing. And, if the dough-faced man in front of her thought for one second that he intimidated her, he'd missed the clues.

Dough-face raised an eyebrow and looked at her, waiting. He didn't have to wait more than a second.

"That's true. I'm not happy," she said in a calm voice that sounded as if she were explaining something to her students. The man in front of her had no idea that it was the calm that had surpassed the storm. The calm that was more deadly than any storm. It was a calm that sweetly announced, "I'll stomp out your sorry heart, pull out your eyeballs, and shove them down your throat, while I spit in your face."

Dough-face interrupted her to say, "I understand you threatened my secretary. You told her that you'd report me to the administrator of the hospital, the medical association, and, possibly, hire an attorney. Is that true?"

"Yes. It's true. And, make no mistake, I will. Although I don't know if an attorney will take a case based on the fact that the doctor has a lousy bedside manner, but I do think that others will listen. Now that we understand one another, I'll continue. I'm not simply unhappy. I'm furious that a doctor will demonstrate such outrageous contempt for a patient and the family, totally disregarding all of their wishes. By walking into a room, with cold-hearted disregard, and giving someone a life sentence. Did you comfort her? No! Did you hold her hand? No! Did you ask if you could call a family member? No! Did you care? No! Did you—"

"I'm not obligated to my patients' families. Medical information is between a doctor and the patient. No one else," he interrupted.

"Mr. Ruthledge, I understand the law," Marley Jane hissed, deliberately refusing to address him as a doctor. "And the law also states that if the patient agrees, in your presence, to share information with someone else, that is what you do. My mother made it clear to you that she agreed with my sister, Laura Faye, that you would not give my mother the results of the tests, until one of her children was in the room with her. You totally disregarded her wishes. And, that is where you made a serious mistake. That is the valid reason for the threats—promises—that I made to your secretary.

"In my opinion, you are a sorry excuse for a doctor and a man. I'm deeply disappointed, hurt, and angry. From your behavior, I don't think that you regret the decision that you made. You have learned nothing," she said and stood to leave.

The doctor looked at his desk and back at Marley Jane. "Perhaps, I was wrong. If so, I apologize for any hurt that I've caused you or your family."

The three sisters paused at the door. Janet and Zelda looked out the window at the Chattahoochee River. Marley Jane said, "I accept your apology, but I'll never respect you. My mother's dying, and you did a cruel thing. Hopefully, you've learned something. Some compassion. Thank you for meeting with us."

She turned her back to the man who was now standing behind his desk; she opened the door and started out, ahead of her sisters. She quickly turned around and said, "We want an oncologist to see Mama. And we want her family doctor called in to take over. Make those two calls. Immediately. When you've done that, the threats will be taken off the table." Her hard eyes held the doctor's eyes, and she was aware that her left eye had begun to twitch, which happened when she was extremely angry. Janet and Zelda had noticed it earlier and knew that Marley Jane had entered a dangerous anger zone.

As they walked back up the hill to the hospital, she said to Janet and Zelda, "Thanks for throwing me under the bus. And, Janet, it was your idea for us to talk to that fool. You went all soft, like the flour you put in your cakes. And, Zelda, you acted like some sweet school girl who was flirting."

When they got to Mavis' room, Beulah and Edith were there, one on each side of the bed, holding Mavis' hands. Edith was telling a story about old man Bell, and the three friends were laughing. At the end of the story, Beulah said, "I'm takin off work a couple of days when you get home. Me and you and Edith is gonna get in the car and just ride. Go wherever you wanna go. Do whatever you wanna do. You be thinkin bout that. Make some plans."

"There ain't any need in me making plans. Bout anything," Mavis said in a tired voice, as she picked at a loose thread on the blanket. "And, of course, the cruise is off." No one replied.

"No, Mavis," Beulah corrected her, "you're wrong bout that. You gotta fight. You gotta live every day the good Lord gives you. And me and Edith, we gonna be there, with you. You hear me, Mavis? We gonna be there." She stroked Mavis' cheek and smiled. "You're a fighter, girl. I ain't never knowed you to give up. Don't give up now. Please, don't."

Mavis nodded her head and smiled at Beulah. "I'll try. I'll try my best."

Bobbie Jo spoke up, "That's all we ask, Mama. Just try. Fight." Her siblings agreed.

"Okay. Now, I want everybody to leave, but Edith and Beulah," Mavis told her family. Each one kissed her and drifted slowly out of the room.

"Stay out of trouble," Richard instructed the three women, as he waved from the doorway.

When they'd gone, Mavis said, "I need y'all both now more than ever. Just to be with me. To stop by and talk. When y'all stop by, I don't want y'all to be all droopy and down. Y'all two know more bout me than my kids. Half of them have no idea who I am. That's okay." She stopped talking and looked at the river. The fog had disappeared.

"When I'm gone, I want y'all to check on Johnny Lee—every now and then. I've got some things at the house I want y'all to have. Edith, you know how much you like them pickles I make every year? You can have all of them, and I'm giving you the recipe. You've been asking for it for a long time. Now, I'm gonna give it to you."

Edith said, "Now, after all this time, you're gonna just give it to me?"

Mavis stared at Edith in disbelief. "Edith, I'm dying. What do I need with a damn recipe? If I go to hell, I'll be what's cooking. If I go to heaven, nobody has to eat."

Beulah sniggered. Edith didn't find it too funny that here Mavis was, on her deathbed, still behaving in a manner that Edith considered blasphemous. "For goodness sake, Mavis, when are you gonna stop testin God?" She reminded herself, more times than she could recall, how useless it was to argue with Mavis. Some things never change.

Mavis shook her head and continued, as if Edith had never spoken, "Beulah, I'm giving you the gold loop earrings. You've been wanting them since the first day that we met.

"I want both of y'all to sing at my funeral. Separately. You sing first, Edith so that I can laugh at death. You next, Beulah, so that I can leave with beautiful sounds in my ears." She looked at Edith's sad face and added, "You know I've always liked to tease you bout your singing. You sing better than me. That's a fact. Now, let's talk bout kicking up our heels before it's too late." Beulah and Edith nodded their heads, but they didn't speak. Tears filled their eyes and they squeezed Mavis' hands.

For over an hour, they planned things that they'd do when Mavis got home. They agreed to take one day at a time, taking advantage of the days that Mavis would feel well enough to get out and about. They verbally completed a list of things that they wanted to do after Mavis was dismissed from the hospital. They were quiet, as sadness began to sweep over them. Then, Edith farted. It was loud and drawn out. The rotten odor caused them to gag and cough.

"Holy moly! Are you trying to bomb us to death? Edith, open the door. Let that awful smell outa here before we die from inhaling too much gas. Beulah, press the button for the nurse. Tell her that we need some oxygen," Mavis said, followed by exaggerated coughs. "My eyes are watering cause they're stinging from all that gas."

Looking embarrassed, Edith opened the door and noticed that the scent moved with her. She turned to face Mavis. "It musta been them big butter beans and onions I ate for dinner. They always give me gas."

Shaking her head and giving a fake cough, Mavis corrected her, "No. It musta been that skunk you ate. That smell is too bad for butter beans and onions."

Beulah was laughing and slapping the side of the bed. Mavis and

Edith joined her. A nurse stuck her head inside the room. She didn't find too much humor in a fart, but she smiled because her patient was laughing. When Laura Faye returned, with an overnight bag, she found the three women howling with laughter.

When they managed to stop laughing, Mavis told Laura Faye that she wanted to spend a week at the condo in Panama City, with Beulah and Edith, soon after she left the hospital. Laura Faye thought that it was a good idea. It pleased her to hear Mavis laughing and making plans.

"You tell me when, Mama. You've got a key. Who's gonna drive y'all to the condo?"

"Edith. Course that might scare two months off my life. Plus, the way she speeds up and slows down, it might take longer than I've got to get there. But, I'll risk it." Beulah laughed and Edith rolled her eyes.

Mavis continued in a melancholy voice, "I wanna hear the ocean and walk on the beach. I wanna watch the sun come up and go down. And I wanna see the moonlight on the waves as they come to shore." The sadness in her voice touched all of them.

"Mama, you know it's gonna be cold. It might be too cold to walk on the beach."

"I don't care. It's what I wanna do." She paused for a long time. They waited. "It'll be the last time I'll see the ocean. I wanna see it one more time."

"Whatever you want, Mama. Just tell me," Laura Faye said as she pushed a strand of hair away from Mavis' right eye.

Mavis looked at Beulah and Edith. "Okay. Y'all leave. I want to sleep. I'm tired. It's been a long day."

Each one kissed Mavis' silky cheek. They blew kisses from the doorway and waved. When they left, Mavis asked Laura Faye to turn off the lights. Soon, soft snoring filled the room, while Laura Faye read by the window. She'd read a page and break into soft tears, as her heart broke into fragments that'd never again be pieced correctly together.

Her heart had become a scattered puzzle, with an important piece missing.

CHAPTER SIXTEEN

After the oncologist and Mavis' family doctor consulted with one another, they decided that no amount of radiation or chemo would have improved the quality or quantity of Mavis' life, but they let her make the decision, which was a quick, firm "No!" Two days later, Mavis went home. Laura Faye and Johnny Lee settled her into the Yukon, and the vehicle left the hospital parking lot.

Mavis looked behind her at the building that held good and bad memories. Her two youngest children were born there, as well as many of her grandchildren. Her mama and daddy had died there, as well as her husband. Soon, she'd be with them, but she didn't want to think about that right now. She gave one final look at the four-story brick building that sat on a cliff, high above the twisting Chattahoochee River that never stopped flowing and gurgling its way to the Gulf of Mexico.

As the vehicle pulled into the gravel driveway, Mavis watched as the rest of her children and several of her grandchildren came and stood on the back porch. Claude took her bag from the trunk of the vehicle. Richard took her left elbow and guided her up the steps. By the time that she reached the sofa, she was exhausted. It was then that she noticed Beulah and Edith at the kitchen door.

"Hi, y'all," she said and waved at them. "Come on in here, near the heater, where it's nice and warm."

"Is it too hot for you, Mama?" Johnny Lee asked.

"No. No, it feels good. I stay cold all the time. What's that I smell cooking?"

"Ms. Beulah made some vegetable soup and Ms. Edith cooked a roast with potatoes and carrots. Janet made a lemon pie. BobbieJo made a chocolate pound cake," Zelda said. "Are you hungry, Mama?"

"Not right now. I'll eat a bite after a while," Mavis answered, as she slipped out of her coat. She really wanted to go to bed, but they'd all come to see her and to eat dinner. So, she smiled and made small talk, allowing her children and grandchildren to fuss over her. All of the talking and questions irritated her, but she continued to smile.

Beulah saw the tired look in Mavis' eyes and noticed her sagging shoulders. She sat beside Mavis and held one of her cool, too bony hands. Patting the soft hand, with the long, slender fingers, Beulah said in a low voice, "If you're tired, go on to bed. We'll understand. You've done a lots this mornin."

"It's okay. I'll stay up a little longer," Mavis said and patted Beulah's hand.

"All right then, I'm gonna bring you a bowl of soup. Stay there. I'm gonna get you some sweet tea with lemon, too." Mavis nodded and smiled.

After Mavis ate a third of the soup, she announced, "I think I'm gonna lay down. Y'all go on and have dinner. Beulah. Edith. I'll see y'all tomorrow, and we'll plan our trip."

She allowed Edith and Beulah to lead her into the bedroom. Edith located a flannel gown that was covered in small blue flowers, while Beulah turned down the covers. Mavis popped a pain pill in her mouth and took a slow drink of water. Afterwards, she put the diaper around her head, didn't remove her socks, and climbed into bed.

"Thank y'all. Now, go get y'all something to eat. Let me sleep late in the morning, and I'll see y'all bout eleven o'clock." By the time her two friends had reached the door, Mavis had turned onto her left side and was falling into a deep sleep.

The next day was cloudy and cold. Dark sooty clouds rolled across a sky that was gloomy and overcast. Mavis slept until eight-thirty. She slipped her feet into fur-lined bed slippers and snuggled into a worn, soft purple chenille housecoat. Not bothering to remove the diaper from around her head, she walked slowly into the living room, where the wood heater roared with yellow and red flames from the abundance of logs that Johnny Lee had stacked inside its flaming belly, before he left for work. He'd wanted to stay with Mavis, but she'd insisted on the way home from the hospital that she'd rather he go to work, because she knew that her children were plotting to take turns staying with her, twenty-four-seven. She planned to delay that as long as she could.

Mavis sat on the sofa and clicked on the television. Another presidential election was gearing up. She listened for ten minutes and thought, "I don't have any more interest in politics. I always enjoyed presidential elections, but I can't seem to care so much these days. I wish I still cared. I do hope folks don't elect no crazy war-thirsty, ass-kicking loony bin. We've done been involved in way too many needless wars." She sighed, got up, and went into the kitchen. She took her pain pill and leaned against the counter, with her eyes closed.

Before she started a pot of coffee, she looked out the window and saw Sadie Smith on the porch. Sadie lived approximately three hundred yards down the road from Mavis. They'd been neighbors and friends for more than thirty years. The Smith family was the only African-American family on Hopewell Road. Their children had played with Mavis' and Edith's children. Sadie had spent many days with Mavis, Beulah, and Edith, preparing fruits and vegetables for canning or freezing. Also, she'd been a fill-in cook at Mid-Way Café, off and on for years.

The big-boned woman held something in her hands. Before Sadie could knock on the door, Mavis sat the coffee can on the counter and opened the side door that led into the kitchen. "Come inside, Sadie. Get in outa that cold. You're just in time. I'm bout to make a pot of coffee. And I got some chocolate pound cake," Mavis said, holding the door wide. Sadie and the cold air entered the warm kitchen.

"Coffee'll be good. It's a good day for hot coffee. I brought you a pan of biscuits, ready to stick in the oven. Didn't figure you'd feel too much like cookin this mornin." She placed the pan of biscuits on the stovetop. "Can I help with anything?"

"No. Take a seat and keep me company. It's good to see you. How's James?" Mavis asked, as she turned on the oven.

"He ain't doin too good these days. Arthritis and bad health done took its toll on him. He can't hardly get round no more. Of course, he uses a cane some, but it's hard for him. But, you knows how he be. Tough as nails."

The smell of coffee permeated the room. Mavis got two cups and saucers, two plates, a jar of her fig preserves, utensils, paper towels for napkins, and butter. Sadie watched as each thing was brought to the table, and she noticed that Mavis moved almost as slow as molasses. Quickly, she turned her attention to what Mavis was saying about fig preserves and how she wanted Sadie to take five or six pints home with her.

"We'll have some coffee, buttered biscuits, and fig preserves. There's nothing better on a day like today. Tell me what you've been up to since I last saw you," Mavis instructed, as she poured coffee into two cups that had a dancing Mickey Mouse on each one.

"Not much. I sho am sorry I didn't git to the hospital to see you. Like I told you, James has been real sick these days. His whole body's done crippled up on him, so bad he can't hardly stand it. It's just me and him. So, I can't leave him too long by hisself," she said, stirring cream and sugar into the strong coffee, until it turned a creamy light brown. "I came to see you. To check on how you're doin. I been mighty worried bout you," she said and laid her left hand on Mavis' right hand.

"Thank you, Sadie. I'm dying," Mavis stated, as matter-of-fact as if she were discussing the weather. She held up her hand to stop her long-time friend from interrupting. "Other than that, I guess I'm doing pretty good." She laughed. "Now, don't misunderstand me. I'm not being a smart-ass. Just stating facts."

Sadie laughed and said, "I know. You good at statin facts. Don't I know it? Lord! The times you shocked me and made me laugh. Ain't nobody else like you, Mavis. God deliberately broke the mold after He made you. That's for sho. Maybe, that's why He think you so special."

"Well, He must not think I'm too special. He's letting me die." She laughed again. "He might be tired of me being a smarty pants. You reckon?"

"No, I don't think that's it a tall. I think He needs another angel. That's my opinion. Now, tell me how you doin?" She sipped the sweet coffee and added, "For real."

Mavis buttered a biscuit, which she had no desire to eat. She smeared fig preserves on top of the melting butter and laid the biscuit on her plate. Finally, she looked up and said, "For real? I'm scared as hell. I'm afraid to die, but I'm working on accepting it. That's hard. I wonder, 'Why me?' You know? Then, I think, 'Why not me. If not me, someone else.' And it's so confusing. But, the bottom line is that I'm scared. I try not to show it. But, I'm not gonna lie. I'm scared."

She picked up the biscuit and took a small bite. After she swallowed, she spoke again. "And I'm mad. Mad as hell. I keep using the word 'Hell.' I hope that doesn't mean anything." They both laughed.

"Them things all seems normal to me. I'd feel the same way. Most folks would, if they was honest. It's human nature. But, trust in the Lord. Is you in a lotta pain?"

"I was in bad pain. Since I went to the hospital, the doctor gave me some pills for pain. They've helped a whole lot. And I'm wearing a pain patch. The pain no longer feels like rats chewing on my insides." Mavis toyed with her knife. "Hospice will be coming to visit me some time this afternoon. You know what that means."

"Are you stayin by yoself? I mean you and Johnny Lee?" Sadie asked, ignoring Mavis' comment about Hospice.

"I am for a while. Beulah, Edith, and I are going to Panama City to Laura Faye's condo for a week. We're leaving tomorrow. I'd like for you to go with us. It'll be cold, but we can see the ocean."

Sadie waved her hand. "No. Thank you for the invite, but I can't go. I gotta stay home with James."

"When I get back home, one of the girls will take turns staying with me every day. I don't too much like the idea, but they insisted. And I don't feel like arguing." Mavis took her time, stirring her coffee before she continued. "I don't really mind. I don't want to listen to their remarks bout Johnny Lee. It's for the best though. I guess. I just don't want to argue bout it," she said and sighed.

Sadie thought about how much Mavis enjoyed a good argument, but she didn't say so. Instead, she said, "It's a good thing they stayin with you. You don't needs to worry bout cleanin, cookin, or washin clothes. None of that stuff. All you needs to do is rest and stay strong. If you needs me, I'm down the road. Give me a call. Most of the time, I can sneak away for a few minutes."

She stood up. "As a matter of fact, I needs to git back." She carried all of the dishes to the sink, rinsed them, and placed them in the dishwasher.

Mavis stood up. "Let me give you the fig preserves. They're on the top shelf on the cabinet in the corner. If you don't mind getting them down for me. My balance ain't so good."

Sadie stood on a chair and took down six jars of preserves. Mavis placed them in one of her favorite straw baskets that she'd used for years to gather vegetables from the garden. "Keep the basket. It's handy for all sorts of stuff." They hugged one another, and Mavis walked with Sadie to the door.

"If you needs me, call. I'll do what I can. You always had my back. Stood up for me and helped me in all sorts a ways. I ain't never forgot none of that. I love you, Mavis. You're a good person. You got a carin heart."

Mavis hugged Sadie again. "You're kind. We've helped one another. You've been there for me, too. It's been equal. Come back soon."

"I will. Bye now," she said, "and lock the door behind me."

◆

As she watched Sadie walk down the steps, Mavis recalled a long ago incident, and she knew that it was one reason Sadie said that Mavis always had her back. Mavis let her mind wander back to a brisk windy March Saturday, many years ago. A ferocious rain had fallen since midnight. The Smith family was awakened by a loud banging on the front door of the run-down weather-beaten wood house that was constructed of paper-thin boards and no insulation. Here and there, throughout the house, were slits that allowed the sun to slide through or the cold to blow into the crooked rooms. Newspaper was stuffed in large cracks in the walls.

Soon, the banging was followed by, "Smith, git out here! Git yo ass to the door, old man!"

Sadie and James sat up in bed. Sadie's short hair stood up in spikes, as if she'd been spooked. James' brown eyes were large with fear. They listened for several minutes.

"It's Mr. Tully. He be here to git the rent. Guess he couldn't wait til daylight," James said, swinging his twisted legs off the bed.

Sadie threw back the covers and reached for her housecoat that was at the foot of the bed. She changed her mind and began to dress. "You go to the door, while I git dressed. We ain't but one day late with the rent.

Why he be so upset?"

Wiggling his twisted legs into a pair of overalls, James answered, "True, but we been late a lotta times. I guess he be real mad. He gonna teach us a lesson. Nothin to do but face the music. You check on the young'uns."

He limped to the front door. His upper body was bent forward as if he walked through a storm. It was obvious that his left leg dragged slightly behind his right leg. All of his life he'd managed with his twisted legs and stooped body. It didn't make him shy away from labor. Since he was thirteen, he'd been employed on the second shift at Langdale Mill.

It wasn't in his nature to complain. Life had dealt him a certain hand. In spite of that, he'd married a good woman and they had seven beautiful children. He had a job, and Sadie worked as a maid to help out. They barely made it from paycheck to paycheck. Life was hard.

By the time that James opened the door, Sadie was standing behind him, peeping over his right shoulder. They were looking at a red face and furious eyes that belonged to a tall, heavy-set man who wore a yellow raincoat.

"It's bout damn time y'all opened the door. My guys here was bout to kick it in. Ain't no need in me tellin y'all that y'all are late—again—with the rent. I done told y'all and told y'all I'm tired of it. So, I'm here to put y'all out."

The two dark faces looked at him in disbelief. Sadie said in anger, before her husband could speak, "We's only one day late. We was gonna pay you today as soon as I could get Mrs. Norrelll to drive me to yo house. You can take the money now."

As she turned her back, he ordered, "Stop! Ain't no need a that. I'm puttin y'all out. Today! I—"

"In the pourin rain? Is you serious?" Sadie asked, with more shock and anger than she intended.

"Yep! Today! Okay, boys, start totin stuff out. Put everything on side a the road."

"Mr. Tully, it's rainin for God's sake. My children's sleepin. It's barely daylight. Why can't you take the money?" Sadie pleaded.

"Cause it's bout time you people learned a lesson," he said in an angry tone. "Start with the kitchen," he ordered the two rough-looking men, and he pointed in the direction of the kitchen.

Sadie turned her back on the red face. Her children stood in the living room, in their nightclothes. They were huddled together, and their eyes were full of fear. The oldest girl held the youngest one close to her side.

"Y'all get dressed. Put y'all's clothes in pillowcases. I'm gonna go and get Ms. Mavis. Stay inside the house, unless that man runs you out. Then, stay on the porch." As she gave instructions, she put on thick socks and heavy shoes. When she finished, she grabbed the almost useless umbrella and headed out the back door. She was thankful that the rain was a weak drizzle, and she prayed that it'd stop.

Sadie half walked and half ran to Mavis' house, which was over a mile from the rain-soaked house that now sagged in shame. She ran onto the back porch and beat on the door, just as Tully Hodnet had done at her house, less than an hour earlier. Through the loud knocking, she heard Mavis yell, "I'm coming! Hold your horses!"

By the time that Mavis opened the door, tears were running down Sadie's face, and she was soaked from the rain. The umbrella hadn't been much help. "He's puttin us out in the rain! We told him we got the money. But, he didn't listen. He said that he gonna teach us a lesson. Please, Ms. Mavis, you gotta help us."

"What? Are you telling me that old man Hodnet is evicting y'all in the rain? That mean-ass-son-of-a-bitch! Let me get on my housecoat and get the car keys," Mavis said. "Come inside, Sadie, and stand near the heater, cause it's still chilly in the mornings, especially with this rain."

Before Sadie could feel the heat from the wood heater, Mavis was motioning for her. As Mavis broke the speed limit over the slippery highway, Sadie told her exactly what had happened. Mavis flew into the muddy driveway and slammed on the brakes. In front of her, two men walked onto the porch, pulling a dolly that carried the stove.

"Put down that stove! And, by god, I mean this very minute!" In her haste to get out of the car, she left the car door open. Suddenly, the rain came down like a mighty force and soaked her within seconds. The men stared at the wild looking woman who resembled a mad drowning animal.

"I said, 'Put down that stove!' Now! And where is that son-of-a-bitch?"

Tully Hodnet appeared on the porch, with his arms folded across his chest. He spread his large legs. "Now, Ms. Mavis, you ain't got no dog in this here fight. Go on back home and mind yo own business."

"The hell I don't! It's my business when I see somebody being mistreated. And, furthermore, I'm gonna show you how much it's my business. If you don't have those men stop what they're doing, and y'all leave, I'm getting in my car, with Sadie, and we're going to Lafayette, right now, and swear out a warrant on you. Now, what's it gonna be?" By then, she was standing on the porch, while water dripped from her hair and ran into her eyes. It fell off of her clothing and made a small puddle at her feet.

Rain echoed around them, and they heard it hit the tin roof. Thunder sounded like a freight train and was followed by a long, white streak of lightening. Two angry faces confronted one another. Tully was considering that he knew Mavis' daddy. He and her daddy had owned most of Hopewell community at one time. Dewey still owned large tracts of land that joined Osnaippi Creek, which ran behind his house. Tully had known Mavis most of her life, and he liked her. Respected her. He had gone to Mid-Way Café every morning for one of her biscuits, smothered in gravy or filled with country ham or butter that oozed out the sides and ran down his hands.

In a softer and lower voice, Mavis said, "They've got the money. How do you think the law's gonna look at that?"

He knew the answer. His son, who was a lawyer and a banker, had warned him not to put the Smiths out in the rain and had explained Alabama law to him. He'd been too mad to listen. He knew the law wouldn't be on his side.

"How are they supposed to get the rent to you when James got paid late yesterday, and they don't have a vehicle? Besides, why don't you bring your ass down here from your fancy house and collect the rent? Or send someone to collect it for you? Huh?"

They glared at one another. Sadie was now on the porch. The two men were getting tired of holding the dolly. James leaned against the wall, and the children were glued to his side. Tears streaked the faces of the two younger ones, and the baby sucked his thumb. The older ones looked sullen and gave Tully Hodnet resentful glances.

Tully was the first one to blink. "Put the stove back," he told the men. Turning to James, he said, "Give me the money. From now on, I'll be here to collect on the day the rent's due, and, by god, I pect y'all to have the money."

Sadie pulled the money from her bra. Right there, in front of everyone. She handed it to her husband. He handed it to Tully, who stalked by Mavis and said to the two men, "I'll be waitin in the truck." He stomped down the worn wood steps that were becoming slick from the rain and dirt. They heard the slamming of doors.

After the truck left the yard, everyone went into the house. James built a fire in the fireplace, while Mavis listened to the laugher of the children who sensed that they were safe. Sadie made biscuits, which they ate with Golden Eagle syrup and butter. She watched as several of the older children dunked biscuits in hot cups of coffee and dipped it out with spoons. Mavis, Sadie, and James sat at the table, drinking coffee. The children had eaten and were sitting on the living room floor in a semi-circle, watching cartoons on a second-hand TV.

"I wanna thank you, Ms. Mavis," James said in his humble voice. "If you hadn't come, we'd be on side a the road, drowned in the rain. I sho do preciate what you done."

"I'm glad I could do something. And, I want y'all to know that the house below me is empty. Why don't you think bout renting it from Calvin Jones? If y'all are interested, I'll drive y'all over to talk with him."

James and Sadie looked at each other. They nodded. "Can you take me this afternoon?" James asked.

"Sure. Just tell me the time." They decided on a time and Mavis left. When she got to her car, she noticed that the driver's door was closed. She assumed that Sadie had closed it when she got out of the car. Then, she remembered that she'd heard two doors slam after Hodnet stalked off the porch.

Since that time, almost thirty years ago, the Smiths had rented the house below Mavis. Sadie's children grew up with and played with Mavis' and Edith's children. When the Smiths needed money, Mavis or Edith hired Sadie to cook or clean for them. Often, Mavis slipped Sadie what little money that she'd managed to save in an old sock. The three women had formed a bond.

♦

Mavis watched until Sadie disappeared from sight. She closed the door on the almost forgotten memory. She closed and locked the door, cut off the kitchen light, got a fresh cup of coffee, and went into the living room. After watching TV for fifteen minutes or so, she cut off the sound. Next, she gave herself a breathing treatment, while she watched the silent screen. Once she completed the breathing treatment, she checked Johnny Lee's room. It was a mess. She had to admit that he was a pig. What would he do when she was gone? Who'd help look after him? She needed to talk with Laura Faye about that. None of the rest of them cared what happened to him. It wasn't that she was afraid of dying. She was afraid of leaving him alone, without anyone who really cared. That worried her more than where her soul was going. Anyway, she figured that the decision had already been made about where her soul was headed.

In the last year, she'd suspected that something was terribly wrong with her body. From that moment on, she began to save money for Johnny Lee and to purchase things that he'd need and that he'd never think about, like socks, underwear, towels, washcloths, sheets, and the list was long. All those things were in her walk-in closet. Someone would find them when she was gone. But, she planned to tell Laura Faye so that she'd see that Johnny Lee got all the bags of items, not some of her other children.

As she wandered throughout the house, she touched things in each room. Memories occupied her mind. In the stillness of the empty house, with dark clouds almost touching the roof, she welcomed the salty tears that she licked from her lips. Tears ran down her cheeks and splattered off her chin onto her housecoat, creating dark stains. Wrapping her arms around her thin body, she returned to the living room. The stove was a hungry animal, needing more food. She fed it. Then, she went to the linen closet to get a blanket and a pillow. She slipped a blue pillowcase over the pinstriped pillow. Afterwards, she arranged the blanket and the pillow on the sofa. Then, she lay down to wait for Beulah and Edith. Sleep came as soon as she sank into the warmth of the sofa, while the television carried on a silent conversation.

The next morning at ten o'clock, Beulah and Edith loaded suitcases into Mavis' red Ford SUV. Mavis stood on the back porch, bossing Edith, telling her where to place each suitcase. Mavis wore a new light blue sweat suit that Marley Jane had given her for Christmas and a mid-length fur coat that had been a Christmas gift from Laura Faye. A wool purple hat, scarf, and gloves completed the outfit.

After arranging and rearranging the bags, they were ready to leave.

Edith drove and Beulah sat in the front passenger's seat. Mavis sat on the back seat, in case she wanted to lie down. It'd be a long drive that most likely would exhaust Mavis. When they entered the bridge over Osanippa Creek, the SUV hit a bump, causing them to bounce on the seats. By the time that they left Smith Station, headed to Dothan, Mavis was asleep. Edith and Beulah talked softly so that they wouldn't disturb her.

Edith's voice was deep with concern. "I hope this trip ain't gonna be a mistake. Mavis is real sick. I don't know if she's gonna hold up. I'm worried. I been worried for more an a year."

"Me, too. But, we'll keep an eye on her and see that she rests and eats good." She watched the road ahead for several minutes and said, "I don't even wanna think bout life without Mavis."

Edith looked at Beulah. She reached across the seat and held Beulah's hand. "Me neither. I've known Mavis forever, it seems. She says what she thinks. Sometimes, she doesn't say a word, but a heap of stuff's goin through her head. I've known her to stay quiet bout a whole lotta things. It never ceases to amaze me how much she cares bout people and things. Her understandin bout people and things is deeper than anyone else I know."

In a sincere tone, filled with emotion, Beulah responded, "She's the nicest, most sincere person I've ever met. And she's the best friend I've ever had. I don't even wanna think bout losin her." She wiped tears from her cheeks with the back of her right hand.

Edith didn't reply. She waited. Then, she requested, "Sing, Beulah."

Beulah looked at Edith and, then, she looked behind her at Mavis, who'd pulled the blanket over her head. Softly, she began to sing "What a Friend We Have in Jesus."

Edith stopped in Dothan for lunch. They pulled into a Hardee's and ordered cheeseburgers with French fries and milk shakes. It didn't go unnoticed by Edith and Beulah that Mavis barely touched her food or that she took two pain pills. As they pulled out of the parking lot, she lay down and pulled the blanket over her head. She didn't wake up until they parked at the condo.

Beulah got a cart near the elevators. Edith and she loaded the suitcases and bags onto the cart. Then, the three women took the elevator to the seventh floor. As soon as she entered the room, Mavis walked across the floor and opened the sliding glass door to the balcony, while her friends unloaded the cart. Edith took the last bag and Beulah pushed the cart into the hall outside the door.

Edith made coffee and took steaming cups to Mavis and Beulah, who were sitting at the round wrought iron table. As they sipped the hot coffee, a strong wind blew off the ocean and intensified the cold. The day was fading. The sun rocked on the waves that occasionally covered a portion of the golden ball, causing it to look as if it were sinking into the ocean. A long wooden pier stretched far out into the loneliness of blue-green water that appeared endless, until it touched a far-away sky that was painted in various tones of pink.

Mavis recalled the last time that the three of them had been to the beach. It was a blistering last July. They'd walked near the water, while the waves nibbled at their toes. They'd felt the briny freshness of the air and tasted the salty sea spray on their parched lips, as a breeze caressed their naked arms and legs that, for Mavis and Edith, shone like alabaster in the aroused sun. Lacy waves rolled onto the beach, washing their feet in gritty water, as white silvery foam tickled their ankles.

She interrupted her thinking to say, "I wanna watch that sun sink every day I'm here. Once we leave, I'll never again see it sink into the ocean." She paused, took a sip of coffee, and continued, "Y'all wake me up in the morning when the sun comes up. We'll sit out here and watch it."

No one spoke. There was no need. They'd do what she asked.

"I wonder if you miss things or people when you die. Or if it's as if nothing ever existed. I find myself remembering things so that I can take the memories with me. But, I don't know if it works that way. Dying is bout the unknown. There are no survivors who can tell us how to die. Ain't that a shame?"

"It could be. And it could be a blessin. You know what I mean?" Edith asked.

Beulah said, "To me, it's a blessin. The Lord can surprise me. I ain't gonna think bout it. But, then, Mavis, you're in a different situation than me and Edith. We ain't the ones on the way to meet death. Well, at least, as far as we know. So, you're lookin at it out of a whole different set of eyes. It's real to you."

No one spoke. But, Beulah noticed that Mavis was nodding her head. Then, Mavis spoke in a soft voice. "This might sound strange to y'all, but I've always believed that a person comes into the world with knowledge that was learned before he or she was born. I call it instincts. I've always had plenty of that. If animals can have inbred knowledge bout things, I don't see why humans can't. There seems to be one difference between animals and humans. Animals know how to die. We don't. I wonder why that is."

The sun was half gone. The three women looked into it, through their dark sunglasses. Mavis added, "I wanna learn how to die." Her friends stood up and hugged her.

They stayed on the balcony until the sun disappeared. Then, they went inside. Edith made breakfast food for them. When they finished eating, they played cards until Mavis took a pain pill and a breathing treatment, followed by a hot bath. Then, she went to bed, with the sound of the ocean outside her room, and the yellow cold moon on the far edge of the water.

◆

The next morning, as she'd do for the remainder of the trip, Edith woke up at five o'clock and made coffee. She cooked biscuits and gravy.

When the food was ready, the sun was beginning to break through the sky. Then, she woke up Beulah and Mavis. They ate on the balcony and watched the sun rise. They wore gloves that made using the knives and forks difficult. Wool caps were pulled over their heads and ears. They wrapped themselves in blankets and laughed at how foolish they looked.

Edith asked, "What do y'all think people would say if they saw three old women huddled against the cold on a balcony that's overlookin an icy ocean?"

They stayed on the balcony after the sun stopped climbing the sky and allowed their faces to soak up the warm rays. Their hands and feet remained cold. Soon after the sun found a place to settle, Mavis returned to bed and slept until lunch. While she slept, Edith and Beulah read or watched television. For lunch, they ate fried bologna sandwiches and drank sweet tea with lemon. By two o'clock, they were dressed and ready to go to the dog track.

On the way to the track, Beulah asked, "Mavis, do you remember that time we went to Biloxi, Mississippi, on that bus to gamble? Did we ever tell you bout that, Edith?"

"You did, but tell me again."

"Well, it was like this. A group of black folks chartered this big ole bus to go to Mississippi to gamble. I signed up to go. When I told Mavis, she wanted to sign up, too. She did. And we get on that bus, and there ain't but one white person on the entire bus. It was Mavis."

"It didn't bother me," Mavis spoke up, "but that rap music drove me slap crazy. My head was bout to split wide open. The whole bus was shaking from that racket. I ain't kidding."

Beulah continued the story, "So, Mavis said to me—not in no whisper, mind you. She said, 'I can't stand no more of this damn noise, Beulah.' So, I stood up and yelled to get everybody's attention, 'Let me have y'all's attention!' It got quiet. Somebody cut the music down real low. And, I said, 'Ms. Mavis don't like this rap music. Y'all gotta play something that ain't so loud.' It got real quiet, and I sat down real quick. And they did. Not play no more rap. We didn't hear another bit of rap music all the way to Mississippi and back."

"Thank, the Lord!" Mavis laughed. "I was bout to get off that bus and walk to Mississippi."

Beulah laughed. "And Mavis' son Claude got so mad cause his mama rode a bus to Mississippi and back with nothin but black folks. He said it'd been different if she'd gone to Mississippi to march or something like that. But not to gamble."

The women laughed, and Mavis said, "I never said a word back to him. There ain't no need in arguing with grown young'uns. Just do what you wanna do."

The dog track could be seen ahead on the right. Edith drove up to the entrance. "Y'all get out here. I'll park the car and meet y'all in the lobby." Beulah opened the back door and helped Mavis out. They went into the building, as Edith drove off. Within five minutes, she joined them. They spent time looking over the race sheet and selecting dogs.

"Okay, girls, time to play." Mavis laughed and slapped a one hundred dollar bill on the counter. She gave her bids to a young tall woman with red hair, who never stopped chewing and popping gum.

"That's a lotta money, Mavis," Edith said.

"What am I gonna do with it? I can't take it to the grave. Don't worry. I'm gonna win big."

And she did. Two thousand five hundred dollars. Bells sounded throughout the area, announcing a winner. She counted out five one hundred dollar bills to both Edith and Beulah. "The rest I'm putting away for Johnny Lee to have when I'm gone. Y'all go ahead and play. I'm through."

Edith and Beulah looked at one another, still holding the crisp bills in their hands. "We are, too. Heck, we got five hundred a piece. I don't wanna lose it. Do you, Beulah?"

"No, I'm ready to go," Beulah replied, putting the money in her large black handbag.

"Good. Now that we've made that decision, I'll go get the car. Y'all wait in the lobby," Edith said, as she put her money in the back pocket of her jeans.

"I'm taking y'all to supper. Pick the restaurant y'all wanna go to. That's where we'll go. My treat," Mavis said and sat on a chair near the entrance. Beulah sat beside her, and they watched as Edith went into the wind to get the car.

They ate at a well-known seafood restaurant and took leftovers with them. Back at the condo, Beulah made coffee. They wrapped themselves in blankets and wore caps and gloves. As the sun disappeared, they drank coffee and talked about the fun that they'd had together throughout the years. When the sun disappeared, Mavis took her fifth breathing treatment of the day and a pain pill. She soaked in a hot tub of water, with bubbles that sparkled around her. She fell into bed, exhausted and more tired than she'd been in a long time. She knew that she'd over-extended herself.

As the sun was fading and streaks of darkness fell the next afternoon, Mavis said, "If it's okay with y'all, I'd like to go home in the morning. If not, we'll stay the rest of the week. I just wanna sleep in my own bed."

Beulah quickly responded, "No! That's fine. We're ready to go when you are." She looked at Edith to get her approval.

Edith added, "We came for you. It's all bout you. We discussed that when you was in the hospital. And, Beulah and me are gonna take turns sittin with you so your girls can take a break now and then. Do you wanna see the sun rise tomorrow or sleep late?"

"I wanna see it one more time. I'll sleep on the way home. Now, I'm taking my bath and going to bed." She stood up. "I can't tell y'all how much y'all both mean to me. Nite."

As Mavis hugged Edith, then, Beulah, each one whispered in her ear,

"I love you, Mavis." They watched her walk, carefully and slightly bent, through the sliding glass doors and down the hall. When she'd disappeared from view, tears fell from their eyes and they looked at the ocean that was beginning to be covered in a thick blanket of darkness, with far-away twinkling stars. Later, they packed as much as they could in the car, ready to leave the following morning as soon as the dishwasher was emptied, the floors vacuumed, and the linens were washed and put away.

Before taking a bath, Edith called Bobbie Jo to tell her that they'd be home the next day and for her or someone to be at Mavis' house when they arrived. Bobbie Jo asked Edith how Mavis was doing, and Edith said, "Not well. She's movin slower and stays tired all the time. I think, maybe, y'all are gonna have to start stayin with her as soon as we get back. It don't look good, BobbieJo.

◆

Mavis slept for almost ten hours when she got home. Bobbie Jo stayed with her for the first two days. Marley Jane came Friday afternoon and left Sunday afternoon. All of Mavis' daughters arrived on Saturday and made a schedule of who would stay when. They agreed that breathing treatments should be given at least six times a day, as the doctor had recommended, as well as several back massages, which would help keep her lungs clear of fluid. She'd use the oxygen, as needed, which they knew would become more frequent. The doctor had told them how important the oxygen would become as the cancer spread and affected the function of various organs.

Before Mavis realized how fast time had gone by, it was March, with unpredictable weather. It was the South, and there'd been years when it snowed in the spring. Mornings were cold, and the days grew warmer as the noon hour approached. In spite of the warmer days, Mavis stayed cold and couldn't stop the chill that crawled inside her bones and made her blood feel like ice water flowing through her veins. The house was never warm enough for her.

Nothing tasted good, and she completely lost her appetite. In spite of that, she forced herself to eat. Breakfast usually consisted of a biscuit that was soaked in coffee, something that she'd loved as a child and something that she'd given her own children when they were small. She preferred Hardee biscuits that were brown and crusty, not like McDonald's biscuits, which Mavis said were half-cooked and for old folks. Therefore, each time the shift changed, one of her daughters would stop by Hardee's to purchase six biscuits.

For weeks, she'd been bothered by something in her head. At first, it felt like maggots were crawling around, eating brain cells that were like gummy bears. They moved from one ear, over the top of her head, to the other ear. She could hear her ears whistle as if the wind was blowing through her head and out of her ears. Several minutes after the maggots stopped feeding on her brain cells, she could feel flies, buzzing in her head, among what she believed was left of her brain. She'd clamp her eyes shut, in hopes of stopping the destructive activity that caused her head to release sudden and violent energy that'd increase powerfully, rapidly, and without control. The pain grasped her temples until the veins in her forehead throbbed visibly. Then, she'd tightly wrap the diaper around her head in an attempt to force the pain to disappear; she'd take a pain pill and fall asleep to escape the terror and violent energy inside her head.

She sat on the back porch in April, with Edith and Beulah. Some flowers had begun to bloom, and the grass was turning green. Leaves were ready to burst open, and they looked like tiny roses about to pop into full bloom. The sun warmed the three friends. Mavis wore a coat, but, still, Beulah draped a blanket over her knees. Edith talked about the garden that she'd planted and the chickens that she'd decided to raise. Ferris had built a chicken pen for her. Soon, there'd be lots of eggs, which she'd share with Mavis and Beulah. She brought Mavis up-to-date on church events and said how everyone missed her.

"If they miss me so much, why hasn't anybody been to see me?" Mavis interrupted. "No one has brought food, sent a card, made a phone call or told me to go to hell. So much for the church."

"Well, Mavis, that could be my fault. I told em not to bother you. That you need to rest."

"Why did you tell them that? Anyway, they could send a card. Couldn't they?"

"Well, I thought I was helpin. I'm sorry. I'll tell em that you'd like to see em."

Mavis' hands were restless and she twisted the blanket. "Don't worry bout it. Cause it ain't your fault. People do what they wanna do. You gave them an excuse. That's all. Forget it. You meant well. And that's a hellava lot more than I can say for them. I will say that the preacher has been by a couple of times. But, he worried the hell outa me, wanting to talk bout my soul being saved. I got news for him. My soul is as saved as his soul. And, I'm gonna tell him that he sure better not talk bout saving souls at my funeral. I mean that!"

Beulah said, "Preachers don't visit or call like they used to. They want your money, but they don't wanna earn it. Lazy. That's what I say. Lazy."

Edith, as always, defended the church. "A church is a big responsibility. Preachers have a lots to do."

Mavis looked at Edith as if she'd lost her marbles. "For real? You're gonna sat there and tell me that tiny little old Hopewell Methodist Church requires so many responsibilities from the preacher that he doesn't have time to do his job? You know better than that. Anyway, Beulah and me don't believe a word of it."

Beulah laughed. "She's right, Edith. You gotta admit Mavis is right. Don't excuse wrong."

"Well, I guess preachers could do better. I like to give em the benefit of the doubt."

Mavis popped back with, "That's okay, but recognize the truth. Stop pretending it's right when it's not. Wrong won't ever become right, and pretending that wrong is right is plain wrong. Make it right!"

After her friends left, Mavis went to bed and thought about right and wrong and truth. She decided that people make up their own truth about what is right or what is wrong, which wasn't a new awareness for her. They simply thought that their ideas and opinions were the truth. Next, they adjusted everything that they saw, read, or heard to fit their truth.

Truth, she knew, is a total of many ideas, opinions, or facts. Mavis firmly believed, in order to determine the fact of truth, a person must be open-minded and willing to be objective and to listen to the ideas and opinions of others and to search for evidence. She didn't know too many people who were willing to do all of those things. Too many people wanted to be right. To hell with facts or evidence.

Mavis thought about how, for years, when she couldn't sleep, she'd often called Beulah at one or two o'clock in the morning. Beulah would get out of bed, get dressed, and drive to Mavis' house. Truth and lies were some of their favorite subjects. They agreed that the truth can hurt, but that a lie can destroy. Those subjects had many sub-subjects, like hypocrites and deceptive lives. They also agreed that everybody lied at one time or another, and if a person denied lying, that person was lying. Some lies were good and necessary. Some were evil and destructive. A person needed to know the difference. They further agreed that it was really sad when a person believed his or her own lies.

Mavis was certain that, after her death, she'd miss Beulah, late night biscuits and gravy, along with deep discussions about people, politics, religion, and life. With all of her heart, she believed that death couldn't steal those memories. She'd begun to treasure days that brought special memories or days that she recalled certain memories.

Sweet memories settled in her head, as she thought about her babies, heavy on her shoulders like limp sacks of flour. She treasured long-ago smiles or laughter, a baby's soft skin that'd been dusted with powder, the smell of a freshly cut watermelon, the heat from the sun on exposed skin, the nightly sounds of unseen creatures, the scent of freshly ironed clothes, wet dogs, and the smells of Christmas. A lover of rain, her mind's eye saw misty rain that was light and fell without a sound, with a softness that caressed the earth, cleansing it. The fresh smell of rain on a dirt road lingered in her nostrils.

She recalled how the wind could sweep across her face and how it billowed around the corner of the house and seeped into the rafters at night. There was a clear memory of lightening striking her twice. Both times the power had thrown her to the ground. Each time, she'd miraculously gotten up, shaken and scared, but not harmed. The sound of thunder like a rapid moving train rumbled in her head.

Her mind took her to the days of her childhood, and she heard the rattle of the black leather buggy as she, an innocent six-year-old, rode dusty country roads with her grandpa. A faded memory of a day that her daddy killed hogs swept over her, and she saw the black pot, filled with hog fat, that she stirred to make soap. She recalled the smoke from the fire beneath the pot and how the smoke made her eyes water.

She remembered the sun sinking into the Gulf of Mexico, the blazing colors of the setting sun above the ocean, and the odor of the sea, as well as the taste of sea salt on her lips. Closing her eyes, she saw the vibrant colors of the sinking sun as it stretched above the ocean. She remembered how Robert's eyes were the color of a bright blue sky. And she missed him.

There were thoughts of how she could fight for one more day, one more week, for more time with her children, especially the ones whom she considered in danger of inhaling too much of life's dangerous fumes. Johnny Lee walked through her mind like a restless ghost, haunting her every breath of life. During those times, she feared dying, because it'd take away any control that she had to protect him.

She told God that she couldn't die and leave Johnny Lee alone. "Why are You doing this to me? To Johnny Lee?" she whispered into her pillow. There was no answer. She waited for some sign, a dream, but there was nothing that she recognized as a sign from God. Still, she had faith. She knew that God was in control. Some things were beyond human comprehension.

When she was told that an enemy had taken permanent residence inside her body and that the enemy was equipped to win the battle that raged throughout her blood and tissue, she'd seriously begun to worry about Johnny Lee. She had a long discussion with Laura Faye, who promised that she'd always look after him. Mavis let go of some of her worry, in spite of the fact that she knew many of her children and grandchildren would resent anything that Laura Faye did for Johnny Lee. She didn't care what they thought, because they'd always been jealous and resentful of him. Mavis trusted Laura Faye to love Johnny Lee and to look out for his best interests.

A cloud hung over Mavis' head. It followed her and clung to her like dust. At times, it was dark and gloomy. At other times, it poured imaginary acid droplets on her shrinking body. Occasionally, in between the dark and light, she'd feel some hint of hope that it was a bad dream and that she'd wake up. The enemy would be gone. She'd tell Beulah and Edith about the nightmare. They'd talk about it, analyzing it from every angle. Finally, they'd make jokes and laugh at the terrible nightmare. But, she always returned to the truth. She couldn't hide from the truth, which followed her like a shadow.

CHAPTER SEVENTEEN

In August, there was an unmistakable change in Mavis. Her body was rapidly deteriorating to bones. She looked dismantled and weary. Her once bright green eyes turned dark. Marley Jane noticed it for the first time one Friday when she went to stay with her mama. She was shocked and thought, "Death lives in her eyes. Death's taking over." A strong urge to rush out of the room, to run into the woods, and to cry loud uncontrollable tears swept over her. She couldn't allow Mavis to read her thoughts or to see her fear.

Mavis's strength was indeed waning, leaving her body a shell. The progress of the disease was evident. Its presence was abundantly clear, from the haggard patient to the cluster of medicine bottles on Mavis' bedside table. There was no mistaking the enemy. Mavis told Marley Jane how simple it seemed to let life slip away, like releasing a butterfly, and to sink into the unknown that she no longer feared. She explained how she saw the image of life breaking away from her, wrapping itself around her. Always, there was the lingering thick silence of being introduced to death, face-to-face. Death was no longer a stranger. It was becoming a companion. Marley Jane listened, with a tight knot in her throat, while her mama told her that she felt the fear and the separateness that had begun to haunt her, until she accepted both the fear and the separateness as a normal process.

Marley Jane felt as if she'd listened to a lesson on dying. She knew that her mama had surrendered to the enemy, that the enemy was no longer the enemy, but a natural part of dying that no one could escape. As she listened to Mavis talk, she was aware that Mavis was dying with dignity and that Hemingway's major theme of dying with dignity was nothing compared to her mama's reality of dying.

◆

The second week of August was hot and humid. Sweat glistened on Beulah's forehead when she walked into Mavis' cool, dark bedroom. She stopped at the doorway and looked at her friend, who was staring out the window. The look on Mavis' face was meditative, and she was, in fact, deep in relaxation. Beulah recognized traces of solemnity, sorrow, and surrender that were derived from acceptance and the courage to face death. But, the most prominent feature on Mavis' face was peace. They'd talked in great depth about courage and death. Beulah knew that time was slipping away and that Mavis had begun to release it, day by day. No longer did she dread tomorrow or regret yesterday. It had become about the present, the now. That, too, she'd discussed with Beulah.

At the moment Beulah stood and watched. She could almost read Mavis' mind. It was as if she saw Mavis' thoughts on the tranquil face. But, she didn't have a clue as to the roads Mavis' mind traveled as she lay, waiting for death.

Mavis savored the sun as it peeped in her window and fell across the foot of her bed. Just as she'd savored the full moon the night before as it lay on a small pane of glass in the same window. She recalled how she'd imagined the taste of rain in her mouth like the taste of pennies and how she could hear the echo of thunder in her heartbeat.

She remembered the winter wind as it howled above the roof, rippling across her nerves and giving her energy. In the spring, she'd heard the songs of birds, which convinced her that life lay beyond the grave. When summer came, bringing flowers, buzzing bees, and heat waves, she felt God's arms around her, and her fear died.

It was then that Mavis knew she was ready. She told Beulah how she felt, and Beulah told Edith. It calmed them and gave them serenity. They no longer worried.

Entering the room, Beulah said, "I'm here, Mavis. To be with you."

Mavis patted the empty space beside her. Beulah lay down next to Mavis and took her left hand. They both closed their eyes. Marley Jane walked by the door, stopped, and took two steps back into the shadows. She smiled at the two friends who didn't need to talk in order to communicate. They shared a special bond that went beyond blood and family. Very quietly, Marley Jane closed the door.

♦

The last week of August sounded the toll bell. Mavis could no longer speak or eat. She lay in a fetal position. Cancer had shrunk her face and body so that every vein showed through paper-thin skin. Her breathing was weak, and one ear made a loud whistling sound that vibrated throughout the room.

By the first day of September, Mavis was barely alive. It was the first Saturday of the month. Bobbie Jo, Laura Faye, Marley Jane, and Bella, as well as Beulah, were spending the night with Mavis. Everyone knew that they were waiting for death, but no one admitted it. They realized that Mavis could die at any time. At midnight, Laura Faye checked on Mavis and touched skin that was cool and damp.

Laura Faye's screams rattled to the ceiling and flew out of the room, where the others heard, "Mama! Oh, God! No, Mama, no!"

They came running into the bedroom. They fell across the bed, hugging any part of Mavis that they could touch. Beulah stood at the end of the bed and felt Mavis' foot beneath the sheet. Her heart seemed to break into thousands of pieces like shattered glass.

Bobbie Jo called Hospice, while Marley Jane called the other siblings. Laura Faye woke Johnny Lee from a deep sleep. Beulah held Mavis' head in her arms as she listened to the voices outside the room. Tears poured down Beulah's cheeks and she wept without shame.

Two Hospice nurses arrived shortly thereafter. They examined Mavis, called the doctor, and the funeral director. Then, they flushed all of the remaining pain medicine down the toilet and cut the pain patches into shreds. When they completed the necessary paper work, they went into the living room. All of the children had arrived. No one spoke. They were all quietly crying and some were hugging one another.

Beulah was in the kitchen, making a pot of coffee and crying large tears that dropped onto the counter. Her hands shook, and she knew that her heart had cracked, as if it had been hit with a hammer. Anger overcame her, as an urge to scream and beat the wall washed over her. The anger was threatening to drown her in its rage. She wanted to run, as far away as she could. But, she couldn't leave, not as long as Mavis' body was in the house, as physically near to her as she'd ever be again in Beulah's lifetime. So, she made coffee and waited for Edith to come.

That night a part of Beulah died with Mavis. When she got home, it was almost daylight. She knew that sleep wouldn't come to her for a long time. She sat at her kitchen table and wrote a song for Mavis. It was a song that she'd sing until the day that she died. Years after Mavis' death, Beulah would come wide-awake and cry. Then, she'd sing the song that'd break a heart.

"Mavis. Mavis./Why did you go?/Mavis. Mavis./Why did you go?/Why did you go?/Mavis. Mavis./Why did you leave me?/ Why did you go?..."

Each word was drawn out in low melancholy notes that vibrated throughout the room and lingered in Beulah's heart. The sound of the song echoed off the walls and fell like teardrops to the floor. It was a pure blues and jazz song from the soul, created out of love and pain. An honest emotion of grief.

◆

Bobbie Jo asked Beulah to sing at Mavis' funeral, but she couldn't, in spite of the fact that she'd promised Mavis that she would. Bobbie Joe understood. It was all that Beulah could do to attend the burial, and she didn't remember a thing about that day. She couldn't recall if it rained or if the sun was out. There were songs, but she didn't hear them. The preacher's words fell into the grave beside Mavis' casket. The children looked defeated, filled with sorrow. Johnny Lee looked lost and clung to Laura Faye. Edith wept loudly, while Beulah was stone-faced and numb. After the funeral, she went home, because she couldn't bear the thought of going back to Mavis' house to be with the family. Instead, she went home, took two sleeping pills, and crawled into bed naked. She awoke the next day at noon. Still drowsy, she thought that she heard Mavis' voice in the distance, followed by her laughter. Beulah buried her face in the pillow and cried.

CHAPTER EIGHTEEN

Beulah rocked slowly on her front porch, while fresh tears seeped down her sharp cheeks and off her chin. The glass of tea that she held in her hand was covered in sweat and the ice had melted. When Beulah took a sip, she frowned at the weak bitter taste. Bending forward in the rocker, she dashed the remaining liquid into the yard and sat the empty glass down beside her. The moon hit the rim of the glass and made a half-moon of light.

A full moon hung in the trees and the sky was lit by millions of stars. One shined brighter than the others. They filtered through the tall, thick trees and spilled under the branches, blinking on the ground like ice cubes that floated in a large bowl. Some unidentifiable animal spoke not too far away, and Beulah heard a mouse running nearby among the pine needles.

Beulah became aware of the tears on her cheeks. She wiped them away with the back of her left hand. A large fist squeezed her heart, and she took a deep breath. Her body was tense, and she felt as if she was walking a tight rope, high above the tallest tree. Sharp pine needles were the only net. If she fell, a needle would puncture her heart.

First, Silas was gone. After his disappearance, she thought that she'd never again know such suffering. Years later, her mama and daddy were gone. After her mama's death, she and Autumn moved into her parents' house, where they still lived. Next, Mavis was gone. And it caused her pain each time that she drove by Mavis' house and thought about Johnny Lee who lived there alone. Now, Edith was gone.

So many people whom she loved had left her. An overwhelming sorrow of being abandoned came over her. In the midst of her deepest well of pity, a small voice spoke in the back of her head and told her that she still had Autumn. It'd always been the two of them. As long as she had Autumn, there was hope, and Beulah could survive. She wiped away a tear and sat up straight. Her back stiffened, and she tried to push the painful memories to another area of her brain. She couldn't push hard enough.

Autumn had married Tyrone Upshaw two years ago, on a spring day that was flooded with sunshine and the smell of new life. Tyrone was a good man who owned his own auto body shop. He was kind to Beulah, who'd invited them to live with her until they could save enough money to purchase their own home. One of the happiest days in Beulah's life had been the night that they took her to dinner and announced that she'd soon be a grandma. Beulah was delighted that they were expecting a child in five months.

As long as she lived, she'd miss Mavis. That was a given, and Beulah knew that the pain of losing Mavis would return again and again, as it had been doing for years. The pain had become a part of Beulah's life, a part that she embraced. Sometimes, at night, when she lay awake in the early hours of the morning, the pain would visit her. It'd wash over her body like furious waves on a beach. Gradually, the waves of pain would be reduced to gentle caresses, as Beulah sang the words to the song that she'd written so long ago after Mavis' death.

Beulah was deep in memories, while the night crept over the earth on soft cats' feet. Her eyes were closed and she sang the song that gave her comfort. It filled the night with its melancholy sound. Now and then, an owl asked, "Whoo?"

She stopped singing, rested her head on the back of the rocker, and recalled some things that'd happened between the deaths of Mavis and Edith. Once she let go of her mind, it surprised her just how much had taken place in those years, how time had flown, and what she'd forgotten.

Preston had been killed in a terrible automobile accident on a bridge not far from Beulah's house. The sound of a car against a metal railing screamed into the late night and awoke her from a deep sleep. She sat up in bed and listened, but could hear nothing else. The silence was broken, and she heard the siren of an ambulance, as it flew through the darkness. Its lights lit up Beulah's bedroom and the siren ended the stillness. Beulah got out of bed, walked onto her front porch and stared into the night that was now blazing with lights from the ambulance and police cars. A knot settled in her stomach, as an unknown fear gripped her.

The next morning, Edith called her. Beulah quickly dressed and rushed to be with her friend. Edith clung to Beulah, as loud animal sounds seeped from her throat and shook her body.

Beulah wondered to herself, "How many more bodies are You gonna snatch from us? Please, Lord, give us some peace."

As soon as she thought those words, she recalled a preacher who once said, "Peace isn't a gift. It's an act of mercy." And, as Beulah well knew, peace often comes after the floors of hell have opened wide to inflict pain and suffering. Too, you had to work at having peace. You had to know when to fight and when to surrender. You had to be objective and remain strong, with a deep faith that time would heal or, at least, ease the suffering, the pain, the anger. All of the important women in Beulah's life had known about suffering and faith.

She remembered Johnie Pearl, Mavis, Edith, Sadie, and all of the other strong women whom she'd known. She thought, "The lives of Southern women is like sweet tea with lemon. They understand that much of life's happiness can be full of pain. But, they learn to take the bitter with the sweet."

Beulah's mind turned to Mavis' children, with whom she'd stayed in touch as best she could, because it kept her in touch with Mavis. In each one, she recognized something of Mavis.

Johnny Lee had been in and out of drug rehab at least four times. Each time that he returned home, his drug habit got worst. The last time that Beulah spoke with Laura Faye, he was doing better, but hadn't completely given up drugs. No one seriously believed that he ever would, but his siblings had become more supportive and protective of him.

It was a long time before anyone in the family knew that Johnny Lee had attempted for years, and repeatedly failed, to self-medicate himself against voices that only he could hear. Each passing year, it took more and more drugs to drown the voices that took up residence in his head and controlled his life.

After listening to Johnny Lee, one sagacious drug counselor recommended that he be given a series of tests. They were administered, and it was discovered that he was schizophrenic, which explained the voices that he'd heard most of his life. Once he began taking medication for the illness, his desire for drugs decreased. Later, Laura Faye helped him to obtain disability, which meant that for the remainder of his life there'd be some financial support.

Occasionally, Beulah stopped by to visit or to take food. Like Mavis, he made her laugh. They'd sit on the back porch of Mavis' house and recall one thing after another. It amazed her how well he could analyze a person's character and how forgiving he was. There was not one ounce of bitterness or anger in him.

Janet's husband Morgan had passed away in his sleep, due to a bad heart. His death was peaceful and shocking. Years later, Janet was diagnosed with cancer and lived three years before the monster took her life. Beulah missed ordering birthday and Christmas cakes from Janet, who was friendly and good-hearted.

Claude still planted a huge garden every spring, using his daddy's old Ford tractor to plow the neat rows. All of his siblings, as well as Beulah and Edith, were invited to gather whatever they wanted from a garden that was the envy of everyone in the community. Other than a bad back, which he didn't allow to conquer his spirit or energy, he and his wife were doing well. Beulah often noted that he was the quietest of Mavis' children, and, like her, you never knew what his silence or grin meant.

Bobbie Jo's husband had died from more complications than Beulah could recall, and his ashes had been dropped in the Gulf of Mexico. Since that time, Bobbie Jo had been diagnosed with cancer. It was now in remission, an enemy that could attack without warning, but she took one day at a time, thankful for every day that she was allowed to be with her children and her siblings. As she grew older, she became quieter and more reflective, more thoughtful. She, too, had a kind heart and helped many people in need.

Richard and Bella were enjoying life. He raised roosters and had developed a close relationship with many Mexicans who indulged in illegal rooster fights. In addition to raising roosters, he liked to be with his grandchildren and to travel to antique car shows throughout the South. Beulah liked his loud voice and laughter, his teasing and twinkling eyes that reminded her of Mavis. He had his mama's way of winning people, and, like her, he didn't tolerate foolishness.

Marley Jane's husband wasn't in good health, but he continued to practice law. She'd retired from teaching in Alabama and had gone to work in Georgia as a media specialist. Many of the things that she said and did made Beulah think about Mavis, but Beulah agreed with Mavis. Marley Jane was different from her brothers and sisters, and, like Mavis, Beulah couldn't quite put her finger on what made her different. She was funny one minute and dead serious the next. Beulah never knew what Marley Jane was thinking, except when she felt strongly about an issue. If that was the case, there was no holding her back.

Zelda and her husband had settled down next door to Mavis' house. She no longer preached, but never stopped quoting Bible verses or reminding people that sin and evil lurked around every corner. Beulah saw her often at church and spent a great deal of time, listening to Zelda talk about a child or a grandchild. Zelda enjoyed being a grandma as much as anyone Beulah had ever known. Now, Beulah would soon have her own grandchild, her own joy.

Laura Faye grieved so much for Mavis that she began to neglect her business, which she lost. She went bankrupt and became something of a recluse. Beulah knew that she didn't withdraw out of shame or regret. Laura Faye was tired of the daily routine of providing for so many family members, for fighting to keep her head above the ordinary, and for denying herself the peace that she'd wanted for years. But, the need to love and to care for others had never left her. She continued to help her family, even when she couldn't do so financially and shouldn't have done so.

In the past two years, Laura Faye and Felton had gotten custody of a great-granddaughter who was a special needs child. The child filled Laura Faye's need to love and to take care of someone. And, of course, she'd taken over Mavis' job of taking care of Johnny Lee. Like Mavis, she had a kind heart, but she, too, didn't suffer fools gladly and would speak her mind as quickly as Mavis or Marley Jane. Beulah felt a deep connection to Laura Faye, because they both had loved Mavis so deeply.

As Beulah was thinking about Laura Faye, she looked into the darkness and was comforted by the warmth of the dark night, by familiar sounds that she took for granted. She hugged herself and took a deep breath, exhaling slowly as she let go of the tension that had tied her body in knots for hours. The letting go felt good and she fell into a relaxed state.

Her eyes were closed and her body was completely at ease. Her mind was empty, no more thinking. She felt peace in her body and sighed softly. For the first time in days, Beulah felt nothing but relaxation. The wind chimes at the far end of the porch moved gently and made soothing sounds in the night.

After some time, she heard the screen door open quietly. She sensed Autumn's presence, holding the door open so that the light from the hallway swept across the porch and made a bright globe in Beulah's lap. She opened her eyes and looked at a star that winked. The moon had gotten caught in the branches of an old oak tree. She stopped rocking and waited for Autumn to speak. She realized that she was holding her breath. Tension was returning to her body. The state of being had disappeared.

"Mama, there's a lawyer from Texas on the phone. He wants to talk to you bout Silas," Autumn said in her soft voice.

ACKNOWLEDGMENTS

The author would like to give special thanks to her sisters—Billie Wayne Weekes, Patricia Meadows, and Cindy White—who shared stories with the author about their mother, Hazel Austin, who is Mavis Norrell in the novel, and about their brother, Randy Lee Austin, who is Johnny Lee Norrell in the novel. Some of the stories were tremendously funny and others were sad. Many of the stories are woven into *Sweet Tea with Lemon*, to develop character or theme.

The author expresses gratitude and thanks to the following people who supported and helped her in producing *Sweet Tea with Lemon*: Judith Ballard, a friend who took the time to read, to edit, and to comment on the manuscript, before it was submitted for publication; Bob Hranichny, the author's son-in-law who created the templates for *Sweet Tea with Lemon*; Austin K. Sanderson, the author's son who helped his life partner, Bob Hranichny, create the cover design; Della D. Sanderson, the author's daughter who encourages the author and offers feedback; to family and friends who inspire and support.

ABOUT THE AUTHOR

Shirley A. Aaron is a retired English teacher and media specialist. She has two children—a son, Austin K. Sanderson, who lives in New Jersey, and a daughter, Della D. Sanderson, who lives in Huntsville, Alabama.

She published a book of poetry, *Drops of Light*, in June, 2014. It is based on her life experiences and how she perceived those experiences. *Troubling the Ashes*, a historical fiction, was her first novel. It is set in Notasulga, Alabama, and deals with the Alabama school desegregation lawsuit, Lee v Macon County Board of Education, that was filed by civil rights attorney, Fred Gray, in 1962.

She is presently working on a sequel to *Sweet Tea with Lemon*, which deals with Beulah's son Silas, who is on Texas' death row. The title of that book is *There Ain't No Sunshine on Death Row*. In addition, she has completed another novel, *Seeking the Holy Ghost*, that is based on the adventures of four young children, ages seven to nine.

http://shirleyaaron.com

Made in the USA
Middletown, DE
27 April 2017